A Restless Wind

A Restless Wind

Shahrukh Husain

PICADOR INDIA

First published in the Indian subcontinent 2013 by Picador
an imprint of Pan Macmillan, a division of Macmillan Publishers Limited
Pan Macmillan, 20 New Wharf Road, London N1 9RR
Basingstoke and Oxford
Associated companies throughout the world
www.panmacmillan.com

ISBN 978-93-82616-11-5

1 3 5 7 9 8 6 4 2

Typeset by InoSoft Systems, Noida
Printed and bound in India by Gopsons Papers Ltd., Noida

To my husband
Christopher Shackle

Prologue

Only the walls of this fortress know my secrets. The thought hovered in Hana's mind as she tried to clutch at a disintegrating dream. But she was awake now and troubled. Sleep did not linger these days – the little time left was too precious to slumber away. She felt a streak of panic. 'I must confess before it's too late.'

She levered herself up on her pillows. The blood drained from her head and she sat still, waiting for the faintness to pass. A memory wavered, of something floating out of her grasp and into the old stone walls of the room that had witnessed so much of her life. There were many things still to do, mistakes to rectify ... The twenty-first century had contaminated her beloved town of Trivikrampur, had even brought the sectarian violence inside the gates of the Ramzi family whose name was a by-word for communal harmony far and wide.

She pulled out her monogrammed writing paper and put aside the envelope addressed to Zara days ago. She would write to her this instant. She could see her now, striding through her London life, lithe and energetic, black hair swirling along with barrister's cloak. With an extra burst of determination, she picked up her pen.

'My beloved Zara ...' She looked at her writing. It wobbled and crawled along the page, giving no hint of its former elegance. Ah, she thought. What it was to experience the machinery rusting while the mind remained agile. 'So many stories,' she scrawled, her hand beginning to shake. 'Stories I should have told long ago. I want to clear up what I can before ...'

She felt the blood rush to the right side of her body, then grow thick. A clip in her wrist was pinching apart her fingers, detaching them from her pen. She clenched them round it, dogged.

'You are the only one who will do exactly as I ask. I want you to take charge of two things. A seventeenth-century manuscript containing the origins of the Ramzi Order – Saif and Pebbles must never know about it. I've written out detailed instructions, tedious, I know but ...'

The pen rolled from her fingers. Hana's mind was wandering now, her arms stretched out to catch the coherence drifting just beyond reach. She struggled to bring her hand to the bell on her table. It tinkled and she saw Littl'un enter in a blurred haze. Littl'un would put Hana's letter in the envelope and send it off before Pebbles saw it. Hana's confession would have to wait.

1

I

Zara put down her briefcase and drew back the curtains. Her office lit up like a theatre set. The colours calmed and focused her – desert and sky resonating in a continual transition of taupe and teal. She'd chosen them as an antidote to the hectic bodies flitting back and forth on Chancery Lane below.

The pile of papers on her desk was inviting. Work would be a balm, take her mind off the tension she'd woken with this morning after a disturbing dream. She pushed it to the back of her mind – it would wait until she got home and told Peter about it.

Judging from Naz Hamid's pleas yesterday, this appeal, due to be heard in two days, would prove a challenge. She slipped into her chair and opened the file Naz had couriered over this morning.

Dear Zara,

Re: Parveen Abdul-Rehman

I'm really grateful you've agreed to talk to this client at such short notice. As I said when we spoke, I am in court today and therefore unable to accompany the client as usual. I hope you have more success with her. Gujarati is her mother tongue but she tells me she is fluent in Hindi/Urdu, which I gather you speak.

I've had to work with an interpreter. I have a hunch there was more interpretation and less accurate translation – it would be useful to get your view.

Many thanks and best wishes,
Yours sincerely,
Naz

Solicitor – Private and Business
Immigration Department
Harman and Manfred Associates

Zara picked up her phone. 'Annabel. When's Miss Rehman coming?'

'10.30,' Annabel answered at once.

'Thanks. Fifteen minutes.' Zara replaced the receiver and riffled through the file for the original client statement.

1. I, Parveen Abdul-Rehman will say as:
2. I am a twenty-four-year-old Muslim woman currently residing at 3, Solihull Road, Peckham Rye, East London.
3. I was born in Mehsana District of Gujarat in the village of Dhanagiri. My parents owned a small farm but were massacred in their home on 28 February 2002.
4. I have three sisters and two brothers. They were all massacred at the same time as my parents except one sister, Nasreen, who was married and lived in a suburb of Ahmedabad.
5. Nasreen, her husband and their newborn baby lost their house – it was burned down during the massacre. I do not know where they are or if they are alive.
6. I had a comfortable upbringing and was well educated. I studied law and had good job prospects. A local firm offered me work and I had an interview set up with a firm of solicitors specializing in family law, in Ahmedabad.
7. My sister was giving birth in Shah Alam area of Ahmedabad. My mother was in bed with a slipped disc so I went to help her.
8. There had been trouble in Ahmedabad. A train full of Hindu pilgrims from Ayodhya was burned in Godhra and people believed Muslims had done it. That night, 28 February 2002, a Muslim MP was murdered by an angry mob, so Nasreen and her husband told me it would be safer for me to go home immediately.
9. When I returned, our fields looked abandoned, I could see no workers. We grew wheat and it was a busy time of the year. I told the rickshaw man to drive right up to the entrance of my home.

My father, mother, brothers and sisters were all dead. They had been beaten, knifed and shot.

10. I returned to Ahmedabad immediately but my sister and her family had disappeared. Their house was burned down. There was mayhem in the settlement where they lived. Some police were joining in the violence.
11. I was beaten and raped by policemen. Later, I was recognized by some business associates of my family. They kept me secretly in their home until I was better. They were a Hindu family so I was safe with them for a while.
12. After a few weeks people started coming to inquire if they were hiding a Muslim. They threatened them with violence. The family who rescued me decided, for the sake of everyone's safety, to send me to a safe place.
13. They spoke to some people about taking me to another part of India and, from there, to send me out of the country.
14. Two days later some people drove me a long way away, into Maharashtra. I do not know their names. They kept me with other women in a deserted house for many days. I had no way of keeping account. We were very crammed. They brought us something to eat sometimes; otherwise we had wild berries and mouldy biscuits and bread.
15. After that they came to get us and took us in a truck to some strange, wild place. We had to walk many weeks, so we were not allowed to carry anything, even food, because it would weigh us down. Some of us had a little money before we started. We bought food – roti, biscuits, pickle – that we could hide on our body.
16. The agent took all our money. We walked through deserted terrain, thick forests, rocky stretches. We were covered in bites and bruises and sores. My back and ankles have never recovered from that journey. I still have bad dreams about it and wake up in a cold sweat. My sleep is bad and the doctor says I suffer from anxiety.
17. The agents took our food, too. We survived nearly ten days on a single biscuit or piece of roti, though we stopped occasionally to make tea. The food we hid was inedible but we ate it because we

were hungry. A man fell ill after eating chicken hidden in a band around his stomach for three days. It finished him. We hid our exhaustion. If anyone got too tired or people hurt themselves, the agent left them where they fell. A woman begged him to kill her because we were far from civilization. He refused. But she started screaming. She said she would tell anyone who passed that he was trafficking humans. He shot her in the head. I see her every time I hear a loud noise.

18. I don't know what these places were. I never knew before that they existed. I thought I was Indian but now I realize I am only Gujarati. In the rest of India I am alien – we don't even speak the same language. It was a strange thing to realize – I lost my country and my identity together and became nobody.
19. I travelled for many months, by truck, train and plane. I do not know by which route I left India or reached Dubai airport. We slept on benches at the airport. We had eaten nothing for many days. An Arab family left food on a table. We shared that and thanked God for His mercy.
20. In Dubai, the agent selected me and two others to board a plane. On board he gave me two tablets and I slept until we arrived at Heathrow airport. I was very sleepy and confused when he got me off the plane. He told me to follow the people in front of me. I did. For a long time, I did not know I had come off the plane. There was no runway, no airport building – just, off my seat, through the airplane door and straight inside a long corridor.
21. I arrived at London airport on 22 June 2003. I can read English. An airport official asked me who I was. I told him my name. He asked for my papers. I had none. He took me to Immigration.
22. The people in Immigration treated me like a common criminal. They called me an 'illegal immigrant'. I told them I am not an illegal immigrant. I am seeking asylum from the bloodbath in my country. I studied law. I was starting a job. I begged not to be sent out of my country. But it was the only way. My English is not good enough to practise law outside India. Away from my homeland I am nothing.
23. In my home state of Gujarat, Hindus and Muslims were always fighting. But we all got by. I had a future. Now I have none.

Everything has changed. I have no family, no protection and I believe that I cannot survive.

24. I confirm that the above information is true and correct to the best of my knowledge and belief.

Parveen Abdul-Rehman

Zara eased off her high-heeled shoes and felt the muscles of her feet relax. Parveen was right, of course. Societies seemed to be coming apart all over the world with age-old subterranean disagreements exploding to the surface. She was relieved she still found the events distressing; some of her colleagues had developed an attitude of indifference. She felt a surge of warmth at the memory of her own hometown, often cited as a model of harmonious communal relations. From there, the whole world seemed peaceful as Zara was growing up. But now, armies of the dispossessed were fleeing their homes to find safety across boundaries of sea and land. And client after client blamed the same demon – religious intolerance. In India, too, politics had been communalized. It had been a conscious process.

Innocent people like Parveen Abdul-Rehman were its casualties. It was incredible that a mosque built in the sixteenth century could still trigger such hatred even if it had been the sacred capital of the god-king Rama. Accusations and counter-accusations were flung about. The English-language press in India accused the Gujarat government of supporting onslaughts against Muslims. But in the state itself, the police forces, the people believed that the trouble was caused by Muslims and wanted them out. The truth didn't matter. Right across Gujarat, bloodshed was followed with retaliation and counter-attack until it was no longer possible to point a finger. Zara had learned that logic and compassion disappeared in conflict situations along with the notion of 'fact'. Everything rested on perception and agenda. There were no good guys and bad guys.

Zara returned to Parveen's statement. It was what the UK Border Agency would base their decision on. But she knew that there was so much more locked away in those lines that she would need to reveal in court before Parveen had a chance of winning her appeal.

The knock was soft, but it startled Zara. She shoved her feet back into her shoes and opened the door to a tiny, neat woman.

'Parveen Abdul-Rehman?' Zara stood back, waving her in towards an armchair by her desk. 'Please, sit down.' Before speaking, Parveen appraised her with small, almond-shaped eyes.

'Thank you. Naz said you speak Gujarati.' Parveen's English was heavily accented but clear, to Zara anyway. She had grown up with it, making amicable jokes about it with her family and playmates. But she had not heard it spoken for a while, except incidentally in a shop or on public transport. She would have to concentrate.

'I understand Gujarati,' she replied. 'But if it's okay with you, I'll ask you to clarify in Hindi if I can't follow.'

Parveen nodded, expressionless. 'Everyone understands Hindi,' she said. 'Because of Hindi picture.'

Zara could hear Parveen's natural language beneath her English, the lost verbs, the erratic articles, the confused plurals and tenses, all smoothed over by the rise and fall of an un-English rhythm and flow.

'I was reading your statement,' Zara continued. 'But maybe you can tell me what happened when you went home to Dhanagiri from your sister's?' Parveen began to speak in her musical, Gujarati-inflected Hindi.

'I took rickshaw from the station. I was worried – first time I took rickshaw alone. When I phoned my house from my sister's no one pick up the phone. So no one came to take me from station. My sister and brother-in-law warned me when I left, to take a Muslim rickshaw-driver – but I couldn't see any Muslim driver, all had Ganesha-god or Krishna-god on mirror. I waited long time, after, it was become dark and I had to take Hindu driver. He had red mark on his forehead but he was only rickshaw present. He told me not to worry – he knew about Godhra incident but he did not blame all the Muslims. He promised to look after me like daughter. At door at my house, sound of humming was coming from inside and dogs and cats were near door. I shoo them away but they move only one or two steps back, as if something pulling them inside. I was frightened. When I opened door, they lower their heads and crane their necks, try to look inside. First thing, I saw the flies. They were everywhere like the black cloud.'

Parveen's gaze drifted into the distance and she grew still except for her fingers knitting and weaving, then she began to rock. When she spoke again, her speech was like a memorized piece – uninflected, continuous, monotonous.

'My father and mother were dead on the floor. My brothers lay on the stairs, back against the ground, as if like they were thrown back by bomb. Flies were all over them – like moving carpet – black. Upstairs both my sisters, twelve and fourteen, lying with legs bare and twisted. Raped and slaughtered in their beds. I ran out after rickshaw-man. The driver let me come in without asking anything. Then he come out. He chase off the dogs and cats and go into the house. He was there for a long time, covering bodies. Then he lock the door from outside and tell me to pray in my religion. He asked me permission to join me with his own prayers because he was a Hindu and couldn't say our Arabic prayers. I said I would be grateful.'

Parveen gasped and stopped, head hanging, struggling not to break down. It gave Zara a moment to regain her own equilibrium. She would never get over these harrowing descriptions. Should anyone, for heaven's sake?

'Take your time,' she said. She poured some water from the carafe on her desk and put it by Parveen's chair.

Parveen shook her head. 'Why are prayers always in languages that don't let us feel properly? I understood meaning of my prayer for the first time, like mullah taught when we were small. *Indeed we belong to Allah and to him we must return.* But like this? Must we return like this? In disgrace and dressed in our insides instead of decent shroud? I could not even bury my family.' She was silent, again, and still for a good few moments. 'The rickshaw-man drove me to station. He said: "Go back where you came from, daughter. And forgive my people if you can. They disgrace our gods. Ram and Shiva never intended this, I swear. Try to think well of them at least." I kept thinking: And Allah? Did Allah intend this? But what is it to do with any god? People use God for their wishes. I didn't blame him for what others were doing.'

Parveen lapsed into Hindi. 'When I got back, my sister's house was burnt down. The rioters had been there. I wandered in the crowds. People were confused, some wailing, some walking, dazed. I was going mad – I was thinking crazy thoughts, as if murderers were following me or they were killing my family because they couldn't kill me. I started screaming: "I'm Parveen, Abdul-Rehman's daughter. Come and kill me. Stop slaughtering my family." Someone forced water down my throat. It tasted of smoke. I saw other houses been burned down. People were saying the rioting was because Muslims abducted three Hindu girls from the burning train. Police vans came but police only watched. In fact, police were beating the victims. A few of them shouted as I passed by: "Get that one. Show her father how we feel." After that, I remember him hitting my head with a truncheon. Then he ... forced me ... he violated ...'

She ran her hands over her face and her words came out in a rush. 'Other people, too, many times that night, I think. Later, two men found me in the gutter. I thought they would rape me, too. It didn't matter. I couldn't feel anymore. But they said they did business with my brother-in-law. They took me to their house. Their womenfolk bathed me. They hid me for a few days. They were a respected Hindu family so no one questioned them. After some days, they said I would be taken to a country where a single woman can live safely. They must have got into debt for that. Some weeks later I arrived here. It's a common story. But the courts here don't believe me. This country doesn't want me.'

Zara went to sit beside Parveen. Sometimes, moving around took the edge off the harrowing narratives of her clients. The stark storytelling forced a confrontation between words and images, as if the teller were somehow squeezing out her suffering through the flatness of her narration, passing it on, through pictures, to the listener. Zara had seen it often in clients trying to escape violence. It was, the experts said, a standard characteristic of post-traumatic stress.

Parveen was enfolded in the armchair like a small animal cowering in its den for safety. Her dark eyes darted around before fixing steadily, disconcertingly, on Zara's face, as if searching for a conclusion to her story.

'I am going to represent you in court at your appeal,' Zara said.

'Naz said you are Muslim. "Zara" is Arabic word for "flower".'

'Yes ...' Was this important to Parveen? Or was she deflecting the memory of her experience?

'Is there anything you'd like to add?'

'It's all in the statement.' Parveen's small mouth turned up at the corners.

'Parveen, the judge sees lots of people in your position. Victims of political or personal violence escaping from danger. He will want to know why he should allow *you* to stay here rather than someone else. You must explain to him how you'd benefit from staying here.'

'Benefit?' she sat forward, puzzled. 'Benefit how? You see, I'm nothing here. But I will live without being terrified.'

Zara tried again. 'Let me ask you – why do you want to remain in the UK?'

'To stay alive.'

'So you fear being killed if you return to India?'

Parveen nodded. 'But I don't fear death.'

Zara stood up. She was beginning to understand why Naz Hamid was baffled. 'If that's what you plan to tell the Appeals Court, there's no point going.'

Parveen recoiled, sinking deeper into her armchair. Zara wished she had not sounded so sharp.

'I won't tell that to the Appeals Court,' Parveen said. I'm telling that to you. Because you're a Muslim. And you let me speak my language.'

Zara forced a smile. 'That's good. And what will you say in court?'

'I will tell the truth. I'll say I'm very torn. I respect your country and I want to stay here because you are honourable people. You don't punish others for their beliefs. Or for being women. But I must be honest – mainly, I want to stay for my safety. If my country is safe, I will go back there at once.'

'Why?'

Parveen looked around the room and began singing.

Like piles of gold, glisten dunes of sand;
Like diamonds and emeralds glow your trees, my land.
Oh star of my eyes, beloved, precious land.

Zara drew a breath. That voice! The raw, pure voice of the gypsies who came to the fortress in Trivikrampur and sang up to the balcony. Afterwards, Aunt Hana would tell Littl'un to take them to the kitchens, to eat all they could. Zara crept off to see the women as they rested in rows, in the cool, covered end of the back terrace by the old kitchen – a brief respite before they walked on, heading to town to sell their wares. Sometimes they'd make bodices and showed her how to tear the pieces of fabric into precise shapes which fitted together like a cloth jigsaw to create the short-sleeved garment with its perfect breast-cups. The little girls jostled each other, giggling as their mothers filled out the cup with rolled fists to check the precision of the sewing. Several of them embroidered scenes on vast cotton friezes, working at once on each piece, as they told stories of heroic battles in places where history met myth. And Zara would imagine men with burnt skin, twirling moustaches and bright turbans, in dark desert spaces and village squares, holding up the vast frieze, lit by lanterns in all corners. They acted out the epic of Pabu Ji, a ruler whose memory survived in the women's dense, colourful stitches.

They told Zara stories, sang her songs about their journeys and the magnificent desert from which they had come. *Dead land*, they called it, because you could walk miles and miles without a sign of vegetation or habitation. But Zara knew the land was not dead. She had seen for herself how the dunes rose and fell and turned, shifting, sliding, morphing into interminable other dunes. They changed colour. Silver by dawnlight and moonlight, the vivid yellow of tungsten lights at high noon and at sunset, the piles of muted gold described in the lyrics.

Parveen was singing Zara's childhood.

Zara stared at the turquoise hood of the lamp on her desk. She reached for a folder and flipped it open. 'You need to be clear about your reasons for staying.'

Parveen's eyes were boring into her. She held her head slightly to one side, gazing at her, sizing her up. Zara shifted uneasily in her chair and forced herself to relax her face muscles to release the tension. Parveen was humming now.

How can I explain to you what it's like?
Being a stray dog's an evil blight.

Zara knew the poem. She'd heard it recited at a gathering of poets in exile. Many, many years ago. It had opened up an abyss of internal wandering that seemed never to lead to a stable destination. She still felt panicky when she heard it. She clenched her fist. *The job at hand: prepare Parveen for the appeal.*

Zara looked across at her large beech desk, longing to separate herself from the psychosis of the despairing. Piles of folders, pots of all kinds to hold pens and other stationery and a covered malachite ashtray in the shape of a large bud and leaf – Annabel had brought it back from a Nigerian holiday. The objects did not make her invincible but they helped her to detach. She placed her hands on her knees, linked her fingers loosely. 'Parveen.' She disliked the intensity in her own voice. 'Try to focus on my questions. I know it's hard ...'

'You speak my language. I can see you are moved by the music and words we share. Do you know what it's been like, not speaking my language? You knew my song. Didn't you? You are Gujarati.'

'I'm not.' Zara clenched her hands. The words felt like a betrayal.

'But you speak my language.'

'I speak Hindi and Urdu. I understand Gujarati.'

'But you knew my song from Gujarat.'

Zara nodded and looked away. Everyone from Gujarat knew that song.

'Which part of Gujarat are you from?'

Zara shrugged. She didn't know the answer.

'Aunty Hana, I'm not from Trivikrampur, am I?'

'No, sweetheart. You're not.'

'But what shall I say when people ask me?'

'Well, I say I'm Indian.'

'But you are Indian. Where was Mama from? What should I say?'

'Tell them you travel around so much you belong to all the world and all the world belongs to you.'

The answer didn't satisfy. It never satisfied. Where was her mother from? 'She's a fairy – not from Pakistan but Peri-stan,' an admirer had quipped once.

'Where were you born, Aunty Hana?'

'In a beautiful place called Saurashtra – green, lush, fragrant.'

'And my mother?'

'Well, Nyla went away to Pakistan but, of course, she was also born in Saurashtra.'

'Then I'll be from Saurashtra, too.'

But Zara had never been to Saurashtra, to her grandparents' state, so she was never truly convinced. All claims to a home had felt false for so long that she was more comfortable with the familiar sense of unbelonging.

Parveen was still gazing at her, a little curious now, her face tilted. 'You knew the poem.'

'It's a well-known poem by a famous poet.'

'You have the soul of a poet.'

'I'm a barrister. Now, we're here because Miss Hamid asked me to talk you through your appeal case.' She looked at her watch without taking in the time. 'I have another appointment soon. We have ten minutes.'

Parveen flinched again. Again, Zara regretted her terseness.

'Then I have time to tell you the rest of the verse.'

No bad thing for me to die,
If it were just once.

Parveen's words were tripping out in Gujarati, fluid and unexpectedly emotional.

'You know, sister, death comes many times for a single woman of my background. If I'm sent back to India, first I'll be violated by the customs, then the police. If I survive, I'll end up in a refuge or as a domestic servant. When they find out I have nothing and no one, I'll be forced into drugs and prostitution. Every sin I'm forced into will be another death.'

Zara frowned. They were both lawyers, for heaven's sake. She felt a wave of nausea. 'You paint a very bleak picture. I'm sure ...'

'I will not go back. *No bad thing for me to die.* I know of women who were received by respectable organizations. They found them jobs, they settled them in hostels and then they left. Afterwards, the hostel owners or employers forced them into vice because they were alone. One hanged herself. The other was forced to be a prostitute and sell drugs also. I will not endure that. If they try to deport me, I will make it happen so that it only happens once.' Parveen stood up. 'Thank you for your time. I can't tell you how happy I am to meet you. I believed I would die without ever again sharing my poetry and my songs with anyone who could truly understand. I feel something coming together – here,' she tapped herself between her breasts with a rolled fist. 'My heart feels cool.'

Her smile, as she turned to leave, was dazzling: it transformed her from plain to beautiful. Then she was gone, leaving Zara drenched in despair. How, in God's name, would she get Parveen to respond appropriately in court?

She looked at her diary. Nothing booked until after lunch. She felt guilty and fearful for sending Parveen away – still, the time was probably better spent looking through her papers and constructing a suitable strategy. Her head throbbed.

2

Peter was getting dinner ready when Zara got home. 'You will love this,' he said, coming out from behind the kitchen counter to greet her. 'It's got your favourite things in it – aubergine, sun-dried tomato, goat cheese.' He stopped when he saw her face and walked over. 'Hard day?'

He put his arm around her and she let herself lean against his chest for a moment before pulling away. She couldn't allow herself to weaken; she had a tough evening ahead. She took off her jacket, walked into the kitchen and slumped against the counter. It was impressive how Peter managed to keep the worktop clear even when he was working with so many ingredients. He continued with his chopping and cutting but she could sense him waiting. Like most psychotherapists, he had no trouble with long silences. She sat down and closed her eyes, playing a game – she wouldn't say anything until he spoke. She massaged her forehead. The pressure brought relief.

'This should help,' Peter placed a glass of water and two paracetamol caplets in front of her.

'Bad night,' she replied. 'Strange dream. Bugged me all day. It was about the Green-clad Man ...'

'The founder of the Ramzi Order?'

Zara nodded.

'What was the story, exactly? A Vamana maharaja, Hindu, adopted a green-clad Muslim sage as his guru, right?'

She winced. '*Reductio ad absurdum*. He's a big deal around Trivikrampur.'

Peter disappeared behind the door of the refrigerator and pulled out a pack of cherry tomatoes. 'Shall I add these to the salad?

They're very sweet. I don't really know the history of the Green Man.'

She could tell he was not interested in her dream. 'That's irrelevant right now.'

'Sure. Of course. The dream. What happened?' She ignored his indifference.

'I've been bottling it up all day. The Green-clad Man's on the edge of an island – a tropical one. I'm meant to know it but I don't recognize it. He beckons to me. I get right up close but he's behind an invisible barrier – as if I'm being kept out of something, as usual.'

Kept out as usual. Why had she said that? Did she mean Peter? She forced herself to carry on. 'But then, he just drifts away on his island, waving. He looks as if he's sorry for me. And suddenly, I know that there's only one prisoner on that island.'

'Your mother?' Peter grasped her hand. She took a large gulp of cold water, forcing down the constriction in her throat. It lodged painfully in her chest. 'Yes, but it was also me.' She closed her eyes for a moment to lock in the tears, but they slid down her cheeks. What had she done all those years ago to make her mother disappear?

Zara took a deep breath and let her body go floppy to get rid of the physical tension. 'My mother wouldn't come out to see me.' Her voice was steady now. 'What do you think it means?'

'Well, it's hard to say, of course.' He was quartering the tiny tomatoes with great care. 'With dreams you can't just glibly give your own take ... hang on, there was something from India this morning.' He walked out to the hall, calling behind him. 'I'll bring it in.'

Zara was hurt. If he didn't want to mix the professional with the personal, fair enough, but it was the subtext that was bothering her. Couldn't he see how desperate she was for his help – or was he choosing to ignore it? She looked around her at the beautifully set table, the gleaming kitchen, his magnificent salad, the carefully halved caplets on the table beside her. If he was unwilling to address the things that mattered, then all this was merely a substitute for caring. Perhaps he didn't mind the shallowness of their present relationship and when she forced a discussion he blamed – no, he *cited* – her obsession with work. When the closeness had gone work filled the deficit. Her twinge of pain quickly turned to irritation because Peter knew how hard it was for her to mention her mother or to ask for help. 'Take risks,' he always said, yet he withdrew the moment she did. She followed him into the hall, half-heartedly wanting to confront him.

Peter held out a pale blue envelope edged with dark blue and red. Zara reached out, her breath solid in her chest as she ripped it open.

'Aunt Hana,' she whispered. 'She's ill. Look ... she couldn't finish.'

Peter took her hand and led her into the dining room. He pulled out the chair closest to the door and guided her into it. She could see him at the fridge, through the hatch, refilling her glass with crushed ice and water.

The shock of the icy liquid in her throat brought her back to the here and now. 'The Green Man. Was he trying to warn me?' She could hear herself conflating her mother with Aunty Hana as Peter shook his head.

'You're upset. Phone Trivikram. It's the only way to put your mind at rest.'

He handed her the phone. Zara dropped her gaze to the gleaming black glass of her dining-table, saw the reflection of the centrepiece: the amethyst obelisk she had found in a pile of rubble in the Ramzi meditation room on her last visit, infused with shades from a mauve whisper to deep purple. The dream had nothing to do with the letter. There was no magic. The incidents were unrelated. Synchronicity, Peter would call it.

She picked up the telephone and dialled.

3

The notes of the flute playing 'Breeze over the Thar Desert' came to an end and Zara opened her eyes. Clouds drifted away, letting in the sun. The furrow between her brows grew smooth, the crinkled edges of her eyes relaxed. It always had this effect on her, the Indian flute. Peter used to be amazed that such a 'primitive' instrument could produce this exquisite sound. He thought it was a waste of the musician's formidable skill. He had said it once in Qila and Saif quoted a verse from Rumi saying the player should 'be the note' – the breath of the Creator, to be breathed rather than to breathe. It was by submitting to the instrument, demonstrating complete trust that the player could be one with it. That was the secret. Peter was enraptured by the explanation. He had never again referred to the unsophisticated nature of the instrument. 'After all,' he said, 'an entity should be evaluated by its capability. Your cousin's views are always so enlightening.'

Saif had been reassuring on the phone last night. 'A little blip,' he said. 'A mini-stroke, they think. It did knock her back a bit but she's recovering.' Aunt Hana was weak but she had not lost any of her functions. It was a relief. Today had been a busy day. First, flattering news from the Senior Partner, Robert, telling her an influential judge had suggested she apply for the position of Queen's Counsel, and then endless interruptions. Parveen's case was testing her skills to the extreme and she still wasn't sure she would convince a judge.

Ten minutes of the music eased Zara's headache and she was ready to face the Underground home. Carefully, she ran through her list and packed the documents for tomorrow's hearing. She flicked off her lamp and stood up.

The door burst open and Stella stood framed by the light from her PA's room, like the subject of an arty photograph, tiny silhouette a little hunched, short, spiked hair, hand poised in mid-air.

'Zara! Congratulations! I've just heard you're taking silk! Not bad! QC at thirty-five! Why you and not me?'

'Political expediency?' The words were out and Zara felt churlish. Her first reaction to the invitation had been guilt. The memo would be out tomorrow. It made her feel apprehensive. Knives in chambers could be as sharp as anywhere full of clever, argumentative people.

Stella stepped into the room and shut the door behind her. 'You've been a Hamilton for sixteen years. You count as one of us.'

'You can share my parents,' Stella had announced when she introduced them all those years ago as they helped themselves to the buffet at the first-term parents' lunch at Oxford. 'They've always wanted a more normal daughter.' Blanche and Stewart welcomed her without reservation.

'Don't wait for Little Miss Elusive here,' Stewart Hamilton said. 'Pop down when you're homesick; we'll look after you. And you can tell us about India. We have a son working out there.'

The first time Zara visited the farm, she found Blanche in a muddy field, assisting a vet to examine a pony. She waved. 'Come on over.'

Zara hitched up her trousers, trying not to laugh at the radical transformation in Blanche from classic drawing-room elegance to farmhand, complete with floppy hat, puffer jacket and jeans tucked into massive Wellies. Zara was dressed for a living room, not a muddy field. But she waved back bravely, slipped through the stile into the field, skidded and almost fell. Blanche looked a bit surprised. 'Sorry,' she called out. 'Should have warned you. It's a bit slippery under the grass in places. You need Wellies, really.'

Zara kept walking. All four inches of her heels sank into the soft, sticky mud and she was sure she could smell something unpleasant on the hem of her trousers. The joke was on her now as Blanche tried to conceal her amusement and converted the incident to a story which she told wittily on many social occasions over the years, drawing laughter at the gaucheness of the 'townie' Oxford undergraduate. The incident bonded them.

When they came into the house after the vet had gone, Blanche picked up Zara's sandals by their delicate straps and pronounced them ridiculous. Then she flung them into the guest bathroom, wondering if they could be salvaged.

The farm became a second home. The Hamiltons were friendly, generous people and the openness of the farm and its acres of land, its constant flow of workers and visitors and diverse activities, gave her a sense of freedom she missed in her life at Oxford. In a way the rambling stone house felt familiar, with its many corridors and wings and people going about their work. Apart from the missing troops of 'servants' and a more egalitarian attitude to the workers, who Blanche called 'helpers' or 'staff', the lifestyle felt familiar and reassuring.

'Let's ring Blanche,' Zara said, turning her lamp back on. 'She'll be pleased.'

Stella threw up her hands. 'You haven't told me properly yet.'

Zara chuckled. Stella always lifted her mood. 'I called by your office earlier.'

'Wasted day. I was stuck in court for hours – loads of delays. But this is great news. QC, eh?'

'What are you up to this evening?' Zara said. 'Come home and celebrate?' Stella would lighten the evening.

'Why not? A chance to see my elusive brother.'

Stella waved long, painted fingernails under Zara's eyes. 'What are we waiting for, girlfriend?' She grabbed Zara's briefcase. 'Let's hit the liquor shelves. It's party time.'

Stella's lithe form darted between customers in the wine section of the supermarket. Zara saw her spiky hair bobbing up and down in the crowd and walked over to her.

'Extra champagne!' Stella said, hugging three bottles of Laurent Perrier, adding, 'What?' with faux truculence. 'The third one's half-price.'

Zara laughed. 'What is it with you and supermarket offers?'

A customer at a nearby till was paying with vouchers and as she moved on, a woman in the queue shoved forward her trolley, snapping:

'Fucking asylum-seekers.'

Zara tensed as Parveen's face flashed in her mind. Fucking asylum-seekers – that's all they were and the opinion endlessly ricocheted back from the people to the Border Control authorities.

'Britain's modern-day slaves,' she said.

Stella's cheerful face crumpled with sympathy. 'I know. There's this swami guy we're preparing an appeal for. Has a PhD and all sorts. I cannot understand why he was denied his stay. We have medical reports proving he's been tortured and beaten. They cut him loose, basically, no NASS allowance, and, of course, no housing and not allowed to work. He shovels crap all day for this plumber guy, then goes home with him and does the housework.'

Zara felt sick. 'They pay him, right?'

'Nahhh! Apparently the guy who he works for doesn't want to break the law by paying him. So he has to be grateful for his food and shelter – he sleeps on the kitchen floor. Never complains. Doesn't even have money for toothpaste. Makes do with salt and soda bicarb from the kitchen cupboard.'

'And we're meant to switch off after doing the legal bit,' Zara said. 'Sorry sir, lost this one. Off to the next.'

Stella squeezed Zara's arm as they joined the queue. 'Let's not take it home with us, Zara. This is a celebration. *Your* night. That's the good part of the job. Recognition. Kudos! We're going to have fun!'

Zara wondered as they jumped on a bus if she could handle Stella's exuberance tonight, then felt immediately guilty. She had become hyper-conscious of how acutely her client group was disliked. A street dog, Parveen had called herself. It was lack of information, she knew, but it was also the fear of being overwhelmed, culturally and economically. Recently, though, she couldn't stop thinking about it – she saw racial and cultural prejudice everywhere. She was frustrated that she could not change attitudes on the streets or with men and women in authority and she sometimes caught herself mentally documenting comments and incidents she witnessed, analysing and re-analysing whether they were really derogatory or if she was reading too much into them. Yet there was a time she had been oblivious to it. Once, she'd travelled on the Underground with a couple of hooligans chanting racist and misogynist obscenities. She was filled with pity for the victim and only realized when she stepped out that she had been the sole woman in the carriage! She still laughed when she recalled it.

Then there were people like her in-laws in the Norfolk countryside, who treated her from the start like a member of the family – Blanche in particular, roped her into baking and jam-making for her fundraising drives. 'I don't suppose you can make samosas?' she had ventured once. 'They go down an absolute storm here.' Zara had called home for the recipe and tracked down the thin wraps in a shop in Willesden.

Stewart had got her involved in his campaign to ban the shopping plaza which would quickly have destroyed the local businesses.

'We witter on about "loss of Englishness",' he said in one of his speeches. 'The corner shop and the country pub characterize us. Our towns and village centres define Englishness: the haberdashers and toyshops and menders of things; the proprietors who know the names and preferences of their "regulars"; the pub curry and mango chutney. Losing these institutions is what erodes Englishness. We lose our identity when we are homogenized through sheer lack of choice, forced into vast car parks and shopping centres, no different from those in America and Dubai and everywhere else. It's the octopus tentacles of international franchisees that strip our identity, not people who come to live and work here.' His words made people think. The campaign was successful. Zara had to keep reminding herself that people were different – God knew she had enough weaknesses of her own. She had no intention of adding negativity and self-righteousness.

The bus turned the corner and the lush greenery of Tiverton Green came into view. Stella pulled off her earphones. 'Home sweet home,' she said as the bus shuddered to a stop.

4

Stella slid off her backpack as they walked down the forecourt to the door. Zara reached for her key but the door swung open. Peter had spotted them coming. He took Zara's shopping bags. 'Decent day?'

'You get more uxorious by the minute, bruv.'

'Oh Lord!' Peter laughed. 'Zara's dragged in some flotsam.'

Stella gave her brother a playful punch in the stomach and shoved her backpack into his arms. 'Prepare to be well and truly outshone, bro.'

Peter looked at the bottles of champagne and raised an eyebrow. 'Found someone to take you on? He's not lurking in the bushes, is he?'

'Give over. It's your eminent wife. Are you telling him, Zara, or shall I?'

'They're suggesting I take silk.' Zara's voice sounded tinny, mutinous. 'It's a long process ...' Peter set down the bags and lifted Zara off the ground.

'Well done, *you*!' She was relieved. 'She's young to be a QC, you know,' Stella said. 'It's quite an honour at any age, but ...'

'It's well deserved,' Peter said. 'She's totally dedicated.'

Totally. Zara wished he hadn't used that word. It left her feeling judged. As if she was ignoring other duties. But Peter had not said that. This was probably one of those 'shadow projections' Peter and his friends talked about. The censure was coming from her.

Stella was threatening to pop a bottle of champagne.

Peter held the bottle between both palms. 'No,' he protested. 'It has to be on ice for at least an hour.'

'An hour?' Stella sounded plaintive. 'But I specially got it out of the cooler.'

'You, little sister, are turning into an alcoholic.'

'Hardly.'

Zara enjoyed listening to Peter and Stella bicker. She let herself be drawn into it, away from the day's concerns. Peter went out to the back porch to prepare the barbecue while Zara unpacked the shopping bags. Stella found a plastic bucket and packed all three bottles in ice. 'Headache still bothering you?' she asked.

Zara could feel a furrow between her eyebrows. 'Aunty Hana wrote.' She reached across the counter for the letter. 'Look at that line. Something happened while she was writing.'

'Did you ring?'

'I spoke to my cousin Saif, and his wife. They say it's not serious. Aunt Hana's had a transient ischaemic attack. Apparently it wasn't much more than a wobble. She's weak but Pebbles reckons she's on the mend. She's eating well. Come to think of it, Pebbles asked a lot of questions about the letter.' Zara stabbed viciously at a piece of chicken breast.

'You can't kill it, it's already dead.' Stella put her arm round Zara. 'It's been getting to you all day, hasn't it?'

Zara nodded. 'A bad night, then this. And another bad night.'

'But she's going to be okay,' Stella said. 'You'll see.'

Zara shrugged. 'I hope she will.' She looked away as tears threatened.

Peter walked in. 'Why so glum, you two?' he said. 'This is a celebration!' He handed Zara a paper bag. 'I was at St Albans Cathedral today. It was wonderful. Gentle sunshine, soft breeze. Singing at morning service.' Zara slid a book out of the bag. *Legends of the Green Man.* 'How thoughtful.' Her voice was flat. She saw a flicker of anxiety on Peter's face before he scooped up the chicken she had cubed.

'Satay? Will you make the peanut sauce, or shall I?' He started to prepare a marinade for the chicken. Stella washed the Romaine lettuce. 'I fancy a Caesar-ish salad.'

'What does that mean, exactly?' Peter grinned.

Stella turned to Zara. 'Is he the geezer from your family?'

'Similar,' Peter said quickly, without looking up. 'There are some interesting connections.' He was on edge, Zara could see. Probably my fault, she thought.

She looked up. 'I dreamt about him. My mother was there – not wanting to see me. At least she's consistent.' She saw a flash of her mother, lost and fey, quoting some verse, and felt guilty for sniping.

That was it! She knew now why the encounter with Parveen had made such an impact! Her mother had a verse for all occasions, too. She had sensed this morning that Parveen used them to carry her emotions, to transfer her pain elsewhere. Perhaps Nyla had done the same.

'Your mother has never actually refused to see you, has she?' Stella scooped up the chopped lettuce and piled it into a large glass bowl. 'I mean, she hasn't contacted you but ... I love this huge brandy-glass bowl of yours.' She wiped her hands on a tea towel. 'Sorry ... we never talked about this before ... but you could find out ...'

Zara shook her head. 'Easier for her to find me.'

Stella shrugged. 'Maybe she's thinking the same.'

'Maybe,' Zara murmured. She could see Stella waiting to regroup and come back for another round. The quality made her a formidable opponent in court.

'I would have to find out,' Stella said. 'I couldn't let it rest until I knew.'

Zara felt tearful. Peter had evaded her question, Stella was engaging. It was what people did when they cared. Why was she so out of step with Peter these days?

She watched him bustling around the barbecue. He'd been a man with strong, direct opinions, determined to help the needy, perhaps start an international charity. His views had been strong, uncomfortable at times, but she had respected him for speaking out. Now he was so 'open-minded' there was a gaping space where conviction had been.

A sick feeling snaked through her. It was an old feeling. She thought she'd seen the last of it: an unreasonable feeling that Peter had betrayed her when he decided to train as a psychotherapist.

She put down her knife and looked at him. He had been true to himself. She was the discontented one. She knew she should not hold him responsible. He had done what he set out do – he *was* helping the needy. Only they were not the kind of needy she'd expected. And they were not in Trivikrampur where they had planned to return to work – together.

5

Two arcs of light curved towards each other, powered by throbbing midnight engines. They crossed, insubstantial, like ghosts. Another light, strong, harsh, was splintering into tiny, painful shards, finding Zara's retina. She clenched her lids, swinging out of bed, then opened them again. Her eyes were acclimatizing to the dark. Her mind lagged behind in some maudlin zone.

The cars stopped coming. For the moment. Zara drifted over to her dressing table, gazing out. She no longer saw the view. Beyond a succession of gates were forecourts or gardens beautifully laid out before freestanding houses but it was hardly the vivid, lively view of the bustling street she had grown up to in Qila. 'We've made it our own,' people said about their homes. Or, 'We've put our stamp on it.' Her experience was different. The Ramzi fortress had put its stamp on her and all its residents. It had existed for generations before her and would survive well after she had gone. Bricks and mortar did not change with a slap of paint or the installation of an electronic track on the curtains.

'So *you*,' Stella had commented, as had others, when the thickly lined and interleaved curtains had gone up in her London home.

She was surprised and gratified they perceived a 'you' in her, a particular someone with an identity substantial enough to equate with a lifestyle, a colour, a shape. But which 'you' were they talking about? The career woman, about to become Queen's Counsel at thirty-five? An orphaned, abandoned child? A voiceless, nameless immigrant? Or the scion of a noble household, brought up to the knowledge of a line that began farther back than the thirteenth century? Aunt Hana used to laugh when she told the story of how, as a child, Zara discovered she had descended, on her mother's side, from Chengiz Khan and Tamerlane.

'With two such violent ancestors, what chance have I of being a peaceful person, Mama?'

Zara remembered the incident only through Hana's retelling but Nyla's perplexed look was imprinted on her eyes. Clearly, Nyla found her puzzling, intrusive; she could not work out how she had produced the bundle of qualities that was her daughter. Zara had stopped looking in the mirror except when she was alone with Hana. In Hana's mirror she was loved and beautiful.

What made her different – the mirrors, the eyes, the light? Maybe there was no self. No definite core but simply a vacillating mass of possibilities seeking a mould. An abyss opened up in her, enveloping her in the darkness that filled the mirror opposite.

She felt her face twist into a grimace. The lowering of vigilance in the night allowed pain to seep through the emotional repositories of the mind into the body. A spear of light cut into her thoughts. The curtains could not stop it – when she was sleeping or dreaming or making love. Making love ... a meaningless phrase for an odd ritual, redolent with significance from the past but in itself not having much to do with love.

Peter looked dignified in sleep. Not the needy creature of a short while ago, pawing at her for gratification. Sex had become an ordeal to her. Was she different or did the world around her make everything so strange?

She was shuddering again. Was her work truly invading her mind, her personal life, so much that she could no longer think normally?

'You're running,' Peter had said last night over hot chocolate after Stella left. 'You use work to shut out what goes on inside.'

'So you've said before,' she said. Peter inclined his head in agreement.

'Take a break from this asylum work, Zara. It underscores your losses. You won't sublimate unresolved issues through fixing your clients' problems.'

He had briefly cut through the foggy space that lately existed between them. She was grateful, humiliated, angry all at the same time. But it was not a reason to give in. Why, in God's name, why, could she not just have said she didn't want to? But no, she just lay there beside him, letting him stroke her arms, feeling him grow more frenetic, more intimate as she wondered about leaving the bed to sleep elsewhere or yet again plead exhaustion or backache. When she could find no excuse for her resistance, she let go, turned to him and responded to his caresses. There was pleasure, of course there was. He was a caring lover who knew her body. But ... inside her there was restlessness. *This is all a tedious waste of time.*

How, when had that happened?

Images flashed in the mirror like shots from a romantic comedy. She watched him from one of the roads fanning out from Trafalgar Square, they crossed towards each other through the scattered jigsaw of traffic. Headlamps like stage lights. When she was halfway across, he ran to meet her, grabbed her in his arms, lifted her above the bonnets of the cars. A startled driver beeped, registered the mad love scene, grinned. She imagined the startled expressions of drivers as they saw her raised above the traffic. They put their hands on their horns, as if in a choreographed scene, and honked a sort of anthem. All of Trafalgar Square was celebrating her success. Time stood still to acknowledge her achievement. Because of Peter. Only because Peter was so happy that she had the job she wanted.

'All the world loves a lover,' a driver shouted from the car. 'Sorry, mate, don't know the rest.' His car slid forward; the 'freeze' button released. There was movement again.

'Nelson's happy for you,' Peter said, grinning at the statue. 'Success is, sort of, his thing.'

She felt she'd drunk her fill of champagne. She wanted to go home, lie in bed with him. 'I don't want to stop making love to you until I die,' she said later.

He rolled over, his body shuddering rhythmically with laughter. 'That's a mighty lie.'

It was rare to feel those surges of passion now – that commitment to sensuality, to pleasure, to gratification.

'Promise me,' she said to him once, 'that we'll never become one of those couples who only ever have sex when they go to bed at night.'

Now, they had sex only when they went to bed at night. Like they brushed their teeth or showered or slid between fresh sheets. That extra, thankfully, only occasional chore to be performed before turning in. But she had never thought of bedtime as sex time. Sex, to her, was a means of locating herself in energetic moments – moments of transformation. That was when the ritual liberated her.

When they first met, sex had frequently happened in the day – in snatched moments carved out for other activities. Worlds ago it was natural to fling off her feather boa and her carefully planned ensemble before a party, to tumble into the bed, to find instant ecstasy, letting Peter muss up her hair, smudge her make-up and then surface later to the image of a youthful Baby Jane staring back at her from the mirror, muzzy with love, eye sockets blackened with mascara, lipstick smearing her chin, knowing the damage was irreparable and not being bothered to start from scratch. She would ask: 'Do you really want to go? Shall I get dressed again?' He always declined, pushed her back into bed. Later, they bought a takeaway.

There had been that one day they had been more disciplined because visiting friends from Trivikrampur were throwing an engagement party. They came back tired and started to make love. She faked her orgasm. He sensed it at once. She cringed inside.

'I can't explain it,' she told him. 'Except, I was enjoying myself but I knew it wasn't going to happen. I thought it best you should ...'

Peter's smooth movements on her body usually lifted and stirred her emotions and senses so much that they drove everything else out of her mind. Even without the orgasm. It was the same that night until she opened her eyes and realized with a shock that in her mind his satiny white arms had been deep brown.

'Never pretend again,' he'd begged, stroking her hair, kissing her eyelids. 'I'd rather just know the truth.'

Something was bothering him, she'd picked up on it at the party. 'I won't,' she promised. 'But you should tell me, too.'

'Stella told me about your ... the maharaja.'

Something ran cold inside her. 'What about him?' Her voice sounded as if it was coming out of someone else.

He rolled away. 'I thought it might have brought things back.'

'Well, if it hadn't, it would now. If it still mattered.'

It was true, she could think of her relationship with Jay and no longer feel pain. She sometimes wondered what made him end it so abruptly but she was over it. The cut had been clean and absolute – he was out of her life.

It was not like Peter to worry about her past relationships but she saw it disturbed him that she had not mentioned Jay. Sexual matters, like everything else between them, were transparent. Theirs wasn't a relationship in which she needed to fake an orgasm. Tonight, more than sixteen years later, she had again underestimated his ability to distinguish between intimacy and pretence.

She looked over at the bed. Peter was gazing at her, propped up on one elbow.

'Restless?' His hair was tousled, a lock fell across his forehead. His looks were as striking as ever. Sadness flooded her for something lost.

'Headlamps. I was thinking you can't do anything about them, however high-tech you get.'

'What's really bothering you, Zara?' His gaze was challenging, boring through her.

'It's late, Peter. We should both sleep.'

The clock read 2.39 am. He dropped to his side, snorted, heaved himself up. That was Peter gearing up for a discussion.

'It's this job of yours. All this thankless work.'

'Invaluable to some of my clients.'

'And to you?'

'My work is being recognized.'

'Ah, the silk.'

Anger stabbed at her. She thought of all the times she could have been snide about his sudden passion for a new career.

'Going to the top of your profession is brilliant,' he said. 'But you're running – upwards, admittedly, but away from your self. I see drivenness, not passion.'

It's your fault, she wanted to say. *Passion went when you changed our life plan.* But she could not say it. He no longer saw that there was nothing left of a self, that she was in crisis. She shook her head to clear away the thought. There was no crisis.

'A trip to Trivikrampur will do you good. Get some balance back. Right now you're lost.'

Zara sank into bed, disappointed. He was saying she was to blame for her own sadness. Where did Peter think she could claw out time to get away? Besides, would that not count as running away? Going back to Trivikram now was out of the question. Pebbles had assured her that Aunty was fine. She buried her face in her pillow, wrapped her arms around it to smother her longing for Aunty Hana. But as she drifted into its softness, she was overwhelmed with a terrible fear of losing Peter.

6

She could remember the silhouette against the French windows of the Hamilton house and the first words he said to her. 'I'm Peter – the prodigal son returned.'

'I'm afraid they're out – a major shopping trip. How come ...?'

Peter stepped out of the shadows and she stopped speaking to take him in. He was a lot taller and stronger than he looked in his pictures. And his skin had tanned during his years in India.

'I go in for surprises in a big way,' he said. 'I'll make myself busy.'

Zara warmed to him. Over lunch with his family, he regaled them with stories of his travels in India and she was struck by how much he had absorbed of its sounds and colours and character. He had an endearing way of including Zara in his experiences, asking her for clarification or confirmation of his comments. This was the first time in her three years at Oxford that she had met someone with his depth of knowledge about India.

After lunch, Peter showed her his favourite spots on the farm and chatted about his childhood.

'I'll be in London next week,' he said as he dropped her at the station. 'There's an exhibition ... perhaps you'd like to come? Indian palaces. They're stunning buildings. There was a sense of noblesse oblige in those days. Rulers helped their people.'

Zara felt stung. 'And when do you reckon they stopped?'

'When the states stopped being kingdoms,' he replied. 'When the people no longer "belonged" to the princes.'

She let it pass; the exhibition would be her chance to explain the facts. She was intrigued by Peter. He seemed as passionate and sure of his point of view as she was of hers.

'You are nothing like the rest of your family,' she told him, as they made their way past the small bookshop at the Brunei Gallery in Russell Square, into the main exhibition space.

'And you?' he said, raising an eyebrow. 'Are you like yours?'

Zara gasped as she spotted a photograph of her grandfather's palace. She crossed the room.

'What is it?' Peter asked. 'What's wrong?'

She grabbed his arm with one hand and pointed wildly with the other. 'My mother grew up there.' She lowered her voice. 'It's my grandfather's palace.'

'Really?' Peter whispered back. 'Have you been there?'

She shook her head. 'I was a baby. I don't remember it.'

'Why are we whispering?' he said suddenly. 'Is it a secret?'

Zara laughed. 'Didn't want to be ostentatious.'

'That you can't help,' he said and laughed when she gave him a playful push.

She peered into the photograph where a few men were playing cricket on the lawn. 'That tall man there. He was from the third generation of cooks in my mother's family. My grandfather noticed how clever he was and sent him to boarding school.'

Peter looked skeptical. 'The nobles strike a blow for equality,' he said. 'What did the education buy him? Was he your uncle's secretary? Or commander of the royal kitchens?'

Zara wondered if Peter intended to offend her. She shrugged her shoulders, controlling the urge to snap back.

'So the family legend only tells of the prince's largesse. Not the low glass ceiling of the class system.'

'Actually,' Zara said, 'I called him "Uncle" when he visited Qila.' She stopped and faced him. 'Kids don't care what grown-ups do for a living. I only know his background because he kept mentioning it. His family drove around in a Bentley and his wife behaved like a prima donna – shopped twice a year in Europe.'

'I salute your grandfather,' Peter said.

She focused on exhibits of homes she had visited, trying not to be annoyed by his bluntness. Peter asked questions and she told him about Hana's work with female artisans and the palace that Jay and his mother had transformed into a hotel collective run by former family retainers when they could no longer afford armies of servants.

'I'll shut up,' she said eventually. 'I'm sorry.'

'Well,' he said. 'I suppose you can take the girl away from the nobility but you can't take the nobility away from the girl.'

'Oh shut up,' she said, laughing. Then, 'If I've changed your mind ...'

'Now I know that a few rich and powerful people care about the underprivileged. Your family seems to ... but largely I'm still not convinced.'

'If you say so ...' she said. She noticed his furrowed brow, his thoughtful expression and tried not to be angry. 'It seems to me you have a problem with my background and your reasons are ... wrong.'

She walked quickly ahead and he grasped her arm to slow her down. 'Does that mean we can't be friends?' he asked.

Zara was startled by his intensity. Her heart was beating but she made no attempt to break away as he ushered her out into the open.

'We should have something to eat,' he said. Zara nodded, wondering what had just happened.

'I'm sorry if I've offended you,' he said over lunch. 'But things are not as they should be in India, even with exceptions like your family.'

'You could say that of any society.'

He shook his head. 'To some extent. My parents eat and shop where our farmhands do.'

'But you're aware of it. "Our farmhands?" Listen to yourself.'

He smiled. 'Truce?' Peter put out his hand and when she put her hand in it, he held on.

The next morning he was at her doorstep with a huge bouquet of flowers.

'You're different,' he said. 'I couldn't go away without asking if you'll spend the day with me.'

He drove her to Sussex along the coast and through chocolate-box villages where they stopped for cream tea in picturesque tea houses.

'Ethnic Britain,' Peter said, handing her a Pontefract cake from a village shop. Zara thanked him, expecting a samosa. She gazed at the strange, shiny black lump of liquorice in her hand.

'Ethnic?' she asked.

He laughed. 'You think "ethnic" means "foreign", right? Well, not necessarily. It's cultural heritage. Anyone's. Like cream tea and Bakewell tart.' He grabbed back the sweet. 'Pontefract Castle,' he said, solemnly tapping the moulded stamp in the middle of the cake. 'It has a highly respectable pedigree. All the way back to the Normans.'

She laughed. 'Indians never think of western communities as "ethnic".'

He was suddenly serious. 'A hangover from colonial times, you think?' He grabbed her hand and dragged her to the car and she realized he was trying to avoid edgy topics. Oddly, she was learning from him and it was interesting to look at her own world from the perspective of an objective observer. Not that Peter lacked opinions.

They returned to north-west London late on Sunday night and she thanked him for the weekend.

'There was just one thing missing ...' He scratched his head. 'If you'd fallen over or been useless at climbing, I could have executed a chivalrous rescue and snatched the chance to kiss you.'

Zara felt a rush inside. Peter leaned forward on the steering wheel and looked into her face. She avoided his gaze.

'Would you have pushed me away, Zara?' He held her face between his palms and kissed her on the top of her head, her brow, her nose. He dropped a kiss on her mouth, then another. She felt her arms go around his neck as she nuzzled her face close to his. He cupped the crown of her head in one hand and drew her face so close she could hardly breathe.

Zara's voice was shaky when she spoke. 'I think we should probably go inside. The neighbours ...'

'I don't think I can be chaste around you,' he said when she told him he could stay the night. She took his hand and led him to the bedroom. They were barely inside when he pulled her to him, ruffling her hair and holding her close, stroking her face and arms, nuzzling her neck and shoulder with soft kisses, sliding down her shoulder straps.'I can't believe my luck,' he said.

The following week, Peter moved to London and got himself a volunteering job on the psychiatric ward of a teaching hospital.

Zara was relieved that Stella accepted the relationship without awkwardness.

'I was worried he'd inflict some weirdo on us,' she said. 'What a relief – you're already part of the family.'

Stella was running ahead. They could hardly plan a future together – in two or three years she would be back in Trivikram. Stella's comment pleased her and worried her.

Zara had never doubted that she would return to Qila – Aunty Hana was waiting anxiously for her return. Yet the thought of separating from Peter was unbearable. He was the only person she had met who could completely abandon inhibition, like that first day he had arrived at her doorstep and wafted her away for the weekend. Or the time when they'd argued, yet again, over their differing perspectives on India and she had battled the Underground in rush hour to find her communal hall filled with flowers and a large note in red ink, saying: 'Flat 5 please ring Flat 1'.

'I couldn't find enough containers for them,' said the woman from Flat 1. 'The rest are in my bathtub. Did you win an Oscar?'

She knew then that the disagreements would not split them – they could each maintain their identity. Peter was the first person she had ever rowed with and she found it satisfying to have her say and get rid of the tension and misunderstanding. But some differences between them went deeper.

There was the time when she was meeting him at the National Theatre. Her heart lifted when she saw him. He was signing a petition. She looked up to read the slogans. 'No more child labour'. 'Indian government! Stop exploiting your children'. 'Legislate against child exploitation'. 'No corporate colonization of India'. She felt her skin burn. What did these do-gooders know about the reality? She wished, too, that it could be different but without the chance to work the children faced terrible things.

'And I don't just mean starvation, Peter,' she said over lunch. 'I mean trading their vital organs, being sold into the sex industry, crime, professional begging ...'

'Pressurizing the government is a starting point,' Peter said.

She huffed out a long breath. 'India is no longer the white man's burden,' she said. The skin of her knuckles was taut, white. 'There are things to be done for kids here, too. But it's easier to patronize people out there.'

'Leave kids to their fate, then?'

'If the alternatives are worse.'

She did not want to eat with him. 'I'm not hungry,' she said. She walked out of the restaurant but he caught up with her.

'Please,' he said. 'Don't be angry. I know you care. But is there another way?'

'Ethics and personal responsibility,' she said. 'Compel western companies to follow a code of ethics when they outsource.'

Peter reached into his pocket for a hanky and dabbed at her tears. She pushed away his hand.

He smoothed back her hair, twisted a curl round his finger. Zara grew still. Peter's closeness was making her entire body tingle. But these moments of ideological conflict were like darkness between them and she wondered if they could be resolved.

Peter put his arms around her. 'Your passion is very exciting,' he said. He took her hand and kissed each fingertip. Zara did not resist. He cared and he was prepared to show it. And his love of India had endeared him to her from the start.

Peter persuaded her to abandon work that afternoon and they went rowing in Regent's Park. Standing on the bridge afterwards, they looked at the tree-lined horizon, slightly hazy and changing from green to autumnal shades.

'Zara,' he said, looking into the water. 'Will you marry me?'

She longed to say yes. 'How?' she said, slipping into his arms, wanting him to understand. 'I'm going back in a year.'

He kissed her. 'I thought I might pre-empt that by proposing.' She glimpsed the sadness on his face before he pulled her to him. 'I can't let you go.'

A few days later, she saw him outside her chambers, looking radiant. 'I'll go to India with you. We could both help with local issues ...'

She put her hands to his cheeks. 'You'd hate it,' she said, trying to keep the tears from her voice. 'We'd disagree about everything and you'd be forced to mix with people like my family. And you're right, some of them speak and think like fascists. You won't be happy.'

He looked troubled. 'Will your family accept me? Would you have the courage ...?'

'Saif and Aunty Hana would support us.'

'Then I'll be fine. I'll have you and the work I love. I can survive the rest. Please, Zara, say yes.'

Slowly, she nodded and let herself rest against him. 'But there'll be some tough times.'

She had not guessed how easily her trust could vanish, how simple it was to let go of the line to happiness – and that just a few years later, giving in to Peter's change of mind without a struggle would change her life.

It was a silver moment when it happened. They were walking over the scrubby growth and bronze-green grasses sprouting from the dunes. An Irish beach in Donegal, the sea, peaceful, edged with smooth, damp sand. Runnels of water cut channels in the ground as river met sea. They walked hand in hand.

Peter said: 'I've decided to train as a psychotherapist.'

There was sudden movement on the surface of the sand. Zara thought it was a swarm of small insects. Her eyes were gritty as she watched the swarm rise as high as her shin. 'What is it?'

'Sand,' Peter said.

They watched the cloud of fine sand swivel and swerve across the surface of the beach to the sea.

'Flinging dust in my eyes,' she murmured. Peter craned his neck, inquiring. 'A translation,' she explained. 'It means "to deceive".'

In that moment, she abandoned the country of her mind and moved elsewhere. She wanted to point out that in order to fulfil his dream Peter would have to tread on hers. That if she had to live elsewhere, then merely visiting Qila would be too painful. The fight seeped out of her.

It was as if Peter decided to compensate for her lack of resistance by removing all conflict from their relationship. It brought constraint into the dynamic between them. She could never make herself ask him why he had changed his mind.

7

Zara felt uneasy as she stepped on to the Tube at Queen's Park Station on her way to meet Naz Hamid. Parveen's appeal was scheduled for two that afternoon.

An Albanian child skipped through the carriage, begging, stopping occasionally to check that her mother was behind her. The passengers reacted in synchronization: the rolling of eyes, the clatter of tut-tutting, the hiss of sighs, people pulling back their feet, moving their objects out of the way as if to avoid contamination. Zara reached into her pocket and gave the child a pound coin. The woman beside her spoke to the air.

'No one starves in this country. The State takes care of them.'

In this country. It was a loaded phrase. Responses gushed into Zara's mind. The empty seat on one side of her was stained a bright yellow. On the other side, some bored passenger had stuck together a large rip in the fabric with blobs of chewing gum, hardened now, and black.

Zara reached into her bag and brought out a twenty-pound note. It was for all the times she and her fellow passengers had tossed a coin into the hat of the alcoholic 'regular' who got on the Underground at Waterloo and lurched through the train, pungent with stale cider and weeks of dried excretion. No doubt he'd refute the claim that no one went without food or shelter *in this country.*

'The English don't encourage begging,' the woman muttered.

Oh yes? Zara thought. I suppose that's why Central London's packed with beggars desperate for a crust. Oh well, a beggar by any other name. Homeless, addict, down-and-out.

'But charity is a glorious British tradition,' Zara said, handing over the note to the Albanians. Her heart was thumping. Childish, maybe, but she felt high as she raced up the escalator and out into Piccadilly.

The sun's glare was breaking up the scene, consuming patches of the cityscape, darkening others, where the shade of towering structures fell. Still treading air, Zara stepped out into the street. Across the road she saw the Green-clad Man.

He was walking towards the Circus. Her eyes followed him and she stepped into oncoming traffic. A bus winged past, so close that the sleeve of her suit was smeared with a trail of grey-black dust and diesel. The heat of its momentum, its closeness hurled her back and she staggered.

People were surrounding her. Concerned voices spoke in her ear. 'Are you okay?' 'Do you need anything?'

Zara shook her head to expel the chaos. 'I'm fine. I must have been ...' She waved down a black cab and jumped in. 'Gray's Inn Road, please.'

She craned her neck for the forest green robe – not a glimpse – and slid back from the edge of the seat. The vision must have been triggered by stress and the disturbing dream of a few days ago.

Her phone vibrated in her pocket and she jumped. 'Zara Hamilton.'

'Zara? It's Naz. Naz Hamid. Could you come immediately to Bart's Hospital. Please. EC1.'

Zara leaned forward and instructed the cabbie then returned to the phone. 'I'm on my way. What's wrong? What's the matter?'

She knew before Naz could answer that Parveen had carried out her threat. 'I will not go back. *No bad thing for me to die.* I will make it happen so that it happens only once.'

All that was visible of Parveen were her eyes, their blackness spilling over through thin slivers of space between the bindings. Could those eyes see through them?

'Parveen.' Zara reached out to grasp her hand and stopped. No part of Parveen was whole. The fire had consumed her skin.

'I told you I would do the job properly.

Somewhere, be a shore for the sluggish wave of night
Somewhere, a stopping place for the boat of a grieving heart.

I needed to say farewell in my language. I wanted someone who could send me on my way with the Fateha.'

'I'm so sorry ...'

'It's no life for a woman alone. Please forgive me for anything I may have said or done to offend you. Alvida. God be with you.'

It was futile now, even insulting, to tell Parveen she would be fine. Her eyelids fluttered. Zara felt a corresponding flutter in her belly.

'Alvida, Parveen.'

Parveen's lips moved. Her voice was part whisper, part grating chant. She raised her mutilated hand then let it drop, her energy depleted. Zara bent closer to listen.

My heart, my wayfarer
Another injunction imposed
For us to become stateless, you and I,
Calling from lane to lane
Wandering from land to land
Searching out traces
Of a message-bearing friend
Asking every stranger
The address that was home.

'My next home will be forever.'

Parveen's head came up for a moment then slumped back. Her eyes streamed through the thick white bindings.

Did I drive her to this? Zara thought. *Please, please, don't let me be responsible for her suicide.* Her throat ached as she swallowed.

'One more favour,' Parveen rasped out her words. 'Women like me should be able to go home safely.'

Zara felt stiff with resistance. All the strength of Parveen's body seemed to drain to her eyes and she fixed them on Zara. No! Zara wanted to shout. No, I won't. What can I do?

Parveen's breath was rattling. Zara panicked; Parveen was dying.

'I will. I will do my best.' Zara's skin felt hot and at the same time she wanted to shiver. The commitment could demand a lifetime's devotion. How could she find the time, the wherewithal, the *will*? The thought was heavy inside. She looked for a chair. She was still framing the reservations and provisos in her mind when Parveen spoke again.

'One last request. Please say the Fateha for me before they take away my body. May Allah have mercy on my soul. Allah Hafiz. May God protect you. May He guide you in your mission.'

Zara struggled to raise her hands in prayer, to recite the once familiar words of the Fateha; it was only the fear of heaping another disappointment on Parveen as she died, that forced her to do it.

8

Swami Ramcharan Das answered the small double-glazed door of the Alperton house. He looked pristine in his white kurta-pyjama and a beige homespun shawl over his shoulder – the 'uniform' of the patriot. He opened the door wide and stepped back to let in Zara. The smell of incense sticks was pervasive, patchouli or rose, a cloying, flowery fragrance very different from the woody, subtle sandalwood she preferred.

'Mrs Zara, welcome. Miss Stella informed me you would come. It is very kind of you.'

It was hard to imagine this man in a soiled tracksuit, sleeves rolled up, arms down a sewage drain. He walked elegantly ahead to the kitchen.

'Can I offer you some tea? Some coffee? Cold water?'

Ramcharan smiled. 'Who drinks cold water here, in such unkind weather? Look at the raining outside. In India, you know, you can't enter any premises, even not the shops, without being offered cold water. But you are Indian, you know that. Please. Sit.' He waved towards the table.

'It's very kind of you to make time for me.'

'Miss Stella said you need some information from me. It is my dharma, you understand dharma, no? I have sworn to spread truth in the cause of unity of nations. What can I tell you? Miss Stella said you want me to provide information about Gujarat situation.' He looked wistful. 'You are from Gujarat?'

Zara hesitated before nodding. 'I grew up in Trivikrampur.' There it was, again, that urge to ensure she wasn't claiming something to which she was not entitled.

Ramcharan was smiling. 'Wonderful, wonderful. A very beautiful place. They call it the country of women. The Rajmata is very active in politics. And there is a very prominent Muslim lady there.'

Zara wondered if she should disclose her relationship with Aunty Hana but he moved on. 'According to the history, when God Vishnu incarnated himself on earth for first time, he came as a dwarf – Vamana – "tri" equals three and "vikram" equals stride. The three strides of Vishnu. It was where Vamana first walked. His three strides covered heaven, earth and hell but three miniature steps were taken here.' He paused. 'It is a great example to the rest of India – the Trivikrampur maharajas are descended from the Vamana incarnation of Vishnu yet for generations their spiritual guide are pirs from the Muslim caste.'

Zara was surprised and pleased that her family, her past was spilling into her work life.

'Did you know, Mrs Zara, there is a fourth footstep, near a small village in Parshad? There is a temple beside a sulphur spring, also. I believe Vishnu in his ten incarnations represented a synthesis of all living things. I'll tell you one example. When Hindu-Muslim massacres were at their worse, one Muslim stonemason from Saurashtra, he was seeking refuge. His family members were killed in hills. Only he was surviving. He came to the temple – it was grand once but now all broken and deserted. He built back the temple stone by stone and guarded until priests came back. A Musalman man. Vishnu stands for preservation. Without cohesion and unity how we can survive?'

Zara wanted to leave. She stood up and paced the room. She had a mission. She had investigated the many international agencies that helped lone women but their support and funding was restricted. They were not always present at the landing, nor beyond an initial set-up. Once apparently settled, the women had to make their own way. Parveen's account confirmed this. Without a support network of family or friends, lone women faced genuine danger. But she had heard of covert national groups who helped integrate deportees within a network and she wanted information that only men like the swami could give. Why should she expect to get it easily?

Ramcharan's host and his wife were at work, his children at school. The kitchen was immaculate. The ceramic wall tiles glistened, even the grouting was free of grease or stains. The floor sparkled and every surface was spotless. Sterile, it looked to Zara. Like a showroom, unlived in and definitely not to her taste. Ramcharan sprinkled spices from small steel bowls into a wok filled with boiled, crushed potatoes.

'Potato filling to stuff parathas,' he explained. He reached into a jute sack filled with wheat flour. 'I need to make too many. God has given them four children. They eat well – may they live long.' He spooned some dry lentils into a bowl and ran the cold tap. 'I will soak the dal now. A little dal is always good to go with bread. Healthy. Father also develops up a good appetite after hard work.'

'I gather you work with him. It must be hard ... with your background.'

Ramcharan leaned forward across the dining table. 'Karma. I am doing penance. I'm doing the work of a bhangi. I am a Brahmin-untouchable. But my faith is most important thing so I accept my karma. If I pay for my evil here, in this world of coming and going, perhaps I will not be sent back again for another lifetime of ignorance and repentance.

'You know, when I was growing, children who studied, like me, in shakha schools – fundamental Hindu schools, you know, equivalent of madrasa – we heard how savage Muslim intruders plundered our country, destroyed our temples, raped our women for a thousand years since Mahmud Ghaznavid created precedent of looting temples of Somnath, in year 1000. Even before that, as early as eighth century, Mohammad bin Qasim ravaged Sindh. He was seventeen but he had violent temperament of Arab faith. In eighties, they said, under every famous mosque in the country lie desecrated remnants of a temple, a humiliated Hindu god. I grew up with the fire in my belly – I was privy to the suppressed history of my own nation, veiled by educated elite, eradicated from the history books, that behind every impoverished Hindu household was story of Muslim greed. In every Hindu widow or orphan's background there was a Muslim living out their stolen destiny. 600 years of oppression before, through the generosity of gods, British came to rid us off this heinous breed. But the memory could not be erased from the victim's minds. For thousands of years, the memory was carried down into the now. And we children were told we were chosen to inherit truth. How to erase the pain?'

He paused, scanning her face for a second. Zara wanted to rush into the silence, validate the misguided beliefs to which Ramcharan was pleading guilty, hold her hands up to the faults of the Muslims. She flinched as Peter's voice rang in her ears. 'Is it a way of dissociating yourself from the "bad" Muslims?' he had asked her once. 'I refuse to be held accountable for what a Christian bomber does. Why should you take responsibility for what a bad Muslim does?' Logic was on Peter's side but in fact she was held responsible – she was 'one of those people' and a flurry of guilt always tempered the anger such accusations sparked. She shifted – voicing agreement now would not make her more acceptable.

Ramcharan continued, 'The wine of martyrdom is intoxicating. The martyr is elevated to sainthood. His admirers progress from victims to aggressors. Rage takes over. You believe you are fighting injustice. The only solution is action. Don't judge such fighters harshly, Mrs Zara. There is a faultline running through this interpretation of faith. Who can we blame? Those who taught this generation were taught before by other generations – who knows where it started? Muslims, they as well do the same. And we innocents, children of few years old, everyday we went to Hindu shakha or Muslim madrasa and learned to hate better.

'The Rashtriya Sevak Sangh were our heroes. They set up system to fill in the gaps about Hindu-ness. Our true legacy, so-called. They created training camps. We young men were named Bajrang Dal – Power Chapter. We joined in masses, ready to give up our hopeless lives for a cause. We learned hand-to-hand, firearms, trident warfare and the use of bricks, stones. We took an oath to serve to the death. Our motto was: Seva, Suraksha, Sanskar. Service, Safety, Culture. Our aim was to build a temple to Ram on the original site in Ayodhya, and death to any who got in the way.

'Then came opportunity to take up arms. These Muslims who had colonized our country for so many years, they came back from working in Gulf States flaunting their money in our country. They had to be taught lessons.

'You can understand, when we heard the cries of resistance, the Shiv Sena, the BJP, the VHP, the RSS – strong Hindu fundamentalist groups – we took up arms and marched to redemption. We knew no judge would protect us. Our state government, we knew, would do its best, it included good men from these parties; like us, they were the guardians of our true history and legacy. All casts were eradicated. All Hindus were one.

'Some twenty years now but it feels like yesterday. What a heady cry it was. "Chalo Ayodhya!" "Come to Ayodhya!" The billboard sang out to us and we marched to its rhythm. We were marching. The epic of our faith was coming to life. We would free God, incarcerated by those brutal Muslims, in the foundations of the Babri Mosque.

'We were there, climbing mosque like a million soldier ants determined to bring down mosque and release our god, returning to vanquish the ominous shadow of Islam, overpowering, necrotizing our entire belief system.'

The insight into the plight of the perpetrator was chilling. How had she managed to remain ignorant of this simmering hatred? Yes, there were occasional sectarian incidents and riots sparked by an event. But this deep-seated hatred? It shook Zara – no one lamented the destruction of demons.

Ramcharan was stuffing the parathas and rolling them out with practised hands. He threw a perfect circle of dough on a frying pan and dribbled some oil around the edges.

'I was swept up in the elation. God had chosen me for this great rescue. Some of my fellow demon slayers lay dead and wounded. But there were more vanquished Muslim demons. I fell to my knees and buried my head in the rubble. "Ram! Ram! You are liberated again!" And before me stood Ram, heartbroken by the devastation. And he asked me a question.

'"Do you really believe I am so small that I can be confined in space?" The question changed me from plunderer to preacher.'

Ramcharan walked over to the sink and filled two glasses of water. He handed Zara one. She took a sip, a little dazed by the vigour of his storytelling and the vision of the other side, the constant interplay of light and shade that vested an incident with so many aspects that an opinion became impossible. Ramcharan picked up his glass of water and drained it. He set it down and wiped his mouth.

'I became Ramcharan Das. The worshipper at Ram's feet. Now, I could distinguish the true from the false. The death cries of my leaders became unbearable. Ram is justice, he could not be misused thus.

'The cries of my leaders were like burning sand in my ears. "We will declare war!" they shouted. "Not a single 'M' will remain in our country. We will burn them alive so that they can suffer in their last moments the burning flame that has oppressed us for centuries."

'I told them the truth and left. For next ten years I took yog – hence my title "swami". I studied and travelled to the heart of my faith and beyond layers of theory and debate, I found peace and beauty. The mightiest parts of struggle are fought here – within us. Ram taught me that day that divinity is boundless. It needs no name, no place. True worship is enlightenment and love.

'My old companions called me a traitor. I was not safe. But the demon is resentment, not any single race. If they do not give me the asylum, I will return to fight my cause unequipped – but fulfil it I will, at any cost to me, bar violence. I will never be violent.'

Zara's eyes smarted as he looked into them. Every asylum story was unique except for the burning desire of the teller to return home.

'Can I ask, Mrs Zara, what was your diaspora moment? You have experienced it, I know. I mean, you know, that moment when you realize your home is no longer your home because you have moved out of belongingness.'

She felt trapped by his gaze. She could hear the poet now, reciting his verse on television.

A lyric, a fragrance, a kafir face
In separation's Nowhereland, a travelling face.

Her diaspora moment – realizing she was in Nowhereland. She relaxed her shoulders, released the tension from her eyebrows and mouth. I'm here to see Ramcharan about a contact, she reminded herself. She cleared her throat and drank some water. She was back in professional mode.

'You must know a lot of people in Gujarat, people willing to meet deportees at the airport and help integrate them. I wonder if you might be willing to give me a contact?'

'You have had a crisis?'

Images of Parveen on fire flared into her eyes, then gave way to the cool white of her bandages. She cleared her throat again. 'My client – she set herself on fire at the airport.'

'Ah. A woman. It is harder for women. Sita's plight has taught us nothing.' His forefinger traced a symbol on the wooden table. 'It can be done. There are official agencies ...'

Zara shook her head. 'I'm looking for something more.'

The swami nodded. 'You are prepared to take risks?'

'I am.'

He sat upright, his voice full of authority. 'These people would be active around all the major airports – Bombay, Delhi for certain. That's where most deportees are sent. Possibly Calcutta and Chennai. My main contacts are in my homeland, Gujarat.'

'That's a good starting point.'

'These men and women, I will put you in touch, they cannot risk communicating by the e-mail or telephone. They will not abandon your clients. You must be prepared to meet them personally.'

'Whatever it takes.' For Parveen. For the guilt and grief she felt every time she heard of a deportation. She squared her shoulders. The risk to her would be minimal. She had connections.

The swami scrawled an address on a piece of paper. 'Ankahi – it means "unspoken". Tell them what you want. They will help you.'

Zara thanked Ramcharan and said goodbye. Her reasons for going to India were piling up. The silk could wait.

9

Zara woke up with a shock. She could still see herself searching for Peter in an empty, grey world but he had gone. Only his words remained in her memory: *You're the damaged one. Look to your own flaws.* Drifting clouds filled her vision and the repetitive voices of the airline staff reciting the menu to passengers were a relief. Peter had never, would never be so cruel. Was the warning from herself? She felt a twinge of guilt, remembering how quickly she became irritated with Peter. Perhaps he had come to the end of his patience. He seemed eager for her to visit Aunt Hana, told her repeatedly to take her time.

She reached down to the side of her seat and released the tray, adjusted her seat. If he did want a divorce, she would return to Trivikram. She could teach at one of Saif's schools for the poor and provide free legal advice. She might even be involved in a reception group for women like Parveen.

A stewardess placed a tray of foil-covered dishes in front of her. She thanked her and looked out of the window. A purple-grey swathe of clouds stretched out as far as she could see. She felt a lingering sense of fear mixed with terrible sadness at the thought of losing Peter but she could see no way to reconnect.

Zara leaned her head against the airplane window. There was one thing Peter wanted from her – the one thing she couldn't give. For her, sexual contact was the product of intimacy, for Peter it was the means to it. To compromise on that would be too great a sacrifice. The biggest lie yet. She closed her eyes. When she awoke, the flight was touching down and her head was whirling with thoughts of Aunty Hana. She handed over her British passport holder's landing form to a passing stewardess. Another reminder that she was now officially non-Indian.

Chhatrapati Shivaji International Airport, Mumbai was enormous. Or so it felt because she had never walked to customs before with this odd assortment of passengers. Someone had always whisked her off the airplane steps, bypassing the crowds and queues. She glazed over as she approached the long lines of people by a sign proclaiming 'IMMIGRATION'.

I am not an immigrant. This is my country. But she counted as an immigrant. Rage flared up inside her. *Peter! This was his fault. He had changed their plans. They should have been living here.* But since they lived in England, travelling on an Indian passport had become enormously complicated, so she had acquired a British one and swapped her status from alien in her adopted country to foreigner in her birthland.

She looked around her and wished she had not over-ridden Saif's offer to meet her at the airport. They would have been on the way to Trivikrampur by now. The thought of Hana brought a gush of self-reproach, relief, love. Her skin prickled and she prayed desperately that Hana was recovering. Thinking of her aunt warmed her. Hana, in Qila, the fortress she called home. *Home.* She shivered.

A harassed woman stood staring at her from further up the queue, weighed down with children, trolley and hand luggage. Zara didn't belong in this place made untidy by numbers. It was like a provincial railway station where the peasantry arrived laden with bundles and bedding. She wanted to be safe in the world she knew. Vile things were happening, she was constantly told, but not in Trivikram. Reality was never as the media depicted. The hatred, the riots were a pan-national belt of bloodshed skirting around her world, outside the sacred circle that was Trivikram. There had always been conflict and killing in the newspapers. But not in the India that was her ancestral world, her inner strength, her source.

A small man pushed past her. Zara's eyes were magnetized to his round middle.

'You don't have any duty-free, isn't it?' he said, positioning himself in front of her. Zara pointed to her duty-free bag. 'But only cigarettes and perfumeries, no?'

She was flummoxed by his cheek. The woman who had been staring at her scuttled away and shoved herself further up the queue, arranging her bags around her. Clearly these two belonged together.

'Kindly take my extra duty-free out with you on remainder of your allowance.'

'Well actually ...' Zara wished again, desperately, that she had let Saif come. The man thrust out his duty-free bag. 'You will please take this ...'

'The rules state clearly that ...'

'It's no problem.' The man was insisting, opening his bag. 'You can check. Only allowance items.'

Oh what the hell, thought Zara. She nodded, shoving her slender Louis Vuitton case forward with her shoe. The man's grin grew large as he held out the bag then produced a garden-rubbish bag wound a dozen times with lurid green string.

'You will kindly take this also.'

Zara gritted her teeth. 'I don't think ...'

'Only children's clothes,' he said. 'Very light.'

'I'm sorry, but ...'

'Very light. Not illegal. I can show you ... no problem.'

It would be too hideous, she thought, to see him reveal the contents of his green garden bag here and now, even worse to deal with the little knots and tangles to get it open for customs. 'No,' she said. 'I'm sorry but the answer is no.'

The man gazed into her face, assessing her, as she stood with her arms firmly folded.

'Tell me,' he said softly, 'you are Muslim?'

Zara was taken aback.

'Tell me one thing, madam,' he continued in a hypnotic tone. 'Why are you people determined to destroy my country?'

'My country too,' Zara said, fighting through a black fog.

'No!' the man said, his voice rose and split. 'Not your country. You are bandits and killers, you Muslim people. Are you coming to spy?'

An electric charge seemed to shoot through the people in the line. They watched, alert, vigilant as security guards turned towards the man.

'Excuse me. Mrs Hamilton?' A uniformed man stood opposite her. 'Please, ma'am, can I speak with you one moment?'

'Of course.' Zara stepped out of the queue, wondering who the man was. Had the commotion attracted him? Was she going to be questioned?

'Captain Arvind Mathur, ma'am. Step this way please, ma'am. Which is your luggage?'

Zara pointed to her case. Before she could ask him who he was, Mathur picked up her slim case and they were marching towards the customs barrier. She could see the small man turn round, grinning at the queue. 'See? I was right. She is arrested.'

Captain Mathur continued walking at a quick pace. Zara's heart thumped as she followed. Who, apart from Saif, knew she was arriving at Mumbai airport tonight? Perhaps it was a hospitality service from the car-hire firm? Zara looked back at the queue. The small man was still smirking. She tensed for a moment then relaxed. The captain would surely not have carried her bag if she was in trouble? At the customs counter, Captain Mathur turned slightly, his head bowed.

'Your passport please, ma'am. We'll go through customs now.'

Zara hesitated a second before handing over her passport. Mathur moved alongside the queue and stopped in front of a customs officer.

'Check this first, please.' He held his identification above the heads of the queue. The customs officer nodded. The car-hire firm wouldn't have the authority to do this, surely? The customs man looked up and then past him, indicating Zara in the queue. 'VIP?'

Mathur nodded.

'Okay. No problem.' The customs officer waved his arms to clear the space in front of him. Zara looked away from the passenger she had displaced. The customs officer scribbled a chalk mark over the constantly repeating LV pattern and waved her on. Then he paused. 'Passport, please.'

Mathur handed back her small maroon booklet. The man flipped through. 'Hamilton?' He took in her sari, her brown skin. 'Husband English?' Zara nodded. The customs man was on a roll. She could see the curiosity in his face. 'You married outside? You have muthrinla?'

Zara bit back a smile. 'Yes, I have a mother-in-law.'

'She's good to you?'

Zara chewed her lip. 'Very good.'

'She lives with you?'

Zara shook her head, not daring to say a word in case she started to giggle.

'Haan! You see, English man will listen to wife. Indian man will listen to mother. You were born where?'

Had she imagined the man tense as the words 'Karachi, Pakistan' leapt from the page of her passport? He flicked through again and saw she hadn't visited Pakistan for the duration of this passport.

'You stay in Britain?' He glanced at the uniformed official who nodded slightly. Once again the customs man looked at Zara's sari. 'Husband treats you well?'

Zara nodded.

'Okay. You can go. No problem.'

Mathur whisked Zara's suitcase off the customs counter and led her out of the crowded, stifling atmosphere into the open.

3 am. Mumbai was humid, sticky. Zara lifted her face to the October night, hoping for a cool breeze as she stepped into the darkness.

'You've been very kind,' she said. 'I should have a car waiting.' Mathur took her suitcase, bowing slightly. 'You're from the car-hire company?'

'Follow me please,' he said. 'The Minister is waiting.'

Zara froze. 'Minister?' The official pointed to a waiting Range Rover and opened the door. Zara stopped. She had no intention of getting into a strange car to meet an anonymous minister.

A man stepped out. He was of medium height but had the imposing air and presence of someone larger.

'The Minister,' said Mathur.

The minister nodded his thanks to Captain Mathur who bowed, saluted and took two steps back before disappearing into the night. Zara turned to the minister, tense, as another uniformed man stepped out of the car and placed himself nearby.

'Zara,' the minister said, holding out his arms. The Oxford voice brought a blast of memory with it. Jayendra Singh Vamana, Maharaja of Trivikrampur. She felt faint, overwhelmed. Why was he here? Had Hana died? But Jay was smiling.

'Jay! What a surprise.' Without thinking she hugged him.

'It's been a long, long time.' She felt Jay's affection as he squeezed her shoulders.

Zara stepped back, stung by her thought. *I wish Peter was still affectionate like that.* 'Sorry,' she said. 'That hug will probably hit the headlines tomorrow.'

Jay helped her into the car. The uniformed chauffeur was beaming widely, saluting her before he leapt to the door on the other side to attend to Jay.

'I didn't guess the captain belonged to you,' Zara laughed. 'No crest on his cap.'

'The days of the crest are gone,' Jay laughed, holding out his ring. 'That's about the only place you'll see it – other than the letterhead.' He pointed to his chauffeur. 'You recognize Raju, old Shamu's grandson.'

'Raju!' Zara stepped forward. 'You're all grown up.'

Raju smiled, a little bashful. 'All of us, Princess.'

'Does your mother still cook like she used to?' Raju nodded. 'Just the same. She will be happy you remember.' He bowed and held open the door. Zara got in.

'Goodness. Do you remember, we could never find him when he hid?'

Jay laughed. 'He's still the same.'

'How did you know I was coming?'

'Saif mentioned it. I was attending a conference in Bombay so I thought I'd see if I could catch you.'

Zara grinned. 'I see your cut-glass accent has survived India.'

He laughed. 'But when it suits me I can say "similyer" and "dev-lup-ment" with the best of them.'

'And "voylent"!' they both chorused as the car moved off.

'You don't!'

'I'm afraid I do.'

Zara laughed. 'Peter says I give my Indian voice an airing when I'm talking to Indians.' Like naughty children who had gone too far, they sobered up.

'Your aunt is not at all well.'

Zara's throat swelled. 'What ...?'

'Weakness, mainly. And the will ... it's gone. You know, these troubles ... they're incomprehensible to us all. For her generation they're cataclysmic. There was ... you know, our families, together, they created a sort of religious synergy.'

What was Jay trying to say? Zara felt sick.

'The fortress was attacked.' Jay bowed his head. 'I am deeply ashamed. But my mother ... I still can't understand the change in her ... after so many years of friendship.'

Zara was alarmed. She had heard that Sita Devi had fallen out with her son. That the two of them were living at extreme ends of the family palace. But surely Jay was not saying his mother was having difficulties with Aunt Hana? They had been closer than sisters since they first met as girl-brides.

'Going to prison changed her,' Jay continued. 'She's become bitter ...'

'Prison must have been hard ...' Zara had to force out the words. She had never felt comfortable with Sita Devi.

Jay fluttered his hand. 'It's different for political prisoners, of course. Also, money and status help ...'

The car curved around the Hanging Gardens and took a left turn.

'But tell me,' Jay resumed a more casual tone. 'How is that green and pleasant land that you've adopted?'

'Well, not always so green nor so pleasant. There's been an awful flu epidemic – Fiji flu, they're calling it. I read an *Evening Standard* headline on the plane. Hospitals are so overcrowded some of them are asking the patients' family members to come and help look after them!'

'Third-world conditions, I expect they compared them to,' Jay wisecracked.

Zara tensed to articulate her question. 'Have you any idea what the doctors are saying ... about Aunty Hana?'

'You know doctors. They're like everyone else here. Superstitious, scared. No one wants to be the messenger who gets shot.'

'So the prognosis is bad.'

'Everyone's worried. She's fragile – can't even chew her food.'

'But Pebbles said she was eating.'

Jay said nothing. The space seemed to grow darker, as if death had come to sit between them.

'So she doesn't have long?'

'I see you're well and truly anglicized.'

Zara heard the discomfort in Jay's voice. He had never liked her bluntness. 'Call it superstition but, you know, in this country we still can't bring ourselves to make predictions like that. If this life is to end then it is not for us to ponder or pre-empt it.'

Zara heard the bitterness in her own laugh. 'What happened to the Oxford radical?'

Jay turned slowly until he was looking into Zara's eyes. 'He grew up. Very cataclysmically. Eighteen years ago.' He paused as if expecting her to help but she said nothing. 'When you accept your duties, the only thing that makes the sacrifices bearable, that helps you shoulder your burden, is the example of your forefathers, your history, the blood that flows in your veins. I have sons, they've got to survive this strife and get on with their lives.'

'You mean,' she said, surprised at the bitterness she felt, 'I'm the one who got away.'

'Got away?' The surprise on his face looked genuine. 'You don't "get away" by not being on the spot. But you got to choose your life. Anyway, Trivikrampur is not your responsibility – you're not ...'

She grew still to hide the painful impact of his words. 'Then what am I?'

He shifted uneasily. 'Saif tells me you are a stupendously successful barrister.'

'I *work* as a barrister. And Saif exaggerates.' Did Jay think she was a foreigner too? 'You know, Jay, India – Trivikram – was always home to me. That's where I grew up. There is nowhere else.'

Jay winced and bowed his head. 'I'm so ...'

Zara waved her hand. 'No. Don't.' She was grateful for the darkness in the car as she steadied herself. 'Trivikrampur was always so rich and giving. But now that I think about it, something had changed on my last visit. Perhaps I've stayed away to avoid confronting it.'

'I'm sorry you feel unwelcome.' Jay's voice was sad.

'I don't want to be told, I suppose, that I'm an outsider. Not in Trivikram. I never felt Pakistani ... how could I? I never lived there. Now India won't let me feel Indian, I've no heritage in Britain ...'

'But long-standing connections.'

Zara nodded. 'I wouldn't live anywhere else in the world. But if I'm asked where I'm from, I have no answer. Not one that feels authentic, at any rate. I'm sort of ... stateless.'

'Your mother said once that you carry your heritage inside you. You are your own nation.'

The atmosphere in the car seemed suddenly to turn liquid. Memories tumbled back from across the years, flowing, swirling through the soft shadows of loss. The car circled around a large roundabout and made its way towards the southern outskirts. Zara did not notice the commotion outside until she sensed Jay stiffen. He leaned forward. 'Do as they say, Raju.'

A mob spilled off the pavement on to the main road. Men were stopping cars and shining torches inside. The Range Rover slid to a stop.

'Your passport, Zara. Quick.'

Jay slipped it beneath the carpet. 'Could I ask you to greet them with a namaste?' She nodded. 'It's just ... ' his hands fluttered. 'You understand.'

The car came to a stop and Raju answered the questions of the mob. A face flattened against Zara's window, lips and nose distorted, eyes bulging. She could not decipher the expressions on the faces in the darkness. Frantically spinning hands signalled her to wind down the window. She turned to Jay. He nodded. 'A little bit.'

She rolled down a third of the pane and brought her palms together in a greeting. 'Namaskar.'

The man at the window moved back. 'English?' he remarked, peering in. 'No speak English. You speak Russian? Hindi-speaking, you?'

Zara responded in fluent Hindi.

'Memsaab, speak very fine Hindi. Good as Indian people,' he replied, delighted. 'Why didn't you tell us English memsaab love Indian language?' he chastised Raju, lapsing back into Hindi. 'Go on, go on. Memsaab must be tired. Jai jai, memsaab. Jai Ramji ki.'

Zara returned the greeting. Jay was looking at her with an indefinable expression. 'What?' she asked.

'Nothing ... just, you don't seem offended by my request; many Muslims would. Greetings have become a statement for both sides – a matter of integrity.'

Zara shrugged. 'You know I've never been religious.'

'It's politics, Zara. Religion is the *prima materia* of politics today – in India, anyway.'

As the car slid forward, Zara heard the crunch of glass. Two formally dressed men were being held by a group. Blood slithered down their faces. One tried to break away, shouting, as a woman was dragged off into the crowd. A small cluster of men surged forward and surrounded him, blocking him from Zara's view. Their arms rose and fell, their torsos swung backward and forward. Their voices were raised. Zara wound down her window slightly.

'Maaro! Maaro!' the crowd shouted encouragement to the men beating the victim. His companion, bleeding copiously from a forehead wound, took little useless runs at the assailants, trying to stop them while his eyes followed the woman being dragged away.

'Can't we do something?' Zara felt frantic.

'I'll call the police,' Jay was already tapping on his mobile. 'It's too dangerous to stop. Chalo, chalo Raju. Why are you hanging about?'

'How long before they get here? Will someone save the woman?' She could hear the hysteria in her voice.

'Not long,' murmured Jay, muttering swiftly down the line in Hindi.

Zara knew without a doubt that the victims were Muslim. 'You know them, don't you?' she demanded.

Jay nodded raising his hand as if to fend off unspoken reprimands. 'Once upon a time,' he muttered, 'I would have been beside them, fighting off the villains.'

'I think I understand.'

There was a wild look in his eyes as he faced her. 'You say you do. But do you understand that this could have been provoked by something as simple as a Muslim greeting? Do you understand that if I get out to help, I'll be recognized and my family could pay? Already I'm a marked man because I oppose my mother's fundamentalist politics. I feel like a bloody Judas.'

'You've been a good friend to Saif.' She resented having to make him feel better. He gave a bitter laugh. 'A good friend! You don't understand. Saif is the guru of the Vamanas, second only to God. I made no public statement about how much my family – all Trivikram – owes the Ramzis. When they tried to burn down Qila, I ordered no mass arrests. You know what I did? I made a telephone call.'

'Mass arrests? Can a minister do that? Everyone knows maharajas don't have that kind of power anymore.'

'Officially, perhaps, but most of those guys have a parent or uncle who worked for us or the Ramzis at some time. Old ties are still effective.'

Burn down Qila? Suddenly the words hit home. When had they tried to burn down Qila? Surely the damage could not have been serious enough for mass arrests?

Two large police vans drove through the crowds, sirens blaring. Zara whirled around in her seat, craning her neck as a string of armed officers crashed through the crowd after the men.

'Thank god,' she gasped, slumping back. 'She's going to be okay. Who is she?'

Jay shook his head. 'She'll be okay. The police know I witnessed the incident.'

'Who are they, Jay?'

'Prominent couple. Wife's Hindu. Enough said.' Jay put his arm around Zara and she let him draw her close, sobbing soundlessly on to his shoulder. She could feel him stroking her hair as he had done in Oxford a lifetime ago. 'Would it have been like this for us, I wonder?' His voice was soft with emotion.

She pulled away. 'I think it worked out for the best.'

'Ah,' his tone was unfathomable. 'But is that the same as right?'

10

Zara opened her eyes as the Range Rover drew into a busy lane filled with shops and stalls. They were in Qila. It was still dark but a few people were about, wrapped in shawls or blankets as they hurried to work, or opened up their shops and lit fires to prepare for the breakfast trade. She felt a rush of pride – she had grown up in the fortress that gave the town its name, Qila. Its flourishing high street was still the same – lined with higgledy-piggledy rows of shops and eateries, studded with brightly coloured fruit and vegetable barrows. On the other side loomed the massive gates of the fortress where she had spent so many happy years. The surrounding walls of the stone building were deep enough to house small shops – a baker, a tailor, two or three grocers, fruit-mongers and street-food sellers. As a child, she called them 'hole-in-the-wall shops' and fantasized about having one for herself and filling it with the potsherds and old coins she found along with small statuettes and endless fragments of beautifully crafted tiles. Occasionally, she would find an unbroken one, like the hexagonal blue, white and lemon block, around which she had designed her London living room. And the centrepiece of her dining table was a three-pound obelisk of unblemished purple stone, once part of the fountain from the meditation room, smashed to pieces during the uprising of 1857. Aunt Hana told her how the Ramzi leader who had built it enjoyed watching the water gush up and then pour down in fast, full rivulets that borrowed the purple from the stone. Later, when he was absorbed in the world of the spirit and took on the leadership of the Ramzi Order, he would meditate for hours to the sound of running water and the spiritual emanations of the amethyst chamber.

The jeep turned and passed in through the enormous iron gates of the fortress which had been left open forever.

'My goodness!' Zara was not sure if she was disappointed or just surprised. New buildings had gone up inside the compound, four- and five-storey blocks where the stables, aviary and menagerie had been.

'Pebbles' initiative,' Jay said. 'She's quite an innovator. Great business woman.'

'The shrine – where's the shrine?' Zara looked wildly around, trying to catch a glimpse of the small, perfectly built piece of architecture known in the family as the dargah. It had been built by Jay's ancestor, a tribute to the Ramzi leader with whom the close relationship began, and continued to be the focus of many ceremonies in the state. The annual Trivikram festival, or Sabz-posh Pir ka Mela, was attended by hundreds. It commemorated the bond of the Green-clad Man or Friend of God, who had saved the life of Jay's ancestor, cementing a relationship that influenced harmony in the entire state. Before every important mission the Vamana ruler paid his respects at the shrine and asked for his venture to be blessed. I'll miss the festival of the Green-clad Man, Zara thought. Or maybe I can come back for it in four months.

The jeep rolled further in. 'I'm getting disoriented by these buildings. It would be ...' Zara let her eyes travel along the majestic structure of the fortress, trying to locate the windows of Aunt Hana's room; there was the Green Room balcony that looked out on to the gate, the high, small window that belonged to the ante-room and, beside it, Aunt Hana's window, half-veiled by the magnificent tamarind tree, looking on to the shrine. She twisted her body around.

'Just about there.' Her heart leaped with joy. She wrenched open the door, jumping from the car before it stopped. It was a moment before she recognized the charred remains of its wall, the blackened side of the exquisite piece of miniature architecture. She could not move. She wished she could hold on to Peter. She did not look at

Jay. The arson was a protest against the Ramzi-Vamana bond and the blurring of religious boundaries.

Jay must feel lost in this new atmosphere of communal hatred in Trivikrampur. His family, like the rest of the maharajas, had lost their actual powers under the British. Insultingly, they were given compensation in the form of the 'privy purse', an allowance barely a fraction of their wealth – but which came from their own state treasury. The title remained, a hollow reminder of former glory. 'Mai-Baap', they had been known as – and still were among the poor of their states – Mother and Father. The power was gone but somehow the responsibility of that ephemeral parental power still weighed heavy. She could see it in Jay's bowed shoulders, the dullness in his voice when he had spoken about it earlier.

She looked at the front of the fortress, its familiar, welcoming stone portico, added no more than a couple of centuries ago, as it was transformed from a defending fortress to a family dwelling. 'Are you coming in?' she asked.

He shook his head. 'I'm seeing Saif later about the Girls' Academy. Give the ladies my regards.'

Zara climbed the steps to the portico and remembered she hadn't thanked Jay. When she turned, he had gone.

She stepped into the inner courtyard. Three tall trees towered up past the gallery railing, their leaves like curtains, veiling the doors to the rooms along the top. They had grown dramatically in the last ten years.

She was at the foot of the stairs now. Above her, the stone gallery with its metal railings mirrored the square shape of the courtyard. She lifted her sari to her ankles and ran up the stairs. With a fleeting glance at the huge, walled terrace to the right, outside the old kitchen, she turned left and ran along the flagstones of the narrow gallery outside the front of the rooms, her fingers trailing along its low railing. She named the spaces as she went past, as she had when she was a child, to keep herself grounded in the dark when the great structure began to produce unfamiliar shadows, strange sounds and, worst of all, darting lizards: the larder, the luggage store, the Green Room directly above the portico, the niche at the turn containing its ancient oil lamp just above eye level. She stopped at the long living-room door a yard before the turn that led to Saif's bedroom.

There was no one there. She dashed across to the door that led out, on the other side, to a large terrace overlooking the Oval Garden. Across the garden was another wing of Qila which Hana had recently given to Mumtaz, her estranged sister-in-law. It had shocked everyone.

Zara came back into the living room. It was eight; she could see the table elaborately laid through the curtained doorway in the dining room. The next moment Pebbles came through smiling and rose on tiptoe to kiss her. Saif followed, brisk and supple, threw his arms around her and held her close for a moment.

'Good heavens. You're here – and we weren't even downstairs to greet you.'

Pebbles gestured towards the dining room, clapping to alert the maids.

'Where is Aunt Hana?' Zara said, distracted. 'Can I see her first?'

Pebbles' scowl made her immediately contrite. 'Tell me how you are. And Sharmeen? Is she up?'

Pebbles snorted. 'Is she up? She's awake before the birds these days. Sharmeen, come for breakfast! Aunty Zara's arrived.' She looked irritated. 'She'll turn up in a minute, I'm sure.' She guided Zara away from the door, towards the dining room. But Zara's gaze was snagged by a patch of cerise fabric stirring behind the deep purple voile of the curtains leading on to the balcony.

'Probably schmoozing with her grandmother again ...' Pebbles' dark skin glowed with embarrassment. 'I mean, she never leaves her grandmother alone. Never lets her rest.'

'Oh, Aunty Hana would send her off if she didn't want her, I'm sure,' Zara said, still distracted by the movement. She squeezed Pebbles' arm. 'I remember being packed off when she was busy.'

'Sharmeen is a young woman now,' Pebbles retorted.

'Well, I was eighteen,' Zara began. She felt uneasy. The curtain was stirring, filling out with a cerise-garbed figure. The figure moved. Zara jumped as a pair of eyes stared at her through the flimsy fabric.

'Sharmeen!' she exploded, relieved. 'Come here, let me look at you.'

Sharmeen darted out from behind the curtain as her mother whirled round.

'Such a practical joker, my little girl!' Saif's voice contained a chuckle. 'Trying to give your poor aunt a shock, eh?'

Saif put his arm around Sharmeen who was standing up straight now. She was tall like her father, slender and willowy, her hair taken up at the crown and flowing down to her hips. She had the eyes of Hana's family – a fawn's eyes, large, dark and fringed with heavy lashes. She floated into Zara's outstretched arms. Zara felt Sharmeen's cheek against her hair.

'I used to be the tall one in the family,' Zara laughed.

'Shorty, shorty,' Sharmeen sang.

'Where were you?' Pebbles sounded angry. 'Why weren't you here to greet your aunt?'

Instantly Sharmeen stopped laughing and faced her mother, head lowered as if to attack.

'She's here now.' Zara put an arm round her waist.

'Please, Zara,' Pebbles interrupted, 'this is between Sharmeen and me.'

'How was the drive from Mumbai?' Saif chimed in.

'Good.' Zara grasped the diversion. 'Unfortunately, I fell asleep.' Zara could wait no more. 'Can I see Aunt Hana?'

'She's asleep.' Pebbles' face seemed to turn shadowy.

Zara ignored her, dashing through the small stone passage at the other end of the long drawing room. She slowed down in the ante-room to Aunty's boudoir and lifted the curtain in the doorway. Aunty was lying in bed, quite still. Zara tiptoed in and stood by her. Her eyes were closed.

'Zara,' she whispered. 'You came. Just in time.' Her lids fluttered but didn't open.

'I'm here, Aunty.' Her words were almost soundless but she saw the flicker on Hana's lips and reached out to hold her hand. It was soft and small – an infant's hand. Zara was shocked. Where had Aunty gone? Those delicate but firm hands had caressed her and held her steady so many times against the attacks of the world. Hana was the one person who had loved her through everything. Ten years ago, when she left after a two-month stay, Aunty had said softly: 'Don't desert me again.' Zara had felt it deep inside then – the conviction that this was her farewell visit, that she would not see her again. But she had pushed it away. Somehow, the customary words of parting had deserted her. And even Aunty had not said them: *Forgive me for anything I might have said.* They had always brought a lump to her throat, those words.

She swallowed painfully, laving her aunt's face and body with her gaze. Somewhere in that body, in that aura, lay the balm that had eased the pain of so many childhood and adolescent memories. And what a storyteller she had been! The tales tripped from her tongue like a dancer – supple and vigorous, frothy and lively. What would she not give this moment to know that Aunty would survive to tell her just one more story? Nyla's story – the answer to the conundrum: what made Nyla abandon her? The missing piece that Peter had talked about.

She dropped a kiss on Hana's forehead. Aunty would have to recover before she had the energy to complete the message in the letter.

A shadow fell across the bed and Zara leaped back. Death. Had it come? It was Pebbles. She stood by the curtain, partially concealed, and Zara was not sure if she was meant to see her. Pebbles clearly realized she had been spotted. Slowly, silently she beckoned to Zara.

'I've prepared the Green Room for you,' she said. 'You'll be near her.'

'No,' Aunty whispered. Zara looked at her – was that a breath or a word? 'No!' Aunty said again. 'Zara will sleep here. In this room. With me.'

No one had slept in the room with Hana since Zara first left for London. She had become so entrenched in her daily prayer rituals that another presence was untenable. Zara and Peter had been put in the Green Room on their visit. Hana raised her hand and pointed to the dais where she prayed.

'There, if you like.'

Zara smiled. 'No. On a mattress. On the floor, here beside your bed. Like I used to.'

The effort of speech and movement had exhausted Aunty. Looking at her stirred up a tempest inside Zara and she struggled to hold back the tears. Pebbles hovered at the door, waiting. Zara walked over to her, eyebrows raised. But Pebbles said nothing. Zara waited. In her years as a barrister interviewing people, she had learned that if the silence was long enough someone said something. Pebbles spoke. 'You'll be very uncomfortable.'

Zara ran her fingertips down her body. 'I'll manage fine on a mattress. I'm still quite supple.'

'As you wish,' she said, shambling off.

Zara's heart was beating as she pulled up a chair and sat down beside Aunty. How full of life and amusing language Aunty had been. At some point during her reverie Littl'un brought in her luggage. She hugged Zara with tears in her eyes.

'I'm so glad you've come, Bibi Saheb,' she wept. 'Things aren't right. They just aren't good.'

'I know,' Zara replied, squeezing her arm. 'It's hard to see her like this.'

Zara could see Littl'un scrutinizing her face. She opened her mouth then shut it again. Zara felt suddenly weary. She squeezed Littl'un's frail arm and bent over to open her suitcase. The suppressed sobs of seven days suddenly tumbled out. She wanted to howl and cry, to stamp her feet and shout, 'It's not fair!' Instead she moved over to her bags, bending over the cases, looking blindly through her clothes.

'Don't cry, Bibi,' Littl'un begged. 'I'm sorry if I've upset you.'

'It's not you, Littl'un,' Zara wept, hugging the minute, flyaway form. 'It's just ...'

'I know,' murmured the old woman, caressing her back, patting it rhythmically as she had when Zara was a small child. 'Everything will be alright. Trust in God. What he does, he does for the best.'

The words were irrationally comforting. What would Littl'un think if she told her she hardly knew if she still believed in God? That she wondered, when she did think of him, whether he had created humankind or humankind had created him as a scapegoat or as a powerhouse on which to depend in moments of haplessness? Omnipotent. Protector. Healer. All-Merciful. All-Merciful? What a joke, she thought.

'Do you need help?' Littl'un's voice startled her. 'Hanging up your clothes? You could use one of the wardrobes.'

'I'll do it myself, Littl'un.' She walked over to the polished mahogany wardrobe with its narrow, mirrored door set in the centre. Jay's mother, Sita Devi, had loved the mirror because, she said, it made her look slim and tall. She grasped the handle and the door swung open with a slight creak, releasing the soft, woody fragrance of sandalwood. Aunty's white saris hung in crisp, starched rows. The side shelves contained piles of shawls, blouses and petticoats. Boxes of sandalwood soap and incense sticks were stacked on each shelf. Aunty loved the fragrance as well as an aphorism from the poet Tagore: *Be like the sandalwood tree which perfumes the axe that lays it low.*

She darted a glance at the bed – Aunty was lying quite still. She tiptoed over to her, bending, staring hard to make sure she was still breathing. Then she circled around the bed and looked at the hole-in-the wall cupboards, searching for the manuscript and pictures Aunty had mentioned in her letter. Gently, she tried the door of one cupboard, then the next. Both opened without resistance. She tapped her lips, reflecting, then opened both doors wide and scanned the shelves. There were several cardboard boxes there – the kind that contained expensive saris, tissue-wrapped – and a couple of jewellery boxes. She lifted one out of the cupboard, concentrating hard to avoid disturbing Aunty. Softly, she set it on the tepoy beside the prayer mat and opened it. An embroidered Kashmir shawl. She tiptoed back to replace it in the cupboard.

Pebbles whirled into the room, her eyes wild, wisps of hair standing up around her face, her lips tight and controlled. Swiftly Zara turned around, her back to the cupboard door. 'What's the matter?'

'Just wondering if you need anything.' Pebbles glanced at the open wardrobe doors, the box in Zara's hand. 'Were you looking for something?' Her voice was thin, constricted. Her fists clenched and reopened in an unnatural way.

'Just nosing around, wondering if I should hang up my clothes.'

'The Green Room's so much more convenient.' Pebbles' expression was strange. 'Lunch will be ready by 12.30,' she said.

'I'll eat after I've fed Aunty.'

'Oh, Littl'un will feed her.'

'I'd like to.'

'It'll be more trouble than it's worth. Littl'un has it all worked out.'

'It's no trouble, really. I want to.'

'Well, I don't want to say this. But, you know, she finds it a bit humiliating to be watched. It's a bit of a messy job nowadays.'

'She cleaned up my mess enough times when I needed her,' Zara could hear the rage in her own voice. How dare Pebbles speak like that in Aunty's presence? 'I don't see why I can't ...'

'As you wish.' Pebbles left, hair bristling as if she were generating static electricity, the tunic of her trouser suit flapping.

Zara stood over Aunty, steadying herself, watching for a glimmer of awareness. The bronze eyes opened and focused on Zara. She was serene and calm and made Zara feel still inside.

'You've become even more beautiful,' Hana murmured. This time her voice sounded stronger. Then she shifted slightly and Zara thought she had drifted away.

'*Who knows how the flowers suffered at autumn's hand/Today the morning breeze passed restless from the garden.* Does that autumnal country still suit you, my darling?'

'Look at you,' Zara said, touching her cheek. 'No one has any business to look as gorgeous as you when ...'

'At my age, you mean?'

'That too,' Zara joked back. 'But I was thinking of your health.'

'It was a kind thing you said,' Aunty said. 'About the mess ...'

'It's true.' She looked at the steaming bowl of porridge-soft rice and lentils.

Aunty smiled a contented smile. 'I'd love you to feed me. Pish-pash and lemony mint chutney with yogurt. You can get your revenge for the dozens of times I fed it to you when you were sick in bed.'

'But I loved it,' Zara laughed. 'I still cook it when I need comfort food.'

Hana turned her head on the pillow and closed her eyes again. Zara panicked. 'Aunty?'

Aunty reached out and held Zara's hand. 'Pebbles. She's suspicious. She must never, ever find out. Nor must Saif.'

'But Aunty, where is the script? And your instructions?'

'They're safe with ...' Aunty's voice was fading.

'Don't worry now. Rest. Tell me when we're having lunch.'

'My work is done,' Hana said. 'I was waiting to see you.' She fell silent. 'Not because of the will. I trust you with that. But, my darling, ten years is a very long time.' She tried to raise her arms and Zara bowed down and let her head touch the feeble chest and arms.

'You've kept your spirit, haven't you, Aunty?'

'Acceptance brings its own serenity,' she whispered. 'I've had to accept my many, many mistakes. We muddle through this life, you know, my darling. We just muddle through. But you're here and I'm going peacefully.'

She tried again to raise her arms and Zara supported them with her own. Aunty's arms tightened round her then they went limp.

The lamp on the tepoy went out. Zara made no effort to get up. Saif was not back yet. It would make no difference if the others had to wait a little. She needed this time with Aunty but she wished Peter was with her. Ten years, as Aunty had said, without a hint of reproach, was a very long time. Aunty had lived them seven times over and Zara knew those years intimately told through Aunty's bitterness, wisdom and passion. Only the last ten years were a blank because Zara had become so embroiled in her own life, her own ambitions and dilemmas that she had not spared the time to visit.

'But,' she thought, holding Aunty's delicate hand to her breast, 'she knew I loved her. She knew I would come. And she knows I'll do whatever it takes.'

II

A river of white flowed from the massive courtyard through the tall iron gates of the fortress and turned right, filling the street with white-clad male bodies. They were all grieving for Hana, all at their individual level, in their own way, because she had somehow touched their lives. Zara strained to see her shroud as it rose above the procession, lifted up on the shoulders of a grieving crowd. She half-recalled some lines from Rumi that a river flowing with love for the sea had 'become the sea'. Aunty had 'become the sea'.

But she was being maudlin. Qila revived poetic images woven into the tapestry of her family's collective mind and transmitted through the generations. She looked around her. Pebbles looked quite beautiful, her dark skin taut and gleaming against the filtered sunlight. She was in a trance-like state since Hana died, absorbed and disturbed by thoughts some way beyond grief.

The tree by the shrine shook, reflecting the rhythm of Zara's sobs earlier today as she had watched Aunty's body by the desecrated shrine before the others arrived. It was being mended, partly in preparation for the festival in February, and the artisans had hurriedly swept their implements and materials out of sight, filled it with flowers and hung it with strings of triangular green flags to conceal the worst signs of damage. Now, as Zara watched from the Green Room balcony, the sunlight sieved through the branches, lighting up the shadowy spaces in between, so that a billion minute specks suddenly seemed to throb into life in the dusty light-strands.

'Sometimes,' Aunty had said once, 'I feel as if I'm trapped in my body. Then I look at this wonderful tamarind tree and I think of the great expanse above it and how it's grown from a tiny thing. And

I soar. You know, Zara, the body can never really restrict the soul. Not if its owner refuses to let it.'

There had been tears in Aunty's eyes as there were, now, in Zara's. But Pebbles was calm, contained in her trance-world until Jay's wife came in.

'Jai jai, Pebbles,' she said in a sing-song voice. She looked elegant to the point of artifice. Pebbles drifted out of her trance to introduce them.

'Her Highness, Anapurna, Maharani of Trivikram. Ana, this is our cousin Zara from London.'

Zara cringed as Ana looked her up and down.

On the road below, they could see Jay walking beside Saif, their shoulders to the shroud, as the funeral flowed steadily towards the graveyard of the Ramzi family – but Sita Devi had chosen not to come.

Anapurna voiced the unspoken thought. 'It feels sooo odd without Rajmata Sa, my mother-in-law. She was present at every single important occasion in Kil-la.' The mispronunciation of Qila jarred on Zara.

'Always. Right up until recently only; they were middle-aged ladies with grandchildren but for every little thing, they were buzzing each other like two teenagers.' She stopped, pensive. 'I went to tell her we were leaving for here and I found her crying. Really, you know, her eyes were red and swollen. I felt so bad. She really loved Begum Sa. So sad.' She dabbed at a teardrop.

Zara could hear the edge in her own voice. 'It might have helped to see her for the last time. Aunty Hana was her oldest friend.'

Ana's look was hostile. 'You've been away too long, hai na? You don't know my mother-in-law. She's never going to change her mind.'

'About what? Why is she so upset?'

Pebbles stepped sharply out of her trance. 'No one will ever know now. Best to leave it.'

The last of the mourners moved out of view and Zara saw that the shops were closed. Never in all her life had she seen all the shops shut like this except for a few hours on occasions such as the festival of the Green-clad Man. All of Qila was in mourning. The people were treating Aunt Hana's passing as a state occasion.

'Where's Littl'un?' Zara asked, suddenly missing the old woman's presence.

'I gave her some time off,' Pebbles replied.

'But surely she needs to be here, doesn't she, Pebbles? I mean, it's the funeral ...'

Pebbles tensed. The balcony felt tight, overfull, like a small box at the theatre. Zara stepped back into the Green Room. Hana was gone but the Venetian glass frames looked just as grand and glamorous as they always had, their joins held in place with emerald-cut crystal. This had been her wedding chamber, the room where she had lived with Sultan Ramzi, her bridegroom.

Zara walked quickly under the curtained arch, through the small middle room, into Hana's present room. Everything was in place. There was no sign even of the ritual bath that had taken place before she was finally laid in her shroud. It felt wrong somehow – wrong that this woman whose emotions and intentions and experiences had infused these walls for so many years, could go with the ease of one moment passing into another and that afterwards life would look the same. Even she had found herself in moments, simply talking to people, discussing trivia, rather than constantly filling the moments and seconds with the weight of Hana's passing. *She's gone!* she thought. And then there was the guilt. It had not yet found a specific cause to wrap itself around but there it was, like liquid in a mud pool, swirling away in an attempt to find its way out. Every time it struck her that Hana would not be back, Zara felt her chest tighten and a weight pushed in on her, making it hard to breathe. She would never see her again. Never.

Zara heard a hissing, flapping noise by the curtains and moved cautiously towards its shuddering, jerky movements. A trapped animal, perhaps? Swiftly, she grabbed the edge of the curtain and pulled.

'Littl'un!'

The old woman lay crouched on the floor, her body racked with sobs. Zara dropped to her knees beside her and held her in her arms. Littl'un seemed to be all fabric and hair, no substance. She was wet with tears. Neither of them spoke for several minutes.

'What will I do now, Bibi?' she asked, her eyes drowning in puddles of water that filled up her deep sockets. 'Where will I go?'

'You'll carry on here for as long as you like. And your son ...'

'A homing pigeon does not find comfort in any other home. One who lives with angels in paradise would be incapable of breathing on earth.' Some of Littl'un's spirit was returning. 'I mean, my mother's eighty-five and still in Qila!'

'Then stay. I'll speak with Saif.'

'But what purpose will my life have?' Littl'un wailed. 'What's a purse without its string? I should have died ...'

Zara was distracted by a movement outside. Through the small window on the left of Aunt Hana's bed, she could see a crowd of men. One in particular seemed to stand out. He was tall, handsome from what she could see and dressed like a Bollywood 'hero'.

Littl'un stood up, smoothing down her clothes, wiping away her tears. 'I must go and get the women,' she said. 'I promised I'd call for them after the funeral procession had left.'

The women arrived in a huge, weeping crowd. Zara recognized several of them, changed by time. Dilkash threw her arms around Zara. She was a tiny, wizened woman, skin burned black with age, hair thick and white, and wavy despite being pulled back.

'I knew you'd be fine,' she muttered, clinging to Zara. 'My precious ruby would no more succumb to illness than an eagle would make its nest in the ground. I told everyone that when they said you'd gone.' Her voice broke. 'And I was right, my life, my own piece of the moon. Here you are.' She collapsed against Zara a moment.

'Oh my god, Pebbles,' Ana whispered loudly. 'She thinks your cousin is Begum Saheb!'

Littl'un darted forward to guide her mother away. 'Sorry Bibi,' she said. 'My mother makes mistakes. Forgets everything.'

'Senile dementia, poor, luckless thing,' Pebbles murmured as Dilkash came to life again, clapped loudly and announced that the guests were lucky to be invited by her mistress to such a grand party.

The women looked startled even though they knew Dilkash. Zara remembered some of them first arriving at Qila. Hana had given them workspace at nominal rents when it was hard to find accommodation without the protection of a man. They were widows, divorcees and spinsters often with a skill or craft passed down the generations. Many had gone on to become successful tradeswomen.

The daughters of Munira, the seamstress, had taken over her business and expanded her clientele. They appeared now, dressed in sleek white salwar-kameez outfits that some Delhi boutiques were proudly beginning to display. The seamstress greeted Zara warmly and introduced her eldest daughter. 'This is Salma, the eldest – you remember even then she used to sew clothes for your doll's weddings?'

The girl smiled, dropped her eyes. 'So many times your same doll got married,' she said. 'And we got nice-nice things for eating.'

'You were always asking when she'd get married again. Now I know it was for the food,' Zara said. They laughed together. Salma had been a regular companion.

'Salma started to copy designs from magazines and movie heroines,' Munira explained. 'She was supplying her designs to a local boutique. But Huzur Saheb said she wasn't getting what she deserved so she sent her and her younger sisters to study fashion in Delhi. They're getting quite a reputation all over the country.'

'We've started designing saris, too,' smiled Salma. 'New-new designs. Different-different kind of pattern and embroidery and beadwork. We have been approached by one film-costume designer.'

Most of the women lived in the small houses behind the fort. Technically, these were rent-paying tradespeople and yet, because of their class and lack of education, they had none of the rights of those who held the purse strings. Their status was little more than that of servants. But Hana had believed in education. As a young woman, she had taught the children to read and write and had provided training for those without a trade. Zara had been hauled in, too, when she was still at school, to teach the children English. The younger ones came in now, so grown up she hardly recognized them. And there were new faces. So many that Zara was bemused.

The unspoken leader of the courtyard dwellers was Amira, the rangrezan. A mistress of the craft of fabric dyeing, Amira was a princess by name and princess by skill. In her hands fabric was transformed from faded to luminous, from dull to exotic, from reject to object of desire. Zara had spent many hours as a child watching her excitedly experiment with a new plant, a piece of stone, powdered iron, a seashell or verdigris. And she had shown Zara how she could extract the most subtle, the most unusual, the downright impossible colours from plants and powders, stones and minerals to match a fabric she had been given. She never failed. No one had ever rejected a piece of fabric, an item of clothing that Amira dyed.

'Don't be selfish, Amira,' Hana had cautioned. 'We all go some day. Pass on your skill to others. Teach people.'

'I've tried, Huzur Saheb,' Amira would wail. 'I get so frustrated. The idiots never learn.'

'Then, Amira, you'll just have to write a book. Write down all your experiments and how you came by the colours.'

Amira cackled loud and long at this pearl of wisdom.

'Are you laughing at me, Amira?'

'You are making fun of me, Huzur. How can an ignorant woman like me write such things?'

'But that's the whole point, Amira. You're not ignorant. You're the mistress of your craft. I don't think anyone in the world is as good as you at this job. Do you remember the American lady whose shirt you dyed? It was a greenish colour.'

'Its base was not green,' Amira said. 'That was the mystery. I think the Americans were starting with green as their base. I thought I'd do that, too, at first. Then I began thinking that in fact its heart was brown.' She pointed in the direction of the hilly slopes that flowed down the side of the back terrace. 'It looks green, especially in summer, but its essence is brown. That led me to the heart of the mystery.'

'You've just proved my point. You saw what no one else could.'

'Well, naturally, Huzur. Colour is a matter of the eye and the heart in collaboration. One sees, the other associates; one reaches the essence, the other observes the manifestation.'

'We're writing a book, Amira. You'll tell me all this and I'll write it down.'

And so a labour of love began. Aunt Hana discovered that dyeing was not Amira's only skill. She held in her mind a vast repertoire of songs and verses about the rangrez, the dyer, who it turned out was quite a figure in medieval verse and lyric: a symbolic figure, sometimes a mystic, sometimes an allegory for God – but always awesome and magnetic with the power to transform. And she collected metaphors and verses about colour and dyeing and even took issue with the accuracy, or lack of it, in the lines of famous sage-poets. And Hana had recalled some verses that Nyla used to sing.

Be not arrogant about wealth and youth, wrote Mira Bai the mystic, medieval queen-turned-mendicant in search of the god Krishna. *This multi-coloured garment is an illusion.*

'It is not true, Huzur Saheb,' Amira complained. 'If the appropriate compounds are used, the colour will not run. It will stay spring-fresh, like the colour of the rose in dew. Saturated, drenched.'

So Hana added the verses, the lyrics and Amira's arguments to the book. And in the years that followed, more than a few academics came from different parts of the world to gain access to Amira's repertoire and the 'ignorant woman' was transformed into a prized 'informant' to scholars.

She stepped forward now, clutching a bundle wrapped in an envelope of white muslin, and addressed Pebbles.

'I want your permission, Bahurani,' she said. Her head was held high but Zara could see the trepidation behind the exterior. 'My heart is breaking at the sight of Huzur Saheb covered in white. I know. I know it's the tradition, the faith, but that is not her colour.' She thumped the fabric. 'Her essence is in these colours. The colours of life. I was blending all night. Please permit me to cover her bed with this.' Her voice wavered. She looked down, fighting tears.

Pebbles did not respond. Zara tensed. Surely she would not refuse? The rest of the women seemed to hold their breath. This was their uncrowned leader and Pebbles was known to be erratic and temperamental.

'Amiran,' Pebbles said eventually, using the affectionate version of her name. 'Of course you can. Huzur Saheb would have been delighted.'

Amira walked proudly into Hana's bedroom, with Littl'un at her side. Her shoulders were stiffly squared, her head held high to disguise her relief and emotion. Zara followed. Amira stood at the foot of the bed for a few moments, then unwrapped her voile envelope and drew out a length of heavy fabric that Zara could only describe as a representation of a spring garden – a mixture of colours and shapes on a bed of the subtlest green that any impressionist painter would have been proud to call his own. Reverently, slowly, she spread it over Hana's bed.

'I saw her once soon after I'd arrived. She was dressed all in green, that exact shade. She looked like the spirit of nature. More beautiful than anything I've ever seen. I held the colour in my mind and mixed it immediately. I never knew then that one day it would be the colour of farewell.'

She stood back, raised her hands. As she said the Fateha, the farewell prayer, opening her palms to the heavens, pleading for Hana's place in paradise, Zara felt her own hands mirror the gesture.

Outside, the women had moved into Hana's terrace and were spreading out thin mattresses on the stone floor, covering them with white cotton sheets. Zara and the others joined them.

'The departing lady was graced by fortune,' Salma the potter said. 'We've already completed the entire Quran Shareef in her name twice since she passed.'

Two younger women staggered forward with bright cloth sacks filled with unshelled walnuts and almonds.

'They were counted out this morning,' the seamstress said. '125,000 of them.'

Pebbles turned to Zara. 'That's how many times we read the Fateha at funerals. They've started using these nuts to count, instead of tasbihs. You can keep count better with them.'

'I'm not a complete outsider,' Zara said.

Pebbles looked contrite. 'No, of course not. I didn't mean ... sorry. I'm not thinking clearly.' She turned away, visibly emotional.

Was this the Pebbles to whom Saif was so devoted, Zara wondered. And had Aunt Hana known this side of her?

12

There was a lingering atmosphere of homecoming in the graveyard, each one a tiny microcosm of the great 'campsite of destruction' – this finite world. Saif thought it natural that such thoughts and feelings should drift through his mind as he stood by his mother's graveside, watching the white procession flow around the deep pit and stop at its ridges of freshly removed soil, black, grainy, fertile, to him the most divine of materials. The swirling whiteness grew still and sharpened into a gathering of men, crowding, clustering close, body to body, inhibition overwhelmed by death. Differing shades of brown marked out individuals, faces upon shoulders, from a blush of gold to deep mahogany, even a slate-like black, faces beautiful with grief, exquisite in their concentration, harsh with pain held back. Eyes that looked at each other for solace, brothers all – Rampyara, the untouchable sweeper, embracing Ghulam Rasul, the Muslim butcher – as their tears flowed and mingled and everyone shared the grace of a god in no need of naming. That was the power of Hana Ramzi – the power that had gathered like a massive ocean swell over the fifty-nine years of his mother's life in Trivikram, as she filled the massive backyard of Qila with labourers and artisans. They were taken in and nurtured and another microcosm was formed in Huzur Saheb's backyard and became a wholesome, creative community, cohesive, loving, sharing.

It was Saif's backyard, too. And that was his mother, beneath her stark shroud, unmarked by red. It had been one of her simpler dreams to have her shroud stained with kumkum, the sacred red powder dusted into the hair parting of Hindu wives. 'I expect nothing from your father,' she had said, her voice gay, 'except to have the decency to stay alive until after I'm gone. Or my shroud will be drab. I want it sprinkled extravagantly with kumkum.' Underneath that light-heartedness, Saif sensed the weight of lost love. She could not bear to live in a world without Sultan.

What could he say? He could not control his father's life span, though God knew if he had the power, he would have made Sultan live on past her if for nothing else, then to witness for himself what an impact Hana had made on her world. So, as in almost every other matter, his father had let her down. But Saif tried not to dwell on his father's failures because it was Sultan's mantle he had been obliged to inherit. And at the hint of faded resentment coming back to oppress him as he stood beside his mother's grave, ready to bury her, he reminded himself that censure was entirely a matter of perspective. Those who had experienced his father's benevolence and his teaching would no doubt feel differently. To them, his shunning of Hana merely signalled that he had abandoned worldly concerns and hearkened to the call of the Divine Beloved. But Saif believed there had to be a compromise – a way to disengage with the knowledge that God was the inevitable and not a rival and that your love for your dear ones endured.

Saif did not deny that there was definitely something in lyrics of love-fervour and sacrificing all to the embrace of the Beloved that created momentary insanity – he had tasted the exquisite ecstasy of that madness. But for him, it came in brief instants. And when the ecstatic instant passed, he felt fleeting doubts about the Green-clad Man – was he a genuine being or a symbol? Or had the Ramzis exploited the enigma of a fertility spirit of the wild and built upon it in a land with an insatiable hunger for divine connection? Had they earned their fame and fortune through the exploitation of a symbol? He felt no rancour when these questions assailed him, just curiosity. But then, when his belief in the One became stronger the doubts were threaded, occasionally, with a sense of revulsion that the Green-clad Man had been elevated, in the folk mind, to a god. And that he, as his attendant, was revered as a spiritual leader on a fallacy. He prayed now that it would not affect his mother's position in the afterlife.

It was through watching his mother and the unspoken drive in her actions that he had come to his own compromise – his job was simply to do his best. Struggling with the significance of the Green-clad Man as he learned and reflected and grew in the Ramzi Order had helped Saif distil his essence to Unity and Healing. 'The great wound in the cosmic psyche needs healing,' his father had quoted one day. And Saif's ancestors had demonstrated over the centuries that if the sweat and blood of all faiths seeped into the same soil, then a synthesis must take root. Until recently, Trivikrampur had been proof of it as had many other pockets of India. The true Seekers pursued their goal so single-mindedly they felt no urge to tamper with the faith of others. In his own teaching, he strove only to level and provide access to a condition where harmony was possible in every atom of life – and beyond to a celebration of faith. For in the end true faith, like the Creator, was the same in all its names. All this he connected with Hana, though he had no specific memory of discussing it with her. Hana, too, believed in the 'greater purpose' that raised people above the banal prejudices that constrained life.

Today was his mother's day. The day she was leaving forever. Yesterday, after Zara told him Hana had passed away, he said his prayers for her soul and rose to leave. But before he left, he paused at her window a moment, watching the branches of the tamarind that his mother had gazed on for so many decades, allowing all the tiny details to be etched in his mind so that he could say a farewell that came from deep within. But the farewell would not come. Then he saw a dove fly out from the heart of the tree, through its top branches and straight up towards the sky, not as a pigeon would fly but soaring like a kite intoxicated by the wind. And the words of farewell swelled up inside him, just as the dove moved from the heart of the branches and glided up on rising currents of air. Goodbye, Mother, goodbye.

And who was he now that she was gone? No longer a man blessed by the shade of the parent tree. His back felt exposed to the burning sun and he had a fresh load to carry.

One thing was sure as he stood watching his mother's body lowered into the grave, amid the chant of the Quran, that he had been redefined. His sense of self, if ever he had one, was shaken. The world shifted out of his vision and back again. The sun seared his back and set the cotton fabric on fire. He started to repeat words that would, he hoped, ground him as they had when he was a child.

'My name is Saif. I am a Ramzi. Together my names mean the Sword of Secrets or, metaphorically, Protector of the Keeper of Mysteries. I believe that my mother chose the name because it is analogous in so many ways to the "ideal man". Upright, straight-backed, protector of good, scourge of evil.' Hana had expected him to be all those so that he could honour his future position.

He often thought of his mother as a goddess – a mother goddess – and her funeral crowd appeared to prove it. His faith forbade him to believe in goddesses or gods other than the One and at first he had fought against the restraint – when he looked at the glowing moon, the majestic mountains and the forests that surrounded and supported Qila and the rivers flowing on either side of it. At the age of ten, when he visited his newly married aunt Nyla in Karachi and saw the roaring ocean yards from the wooden gate of Nyla's home, he understood the meaning of infinity. It was strange, then, being in a country full of people who believed in one god – a country which the Ramzis had opted not to emigrate to. In Pakistan, in those days, people made no issue of their faith. It simply was. It was an alien but welcome experience, knowing a universe in which God, just the one God, was taken for granted and was present in the prayers of numerous people who chose whether or not to pray – from Nyla's sybaritic in-laws to domestic servants.

Faith was manifest in cyclical surges. The moment-to-moment saying of grace and offering of thanks, and offering of daily prayers by some was free from a sense of compulsion. In contrast, here in Gujarat, a small but visible group of Muslims impressed upon their children that knowledge and observance of their faith was vital to its survival. They were aware that every religious action or utterance may be perceived as a deliberate statement of difference. Even in Trivikram, he wondered if at times his Hindu friends and employees felt overwhelmed by the rigorous 'outsiders' with their strident ways and determined devoutness. He wondered if it had simmered for the thousand years of Muslim presence in India or if the resentment had seeped in from other, contaminated places. When the protestors finally came to Trivikram, to Qila, two years ago, demanding that the 'outsiders' leave India for the Indians, he asked himself: 'After a thousand years, are we still outsiders? The "Ms" we're called today, as if the name "Muslim" might contaminate the tongue of the speakers – the incomers. And if India is not my home, then what is?' But essentially humankind was set on earth to wander – as eternal outsiders – because the ultimate home lay only within the One. And his mother was now part of it as he yearned, one day, to be.

Bhola, son of Rampyara the gardener, had placed a brass incense holder by the grave. The incense sticks wafted out their smoky scent – sandalwood – elegant, deep and wholesome without being heady or pervasive like some of the floral kind. Deep, wrenching sobs came from him as he fumbled in his pocket and pulled out three garlands – one of roses, deep red; the other of the fragrant motia, gardenia blooms, feathery snowballs interspersed with roses; and, finally, a long, winding string of jasmine buds. Saif could see from the series of wheels forming a luscious, rounded garland, that Bhola had woven it himself.

Saif remembered his mother in the Oval Garden with Bhola as a little boy, teaching him with endless patience how to weave the tight buds the way his late mother had – they had a ritual. They would place the garlands in plastic bags and leave them in the refrigerator until it was time for Hana to adorn her hair with them in time for afternoon tea, or to tie them around her wrist. As the hours wore on, the warmth of her body would transform the slim, firm buds into soft flowers so fragrant, that he could have sworn Bhola sniffed the moment of blooming and appeared beside her, smiling, pointing to the mature blooms. Mother said he was a child of nature, so pure that he still contained the instincts and intuition of those who have not been corrupted and distorted by the fruit of the Tree of Knowledge. She objected to his nickname, even imposing a ban on it, and tried to bestow other titles on him.

Saif smiled, remembering Hana's tendency to rail against the inevitable and grow angry when she failed. But names, like scandals and bad reputations, had a way of finding their target and clinging to it. Bhola's mother Mala had turned mad and run away, leaving her baby boy. His father had brought him up but he could not stop the warm-hearted storytelling or strike out the pity in people's eyes; the boy's loss had taken root and grown into a jungle of self-protection in his mind, so that he knew nothing but the simple pleasures of life which played in his constant smile. Saif often thought that if he could see inside Bhola's head, he would find a vale burgeoning with soft grasses, fragrant heather and flowers of so many colours and such a profusion of scents that the outside could never invade.

Saif leant forward and stroked Bhola's shoulder. Bhola stepped back and a stream of petals rained down the length of the shroud, from his shirt and his sleeve. Hana's wish was granted, Saif thought. Nature had granted it through Bhola's simple connection with her. Her shroud danced with red.

Saif looked at the faces around him. The white of mourning was supplanted by the colour of life. The vivid patches of red on Hana's shroud seemed to say that death could not stop flowers blooming.

13

125,000 readings of the Fateha were swiftly completed by the large number of women, some counting with walnuts and almonds, others using their prayer-beads.

Littl'un arose as the sounds of the returning procession were heard. A woman, the bhatyaran, crept silently out of the gathering and made for the terrace by the kitchens where, years ago, the gypsy women used to rest. Littl'un signalled to Zara to follow and they walked along the gallery, past the open stairway from the inner courtyard, to the disused kitchen.

There, in the courtyard, directly behind the kitchen in a pit used at weddings and public functions, a huge fire roared beneath a massive cauldron. Beyond was a shamiana large enough for hundreds of guests who would be fed throughout the day. The first to be served would be the women who had come to pray.

The steam from the cauldron was white and fragrant with cloves, cardamom, cinnamon.

'We kept it simple,' Littl'un said. 'Chicken qorma and naan. The bhatyaran and her family were up all last night preparing. Mumtaz Bibi sent the chickens. 260 of them.'

Zara felt a band snap inside. She fought for control but the tears flowed and she sobbed. 'Why didn't she come, Littl'un? Why couldn't she put aside her resentment – this last time? Just to come and pray?'

Littl'un put her arms around Zara. 'Never mind, Bibi. Come on. A jackal only knows its own hunger. What does it know of compassion? You've been up all night.'

'So have you.'

She looked at the blazing pit and the tandoors with their open mouths gaping heat from under the ground. The bhatyaran climbed a ladder to the neck of the cauldron and leaned inside, stirring with a massive wooden rod. Clearly she wanted to do the job herself, ensure that everything was perfect for Hana's farewell feast. Twelve young women in white joined her. They were her ten daughters and two daughters-in-law returned from the prayer reading. Now they set to work, chopping, grinding, mixing. Twelve men, their brothers and their husbands, stood in a row, a chain of hands, passing down heavy trays loaded with dough. And every time they heaved a load, a cry of 'Allah' went up.

'They must be exhausted.'

'They're working people, Bibi,' Littl'un said. 'They save their tiredness for bedtime.'

This was a labour of love. The job of jobs, a way of offering up their affection and gratitude to Hana. Zara felt humble. They were a proud lot – in the best possible way. Hana had always known and respected it. 'I have learned so much from them,' she'd said to Zara and Peter when they came ten years ago. 'They're never proud but they never lose pride.'

'You should rest,' Littl'un said, shoving Zara in the direction of Hana's bedroom.

She smoothed the sheets on the bed. 'Here, lie down for a few minutes.'

Zara looked at Amira's gift, like spring spread across Aunty's bed. 'I'll use the middle room for now,' she said.

Littl'un hobbled up two stone steps and busied herself getting the bed linen from the small chest of drawers in the corner.

'What do you think she wanted me to do, Littl'un?' Zara felt lost. 'Have you any idea at all? Did she tell you?'

Littl'un looked perplexed. 'What she wanted you to do?'

'She said she wanted to give me something.'

Littl'un looked relieved. 'I think it was those wretched bangles – you kept going to museums to find out about them. Don't you remember?'

'Where are they now?'

Littl'un looked around as if she was surrounded by spies. She cupped her mouth with her hands, leaned up and spoke in a squawky whisper. 'Bahurani thinks Huzur Saheb stole them. Stole her own bangles, I ask you?'

Littl'un was rambling, surely? 'I'm talking about a book ... maybe some papers?'

Littl'un shook her head. 'Maybe she told Sita Devi, who knows? They don't talk anymore. All I know is she did not want Bahurani to know.' She walked towards the door. 'Do you remember that fancy jeweller, Hirani? Maybe you should ... Anyway, you sleep now. Worry about all that afterwards.'

Hirani the jeweller? Had Aunty given him something to sell? Or for safekeeping? The bangles, perhaps?

The branches of the tamarind tree swept in horizontal curves above the shrine, as if veiling its humiliation. Zara could see Sharmeen beside the remains of the small edifice. She looked lost, as if waiting for someone. Zara moved closer to the window. Someone was approaching Sharmeen. It was the Bollywood 'hero' from the street. He took a few urgent strides towards Sharmeen then grabbed her by the shoulders and shoved her into the Oval Garden.

Zara turned from the window and flew down the stairs. She brushed through the crowds of men in the dining room, ignoring the startled heads that turned to look, then whipped into a side door to throw them off-track, and into the Oval Garden. The garden was empty. She whirled around, looking in all directions, stopping herself from calling out. She had attracted attention and the men would be alert for anything untoward.

'Zara? What's the matter?' Jay was standing beside her.

'It's Sharmeen. A man grabbed her. He pulled her in here.'

'A man?' Jay looked puzzled.

'She was at the shrine and then ...'

In a grotesque imitation of what she had seen, Jay grabbed Zara and pulled her back into the dining room. The next moment a violent cry went up, calling for the death of Saif and his family. 'Ramzi jaati, murdabad.' Death to the Ramzi clan.

Zara saw Saif stride to the entrance. 'Saif? Where's he going?'

Jay darted through the drawing room and grasped Saif's shoulder. 'What are you doing?'

'I have to talk to them.'

Jay listened to the chanting. 'Close down girls' school!' 'No conversions to Islam.' 'End campaign of conversions.' 'Out Muslim traitors.'

Jay blanched and grabbed at Saif. 'What on earth are you thinking, man? No! I'll talk to them.'

Jay's aide-de-camp rushed to his side. 'It would not be wise, Maharaja Saheb.'

Several men pushed forward, offering to reason with the rioters, but their negotiations were disrupted by the sound of police sirens.

A pistol shot cracked out. The shouts died down. A voice on a police loudspeaker dispersed the crowd. Saif, Jay and a number of important guests surged towards the police inspector as he entered.

'Thank you, Inspector Pandey,' Saif said. 'I'm impressed. You were here very fast.'

'Well done,' Jay said. 'Very impressive.'

The inspector saluted and bowed slightly. 'We had a tip-off, sir.'

'A tip-off?' Jay frowned. 'When?'

'Twenty minutes before the event, Your Highness. Some young men were spotted near Qila. We recognized the description of some of them – well-known troublemakers. They come from outside Trivikrampur for the express purpose to create disturbances.'

Inspector Pandey turned to go then turned back. 'May I offer my condolences, sir. We have lost a magnificent personage in your mother.'

Zara looked anxiously through the door to the Oval Garden. The crisis was over. But where was Sharmeen?

An army of servants marched in, carrying silver tureens of steaming chicken qorma and oval dishes containing yellow lentils cooked with peanuts and a blend of unusual spices, and stuffed aubergine in a sauce of ground poppy seed, sesame seeds and the subtlest touch of tamarind. Engraved silver platters were piled with freshly baked naan; crystal bowls were filled with raita flavoured with mint and grated cucumber; smaller, deeper bowls held kachumbar, a salsa of finely chopped tomato, onion, green chilli and coriander, steeped in lime juice. These were scattered along tables covered in white damask. The bhatyaran had observed the protocol for a funeral meal never to be confused with a banquet. But she had maintained the lavishness and haute cuisine for which the Ramzi table was renowned. And for dessert, Zara knew there would be the original shahi tukra – royal portions – a grand version of bread and butter pudding from a recipe in a Mughal manuscript.

Saif and Jay were ushering the men towards the dining table. Zara slipped away and crossed the Oval Garden, walking along the adjacent wall to the front door of Mumtaz's wing. She snatched the handle. The shiny brass knocker with the face of a grotesque man had replaced the original 300-year-old iron piece bearing a benign pair of eyes and smiling lips, surrounded with a foliate mane which had been part of her childhood, an object of reassurance; an immovable thing, fixed firmly on to a solid, square base. Wasn't it enough for Mumtaz that Hana had split up the family property to give her this portion? Did she really have to destroy the fabric of the place, too?

Zara let go of the knocker and it clanged loudly. A young woman answered dressed in a salwar-kameez. Her hair was cut in a short fringe and her head was uncovered. She looked sullenly at Zara.

'Is Mumtaz Begum in?'

The woman stood back and pointed to some chairs in the dark and massive hall. 'Sit. I'll see.'

A few moments later, she scuttled back, looking disgruntled. 'Come with me, please.'

After twenty-five years, the stairs were still familiar. The place was clearly under-used. Why had Mumtaz demanded this vast section of the fortress when, clearly, she had no use for it?

Bright sunlight blinded Zara's eyes as she emerged into the terrace adjoining the rooms that overlooked the Oval Garden. It had been built as the mirror to Aunty Hana's terrace but new rooms had been added, and a trellis. Painful memories of Nyla flitted through Zara's mind. Hana had still used this part of the fort when her mother left and it was here that she had seen her for the last time.

'So you are Zara. You are not so beautiful as your mother. Come in.' Mumtaz was a tall woman. Late middle age had made her handsome, different from pictures of her youth, which showed a masculine body and plain, crude features – the antithesis, in fact, of Hana. The story went that each time a family arrived with a proposal of marriage for her, they were so bowled over by Hana's beauty that they changed their mind and went away without asking for Mumtaz's hand.

'How do you come to be visiting?' Mumtaz asked. 'There is a function in progress in your house.'

She spoke crudely. There was nothing that could link her to the Ramzis. Yet she was a daughter of their house. *She's nothing like us.* Us? Well, she had the right. She was more of a loyal Ramzi than Mumtaz, even without their blood running in her veins.

Zara wanted to ask why she had not attended the funeral prayers but bit back her words. 'Just before the protest, I saw a man grab my niece, Sharmeen, from near the shrine.' Mumtaz's eyes flickered. 'He pulled her into the Oval Garden. They were gone when I came down.'

'And you want to know if I saw her?'

'I want you to have your place searched. She could be downstairs. I gather it's unused.'

Mumtaz took a deep breath. 'What did this man look like?'

'Tall. Very carefully dressed. A bit like ...'

'A "hero".'

Zara nodded. 'You know him?'

'He's my grandson, God save me.'

'Your grandson?'

'Kamran. I've told him not to hang around that girl. She's a simpleton. She'll get impregnated and there'll be hell to pay.'

'Please! Don't talk like that about my niece.'

'Hana's blood purifies the child, does it? Puts her above the weakness of humankind? Well it didn't purify my brother.'

Zara pulled herself together. 'Your grandson. Before he took Sharmeen, he was with the troublemakers.'

Mumtaz stood up. 'I will send for your niece. She was not abducted, as you seem to suggest. She seeks out my grandson and I'm doing everything in my power to keep him away from her. She's probably right now with him downstairs. Gives no thought to consequences.'

This woman was repulsive. Her elegantly greying hair and strong, dignified demeanour emphasized the crudeness of her language. She shouted loudly for the maid to fetch Sharmeen then turned to Zara, shaking her forefinger.

'Take the fool and get out. And don't you dare accuse my grandson of violating young girls.'

Zara shook all over. Sharmeen was safe. But was she hankering after Kamran?

Sharmeen came up the stairs, wailing. She minced up to Zara and threw her arms around her. 'Please, please, Aunty Zara, don't tell Mummy and Papa I was with Kamran.' She cupped Zara's face in her hands. 'You understand. You had a love marriage, didn't you?'

Zara snatched Sharmeen's hands from her face. 'We should go, Sharmeen. We'll talk later.' A 'love marriage', she thought, is no guarantee of happiness.

She heard Sharmeen whimpering, 'Just you and I?'

'You and I?'

'We'll talk, you said. Just you and I? Not Mummy and Daddy?'

'Just you and I – for now.' Zara led her away.

'Don't be angry, Aunty Zara. Please. I'm so sad about my grandmother. I was standing by the shrine – you know where her body was laid earlier, and I was trying to imagine it back there instead of inside a dark grave.' She shivered. 'It must be so cold in there. And then all the stone on top.'

'I know, it's very hard.'

'The stone? I know. So I thought if I could conjure up her vision right here again, and then light a small lamp, that might ...' She shuddered. 'A lamp would not be enough. I needed a bigger fire. And then I felt so sad, I thought I would die too. I wanted to climb up and lie down where she had been. And just then, Kamran came. He dragged me in and comforted me ... and just then the men broke in.' She smiled, lost in her own world. 'He's so handsome, just like a film star. And if he hadn't saved me when he did, I'd have still been there when the rioters came. They would have got me. They want to kill the Ramzis – I don't understand why.'

Zara held her tight. She wanted to ask what she was doing with Kamran so long but something stopped her. *I've changed. I'm not Indian enough anymore.* Pebbles would surely have asked. But Indian or not, Zara could not resist scanning Sharmeen's clothes. There was no sign of damp or grit. No indication that anything untoward had happened. *She's nearly twenty, for god's sake. It's not for me to start telling her what to do.*

Her uneasiness persisted as she stepped back into the house with Sharmeen. Had Kamran rescued her from the rioters or tried to help her through her grief? Or was he hoping to get a beautiful bride and become master of the fortress in one, sharp move?

And what of love, plain and simple? In Europe, perhaps, but she had worked with far too many casualties from the strife-torn, sectarian sub-continent where mixed marriages and alliances between feuding families led to slaughter and destruction. Kamran must know that. He would not take such risks for love; Jay had not.

They walked through the main entrance to avoid the dining room. Sharmeen grabbed Zara by both shoulders and whispered passionately. 'Please, Aunty Zara. You won't tell?'

Zara smiled and the relief on Sharmeen's face warmed her. Sharmeen sprinted up the side staircase and Zara threaded her way through the corridor behind the dining room, to the inner courtyard.

A sing-song voice was complaining from behind one of the tall trees. 'I saw you from Begum Saheb's terrace. You came up behind that Zara. Looked like you wanted to just hug her. Your lips were in her hair like you were kissing her. You told me all this was finished ... that you would stop your flirting and your Casanova ways.'

Zara crept quietly up the stairs to avoid being seen by Jay and Anapurna. Why in heaven's name did Jay not tell Anapurna that she was firmly married to Peter, that it was a 'love marriage'? At the top of the stairs, she turned left and stepped into the refuge of the Green Room.

II

14

Zara put down her fork. She felt queasy. 'I'd like to stay on for a bit, if that's okay.'

Pebbles' head jerked up. 'How long?'

Zara could see that her brusque response disturbed Saif. 'Of course,' he said. His tone was warm. 'As long as you like.'

'How long?' Pebbles repeated. 'There's trouble brewing here.'

'Well, I'm not sure. I've come back after ...'

'What about Peter? Isn't he going to mind?'

Zara pushed her scrambled eggs on to the edge of her plate. 'He was the one who suggested it, last night when we spoke.'

Peter's voice had brought a warm rush. 'I've been worried about you. Did you sleep any better last night?'

'Things on my mind,' she said.

'Look, stay as long as you need to.' His response came as a surprise. Once he would have pinned her to a return date.

'Maybe I should come back and tie up a few ends first.'

'That's silly,' he said. 'You're there now. Do what you need to. Stay focused.'

Zara wasn't sure what she'd hoped for from Peter but she felt disappointed. 'My case load ...'

'Let someone else do it. You've lost Hana.'

'But that's just why I ...'

'Give yourself time to grieve,' he insisted. 'Spend time with Saif and Littl'un. Then look out that group. You made a commitment.'

'To be honest, that's gone right out of my mind, Peter,' she said. 'I keep obsessing about Aunty's will – how will I ever find it?'

'More reason to stay.' She wanted to be near Peter. 'You'll feel unsettled until you get closure. Stay put; as Father would say – finish the job.'

Zara wilted. 'I'm not sure ...'

'You were really fired up when you left,' Peter said. 'If you don't make contact with that group, you'll regret it. You know you won't get away from work again. Think how long it's been since the last time.'

Peter did not want her and neither did Pebbles.

Saif patted her hand. 'It's your home, Zara. Stay as long as you like – everything here is at your disposal.' He stood up. 'I'm driving to Ramzi Bagh.' He looked at Pebbles. 'Jay and I are pressing on with the final plans for the Academy then we advertise for teachers in the national press. There'll be a thanksgiving prayer at Ramzi Bagh. Exciting times. I'll be back tomorrow morning.' He squeezed Pebbles' shoulder. 'And, Zara, remember what I said. This is your home, too.'

Pebbles slammed down her glass. Water splashed over her plate. 'Damn!' She turned towards the kitchen, yelling loudly. 'Anyone there? Where do all these wretches go to die, when they're needed?'

Sharmeen put her hands to her ears as two or three anxious women fell into the room. 'For god's sake, Mummy. Why d'you always do this? They need a minute to get here. You know they're standing outside the door. You know it.'

'Ai, tauba, tauba, tauba. Mumtaz Bibi, have some respect for the food God gave you.' Pebbles looked, startled at the sight of Dilkash's wizened form swaying by the door.

'What's she doing in the main house? Did you ask her to stay?' Pebbles looked accusingly at Zara as several maids scurried around her. 'Take away this food. It's all soaked. Fling it in the bin. What a waste!'

Three women rushed in wearing expressionless faces. They had all heard Dilkash mistake Pebbles for Mumtaz. One of them removed the plate; another mopped up the splash; a third put a clean plate in front of Pebbles and served her. Pebbles shoved away the dish.

'Stop crowding me. Did I ask for more? I'll ask if I need more. Am I not the mistress of this house? Now go! Get out. And you!' she hissed at Sharmeen as the women retreated, 'you will never talk to me like that in front of the servants. Or ever.'

Sharmeen shrank into her chair, her expression still defiant. Pebbles turned her wrath on Zara, ignoring Dilkash's burbling.

'Why did you come here, Zara? And why do you want to stay? If you came to see your aunt, then it's all over. But you didn't come to say goodbye to my mother-in-law, did you? What is it you want from us?'

Zara struggled to find words but Pebbles' claim jangled in her ears. *'I am the mistress.'* How easily the words had come. Hana had been laid to rest yesterday and already Pebbles had appropriated her place. This was Saif's home. And yes, it was her home, too – she had lived here for most of the first nineteen years of her life and knew its nooks and crannies and its history better than Pebbles ever would. Zara would stay. She would make contact with Ankahi, and she would investigate Hana's will. Qila would be her base while she completed her tasks.

'What do you think I want, Pebbles?' Thankfully, her voice sounded calm.

'You're asking, so I'll tell you. You always wanted to be a Ramzi. You've always dressed in borrowed feathers. I heard you, with my own ears, calling Noor Jehan's bangles "my bangles". But they aren't, are they, Zara? They're Ramzi bangles.'

Pebbles couldn't have hit her harder if she had tried. It was true that Zara had jokingly called the Ramzi heirlooms 'her' bangles but only because she had spent time researching their provenance. The experts agreed they could not be the seventeenth-century Empress Noor Jehan's own because of a microscopic difference in the lions' heads on the original pair and because, small as they were, they would have hung loose and heavy on the empress' famously tiny wrist. Zara had discovered that the empress had set a trap to find whose wrist her husband had used for size. She commissioned a dozen pairs to distribute among her ladies and slipped hers among them. The woman who could wear those tiny originals would be the one who had betrayed her with her husband. In one version she found the treacherous lady and tormented her to the end. Aunt Hana was exultant that Zara had discovered so much.

'I'll always think of these as your bangles, Zara,' she said. 'When my daughter Sama was born, my husband wanted to give them to her. She became dear to God – but then He sent you. And I shall always think of these as yours.' She looked downcast. 'But they say they weigh heavy on the owner.'

It struck Zara that the arrival of the bangles had coincided with Hana's greatest losses.

Zara glared back at Pebbles. 'But where are the bangles, Pebbles?'

'That's no concern of yours. They will be found and when they are, they will be returned to their rightful owner – Sharmeen. They are part of her inheritance. As is Qila.'

Zara stood up, trying to shake off painful thoughts. 'I'm not after the Ramzi fortune, Pebbles. The Ramzi jewellery is far too grand for the very ordinary life of Mrs Hamilton.'

She slipped through the curtains in the doorway, crossed the long living room and passed through the ante-room into Hana's bedroom. Hana had moved to the boudoir years before when it became clear that Sultan would not return to their marriage bed and the jewel-like splendour of the Green Room seemed to mock her. She could still look out on the shrine and the tamarind tree and the gate that opened on to the busy road. She had seen the street grow gradually from a lane housing half a dozen artisans and food sellers to the thriving market centre it was now. She also loved the vast terrace on its other side that allowed her to watch the sun rise and set on the Oval Garden and across to the wing that now belonged to Mumtaz. Hana had once built a roof-garden there which she nurtured herself, in all seasons, filled with roses and lilies, narcissi and eglantine – and to one side a vast clump of tulips. She had told Zara once that when her husband Sultan first saw it he enfolded her in his arms, realizing at once that this was a memorial to their daughter, Sama. But Zara had sensed Hana's unbearable loss and grief in the memory because Sultan had never embraced her again.

Saif told Peter and Zara on their visit that there was a void in Hana where Sama should have been and he shied away from invading it while his mother never attempted to cross it. He was a gentle soul, Hana recognized that. She had wondered aloud to Zara and Peter on that same visit, 'Did I drive him away by always striving to force the best out of him?' She told Zara how she had searched her soul, asking if her concern with the honour and dignity of the Ramzi line had become an obsession and alienated her only son. Peter thought that Hana was defending herself against loving Saif too much.

Zara ignored a twinge of guilt as she sat down on the spring-garden of Hana's bed and stroked the colours produced by Amira's magical fingers. *What will happen to this when I go back to London? Will Pebbles do something nice with it?* She shuddered at the thought of someone else sleeping in Hana's bed.

Zara's chest tightened. She felt breathless and panicky. She pressed down on her stomach and forced herself to inhale deeply. Then she got up and tidied the bed, straightening the sheet, plumping the pillows. Something felt wrong about the goings-on in Qila. Perhaps, she thought, Sita Devi could help.

The road to Ramzi Bagh grew shorter every time he drove there, so familiar now that he could allow his mind to follow its own routes. The constantly changing scenery, from modern highways to dirt roads, through cities and woods, scrubland and rivers seemed to bring back the contrast between the natural world and the man-made one and he could recall a poem by Urdu's most famous poet which began with a reference to stones and bricks and soared within a few couplets to a dazzling evocation of the manifestation of divine light in the Burning Bush. He felt a surge of emotion. The vision of light – the Dazzling Hand as they called it in Urdu – reduced such specks of dirt as the protest at the funeral to trivia. For an hour or two after the event he would have liked to reassure the rioters that he had never in his life converted anyone nor intended to. The accusation of religious contamination was fabricated by the accusers, most people would know that. Saif's convictions obliged him to do his best to fulfil his function – the result was in the hands of the Almighty and not his to worry about.

But how would it reflect on Jay, he wondered. A maharaja's reputation was important in his state no matter how the national government viewed him. News of the protest had travelled and a few English-language dailies had expressed distaste at the lack of respect shown to the dead. The consensus was that this was not a spontaneous protest, that it was being masterminded by a sectarian group. Jay called to say that the local papers had asked for a quote from Saif but the general feeling was that the protestors' claims were unfounded. Of course, Saif knew people weren't interested in proof; if something was repeated enough, it took on the resonance of fact.

Years ago, Anapurna had been a victim of that effect. Her small, anxious face floated into Saif's eyes, needy with rage and humiliation when her trust in Jay's fidelity was first challenged.

Saif shifted in his seat. The memory was invasive. It made him uneasy. Of all people, he should have rejected the rumour when Ana came to him flushed and furious and begging for reassurance. But the gossip had lingered. He had never asked Jay if he was unfaithful but, sadly, Anapurna had been plagued by suspicion for years. Judging from her anxious look at the end of the funeral lunch, she still was.

The unrest caused by the 'funeral protest', as people were calling it, did not affect the atmosphere of remembrance in the days that followed Hana's funeral. Everyone had an anecdote, a parable, a joke even, to tell about an experience with her, something she had said to them, an act of kindness or indeed hauteur; how she inspired, how she spoke out and how she could never be forced to do anything in which she did not believe. He had looked around at the faces surrounding him – friends, a few relatives, acquaintances – wondering who really *knew* his mother. And was there an unconscious competition commonly at play at funerals about who among the mourners knew the deceased best?

Saif knew her ability to love and give. He saw her affection for Nyla and her almost painful adoration of Zara. And he could be honest now about the envy he had felt when she spent hours with motherless Bhola, telling him stories about his mother's singing voice. It did not hurt anymore when he remembered how once, when he had asked to share in those moments, she was shocked by his lack of generosity – that a Ramzi heir, the son of her blood could begrudge the crumbs cast to an orphan. In fact, he would have traded anything for his mother's closeness. He had spent his life yearning for a connection with her. Now it would never be.

Ironic that he, the Ramzi son, groomed for detachment from the world, yearned so profoundly for human connection. At barely twenty, when his father died and he was plunged into the business of leading the Order, he felt himself come to life if little Zara was by his side; or when he drove out with Jay to the remoter parts of Trivikrampur, speaking to the villagers, discovering their needs. It felt like a blessing to be in a position to facilitate the boring of a well or to install irrigation channels and a short while later to see fields of yellow, green and gold stretching into the distance. The more ambitious projects excited him, too, like raising funds to train a doctor and nurses, set up small, local medical centres and persuade health professionals to settle in rural areas. Dearest to his heart was the scholarship which provided an opportunity for clever children to secure a sound future.

'We'll call it the Saif Ramzi Scholarship,' Jay said when he first mentioned the idea. Saif declined; the idea was not his. Besides, the potential and the grace to carry it through came from the Divine. Was it not hubris to imagine that the Divinity powering the universe had time to oversee individual concerns – his concerns? It made him more determined to work hard for his aims so he and

Jay initiated a bigger project – they set up a network of schools in the rural areas for the entire population of Trivikram. Over the years, he hoped, it would improve lives and convince people of the benefits of education. He and Jay had achieved the first part; their schools studded the rural landscape but it was hard to demonstrate the long-term benefits of education to the hungry and the naked. Some children had to work or the family would not eat. Girls, especially, because they readily found work in the houses of the wealthy and counted as cheap labour on construction sites where they were seen in lengthy rows, colourfully clad, passing concrete-laden vessels along, one to the other, until they reached the men who did the skilled jobs.

Two decades later, he and Jay had not made even a wheat-grain's worth of progress towards changing old attitudes. Women were going into outer space in rockets but here they could only recall the one who died. Still they ploughed on, he and Jay, doggedly set on making inroads, however small.

The Trivikrampur Academy for Girls, strong on practical and technical skills, might be the one to make an impact. This was his highest purpose in the work he must do on earth. To be accused of planning religious contamination might rankle but it was a mere irritation, a challenge to his ego. No one could prevent them going ahead with the Academy. They could slow things down to make life more difficult, but even if every line of the school curriculum, the policies and anything that could be interpolated between the lines was raked over with a fine-tooth comb, there would be nothing that the government or any individual could reasonably use to prevent the school opening. His was to do and die and not to reason why. This was a tribute to his grandmother, Her Highness the Begum Jahan Parvar.

Saif's only sense of belonging, of family, came from his grandmother, when he visited his grandfather's state of Daulatnagar in the salt marshes of Saurashtra. Saif remembered the delicious lead-up to the end of the school year when he prepared to spend the summer with her in Daulatnagar.

Under his grandmother's supervision, Saif experienced freedom. She believed in the magic of the outdoors: she would pack him off on horseback with a small retinue of bodyguards and a band of cousins to gallop free in the desert and marshes to explore and experiment between lavish 'picnics' complete with tables covered in white damask.

The Begum Jehan Parvar, like the meaning of her name, was a world nourisher, at least of her world. Her husband's state, small in comparison with her father's large kingdom, was more a collection of villages and rural stretches and its outskirts swirled into the salt marshes and rivers, savannahs and seas of the western coast. His grandparents had a happy marriage. Despite his sober temperament, the Nawab of Daulatnagar adored his wife and though he never gave in to her chiding and demands for liberalism, Saif learned to see from the flicker of his twirling moustaches, a subtle twist of his mouth, how much he really enjoyed it and wondered what he would be like if he allowed his feelings to come out and walk about. But the Nawab was a sentinel to tradition, standing guard all day, everyday, treating every step as one which would yield consequences.

His grandmother exulted in her small victories. 'I managed to give my daughters modern names,' she told him once. 'If I'd given in to your grandfather, they would have had horrible ones.' She lowered her head to Saif's and pressed the back of his head with her hand so that their foreheads rested together. He could feel that touch even now.

'You know what your mother's official name is? Aijaz Zamani. How terrible that is. Miracle of the Age. What a burden to carry. In England, that would be like calling your daughter Frederika or Anunciata. And Nyla's official name is Jalva-Afroze. I ask you. Do you know what that means, young man? Manifestation of Light. A reference to the Burning Bush – when the light appeared to Moses. Can you believe it?' She barely paused before continuing. 'But I got my way and they had modern names, too. And the others are just for fusty documents.' She paused a moment and then looked across at the English nanny dozing in a chair. 'Even provincials can pronounce my daughters' names.'

Grandmother always referred to England by its Indian name – vilayat – always adding how ironic it was that the Arabic origin of the word meant 'province' or 'outpost'. Saif smiled when she said it, pointing out how the folk of Daulatnagar were as likely to mispronounce the exotic names the Nawab chose for his daughters as the British. Grandmother flicked his arm playfully and nodded.

'Pure grandiosity,' she said. 'Of course if Mrs Venerable had her way, they'd have had names at the other extreme. I swear by God, if they'd been born in the appropriate month she would have called them May, June or Julia.' She looked at old Venables, in her wing chair. 'Or Augusta or Octavia.' She giggled. 'Or maybe she wouldn't have gone that far.'

She fixed her gaze on the former governess. 'Mrs Venerable, what do you say?'

The old woman opened her eyes, waved a lethargic hand over her drowsing lids and muttered. 'Venables, Your Highness, Venables.' She shifted her position and dozed off again, muttering. 'Twenty-five years in her service and she still can't say my name.'

Grandmother raised her eyebrows, only a little shocked at the riposte. 'Her mind's gone bad, poor old woman. She keeps being rude to me but I say "let it go" because her mind's gone bad.'

Then Grandmother would launch into the account of the British Resident on whose recommendation Mrs Venables, the governess, had been employed. According to his grandmother, she regularly sent messages to the Resident, letting him know of any unusual or significant events in the state – or even in the Nawab's private life. From all accounts, she was not a very good spy because everyone knew what she was up to. But since the Daulatnagars had nothing to hide, Grandfather didn't think it worth acting on. Of course, Grandmother regularly castigated Venables and warned that she'd turn her out if she caught her at it again. Several other palace servants took it upon themselves to watch the 'spy'; in their vanguard was the ayah, the Indian children's maid, Ganga

Bai, black as tar with a crumpled face, the figure and mannerisms of a flirtatious milkmaid and a flair for comedy. Saif had caught Grandmother hiding a smile when Ganga put a hand on her slender hip and wriggled, chanting, 'Aha, oh Ganga Bai, how her hips can sway!'

'She was sooo jealous of Venerable,' Grandmother said. 'Always carrying little-little tales about her. "She used His Highness' personal telephone." "She was sniffing your perfume." "She tried on your ring." "She walks around her room in the deep of the night." When she started to hint she was doing black magic to make people ill, I ordered her to stop. I didn't want people thinking Venerable was some kind of a blood-sucking vampire.' She stopped, reflecting. 'You know, Saif, we marvel here about the freedom of European women. How they can leave home and live away, work and earn independence and the freedom to make decisions – big decisions. But no life is as it looks. Which woman would choose a life like Venables'? She was young and very handsome when she came – her husband had died. She was well educated but without the contacts to get a good job or the wherewithal to rent accommodation anywhere in England so here she was – living in a palace, all found, but no hope of any other kind of future. This palace was her cage. She never wanted to leave. Like that prisoner in Spain that Lord Byron wrote about, she told me ... I think she said that when he's set free after yearning to get out of his prison for years, he says, *"Even I, regained my freedom with a sigh."* So, so sad. I have never wanted to beg,' Grandmother said. 'But I came near to it when Nyla got married. What did Venables have to look forward to here? I told her she should travel, write a journal ...'

Grandmother stopped and in that pause before she launched into another speech, Saif glimpsed her yearning for Venables to become her ambassador, her luxuriously captive self to be set free to the experiences of a wider world. 'She will die clutching her lost hopes to her breast.' She gestured to the splendour around her. 'All this ... it's not enough. It cannot be all there is.'

They laughed together but Saif always wondered what it was that translated into 'not enough' for his grandmother. He comforted himself that it was a mercurial thought, on the hoof as soon as it appeared.

When Saif was twelve, Grandmother handed him some documents. 'I found a few acres of land on the edge of Qila,' she said, 'Gree-een, really green, I saw its picture. And a river curves along one side. I want you to build a girls' school there one day. A good one, like the English schools where girls learn everything. Prepare them for any profession they choose. Mechanical engineering and forest protection even, if that's what they want. The point is they should come out employable in their field of choice. And their education should speak for them so that they don't need social connections.' She closed his hands around the document. 'You will do this for me, won't you?'

Saif nodded. 'But you already have a school in Daulatnagar.'

Grandmother waved her hand, frustrated. 'But look who goes there. Rich girls who'll never work even if they want. They'll marry in their twenties. At most, one will start a reading group. I might as well have made a finishing school.' She grasped his hands. 'No, Saif, this new place will challenge social barriers. My dear friend Colonel Deendayal will arrange it all when the time comes.'

Saif had carried the depth of Grandmother's passion with him for forty years. He would not let it go.

The grassy approach to Ramzi Bagh always looked as if the earth was gently breathing, creating small hillocks as it inhaled. He would fight for the Girls' Academy. He would bring the project to fruition, for the triumph of his mother's and aunt's modern names, for the educated girls whose only option was to marry, for Venables and for the dream which Grandmother had tried to ensure would live beyond her.

He relaxed his hand on the wheel. Groundless accusations disintegrated in time. He would wait. He hated to shut the gates of Qila but for now he would do it for the safety of its residents.

His heart lifted as he saw the waterfall and the profusion of trees in the distance, surrounding the low buildings of the retreat.

How far this translucent world of light was from the world of colour and scent and travail!

15

Zara was not looking forward to this meeting so soon after Hana's funeral. Sita Devi, thin and white-clad, gestured to the sofa with vigour and then dropped into the hollow jaws of an Edwardian wing armchair. On a small mahogany table beside it sat a tinted crystal jug of water and a matching glass, each covered with a piece of white net weighed down with an edging of beads – topaz, peridot, citron and aquamarine. Beside it was a book, marked halfway through with a strip of filigreed gold.

Zara kept wondering how tall the Rajmata had been when she had last seen her. Surely she had shrunk – she was no higher than Zara's chest. One thing was certain: she had changed from an international maharani – the kind Cecil Beaton photographed and for whom Chaumet and Cartier designed jewellery – to a politician maharani. Her crisp white sari was cotton, as much, Zara thought, to indicate her widowhood as her new identity of Member of Parliament for the major right-wing party. The once pert and animated face, displayed in the baroque silver frames dotted around the room, was full and somber now. Dominating the room was a portrait of Hari, her husband the late maharaja, mahogany-skinned, stocky in his much decorated uniform but handsome anyway. Jay had inherited his large, dreamy eyes.

Zara sat on the other side of the low coffee table, facing Sita Devi, and wondered if she had deliberately chosen a confrontational position. She felt restless here in Vikram Bhavan, where generations of Vamanas had grown up. Aunty Hana had dragged her here eighteen years ago, before she left for Oxford. It was a rare event because, after the death of Sultan, Aunty Hana did not step out of Qila.

Sita Devi struck the bell and a knock sounded on the door.

'Come!' she said. 'Aao.' A peach-and-gold liveried footman entered and bowed, his hands folded. 'Bring tea.' The footman backed out, bowing. Sita Devi turned bird-like eyes on Zara and waited. Zara tried to find the words, unsure of what exactly she thought this woman could tell her.

Sita Devi made a quick, impatient movement and Zara noticed her feet did not quite reach the floor. 'No doubt,' she said, 'you want to know why I did not attend Begum Saheb's ... to say goodbye.'

Instinctively, Zara offered a justification. 'Politics, I suppose ...' But it wasn't her job to make Sita Devi feel better. She would say what she thought and to hell with protocol. 'People have been wondering.'

Sita Devi bristled. 'And what exactly did *you* wonder?'

'Aunty Hana must have done something terrible to you.'

Sita Devi produced a sound close to a snort. 'You have no idea. We were inseparable, Begum Saheba Hana and I.' She locked her fingers together. 'Like this. More than fifty years. Sixteen when we met. We grew together, learned together, gave birth together. We were so close we knew how the other breathed.' She paused, raising her chin high. 'I don't need to say goodbye. You say goodbye only to those you lose.'

'Pardon me, Rajmata Saheb. If nothing else, there's protocol.'

'I don't have to explain to you. Or anyone else.'

'Except, perhaps, your constituents.'

Sita Devi looked shocked, incredulous. 'You think I did this for votes? You are our Pir Saheb's cousin, or I would ask you to leave.'

'I apologize. I didn't come here to ask about my aunt's funeral.' A nominal apology was no come-down for Zara. She had done it a hundred times in court.

'Why then?'

Zara pulled out Hana's letter. 'She sent me this. About a week before I came.' Sita Devi held the letter gingerly, as if she expected it to produce toxic fumes. 'She died before telling me where it is.'

'I haven't seen her since eighteen months. How would I know?'

'She'd probably been thinking about it for a while.'

Sita's expression was scathing. 'And since when do you care so much for your aunt's needs? You stayed away ten years. Now you come running to do her will when she's dead. You abandoned her. Do you know how much she felt it?'

Zara clung to her self-control. She wanted to get up and pace the room. The truth was hard to take. Sita Devi must know she had played a part in Zara's reluctance to return. 'Perhaps,' she said, 'I want to make up for it.'

'After she's gone.' Sita's voice was dull. 'I suppose it still counts.'

'Can you help me? Please? I want to do what she wished and go back to London.'

Sita Devi capitulated. 'I know nothing for sure. But if it will help you conclude your business quicker, it's worth trying. When I last saw Hana she ... there was some manuscript. Also, she gave Mumtaz a share of Qila. She was so obsessed with the honour of the Ramzi name she gave away all that property to avoid old-old family secrets coming out ... well, that's what she told me. In the end I was never sure if she was ...' Her voice trailed away. 'Let it go. Hana's only fault was her secretive nature. Even when it was obvious she should consult.'

'How do you think I could have helped?'

Sita shrugged. 'Legal advice?'

'Try to think, please, Rajmata Saheb. She said, Aunty said: "*You're the only one I can trust.*"' Sita Devi flinched. 'And she said Pebbles and Saif mustn't know.'

'She never wanted Pebbles to know anything. But Pir Saheb would definitely have told her so better not tell him also. Do you know she never even consulted him? He was away at the Ramzi Bagh retreat and when he came back Mumtaz and her grandson were there. All that negotiation and all, must have taken time, no? But no one knew. Only myself, two-three months beforehand.'

'Do you think it was something to do with inheriting Qila ...?'

If anyone could explode and remain silent and still, then Sita Devi did it in that moment. 'Now you want Qila!'

'Of course not!' Zara was shocked by Sita's vehemence.

'Your presence isn't helping. Pebbles will be distressed with you here. Anapurna is already beside herself and she's making Jay and the children miserable.' She slipped off the chair and walked to the window. 'Just like your mother. She spread disruption and misery also. We get on fine in our unsophisticated ways without your help. I wish you would say your farewells.'

Zara stared steadily at Sita Devi. 'You have never liked me.'

'No, I have not,' Sita admitted. 'Nor your mother, also. Like mother, like daughter, I always thought. And you never liked me.'

'Frankly,' Zara said, 'I never ... you were Aunty Hana's friend, that's all. Now you're not even that.'

Sita Devi stiffened; she flushed beneath her golden skin. 'You will never understand my relationship with Hana even if you are reborn seven times.'

Zara held up her hands. 'All I want is to find this manuscript and the instructions with it.'

Sita Devi clanged her bell and rose. She handed back the letter. 'I can't help with your inquiries.'

Zara nodded and walked to the door just as the footman entered, pushing a trolley bearing tea in opulent silverware.

'Please, Aunty,' Zara pleaded wildly, silently, as she walked through the cool darkness of the Vamana Palace to the top of a marble staircase. The sun poured in through the tall casement. *You must be somewhere still. You must be able to listen. Tell me where to go next.* Surely, surely people didn't just dissolve when they died. They must be able to hear and see the people they left behind. They must want to help. She looked through the glass.

The brilliant sunlight hurt her eyes. Its beams clustered together, forming a small cloud of pale yellow just above the flower beds. For a moment she felt faint and dizzy. Her legs began to shake. She stopped walking and leaned against the banister. *Pinch yourself.*

The phrase came from out of nowhere. It was a panic attack. She pinched herself, stood still until she was breathing evenly and walked through the door.

She had not expected to be here. A long, formal lawn stretched more than 300 feet before vanishing into a drop. She had played here before – years ago. There was a wooded area below known as the Deer Park, sloping down the side of the mountain to a forest. Where was the driveway? *Oh Lord, what do I do now?*

The yellow cloud began to morph, elongating, then closing up, thinning, thickening, flickering, hovering always above the flower beds. She wrenched her gaze away and walked back to the door but it had locked itself behind her. Surely the drive couldn't be too far? She walked through an arch clenching her clammy hands. A man sat at a table on a patio while another talked him through some plans on a clipboard. He stood up as he saw Zara.

'Good morning, Ma'am. Can I help?'

Zara placed him just as he recognized her. 'Miss Zara. Pir Saheb's cousin sister.'

'It's Karan Singh, isn't it?'

The man in the chair whirled round. 'Zara! Welcome, welcome.' Jay stood up, smiling warmly. 'What a pleasant surprise.'

'I'm so sorry to disturb you, Jay. Really. I came to call on Rajmata Saheba.'

'Let me take you to her.'

'No, no, sorry. I've seen her already. I got lost ... I feel so foolish. I managed to come out of the wrong entrance, er, exit.' She held up her hands, giving up.

'It's tricky – did no one show you out? Someone should have ...'

'I left quite quickly. I ...'

Jay dismissed Karan Singh who hovered, reluctant to go. They had all played together as children; he was the son of a general from an old, local land-owning family. Now he was Jay's aide. She shuddered. Did he know Ana suspected an 'affair' between her and Jay? Her skin felt hot. 'Perhaps you can show me the way to the car?'

'Certainly, Zara Ma'am.'

'Just Zara,' she said.

'I'll see you to your car,' Jay said firmly, looking at Karan as he walked to Zara's side. Karan walked away. 'But first, how about some tea? Coffee? A cold drink?'

'I should go, Jay.'

His voice was almost a whisper. 'Stay, Zara. I don't know when we'll get another chance to talk alone.'

Zara looked at him now, intrigued by the plea in his voice, relieved to find one person here who did not want to get rid of her. But the last thing she needed now was another problem.

'It was very tough with your mother. She's got a razor for a tongue. I should go.'

Jay winced then smiled. 'Ah, I apologize. Her Highness was in fighting form. Sorry.' He was near her, touching her elbow. She could feel his breath. Gently, silently, he guided her to the driveway. Zara felt a prickle under her eyelids.

'The sunlight – it's very strong.' And there was that cloud again. 'I keep seeing this little yellow cloud floating over the flower beds.'

Jay looked surprised. 'You've forgotten? Come, let me show you.'

Mindlessly, she followed Jay until they were very close to the yellow formation. Jay reached out his hand. The cloud dispersed.

'Butterflies,' Zara whispered. 'I remember them. They were everywhere.'

Jay nodded. 'Coliadinae, Yellow Migrant. Very common.'

16

Zara paced the floor of Aunty's room as she spoke to Peter, trying to release the frustration of meeting Sita Devi and being left with the message that yet another person resented her presence here.

Trivikram was her home! And then losing her way in a place where she'd played all through her childhood. She leapt from one shock to the next, feeling more volatile with every complaint. There seemed no release.

'Lemon Migrant. I can't believe they classify absolutely everything by colour and place of origin. Even butterflies.'

'Well, at least butterflies don't care.'

'It's not the point. Why do we always have to define creatures as the "other". Not my colour, not my country, not my type.'

Peter's voice on the telephone was a relief, but her own complaining voice palled on her.

'It's your ...'

'*Don't*, Peter. Don't say it.'

'What?'

'Say it's my "wounded self" speaking, or some such crap ...'

'I wasn't going to.' His voice was quiet, hurt. There was silence on both ends of the line.

'Sorry,' Zara said.

'I wish I knew what you wanted me to say, Zara. A special word? Reassurance? But I keep getting it wrong.'

'Just some engagement, Peter.' It was like a shouting voice inside, watching everyone drifting away, cutting off, becoming soundless. She felt voiceless but undesirably visible, disconnected. She had not known in her childhood as she watched those common Indian butterflies perching beneath the leaves at night, camouflaged, that they were migrants like her, taking shelter, trying to blend in, be part of their environment. Yes, she wanted something from Peter, something too indefinable to ask for. She did not want him to be her reason to belong in London. She wanted him to engage with her as he used to do, even to have a row. She wished he had kept the promise that made her agree to marry him.

'I'm sorry,' Zara said, returning to the present. She had to stop living in the past. The tension, the panic attacks, the painful memories were becoming too frequent. She had to stop running, as Peter said, and confront her demons. She stood still a moment. 'So you don't mind if I'm here a good few weeks more?'

They ended the call with a few practical details but Zara could not stop thinking back to the time they had bought their house. She had seen it advertised just after they married, and fallen in love with it. Weeks of argument followed.

'Why, if we're going away?' Peter kept asking.

'We can let it,' she'd answer. 'It'll bring in a packet.'

He was impatient. 'It's a wreck, just look at it'. But Zara was determined she could refurbish it. 'I don't understand why you want to take on such a white elephant.' he said. 'You're going to haemorrhage money on it.'

Zara was determined. 'My money. I can spend it how like. It will improve our quality of life.' Passionate discussions followed on the moral use of money and whether partners had a right to impose their will. Who would look after the house when they went away to India?

She saw now that when they stopped the cut and thrust of their passionate discussions, the spark went out. Perhaps it was her fault – it was a recurring pattern, she chased away those close to her.

She looked over at the photograph of her mother on the shelf, her hair streaming behind her as if she were flying. Hedy Lamarr, a guest had once compared her to, and Sita Devi had said in a stage whisper, 'Delilah'. At eight or nine, Zara had missed the significance of Sita Devi's comment but she recalled Aunty Hana bristling. Had Nyla been involved in a scandal? She went over to the picture and picked it up. 'What did you do to upset people so much?' she said.

Littl'un came in, leading Dilkash. 'She is blessed her mind's lost somewhere in the past,' she sighed. 'For her, Huzur Saheb is always going to be alive and well.' Her eyes were puffed with three days of weeping. She frowned as she took Nyla's picture from Zara.

'What do you remember about my mother, Littl'un?'

'I was very young. What does it matter anyhow, what I remember? My thoughts are not even worth a handful of mud.'

Dilkash looked at Littl'un with blurred eyes. 'To disguise the truth, a Brahmin may read the Quran,' she murmured. 'You were the same age, you two.' Zara realized with a shock how severely Littl'un had aged compared to Hana.

'You were here the last time she came to Trivikram, Littl'un. I remember.'

Littl'un was scowling now. 'Why pick over dead bones, child? She's gone. She went where her destiny took her. That's the important thing. Nothing else matters. It was all long ago.'

'Was I a bad child, Littl'un?'

'Everyone adored you.'

Zara could see the comforting pink-tinged beige stone of the terrace and the solid wall beyond. Perhaps Nyla had not left because of her. Perhaps she had some reason of her own.

The sun wallowed in golden streams threaded with pink and orange. The Oval Garden below was magnificent with the colours reflected in the small pond. Zara walked down to it. The garden was full of memories of being cherished and wanted.

As she stepped down towards the French windows, she could hear a man's voice. 'I will reach for the skies and fetch the pinkness of the sunset for your lips, its golden streams for your hair ...' Someone watching a movie or listening to the radio?

The speech was interrupted by happy laughter, a delighted squeal. 'Dialogue!'

Sharmeen, Zara thought. She's with that troublemaker again.

Zara walked down to the Oval Garden. Kamran saw her coming but continued to fasten a flower in Sharmeen's hair. Sharmeen tiptoed to kiss him but he appeared to be deflecting her. Zara felt uneasy. Sharmeen turned.

'Oh. Aunty Zara! Creepy-creepy. When did you come?'

'Just got here. The sunset looked so ...'

'Kamran! Kamran! Do that dialogue for my Aunty. Aunty Zara, it's from an old movie. A black-and-white one. Kamran can mimic so many actors.' She seemed to notice, suddenly, the tension between Zara and Kamran.

'My Aunty Zara had a love marriage,' Sharmeen said slowly, deliberately. 'She is on our side. She'll help us.'

Kamran raised his eyebrows from behind Sharmeen. His voice was challenging. He was looking into Zara's eyes. 'Will you, Aunty Zara?'

He's hiding behind her skirts, literally, thought Zara. Pretty symbolic, I guess, for someone who wants to sneak in and nab the Ramzi fortune.

As if he'd read her mind, he was stepping forward now, holding out his hand, introducing himself. This isn't normal at all, this handshaking. He's got this from the movies, too. Men here don't shake hands with women.

Before she could curb her response, her hand was out and she was shaking his, in a daze. Her discomfort increased as Sharmeen did a little jig, chanting, 'She's going to help us! She's going to help us!' in the repetitive, mocking tune of the playground.

Kamran was following Zara's gaze. A vein stood out on his temple. He put a protective arm around Sharmeen's shoulder and calmed her.

Zara felt a chill. This beautiful, spirited, affectionate young woman had the mind of a child!

17

Pebbles was obviously relieved that Zara had broached the subject of Sharmeen's childlike nature.

'But she's not damaged goods, you know, Zara. She will make a good wife. She's capable of running a house.' She wiped a tear with the corner of her sari and nodded in the direction of the kitchen where Millo was fiddling with some scales as she waited.

The back terrace where they were sitting was new. Hana had persuaded Amira to start a school for fabric dyers and now there was a workroom-cum-gallery on the ground floor to accommodate visitors, craft tourists from other Indian cities and from the rest of the world: scholars, students, who needed somewhere to stay. She had built above at the same time, not that she ever stepped beyond the dining room herself.

Pebbles and Saif lived in this wing; the extension was her gift to them. Half the terrace had been covered to provide shade. It was where the sun lingered most from high noon until it sidled over the main dining room, back terrace and across the long drawing room and open inner courtyard to set over the old kitchen.

Zara walked among the sun-loving plants that Saif had grown on a third of the terrace, identifying the species of palm among sunflowers. He had created a micro-climate in which less hardy plants could grow – ferns and herbs and flowering bushes – softening the edges of the raised beds and massive pots.

Sharmeen came in to supervise the weighing out of the daily rations – rice, flour and lentils for the family and the servants – accounting for the possibility of condolence guests who still trooped in throughout the day to pay their respects to Hana's family. It was amazing to see that Sharmeen was so keenly aware not only of how much extra to allow but also of what to serve visitors at this time of loss – nothing too fancy, nothing that could possibly cause confusion between hospitality and festivity. Chutney sandwiches, samosas but without a dip to avoid frivolity and the suggestion of indulgence.

'Tell Razia to send some savouries from the bakery,' she said. 'Very plain. No flaky pastry, nothing sweet. She can send something every three-four hours.'

'I'm impressed,' Zara said. 'I couldn't do all that.'

Pebbles' reaction was something between a snort and chuckle. 'You're soft. And a little bit too British. Always were, even before you went away. I'm told you hung around with the servants and treated them like friends.'

Zara tensed but Pebbles was smiling. She smiled back, feeling unexpectedly warm, and went to sit down on the divan beside her. The complex dynamics of life at the Ramzi fortress must be hard. Hana had not been the easiest person to live with. She wondered when Pebbles had discovered that Sharmeen was 'different'. Had she shared it with Hana? Was this formidable training in home craft meant to conceal her disadvantage?

Sharmeen was checking her shopping list against the fresh produce from the market laid out on the ancient wooden trestle table. There was no indication that she was 'different'. Pebbles had done her job phenomenally well. Sharmeen scanned the vegetables and fruit, commenting on their price and quality. She turned over a bunch of carrots, shaking them expertly to check for damage or infestation inside the bunch, and then turned her attention to the tomatoes. This was not the girl Zara had to keep rescuing from Kamran.

'These tomatoes are a bit soft,' Sharmeen said. 'Better make a sambal for lunch. Use them up quickly.' Sharmeen put down the tomatoes, leaned forward and poked Millo's cheeks with her forefingers. She leant her forehead against the small woman's and sang out. 'Not getting a bit of money on the side, are we? Striking little deals with the grocer, buying up his end-of-line produce cheaply before it rots?'

'Sharmeen!' Pebbles' voice lashed out. Sharmeen came to attention, scowling, jaw set. 'Don't be familiar with the servants.'

'She's only playing,' the cook protested.

'Children play, Millo. She's a grown woman. Remember that.'

Millo heaved the round tray containing vegetables and pulses off the table and staggered off towards the kitchen, muttering. 'You bring them up from a tiddly thing, you wash their bottoms and get drenched in their piddle and tears but you have to think of them as grown-ups. I'll never know how.'

'Someone said Millo caused the problem by mixing opium in Sharmeen's milk to make her sleep more. Ayahs do it to make babies drowsy and placid. I used to hide and watch. And never ever did she do anything suspicious.' She pulled herself together. Her voice sounded normal now. 'If only, if only I hadn't missed the moment. Maybe I could have pin-pointed the problem. But, you know, she was always fantastic at practical things. She learned fast: brick-building, jigsaws, even reading. It seems to be a personality thing. I despair about her marriage. She may marry, have children, but how long will any man endure, you know, her childishness?'

Zara opened her mouth to tell Pebbles about Kamran but his face superimposed itself on her thoughts. That look of – what was it – protectiveness, devotion, love? 'She's a very beautiful young woman. Affectionate. I'm sure there's someone out there for her.'

'What if there isn't? What if he sends her back when he realizes? The shame would be too much – and the heartbreak! It sounds awful but thank god her grandmother won't see it. She adored Sharmeen. She could never handle her pain.'

'She didn't know?'

Pebbles bristled. 'She infantilized her.'

'What does Saif think?'

Pebbles spat out her words. 'He teaches her poetry and talks to her in parables and thinks everything is okay. He's cutting himself off. I just live in a permanent state of suspense waiting for him to take off into the woods to ...' She shut her eyes as if she couldn't bear to say the words. 'Sometimes I wish he'd just do it.'

'Is he showing signs?'

Pebbles latched on to a hope. 'Withdrawn, definitely withdrawn. But the Girls' Academy keeps him in our world. He won't abandon it, I know that much. These official things roll on for years.' She looked over at the flowers and foliage. 'That's a good sign, too. He's emotionally investing in this home.'

'Nothing about "merging with the Beloved"?'

Pebbles grinned sheepishly and shook her head. 'But Sharmeen keeps spouting mystical phrases; she could have got them from him only. So it's going on somewhere there in the background, at least.'

'We need to find out what he wants to do about his daughter.'

Pebbles took a deep, shuddering breath. 'I've thought about this myself for years. She needs to have a massive settlement, mehr, you know. And in return we give her a massive allowance. The sheer financial loss of sending her back ... well, it will deter her in-laws. We need to choose a noble family that's a bit hard up.'

'But they'll make her miserable if they feel trapped.'

Pebbles shrugged. 'We'll ensure that she's treated well. Millo, at least, will go with her.'

'But surely being treated decently isn't the same as ...'

'Do you think she'll be happier rejected and living back at home? What about Hana? Was she trapped? Her marriage wasn't exactly an example of the perfect match.' Pebbles sighed again. 'I am her mother. If I don't think about these things, then who will? If she is sent back after I am gone, there will be a plan in place to see her through to the end of her days. We will say she is back to take her place as the Ramzi heiress. Perhaps God will give her a son. We can take steps to ensure ...'

'Take steps ...?'

'Trustees will be appointed. She will be comfortable to the end of her days. Maybe wealth doesn't buy happiness but it is a great buffer against adversity. She must have her own fortune, Zara. And her own son. And her own home.' She had an almost pleading look on her face. 'Please understand.' Her narrow eyes were intense. 'I'm convinced that if her grandmother knew, she would have wanted the same.'

Zara wondered if Hana had made provision for Sharmeen.

'Did Aunty ever talk about Sharmeen's future?' she asked Littl'un later.

But Littl'un was distracted by a dry, choking noise and shuffled over, still in a squatting position, to comfort Dilkash.

'She's at peace now, Ma,' she said in a shaky voice. 'Why are you upsetting yourself?' Littl'un stared at her hands, tangling and untangling her gnarled fingers. 'I never dared say this in the presence of Huzur, God forgive me for saying it now. It's this place. Bahurani is not the only one to be stricken by this lunacy.' She looked around as if making sure she wasn't being watched. 'Unlucky babies, madness, deserting husbands ... curses lurk in these walls.'

Zara could see what Littl'un meant. The stories Hana had told Zara were, right at this moment, resonating in Pebbles' life. Despite it all, she had lived out her life as mistress of her magnificent home.

Dilkash's hissing mumble became audible. '... just seventeen when Sama Bibi was born. Tauba, tauba, tauba.' She chanted her penitence and pinched the lobes of her ears to call God's mercy upon her. 'May God never show any woman such a year. That year would have destroyed a lesser person. But my mistress stood firm, head held high, as destiny hurled boulders at her chest, her head, her heart. Never were so many threads of one destiny plucked away so quickly and brutally. And none of it was my moon-child's fault. None of it.'

18

Zara slipped through the arched passageway to the meditation chamber beneath the ante-room by Hana's bedroom. Its seclusion had always brought her peace when she was a child and she felt restless with the turmoil in Qila the past few days.

The door that divided the dining room from the passage leading to the meditation room was rarely closed except at night, for security. The 'secret passage', she called it as a child, because the passage to the unused room was veiled by a thick curtain of jasmine trailing fragrant vines to the ground.

Zara could hear Sharmeen and Saif speaking. She stopped, reluctant to intrude.

'... but Abba, that patch of earth you said about ... you know, where suddenly something starts sprouting? How do you know it's from God? Because you said, you remember, that the seed is sprouting from God. But how do you know for sure?'

'Does this seedling hurt anyone?' Saif asked, gently. 'Can it cause damage or dissent?'

Zara stepped forward to a gap in the jasmine vine. Saif was stroking Sharmeen's hair.

'Diss- what?' Sharmeen made an impatient movement, like stamping. 'Oh Abba, use words I can understand.'

'Dissent, darling. It means fighting or disagreement.'

'Oh, no no no no. Not at all.'

'Makes you feel good? Happy?'

Sharmeen cuddled herself. 'Warm and happy.'

Saif put his arms around his daughter and patted her back, cradling her like an infant. 'Then it is from God.'

Sharmeen pulled back, worried. 'But it makes me break the rules. Maybe ...'

Zara stepped away from the archway, repulsed by her own eavesdropping, then stepped back again as Sharmeen and Saif emerged into the courtyard through the main door.

'Then it is love. And, my sweet child, love has no rules.'

Sharmeen's voice was anxious. 'But what if the seedling is not the right kind?'

Saif threw his arms up into the air. 'There is no right or wrong in love. I saw your mother for the first time late at night on the deck of a ship. All I saw in the darkness was the flimsy pallu of her sari. A misty veil flitting around in the sea breeze. I had no idea who it belonged to or what she looked like ...'

Sharmeen recited the words with him in a happy, well-rehearsed chant. '"I fell headlong in love and the rest you know." Can I go now, Abba?'

Zara was relieved she hadn't interrupted. She slipped into the meditation chamber.

It looked much the same as always. Mounds of amethyst rubble and rocks were heaped neatly in the corners of the room; the floor was swept clean. The fountain rose intact from its highly polished amethyst base. The sun poured in through the openings in the dome, falling on it like a second cascade. The crystal points in the wall flashed and sparkled.

She walked over to the fountain-head, grasped its lever and pushed hard to turn it. There was a rumbling, resisting noise, then a few dribbles of water. It had dried from disuse. Zara was disappointed. The drops on her hand were brown and had the blood-like smell of iron.

Her hands shook visibly. Why had she come here? She wasn't even sure if she believed any of it – the so-called miracles, the power of meditation. It had been rinsed out of her, dried out like the fountain. When she had moved out of this place, this place had moved out of her mind. She began to rise.

'Stay,' Saif's voice said. He walked over to her and she rested her head on his shoulder.

'I was always happy here. Even after my mother went away. I was going to live here, work with the people in the courtyard, set up a school, reform some laws, *work for the women ...*'

Parveen's words ... another thing she had to follow up on – Aunt Hana's legacy to be a beacon for women who had no one else.

'That is the Daulatnagar legacy,' Saif said. 'And there's work to be done.'

'I know,' Zara was troubled. 'But those threats and accusations ... Saif, it's not just a gut feeling ... you must put it on a legal footing.'

Saif raised his hand. 'It'll all work out.'

Zara shook her head. 'It could be a strategy ...'

There was an edge to Saif's laugh that Zara had not heard before. 'Not worth the time.'

Zara stared at the fountain. 'Tell your side of the story to the media or the courts or your plans may not ...'

Saif breathed deeply. 'That line of thinking assumes that outcomes depend on human action. I believe they are the intent of God ...'

There was no point competing with God. Saif squeezed her arm. 'I should have done more for you after your mother left.'

His remark took her by surprise. 'I wondered if you knew why she left. You and Aunty ... I wouldn't have survived without you.'

The water was forming into a flower at the top of the fountainhead. Gushing white water streamed down the sides, picking up tints of purple from the stone.

19

Saif believed that he should have encouraged Zara to speak more about Nyla's abandonment instead of watching as if nothing was the matter. The truth was that he was disillusioned and confused himself and had no idea what to say. Because, despite being nearly twenty, he too had felt abandoned. And when Zara seemed to get past the desertion and asked for childhood accounts of her mother, he was always conscious that she yearned to glean from those stories some reassurance, some shining truth about how her mother truly adored her deep down. But he had never seen it.

Nyla did eventually write to him from Italy and stayed intermittently in touch, but their bond had come adrift when she vanished. She had, after many years, tried to explain her reasons for leaving, but he realized there would always be a knot to mark the break. The wrench was not so much that she left but the way she went – leaving behind self-doubt and self-blame.

He walked towards the sound of Sharmeen's voice coming from the direction of the formal sitting room downstairs. She was in the Oval Garden with Zara, by the pond. It was years since he had seen women sitting outside for leisure. He stood for several moments at the French windows, watching Sharmeen and Zara laugh and talk in the gloaming. A thin strand of smoke wafted through Sharmeen's hair, then another. Zara adjusted the position of the pierced brass holder from which the burning incense drifted up to perfume his daughter's hair.

He could not imagine walking away from this girl, flesh of his flesh, blood of his blood, without a proper leave-taking. The day would come, he knew, when he would have to shoulder the Ramzi burden exclusively; he would try to make sure Sharmeen understood. It would be a source of great comfort to him if she was settled with her own beloved, ideally within the walls of Qila.

'There was a very famous poet,' said Sharmeen like a patient teacher explaining to a backward child. 'His name was Iqbal. He said many wise things to children – and to other people. Abba says we can learn lines that will help us lead our lives well and be, you know, like special advice. And I like this one.

Create your own world, if you are truly alive
That is the secret of Adam, the essence of 'Be! And it was!'

'What it means is that you can make your own world, the way you want it, if you use your will like Adam did – just like God created the world from His will by saying "Be!". Iqbal, you see, thinks God wants humans to have their own will.'

She snapped her fingers and clapped her hands and Saif felt a warm hand grasp his heart. He had never seen his daughter downcast except once when she had confided to him that her 'heart was a bit different' from those of her classmates.

He brought his hands together in a soft clapping motion as he walked into the garden. 'I hope I'm not interrupting you ladies?'

Sharmeen leapt up and threw her arms around his neck. He stroked her arms. She laid her head on his chest for a moment. 'Look, Abba,' she said. 'We're sitting in the Oval Garden. I was just teaching Aunty Zara about Iqbal.'

'Pretty profound stuff.' Zara looked bemused. 'Sharmeen seems to understand it well. Don't you, sweetheart?'

Saif felt that sweet, familiar tingle on his lips at Sharmeen's nearness and dropped a kiss on her head. She turned to Zara, glowing and smiling, and he felt a distinct stab in his heart. He sent a legion of thanks to God for all his gifts, particularly for his ample share of the ability to love and communicate with his child. Watching Sharmeen turn up her face like a heliotrope to his warmth made up for the devastating moments in which he had faced, as a child, that he would never experience the love of his parents. What was it like for Zara, he wondered, to witness his affection for Sharmeen, having, like him, missed out on the love of her parents? And then that familiar susurration of guilt through his veins, one of the reasons why he had found it so difficult to speak to Zara about her mother.

Could he tell her that it was he who had stolen Nyla's love long before Zara was born, when Nyla was barely twelve and he not yet a toddler? She came to visit them in Qila several times a year, brought by his mother to keep her company. And to give Nyla somewhere to go, something to do that would take her away from her dull existence in Daulatnagar. 'How often, after all, can we spend afternoons dozing and reading and evenings hauling in local folk troupes to entertain us,' her mother had said. 'The girl can sing every folk song in the canon, written or unwritten, and every movie song, appropriate and inappropriate.'

His earliest memory was of Nyla holding him in her arms, feeding him a bottle and singing. They were simple songs, lullabies mostly, which she sang just loud enough for him to hear. By the time he was a toddler, he could understand the words.

Little Saifu's fair-skinned, I'm dark as a raincloud.

Lord, what a jewel of a voice, with all the hidden depths and darkness of a mountain stream on a thundery day, turning effortlessly into a song brook when the weather was sunny and fair. He was always mortified when she described herself as a dark raincloud. For she was not. Nyla had the gold-kissed skin of a daughter of the sun, burnished but transparent. Her hair was like a freshly opened corn-pod, silken, somehow whispering of gold like a halo over its rich darkness. And he would cry: 'No, Aunty Nyla, you're not dark, I'm the dark one.'

Nyla's laughter would tinkle and she'd soothe him and calm him. 'It's just a song, little man,' she'd say. 'Now you go to sleep.' When she started again, his chubby fingers found their way to her lips and she blew on them and kissed them and promised to sing another song, instead.

'Sleep, my little prince', he discovered, when Hana mocked her sister, was part of a movie song's lyrics which Nyla had adapted somewhat.

He wondered about the accuracy of many of the images that formed his memories. But he could feel so vividly, even now, his heart thumping so loud it blotted out all other sounds.

Saif didn't like his mother to chide Nyla. When Hana floated in the background waiting for him to fall asleep so that she could claim Nyla, he was so conscious of her presence, so fearful of a slur that he became fretful and anxious and sleep eluded him. Yet, he could only have understood the exchanges from sensing and experiencing.

'Sleep, Baba, sleep,' Nyla would trill, *'Butter, bread, sugar. Butter and bread has all been eat, sleepy Baba's gone to sleep.'*

'Such rubbish, that song. Makes no sense at all. It's invented by Brit nannies, pretending they can speak Hindi.'

Nyla smiled. 'Or ayahs pretending they can speak English.'

Nyla never challenged Hana so she did not quote examples she had read about from the hallowed tradition of nonsense rhymes, and he only learned about them much later. Nyla adored and even idolized Hana, Saif never understood why. But then, she gave him what Hana never did or could. Tenderness was not his mother's forte. Looking back, he could see her plan was to make a saint out of him. He was the means by which she would show his father that she was capable and strong enough to build a Ramzi leader. Nyla, on the other hand, loved him more each year, just as his own mother loved Zara in years to come. But these recollections would not bring succour to Zara, he decided, sitting on the divan beside her. He would begin the story later – he would build a context for Zara, create a living picture of her mother's life leading up to Zara's arrival.

He took her hand, troubled. This task was a test – one of the hardest he had faced. But it was a process that had to be started whatever the pitfalls. *Zara just wants to know about her mother,* Pebbles had said. How simply his wonderful bride could see to the heart of an issue! He would hold on to her sentence. He would let her guide him through the guilt and self-censorship that was necessary if he was to help Zara instead of hurting her.

Dilkash shuffled out of the shade of Zara and sniffed, her face full of disapproval as she fixed her filmy eyes on his hand holding hers. 'So unseemly. A man holding his bride's hand in public. There was a time it would never have happened in a noble house!' Poor woman, Saif thought, she's gone into one of her delusions.

'Dilkash!' Zara looked shocked. The old woman muttered something unintelligible.

'She thinks I'm my father,' Saif said. 'So you are my mother.'

'Hey, what about me?' Sharmeen said. 'Who am I, Dilkash?'

'What kind of a question's that?' Dilkash said.

'But who?' Sharmeen insisted.

'Nyla Bibi, of course. I've still got an intact brain, you know.'

Sharmeen squealed, standing up to spread her hair more evenly around the incense pot.

'I remember when you were spotted, Nyla Bibi,' Dilkash said, her tiny eyes lighting up as she watched the black waterfall with tendrils of smoke emerging through it.

Saif leaned back. It looked as if Dilkash might begin his job for him.

'Tell us, Dilkash,' he said. 'You saw it all.' Silently, he thanked God for easing his mission.

'I will never forget that day,' Dilkash began, 'when that moon-like child brought a wedding procession to a halt. The groom's cousin stopped his horse to admire her – she just stood on the rooftop drying her hair in the smoke of a loban, oblivious to the bewitched man on his horse. Music blared, horses danced and glittering females passed around sweets to the crowd until the groom dragged them away.

'The next day, the bridegroom and his cousin Jameel Usman presented themselves to the Nawab and asked for her hand. The local mullah came with them, you know, for the sake of propriety. The Nawab said he would make appropriate inquiries and then respond to the proposal.

'He said: "It would have been more appropriate, of course, if your parents had come. Or Maulana Saheb here had brought your credentials before you. This is a matter of lives, families, dynasties coming together, beta. Not a story from a fil-im." We were relieved he had added the word "beta" – a son gets away with all sorts of mistakes, after all.

'Inquiries revealed that Jameel Usman had the reputation of one purified by the sacred waters of the Ganges and the family had strong connections with noble lines of whom the Nawab knew. There were two factors at which he balked. Usman Ahmed, Jameel's father, was a manufacturer, a "businessman". Oh Lord, a weasel woos a princess! His face was red with the fury of a king when he heard the word "business".

' "There has never been a tradesman in our family, Begum Saheb," he said to his wife. "Shall I give my daughter to a tradesman?" It mattered not that Usman Ahmed Mills were an industrial empire possessing more land and wealth than the entire kingdom of Daulatnagar.

'The second reason, much more daunting because it was of the heart and not the head, was that Jameel Usman and his family lived in Pakistan – a country which is like a child who breaks his father's house in half. The feelings of kings are as private as unmentionable body parts but he was, after all, human and those who knew him knew, too, that he adored his youngest and wished to keep her by him, maybe marry her to the son of a senior courtier. But Nyla Bibi overrode all of this. Pakistan, she said, was a young and energetic country made by Muslims. They recognized neither king nor prince (may Satan's ears be deaf) and men were judged on accomplishment alone. Time was when accomplishment could only be noticed among people with a noble bloodline. Instead, the aristocracy and backbone of this country would be built on manufacture.

'"The Prophet Muhammad, peace be upon him, was a merchant," Nyla Bibi said. Her father was profoundly shocked to hear this fact thrown at his discomfiture. But then, the mullah spoke up in support of Nyla's words and everything was settled.'

Saif was suddenly overcome. He got up and walked over to a rose-and-gardenia border, squatting to pick out the dead blooms. When Nyla had told him she was to marry Jameel, he had been stung. His eyes stung with tears, his heart stung with pain and jealousy and the stark fear of losing his mother surrogate. He was not quite nine and the agony of Nyla going faraway to a country of terrible differences was unbearable. The romantic quality of events which seemed to inspire and fascinate everyone else meant nothing to him. He did not want to hear about it. But it became his mother's favourite story for a while and he was not spared.

He set down the flowers to the side of the table. 'Your mother invited me to Karachi just six months later,' he said, as he walked back to the divan. 'It was a long, straight road, tarmacked and smooth, from Karachi airport all the way into town. The roads' names were very British. There was a Drigh Road and a Victoria Road. Your father turned the car into Frere Road after we drove past a hotel called the Metropole. After that, tall, leafy trees, a park, a statue of Queen Victoria – in Frere Park, I think. I must have dozed off. The next I knew we were driving through tall iron gates and my eyes were fixed on something massive – as if the sky was covering the ground, writhing and heaving to get up again. We stopped at a magnificent mansion with a long row of outhouses to one side. And from the porch, I could see this mysterious thing up close, so vast that it made no sense. Something alive in shades of green, blue and grey. It was the sea. I had seen rivers and lakes but this water breathed and with every breath the entire mass of it undulated, rolled, heaved and danced, sending up bouquets of spray. I was thrilled and terrified.'

Uncle Jameel invited Saif to walk down as soon as he got out of the car. The servants would deal with his luggage. The sandy beach that led to it was the colour of slate mixed with sparkling silver;

it curled at the edges and threw up foamy spray. He had never seen an adult with the abandon of his uncle. Jameel kicked off his shoes and socks, pulled off his jacket and made Saif do the same. He grabbed his hand and raced him down to the water's edge. That was the first time Saif touched the ocean and confirmed to himself that it was water, it was tangible and, therefore, real. He flirted with the foam but did not dare to swim in it yet.

'Your mother kept yelling at us from the porch, "Don't swim, Saif. You're not used to it. Jameel, bring him in. It's getting dark." Uncle Jameel yelled back, asking her to join us. But Aunty Nyla had no intention of ruining her chiffon sari or the Chanel sandals she had bought on her French honeymoon.'

As they walked on the beach they curled their toes, sending up squidgy worms of wet sand. Uncle Jameel showed him how he could stand on an apparently solid piece of land and watch his weight cause a pool of water to rise around his feet.

'Like water from sand, instead of stone,' he said, and Uncle Jameel laughed and threw back his head.

'That's wonderful to know,' said Zara. 'I knew nothing about my father except that he was ill and died in his mid-twenties. Quite a morbid image, really. It's good to think of him laughing and enjoying himself.'

Saif reached out and laid his hand on her arm.

'Tell me more,' Zara said. Saif continued.

The house was sprawling and somehow low-lying and very modern. Its rooms were large, with plaster as smooth and almost as shiny as glass. Everything was new and fresh. And it was sparsely furnished to display ornate carpets from Bokhara and Samarkand and Qom, different to the traditionally woven ones. Looking back, he could not remember seeing a single piece of antique furniture. Aunty Nyla said she wanted to get away from the aged grandeur of the furniture in Daulatnagar and Qila. She liked her surroundings modern and light and bright. Even her picture frames were sleek and minimal and white. It was strange for Saif to hear the voice of authority come from her. He put it down, with the wisdom of his ten years, to being married.

'Sometimes,' Jameel said, a few days later, 'I feel you're a little serious. Is there something you'd like to talk about?'

'It could be,' Saif replied, 'because after this holiday, I have to spend all my summers at Ramzi Bagh – I start my training.'

'That sounds fascinating – daunting, too. Do you know what you'll do there? Do they focus equally on studies and physical exercise?'

Jameel spoke differently from other people. He had the same slightly Anglicized accent as many of the maharajas, including Jay's father, but his speech was more flowing, less clipped and somehow more natural. And he lisped the 'th' in some words, like the English.

'He's lived in England a long time,' Nyla explained.

Saif noticed that she looked sad and so, for that matter, did Jameel. But he did not like to ask so he kept his mind on the way they smiled at each other, the way Jameel would brush away a tiny strand of stray hair from her brow, or she'd stroke his hand or cheek unobtrusively with her forefinger. Then it was nearly time for him to go and as Nyla packed his things, the question exploded from him.

'Please, Aunty Nyla, tell me why you and Uncle Jameel are sad.'

She cupped his face in both palms and pulled his head to her chest. 'My darling, darling child. You weren't meant to notice. I'm so sorry.'

'But are you happy? Is Uncle Jameel nice ... I mean, my father is hardly at home to bother Mummy. But Uncle Jameel – he seems to be here all the time ...'

She laughed and reassured him it was wonderful to have Jameel with her.

'Then why?' asked Saif.

'Uncle Jameel isn't very well,' she said.

'Is that why you wander about at night, alone?'

She nodded.

'When did he get ill?'

Saif never forgot the expression on Nyla's face when she responded – sorrow and despair and betrayal, all in one vessel of fate.

'Saif,' his name seemed to be wrung from her. 'He was already ill when we married. He didn't tell me. Until the middle of our second night together.'

'But why?'

'He said he wanted me to be happy on my wedding day.'

Saif remembered the sick horror he felt and realized much later that he was experiencing Nyla's sense of betrayal

'Would you have refused to marry him if he had told you?'

Her eyes grazed the ground beside her feet, long lashes curling up; she shook her head. 'Never. But the choice would have been mine.'

It was strange how, for the rest of the day, they behaved as if nothing had changed. As she saw him on to the plane at midnight, she hugged him more intensely than usual and said, 'I'll miss you.' As Saif clung to her he heard a sigh and, hidden inside it, an unspoken lament.

The next time Saif saw Nyla, she was twenty and a widow – and Saif was about to leave with his father for a six-month stay at the Ramzi shrine. Afterwards, Nyla was never the same. It was as if life had leached her sap.

Tears ran down Zara's face. Saif moved close to her, put his arms around her, kissed her forehead. 'I'm sorry. I didn't think. I didn't want to hold back anymore.'

'It must have been terrible for her.'

Saif held Zara at arm's length. 'Perhaps. But you should know, it was only with you that a certain spark returned. She would teach you jingles and dances and read to you, and play silly games – I remember the two of you marching up and down and round and round the house pretending to be Jambavan's army of bears from the *Ramayana*. It annoyed my mother no end.'

Saif stood up. Now that he had unblocked a channel he would continue to tell her what he remembered. He could not change the anomalies of the past: of her mother singing him songs and his mother telling her stories and each of them growing up cushioned and cradled by the other's mother. His experience of being fathered, on the other hand, bore no semblance to love.

As he walked into the living room he glimpsed Zara's expectant face and knew he had not answered her desperate question.

'Why was it, do you think, that my mother didn't love me?'

Saif froze. His voice sounded strangulated even to himself. 'She did love you.' *She must have. All mothers love their children in some way.*

Zara examined her cuticles, shaking her head. 'Aunty Hana loved me. My mother was ... different.'

Saif felt a rare flame of anger. 'My mother had a way of upstaging Nyla. She wanted you for herself.' He took a deep breath and paused. 'Yes, she did love you. Very much, but so did your mother. With what she had left. But Aunty Nyla never had the chance to recover and develop a proper relationship with you. My mother got in the way.'

His worst fear had been realized. But time was a great provider of opportunity. He would have a chance to make restitution. It disturbed him that he had lost his equilibrium and come close to turning Zara's world upside down.

20

Sharmeen moved from her chair on to Zara's lap and dabbed at her tears with her dupatta. Saif dropped, exhausted, on the divan.

Dilkash emerged again, disgruntled, from near Zara's legs.

'Those scalded by milk,' she mumbled, 'blow on buttermilk before drinking it.'

'Dilkash!' Zara said. 'I'd forgotten you were here.'

Dilkash ignored Zara. 'He looked as beautiful as the sun.' Dilkash knew her head held the archive of information and opinions on the lives of the Daulatnagars and the Ramzis. It was because she had a knack for disappearing and life and its inhabitants went on as if she wasn't there. 'But what good is beauty that burns with its heartlessness? He singed her youth to a cinder and left her flapping without air like a fish on dry land.' She flicked a tear away from her withered face. 'Why do you think she was so ferocious about protecting other women?' She shuffled her minute body around to face Saif. 'And you – it was because your father was no father at all that she was so afraid her company would turn you into a woman's boy. One who ran to his mother every five minutes for help and advice. When you went to Ramzi Bagh to become a disciple, she was like a flower giving up its scent. Severed from its branch. "Dilkash," she used to tell me, "when you love someone you want the best for them. My boy is a gentle soul – that might please me but it would damage him. I must protect him from derision."

'Sometimes I found her weeping and she would cling to me, saying again and again, "Am I a monster? He's so young." That was how it was. "I think I've lost him," she would say sometimes. "I think I lost him long ago – first to Nyla, now to the Ramzi destiny. I hope he's happy. I hope he's not lonely." '

Dilkash did not like to see Saif look stricken as he did now. He had taught himself to say little about his emotions but Dilkash needed to correct his impressions. They thought she was mad and, true, the old, drying stream meandered sometimes and sometimes flowed backwards but during her long life she had observed all of these people and what you know once, you always know, even if sometimes it eludes your grasp. Zara was sad, too, she could see. Was love such a finite commodity, then, that it got divided and used up?

'They thought because my little jewel was strong and outspoken that she had no feelings but, you understand, being strong doesn't mean you don't feel the hurt – just that you endure it and get on with your duty.'

Saif stood up for the third time. 'I'll see you later,' he said.

Dilkash could see Zara wanted to stop him. He had always been able to remove himself from troubling talk but moving the body resolves nothing – sadness, after all, travels in the mind. Shaikh Saheb, they called him – he should have known that by now, a man of his age and supposed learning. If he stayed to listen some gem of healing may come from what she could tell him.

He smiled at Zara. 'The temptation to engage with these disclosures from a long-ago past – they're the stuff of discontent. They may bring a seed of solace but the reverse is also true; why waste energy lamenting what could have happened?'

And what did that mean, Dilkash wondered, letting Zara take her hand.

'Let's go up to the Green Room,' Zara said. Sharmeen's eyes kept making pilgrimages to the terrace where the boy came out, morning and evening, like a shadowy moon. The evening was drawing in.

'I think you should come in, too, Sharmeen,' Zara said. The mosquitoes had formed a tornado above her head. She slashed at it. Naturally, it reformed in a moment.

'Ooh,' said Sharmeen. 'Better go and see about dinner.' She skipped up the stairs and disappeared into the long drawing room while Dilkash climbed up slowly, hanging on to Zara's arm.

As they entered, the sun's rays caught the green glass frames of the Venetian mirrors and filled Dilkash's heart with freshness and vigour.

'The bridal chamber,' Dilkash breathed, slumping down by the bed. 'The world where your Aunty's married life began and ended.'

Dilkash's tears began to flow; she pulled up her knees to her chin and rocked back and forth. Hana had not long gone and memories kept tumbling in like dead leaves in the wind.

Kismet, that old vixen, gives with one hand and takes with the other. And who's to tell when she'll give with one and take with both? The news of her beloved mistress Hana's wedding had struck her in the heart like a knife. The forging of a marriage was a joy. It was named after the word 'joy' – shaadi, happiness – so she was overjoyed. But then it struck her that this suitor, Sultan Ramzi, was not good enough. He was not from a princely background and would lower Hana's status though everyone knew nowadays that money made class. And second, no one in the world would be handsome enough to match her beauty. But the child seemed happy enough. She did not know what it was to be less in beauty than someone else.

Old Dilkash knew she was as ugly as a crow, so her name was a grotesque joke because it meant 'alluring'. Her mother had hoped, when she looked at the wizened, sooty face of her newborn, that naming her 'Alluring' would shame fate into relenting. A pig lusts after a palace! Kismet was a malicious old creature who delighted in creating problems. Well, Dilkash had the last laugh because, ugly as she was, the face she looked into day and night was the most beautiful to be seen anywhere. God had compensated her amply – she worked in a palace of fairy-faced women, ate well, dressed well. Not like others who led a life which kicked them as they stood and punched them as they sat. Still, she was careful to name her daughter appropriately – Munni, Tiny. It described her minuscule frame which was why Hana and her sister called her Littl'un, just as they had nicknamed her Dilkash, Beauty. Let them have fun, what else could she give them but devoted service and the occasional laugh? If her ugliness had the power to give pleasure then here was one good thing about it. The Prophet, peace upon his soul, charged humankind with the duty of making people smile. How much more rewarding it must be then to make them laugh!

Dilkash worshipped the ground Hana walked on. She would go with her as part of her dowry when she was married off into the Ramzi family. She'd had her doubts when she heard about the strange Ramzi connection with shrines and forest dwellings but, as it turned out, the bride was taken to a magnificent castle – a fortress, they called it – which gave the town its name, Qila. Her mistress had married into the most powerful family in Trivikrampur other than its royal family. Of course, it could be said that the Ramzis were more important because who isn't aware that to grab the king's ear is to be supreme master? The Ramzis had been the spiritual guides of the maharajas for generations.

The forest dwelling was a different part of the bridegroom's life. Old retainers in the fortress told Dilkash that he spent much of his time there as leader of a religious sect, directing their training and tending the shrine of the sect's founder who had come to Ramzi Bagh hundreds of years ago during the reign of the Mughul emperor Jehangir. Dilkash knew all about Jehangir from a movie called *Mughal-e-Azam*. It was a grand movie about Jehangir when he was still a prince and fell madly in love with a palace dancer called Anarkali – a famous and heart-breaking legend. She had lamented the fact that the prince allowed an actress as beautiful as that to go to her death without a fight. But some months later, she turned up on the poster for another movie and her mistress laughed at her when she explained that Anarkali was played by an actress who had not really been put to death.

They said that this Jehangir, when he became emperor, had visited the first Ramzi sage in his sanctuary – it was not Ramzi

Bagh at the time but a jungle. He wanted to learn about the healing power of herbs. He must have been impressed because he asked the pir to go to court and be the royal physician but the pir refused. The Ramzi servants told Dilkash that some centuries later, a Vamana maharaja found the Pir Saheb in his hermitage, appointed him the spiritual guide of the Vamanas and brought him to spend part of his year in Qila. So, of course it was understandable that Dilkash was worried at first that they would live in a forest where she had only ever seen hovels.

In the event it turned out well. Sir bridegroom, holy and chaste as he might have been, stayed on after the wedding. And on and on and on. Never far from Hana's bed where he spent all his nights. Dilkash would have rationed Sultan's visits to twice a week and for the rest put him in his meditation chamber to pray. Good for his soul and, undoubtedly, for Hana. Too many demands on her delicate body could drain her energy, make her ill. Besides it was unseemly. It was an embarrassment to her that the servants stopped talking when she came in – dirty gossips – as if they didn't have enough work to be getting on with, instead of cracking smutty jokes about how their master found her mistress. Well, she had been taught better and she would maintain the dignity of silence. But she did speak to her mistress.

'Beautiful hair,' she muttered, 'is an adornment and a curse.'

'For heaven's sake, Dilkash,' Hana said, 'he's my husband.'

She couldn't blame the girl, her husband was handsome. Hopefully, the first throes of romance would soon be over and she would gain the confidence to turn him away more often. Then he might get back to touring his property and his holy schools and behave more like a man with responsibilities than a love-sick monkey.

'They are not schools,' Hana told her when she broached the subject. 'It is a retreat where people receive spiritual guidance. They're known as Sufis.'

Dilkash could feel her eyes popping from her head. 'Sufis? I thought Sufis were dead.'

'Dilkash, you're a fool. That's like saying Muslims are dead. Do you know who the Sufis are?'

'Those babas – they wrote religious poems a thousand years ago that people sing at shrines.' She had heard them when her mother dragged her around on pilgrimage, praying she would one day become worthy of marriage.

Hana tried to explain something about these men wanting to devote their lives to God and give up the world in search of the great universal truth. Dilkash understood they were men of God but she was not a reading-writing woman so a lot of it passed her by. Especially when Hana spoke of these men 'falling in love' with God. Profane language – she hoped God would not punish her for listening – but what could she do? You served for the sake of your belly and you ate what you were fed – even profanity and beatings. But how did Hana expect her to understand? Especially when she saw every day – or rather night – that Sultan was here in Trivikrampur, clearly impassioned and striding bold as a baboon from the Simla mountains into Hana's bed. And he was definitely not praying while he was there. That she knew for sure.

'When will he go to his other Beloved?' she asked. 'He's been here a whole month.'

'What's the matter, Dilkash? Don't you want me to be happy?'

Dilkash was appalled by the accusation. She beat herself on the forehead in despair and distress and cursed her fortune that she had lived to see the day when she could be so unjustly accused. Well, it was the function of the blanket to be crushed, twisted and farted on while it warmed and cocooned.

'I would kill myself but what would I say when I faced my Maker? I promised your mother I would take care of you and keep you well and healthy. How would I stand in God's great court and tell him with my face blackened, nose chopped that I'd broken my promise? You've left me homeless. I belong nowhere.'

'Don't be so dramatic, silly woman. I love my husband, my husband loves me. It's normal to ...'

Dilkash did not want to be contaminated. She grabbed her ears, smacked her cheeks, caught her tongue between her teeth and clenched her eyes tight. 'Tauba, tauba, tauba. Istaghfirullah. God forgive us!'

Hana couldn't stop laughing. She laughed at everything these days. Always laughing, inappropriately and unnecessarily. Too much laughing brought tears, she reflected, and then cursed the thought. But such indiscriminate laughter was certainly not part of her upbringing.

'It's fine,' she said. 'Laugh at me. I was sent to make you happy; what other function does my life have?'

Hana and Sultan continued to cohabit and when her predictions came true, she swallowed her emotions and soothed Hana's slender, sturdy body as it conceived and then convulsed, and bled away its contents. For a while, she was the only witness to these small sagas of life and death.

'Why, my beauty, why my heart, why?' she would lament, terrified that Hana, at barely sixteen, was about to be declared useless as a child-bearer. For the next two years she conceived and bled away goodness only knew how many potential Ramzi heirs. Thankfully, Sultan was away when these tragedies occurred. Men always got off unscathed by such disasters. They spawned their seed and went – flirt, squirt and desert. Women paid for their lust with body and mind. Perhaps it was best he didn't know, because who knew what terrible thing he might decide if he suspected that Hana may never carry a child?

She was the wife of Sultan Ramzi, sole son of an important family with lands and fields and titles and this strange spiritual legacy which sealed the relationship between the Vamana dynasty and their Ramzi gurus. Sultan was looking to her to provide the heirs who would carry the family name forward to the next generation. So Hana and Dilkash kept the tragedies secret until at last Hana grew so concerned that Dilkash called in Sultan's old wet-nurse.

'There's a curse on you,' the old woman cried and invited in a shaman. What a hoo-haa and a storm he raised up to expel the jinx. He might as well have summoned thunder and lightning and a restless wind and commanded them to tom-tom Hana's secret to the world. Everyone in the fortress gathered around in the back courtyard, staring up at the terrace by the old kitchen to see what was going on, and the secret of Hana's failures not only became common knowledge but travelled elsewhere.

'She's just overbred,' Sultan's fat great-aunt declared, turning up bag and baggage to stay on the pretext of taking care of her. What a case of Mrs Delicate, claiming to nibble a gram when really she swallowed mounds. 'Married at fifteen, finished at seventeen without even a brat to show for it. These high-class fillies are useless. Their hips aren't made to bear a proper woman's burden. That's why we get the little bastards their husbands father. God grant her forebearance. Good job her mother sent an ugly crow to wait on her.'

Dilkash held her breath as Hana's bronze eyes flashed but, thankfully, she threw the old buffalo-cow no fodder. There were no bastards in Hana's family. Not a single one. Her father and his before him had been entirely faithful to their wives. So were her cousin brothers, may they live as long as date palms. But that was not so of her husband. Madame Rumour travels in haste but her tracks are indelible. Sultan, they heard, had a wandering eye but people snatched at nasty gossip like gold coins flung at their feet.

'No wonder,' exclaimed the fat aunt, pouring roasted gram down her throat from a paper cone out of a barrow-sized basket. Dilkash could hardly unglue her eyes from her gelatinous belly, pumping up and down like a vast heap. 'She's probably too snooty to please him. He has to go sowing his seed in other stables if this high-bred filly won't give him his oats. A good wife is a lady in the drawing room and a whore in bed.'

She was on to an apple now, gnawing, munching, grinding, swallowing every part of it except the little woody stalk. Coarse mind, coarse words, coarse palate. It made her shudder to think of this woman being related, however tenuously, to her mistress. What people risked when they made marriages!

'Do something,' her sister-in-law Mumtaz hissed to Hana, pretending to be concerned. 'She's looking for a replacement for you. It's one thing to be Wife No. 1 if you've got a son; childless you'll be nothing. No status at all.'

'And how is it,' Hana replied, 'to be unmarried at twenty-five in your virtuous family?'

Dilkash could see Mumtaz hated Hana for all she herself was not. Mumtaz! Naming a bullock Matchless changed neither its sex nor its appearance. Kismet was not so easily deluded, and who knew it better than Dilkash? At fourteen Hana's beauty was already famous. Proposals piled up till the rubbish baskets had to be emptied five times a day and callers had to be sent away without an audience with either of Hana's parents. It was only through intrigue and pressure and the influence of rulers like the Vamanas that the Ramzis had managed to win her hand. And what was it all worth? Here she was, bleeding and bleeding away their heirs. The way of things had to change.

It was one of the few times Dilkash had seen Hana wilt, behind the toss of the hair and the scornful look. It broke her heart. Oh, she could see it even if others did not. Dilkash wasn't having any of that insulting talk from Mumtaz or the fat aunt.

'There's nothing wrong with her noble soil,' she responded, as the servants in the kitchens took up the carping and questioning of their mistresses. 'It's the seed that's faulty; spreading it around so much must have weakened it.'

Dilkash comforted Hana, brought her herbs and potions to strengthen her and told her to lie with her feet up the next time she became pregnant.

Other than the Maharani of Trivikram, Sita Devi, Hana had no friends. How could she? Like Sita Devi, she had no equals in the land. There were visitors, wives of landowners, local nobility – but Hana didn't socialize readily.

Then one day, Sita Devi had news. She had heard of a woman who had the same problem as Hana. A clever doctor woman discovered that a certain lady's womb was tipped slightly which made the seed spill out. So she had tried a medical trick which was to put a stitch into the woman's womb to close up the gap and hold the seed in. After that the woman popped them out every time like popping pips from limes. Six of them, she had now, by God's grace, all healthy.

Sita Devi handed her a slip of paper. 'I've found out where you can contact her, Hana,' she whispered, as if people were listening. 'She works in Bombay. But she's very much in demand and this special technique of hers has broken new ground. She's always off in Europe demonstrating it to the doctors there. It's called the Shirodkar suture.'

Hana summoned Munshi ji, the Ramzi major-domo, and instructed him to track down the doctor at once. She discovered that indeed this doctor lady had perfected the job. The next time Hana's 'monthly' was delayed, the doctor lady was summoned. A clinic was set up in Hana's boudoir and the stitch inserted. Sita Devi and Dilkash were by her side when the procedure took place in complete secrecy. And this time, the weeks went by without mishap. As Hana passed her sixth month, Dilkash was so swollen with pride she felt her skin could burst.

'Now who is an overbred filly who can't carry a child to term?' she demanded as she strutted about the stone corridors or pranced up the stairs or massaged her beloved mistress's aching back.

'Remember your place,' Hana chided, 'You can't speak like that to your master's family.'

'My only master is God, other than that I have a mistress,' argued Dilkash. She was never hurt by Hana's scolding. Deep down the child loved her, however she might snap and snarl.

'Well, your mistress is telling you to control yourself and remember your manners, Dilkash, or that vicious tongue of yours will get us all into trouble.'

Dilkash tossed her head. 'One stitch, that's all it took.'

The baby turned and, as if that was not embarrassing enough, Hana watched the surface of her stomach undulate. It was a wonder to Dilkash how Hana's petite body could contain an entire human child. She watched her place her hand on the distorting movement as it waved through from one side of the bulge to the other. These modern ways were strange. She herself had always looked away from her bulge, tiny as it was, even in private. And the trouble she took to cover it up! After all, it was a shameful thing. A woman's bloated belly was instant proof of shameful activity. Whatever the Christian missionaries might claim, there was only one way of having a baby. It was when your husband entered your body.

Fate decided to thwart her. She soon came to term and as she lay sweating and pushing, refusing to let out a sound louder than a gasp, a huge head, deluged in matted black curls, pushed its way out of her body. The baby was healthy and enormous, but a girl, not the much-needed heir to the Ramzi estate.

Hana called her daughter Sama which Dilkash knew meant 'ambience', but her mistress claimed it was the name for the meditation time of Sufis. Hana thought it would please her husband, though no doubt a proper name would be selected at a ceremony after the Quran was duly consulted. She was instantly devoted to the baby but, like most women born to high households, she was not brought up to pet and cosset her infant at all times of night and day. She employed a sister to nurse her – a proper Anglo-Indian sister who could speak English and who sat on a chair instead of on the carpet and had food brought to her on a tray in her room, and an ayah who would be properly trained to take care of the daughter of a noble house.

The maharani came to visit Hana and commiserated. Sita Devi was a true friend with a daughter of her own now. Massive platters of sweetmeats were sent out to all the important households. In return, congratulatory sweets were sent to Qila and gifts of clothes and toys for the infant. The mosques were given food and money to feed the millions and a massive vat of food was cooked for the household and all the courtyard dwellers. The army of staff all received money, new clothes, food that they would remember all their lives. The fat aunt gorged herself so excessively on celebratory foods that she died. Mumtaz wafted around on a cloud of glee, wretched creature.

'Oh Bhabhi, I'm so sad for you. You don't know what it's like to be a girl in a family like this with a vital need for a son. Look at me. I'm nothing. No status, no rights – not even a share in the property. But at least I have a brother to take over the Ramzi leadership and to support me. Sama will be a charity case, living on the mercy of other women.'

'Don't worry,' Hana snapped, her face even more beautiful with the dewiness of feeding her daughter. 'The nobility know how to treat girls. Nyla and I wanted for nothing. She'll have plenty from my side. I'll give your brother the heir he needs and still make sure you get a share of the estate so that you're not a dependent spinster guzzling away your life like the f... like your aunt.'

When the forty days of confinement were over, Sultan arrived. More gifts poured in: platters of silver, gold jewellery, animals and rare birds. The fortress was transformed into a fairground. Sound and colour everywhere – cars and carriages, guests at all hours of the day – everything in motion. Entertainers arrived to sing, dance, perform acrobatics, offer prayers and perform religious chants.

Doubts put down deep roots in Hana, Dilkash could see. Was Sultan disappointed? Was he here for her and their daughter or to uphold tradition? Would he have come if the Festival of the Green-clad Man was not due soon?

A feast was organized for the maharaja and Sita Devi in the formal dining room downstairs. Dilkash watched, amazed to see how easily Hana played hostess to the guests – men and women. The poor girl had swallowed buckets of rage for two years of her marriage, being openly excluded because she was barren. It was like filling her wound with chilli powder. And it was like a horsewhip on Dilkash's heart. But now she had mothered a Ramzi child, so she was eligible to take part in the private annual ritual between the Vamanas and the Ramzis before the spring festival.

She may have been barred from Ramzi rituals but she was no novice to social graces. And so she moved with perfect poise, talking to the women and men, with her husband's forefathers looking down at her from their portraits, standing down the generations with left arm behind their back, right arm slightly skewed by the hilt of the sword. On the head of each one, the eternal turban with its jaunty, jewelled feather attached, the brocade coats of deep blues and purples, the same hint of a curve to the lips suggesting, but not quite bestowing, a slight smile. Despite searching, Dilkash found no sign of humility or asceticism. Oh well, what does a horse know of courtrooms? It was not for her to judge the Ramzi devotion to God.

But she did wince as she watched Hana circulate. There had to be a touch of immodesty in her make-up to be so comfortable with all these unrelated men. Looking at the portraits, she prayed hard that Hana would not overstep the bounds of decency; how easy it would be for that same suggestion of a smile to turn into a sneer of disapproval for this young newcomer to the family. Thank heaven there were no disasters.

'I admit,' Hana confided to Sita Devi, as she imbibed some of her relaxed religious tolerance over the weeks and months, 'you look at the whole thing so much more sensibly than I do.'

'Well,' said Sita Devi, when she finally finished laughing, 'you know, India's had many invaders; each one brings his own little bit of God with him. Obviously you can't know which one is right or wrong. Or if they're the same or different. So it's best to have your cake and eat it. Why take chances? Worship them all. Same difference. What's in a name?'

Her mistress would do well to learn from Sita Devi that a lizard cannot hew down a mountain. After all, it had gone on for years and no calamity had struck the Ramzis. Nothing was broken, so nothing needed mending. Besides, there were other, more important matters to occupy her mistress' mind. She and Sita Devi were under severe pressure – everyone knows a woman is not fully realized until she mothers a son.

21

Sultan Ramzi hoisted the burden of the Ramzi calling on his shoulders when he was still young and carried it with gusto. They said his father's mind was not so strong anymore. Who knows what's true? If they're strung together, then they're pearls. What they did know was that he did not spend much time at Qila, except for that unnatural deviation when he was newly married. His visits were irregular and often quite far apart. Dilkash wondered, when she heard those scurrilous gossips in the kitchens, if they were right, and the only reason Sultan could keep away from his bride so long was because he found gratification in the bug-ridden beds of the sluts in the vicinity of Ramzi Bagh. How she suffered to see Hana cleave to the 'official' truth that her husband was away talking to the Almighty.

'I just have to accept that I'm part of his worldly pleasures, Dilkash,' she said. 'Can I compete with God? Would I dare to, or even want to? His duty is first to the Divine.'

Dilkash thought it best to shut her mouth. The child was trying to convince herself, as if speaking aloud somehow turned excuses into facts. Hana was a princess – his wife. Those other women that he bedded while he was away touring his estates were whores. He was a Ramzi – one day his destiny would be ripped from hers, he would go off to meld and merge with the Almighty. Could any wife build a lasting house from sand?

'No,' she told Sita Devi, as Dilkash sat silently in a corner with her mending basket. 'I'm not going to be cast away like a lot of hairs from his brush. I am worth more than that.'

The dancing and singing groups she organized, the gatherings of women discussing the latest fashions in beauty and entertainment, the flower-arranging sessions, even the man who came with his machine and showed movie pictures – none of it seemed to help.

'You've fallen in love with him,' Sita Devi teased. 'Now you'll just miss him and long for him. Look at you just pining away. You're pale and you're thin.'

Hana said nothing – without a player, the sitar is mute. She waited for his letters, frequent and full of love, more handfuls of sand to beguile her for some hours before slipping through her fingers. As Sita Devi had predicted, nothing else pleased her. But then, Sita Devi knew about marital love and often said that she would die if even the slightest shadow fell on her relationship.

The cook prepared Hana delicate dishes but they returned to the kitchen untouched. Mala, the gardener's wife, brought her flowers morning and evening but the bursting jasmine buds on her pillow, the rose petals scattered over the bed only reminded her that he was gone.

Finally the cook came to her. 'If I've offended you, punish me,' she wept. 'If my food has become tasteless, sack me. But in God's name, Huzur, don't make a sinner of me by refusing God's blessings. What does my food lack? If it is not fragrant, let me infuse it with more cardamom and cloves. If it lacks colour, let me drench it in saffron and dill. But for heaven's sake, don't disgrace me by rejecting it untouched.'

'Shush, shush Billo. Be quiet. The food is excellent. It's me. I'm not well.'

Billo let out a squeal. 'Then surely everyone will blame me. I'll be packed off from here in disgrace and no one will ever give me a job again. My family will die of starvation.'

Several servants tumbled into the room. Mumtaz came, too, carrying Sama. The baby seemed to have a softening effect on her.

'You have to eat,' Dilkash insisted. Mumtaz, blooming and benevolent, placed the baby in Hana's arms and cosseted her for a moment or two before taking her back.

Hana looked in the huge Venetian glass mirror which gave the Green Room its name and then at Mumtaz. When youth alights on her, even a she-ass looks pretty. Mumtaz's skin glowed and her scraggy, unwieldy tree trunk of a body looked statuesque.

'She's looking like an apsara,' agreed Sita Devi, when Mumtaz left the room. 'She must be in love.'

Dilkash thought the comment inappropriate – accusing a virgin of being in love was dirty even though Dilkash found it unseemly that Mumtaz consulted Munshi ji quite so often these days. Still, he looked after domestic affairs and since Hana's heart was not in running them, the girl was doing her best.

'But with whom?' Hana asked. 'If you tell me,' she insisted, when she was next alone with Mumtaz, 'maybe I can do something about it.'

But Mumtaz blushed and asked Hana not to embarrass her. 'How can you talk to me like this, Bhabhi, I'm an unmarried girl. You're sullying my good name.'

The Lord guided her to let the subject go – she was seeing love and gratification everywhere because she missed her husband desperately. Sita Devi was pregnant for the third time, and Hari was more devoted to her than ever despite the two last babies being girls.

Bodies seemed to occupy Hana's mind. Mala, the gardener's wife, was getting plumper in the face and Hana noticed a definite swell on her thin belly.

'Are you having a baby?' she asked boldly, sending the girl into a frenzy of embarrassed laughter. Mala tried to choke it back by stuffing her sari pallu in her mouth and swaying in semi-circles. 'Well, are you?'

The girl shrugged, trying to make her face disappear into her chest.

'It's okay. We're all married women here. We're supposed to have children.'

Dilkash smacked her own cheeks and shook her head. Why didn't her mistress let it go? 'Huzur Saheb, you're making the poor girl uncomfortable.' She looked sternly at Mala. 'You. Answer the mistress and be done with it.'

'Don't know, truly don't.' The girl's spit flew, she hid her face.

'So what do you think's happening to your belly?' Dilkash said. 'Just bloating with the smell of the earth?'

The girl tried to camouflage her bulge in the folds of her sari. 'Mother-in-law says I eat too much.'

'Has a crow flown off with her brain? Does food make a girl fat on her belly and nowhere else? Look at the sight of you – skinny legs, scrawny arms and a fat belly.' Dilkash was just getting somewhere with the girl when Hana raised a hand to silence her.

'I think you're going to have a baby,' she told Mala. 'How old are you?'

Mala gestured with her hand. At times, Hana did not bother to think how different the lives of the poor were from her own. How could the girl know her age? Did they keep records in villages? Her own father knew when he was born because the wheat crop had been exceptional that year and after the harvest, the locusts had come. Her birthday was determined by the terrible fire in the village next door which had forced her parents to flee to the nearest town which happened, by God's great glory, to be Daulatnagar. And what a day it was. Fate had made it up to her – because she had been born in a palace and lived there until the day she accompanied Hana away with her wedding party.

The girl Mala could be no more than thirteen or fourteen. Her breasts were still little green papayas. 'Do you feel like eating sour things?' Dilkash asked.

The girl nodded, like a chameleon spotting its prey.

'I thought so,' Dilkash muttered smugly. 'Craving pickle and raw mango and lemon.' The girl nodded. 'Then you're pregnant. Tell your husband to let you eat what you want.'

'Come to the big kitchen whenever you're hungry,' Hana said as Mala stood grinning without a hint of joy. Dilkash noticed Hana was always thinking about food these days, always fantasizing about her mother's home – but then, which girl doesn't crave the delights and love of her maika. Somehow the food here didn't appeal and it was only fear of divine retribution that stopped Billo immolating herself in the coals of her own stove because Huzur kept turning it away. Even when Dilkash showed the cook how to produce the food of her maika, Hana couldn't face it and said it was not the same. It was Sultan's absence that was doing it. Two months without a sign of him. Anyone could see the girl was pining.

Hana's hand strayed to her stomach and she began stroking it. Dilkash was alert. Could she be pregnant? She noticed none of the symptoms Hana had experienced before. Panic seized her. Where was the doctor lady at this moment? What if Hana couldn't find her in time and another baby was lost? She must get Munshi ji to locate her and alert her to the possibility of visiting at the first sign of pregnancy.

'What are you staring at? Go. Leave me alone. Dilkash, tell them in the kitchen to feed Mala any time she comes, give her whatever she wants. I don't want her mother-in-law picking on her.'

Dilkash watched her walk on to the balcony and look out on the crooked road past the open gates. The road was tarred now, and hard, but it still produced clouds of dirt that looked like little dust trees every time a vehicle drove past. As usual, the food shops were trading frenetically. The afternoon sun had waned, the coolness enticed the customers out. Small clusters waited like flocks of birds for the hot puffed puris being lifted from smoking cauldrons on to banana leaves. It pleased Dilkash to see Hana relax and enjoy the sight of the banya swirl his saffron-tinted syrup in spirals on to the oil, seeing them turn into jalebis – crisp orange coils – which he lifted out with his slatted spoon to serve in nests made of dry leaves. Dilkash saw Hana retch slightly, probably from a whiff of the hot oil, and turn her gaze from the food to the people. She held her hand to her mouth and swallowed hard, obviously nauseous.

Dilkash was distracted by a head towering above the others. A yogi shouldered his way through the crowd, strands of hair trailing down from the tight knot on top of his head. Whatever he said widened their eyes and opened their mouths wide. They drew back from him then followed at a distance. The puri-walla wrapped some freshly retrieved puris on a banana leaf, piled it high with pulses and vegetables and wrapped it firmly to drop into the yogi's satchel as he passed. The jalebi-walla did the same.

The yogi was striding towards the iron gates of the fortress.

Dilkash knew immediately he had a message for her mistress.

'Huzur Saheb, Huzur Saheb,' she shrieked. 'The maharaj is here. He wants to tell your fortune.'

Hana looked astonished. 'The maharaj wants to tell my fortune? What ...?'

'No, no, no. Not the maharaja. Maharaj, the yogi maharaj. He's asking if anyone here wants their fortune told.'

'Dilkash, you just made that up. How can you tell from here? Anyway, I don't believe in that nonsense.'

'But what's the harm?' Dilkash wished that, just sometimes, her mistress would listen. Even idiots occasionally dribbled words of wisdom. 'People say he's always right. He could tell us if you have a son written in your destiny.'

'A son.' Hana looked down from her balcony. A woman hung behind the yogi, one tiny child wrapped around her hip, another one sucking her shrivelled breast dry – a blessing can be a curse in the wrong places. The yogi maharaj fixed his eyes on the balcony, she could see him narrow them. He reached into his bag and handed the woman his two parcels of food. The woman fell to his feet, babies dangling from her like panniers from a donkey. What does a starving mouse do with a fantasy? She had probably never eaten such food even in her dreams. The yogi did not see them anymore. He was still staring up at Hana. Slowly, he shook his head, as if he had seen a terrible tragedy, and turned to go.

'No,' gasped Hana. 'Go, Dilkash. Run after him. Fetch him back. To the Oval Garden.'

Dilkash raced out to the street, waving and flailing. She could see, as she led him in through the gates, that Hana was already waiting in the Oval Garden on the square dais laid out by Mala every evening with a velvet cloth the colour of heather and large cushions and bolsters to match. The gardener and Mala stood in attendance.

'Bring the yogi directly to me, when he comes,' she instructed. The gardener moved silently to the gate. Mala watched over Hana until the yogi charged in.

'This young woman,' he declared, pointing at Hana. 'She has many unfulfilled yearnings, many fears inside.'

Dilkash cringed. 'Tell her, Maharaj,' she begged, 'tell her what the future holds.'

The yogi was like a saffron temple towering over her precious girl. 'Give me your left hand.'

Dilkash shuddered at Hana's resistance, shrinking at first like the chhui-mui plant then putting out both hands. The yogi gestured for her to raise them higher then peered into the fine lines and creases. It was a wonder how anyone could read messages from little loops and mounds.

'Your birth date?'

Hana told him. The yogi hesitated, pondered, then grasped his long beard at the chin and slid his fist down its length before speaking.

'You will know great happiness and great unhappiness. But remember, nothing is gained from refusing the quest. With your husband there need be no pride or withholding.'

Dilkash flinched as Hana yanked back her hand, praying she would not say anything to offend him, even though, holy man or not, God knew he was getting above his station. How could he speak to her mistress like this? What did he know? And how could he tell something so personal from the creases in her palm? Surely not – did images of events float in front of his eyes like movie pictures? She could feel her skin grow hot and throb.

Hana retched. Her skirts swirled over the side of the dais as she rose to go.

'Wait, girl!' the yogi's voice commanded. 'Listen. The yogi does not care about offence or defence. He speaks only the truth. And this is the truth I came to tell. You will have a son – but when he arrives, your husband will leave you. But first,' his voice thundered on, 'the ailing fruit of your womb will drop and rejoin the circle of eternity.'

Dilkash followed Hana across the garden through the side entrance to the formal dining room and into the inner courtyard. Plait swaying, blazing with fury, the child stumbled up the stairs and into the long drawing room.

'Ignore him, Bibi,' Dilkash crooned. 'God will protect you. What does he know, the ignorant so-and-so?'

'Pay him,' Hana ordered. 'And feed him before he goes.' Her voice was dull as the beat of rain on slate, her face yellow like the pages of an old notebook. She walked out on to the terrace, pacing up and down, fanning herself.

Mala's voice drifted up asking, 'What about me, Maharaj?'

The yogi's voice rang out more menaces. 'You too will have a son,' he thundered. 'But you? Ah you, beloved of God, little gardener, grower of flowers. You will bear a son and go mad.'

Mala shrieked twice. Dilkash and Hana rushed to the parapet in time to see her swoon. Her husband fell to his knees, fanning her desperately with a palm frond.

'Dilkash!' Hana called clutching her belly, twisting with pain. 'Dilkash! Someone! Come.'

Two new maids rushed in to Hana, looking terrified.

'One of you, go down and help Mala into the house. Call the doctor. Tell the gardener that Mala will stay with me till she's better.'

Dilkash could hear her breath catch in pain. Both girls scuttled away, frightened.

'I need you, Dilkash,' Hana said. Dilkash died a thousand deaths as her beloved Hana held out her hand like a child, then doubled over in pain. 'Help me to the hamam.'

How many more times, Lord? Dilkash thought as Hana tore off her clothes. She checked that the huge brass cauldron was filled with water. The chimney of the samovar emitted wisps of smoke – the girls had done their work, cleaning and filling it. The store of coals at its base was reduced to a few embers wrapped in a silvery coating of ashes. The water was scalding hot. She lifted a jug of water from the cauldron and poured it into a metal bucket, then another and another until it was half-full, then dragged the bucket under the samovar tap.

She put her arms around Hana, seating her on the wooden bath-stool. She could feel blood seep through Hana's kurta on to her arm, still warm as it streaked down Hana's legs and mixed with the warm water, flowing along the rippled brown stone floor. Billows of red swirled into the drain.

'What do you think, Dilkash?' Hana asked. 'Is that my son or my daughter?'

22

Sultan wasted no time coming. He must have leapt on to his horse as soon as he heard of his wife's miscarriage and charged the thirty miles to Trivikram from the mango groves where he was overseeing the harvest. What a sight he was as he burst into her room, hair dishevelled, eyes wild. He looked like a possessed man but even stones would have swooned at his beauty! In a flash he was by her side, holding her, and even though Dilkash made herself invisible, she knew he was smothering her hair and face with kisses.

'The doctor sent word that you were ill.'

Even her smile proclaimed her weakness. 'I'm going to be fit again soon. Then you shall have your heir.'

'Damn the heir,' he said.

Hana gasped. She put her hand to his mouth, crushing his lips against his teeth. 'No! What are you saying? Don't curse your child!'

'I don't want a son. Not if it does this to you ...'

Hot tears poured down Hana's face. She knew well enough that words like these tempted Fate who, at best, was uncharitable; at worst, well, evil (may the Devil be deaf). Dilkash shrank into the adjacent ante-room from where she could watch out for Hana.

'Please don't,' she begged. 'The estate ... your calling. I'd be failing if I couldn't give you a son. I swear, I swear on all that's dear to me, I will give you the Ramzi heir and preserve it all.'

Dilkash could see her pause, taking in the intensity of her husband's embrace, of his hands stroking her back. What they said about holy men was true, it seemed – that their robes hid passions stronger than those of ordinary men.

Dilkash found Sultan's tears embarrassing. She patted her cheeks and shook her head, knowing she was invisible and inaudible in her little corner – the joint curse and blessing of the servant.

'You know,' he said, 'there are promising young men among my students ...'

'I *want* a son,' Hana insisted. 'Every woman does.'

Sultan spoke to several doctors over the next few months and not once did Dilkash hear him talk of leaving. Hana was not ill but she was weak. She had lost buckets of blood and she needed to recover. Sultan vowed to stay until he knew for sure that she was healthy and out of danger.

'My life is not in danger,' Hana insisted. But his words softened her face and plumped her lips as if her blood was increasing by the fistful. 'I'm strong. Besides, the yogi said ...'

'Yogi?'

Dilkash flinched as Hana's hand flew to her mouth – a giveaway gesture for sure. Naturally, she didn't want her enlightened lord to think her an ignorant, superstitious woman.

'There was this yogi,' she said. Dilkash grabbed the hair at her temples, clenched her eyes. The master would send her out with her bundles and bags if he knew she'd had a part in it.

'He was at the gates,' Hana was saying, 'and I sent for him. He predicted I would have a son and ...' She stopped. Dilkash could breathe again – better to keep some truths covered.

'Since when have you started to listen to the ravings of fortune-tellers?' he demanded.

'I haven't really. But he said Mala would have a boy and she's at least five months pregnant so we'll know in a few months.'

Hana must have seen the flash of rage in his eyes if Dilkash could see it from her shadowy corner but he put an arm around her, stroked her hair, smoothed her brow. 'Don't be anxious. You've worried yourself too much. We are blessed with a daughter. We don't need any more children. She'll rule over all my estates. Like a queen.'

Hana turned away. 'How can a girl rule over your estates? They're vast. And dealing with all those men ...?'

'You, my little fireball, could deal with anyone!' Sultan said. 'And so will any daughter of yours.'

Dilkash's heart bloomed like a garden as they both laughed and were, for a moment, distracted. Then he grasped her hands. 'Are you really okay?' he asked.

Hana nodded.

'When you gave birth to a healthy daughter, I thought you ... were cured.'

'I was never sick!' Hana flushed, and Dilkash vowed to give up meat for a month if only God stopped her telling Sultan about the Shirodkar suture. Thankfully, Hana said, 'I *am* better. I was careless. I hadn't realized I was pregnant. But I'm getting better by the minute.'

'Are you?' His voice was full of pleading.

She nodded, believing that, at last, she was beginning to live a normal married life. The magic had happened, whatever it was; the spell to keep her husband by her side had taken effect. She was, at last, an ordinary married woman. Dilkash had to confess Sultan's affection seemed to grow daily.

'You know,' he said, looking Hana directly in the face, 'I love you. I don't regard you as a child-bearer. Sama really will be queen of all I own.'

Then, one day as he declared his love yet again, Sultan's eyes wandered. 'I have something to attend to. Nothing bad. But I'll have to be away again. For a day or two.'

Hana was bereft. 'Already?'

'I'll be back in a flash.' He stood up.

Hana was horrified. 'This minute? Won't you even have something to eat?'

'No time,' he grinned. 'Only to wish my beautiful bride a proper goodbye.'

He pushed her gently back on the bed and kissed her deeply. For the rest of the night Dilkash was locked out and woke abruptly when he flashed through the door, laughing. 'The sooner I go, the sooner I'll be back,' he called over his shoulder, prancing down the stairs to the inner courtyard like a stallion on show.

Hana watched from the balcony as he drove out of the courtyard and through the enormous iron gates. What was so important that he had to go away now, so early in the morning?

She went about her routine like a sleeping beauty, coming to life briefly when Sister brought Sama to her and she coddled the infant for a while then returned to the balcony. Night must have fallen as she sat staring at the empty courtyard and the silent gate. The rain had driven most of this evening's visitors away from the streets and the last of the vendors had locked up and gone.

Dilkash carried in the yakhni, the rich bouillon she made her mistress afternoon and evening, flavoured with cloves, cinnamon and black pepper, to make Hana strong. And Hana admitted she could feel the strength return to her body, especially now after Sultan had come so swiftly and stayed so long.

But his departure made her sad again and Dilkash had to keep reminding her that he had promised to be back soon. In the two days that he was gone, she would build her strength even further. She would eat and walk and allow Dilkash to massage her so that her circulation improved. She told Dilkash she would send word to Dr Shirodkar to make sure she was standing by and mortified Dilkash by telling her that the moment Sultan returned, she intended to get pregnant again. And this time she would have the son that the yogi promised because he had predicted she would have a boy.

'Come and eat,' Dilkash wheedled, unbearably embarrassed. 'Your food's getting cold.'

As she picked up the spoon, a shadow-like form flitted across the courtyard towards the house, catching the periphery of Dilkash's vision. Hana must have seen it too, for she asked, 'How is poor Mala? That was a horrible thing the yogi told her.'

Dilkash shook her head and muttered a stream of curses under her breath. 'What can I say? She knows that yogis' words come true.'

'How does she know?' Hana's voice was sharp.

Dilkash looked at her from beneath lowered lids. 'You believe him, don't you?'

'That doesn't mean he's right about everything. There's a fifty-fifty chance when you predict the gender of a baby.'

'So you can just choose to believe some predictions and ignore the rest?'

Hana bristled. 'That's not what I mean. I have a feeling about having a son.'

'Well, Mala has gone strange,' Dilkash said. 'Since she's known what happened to you, she does nothing but weave garlands and sing sad songs about her husband leaving her.'

Hana recalled the form she had just seen outside. 'But I saw her. Crossing the courtyard towards the house. She wasn't singing.'

Dilkash looked puzzled. 'Mala?'

'I think so,' Hana confirmed.

Dilkash shook her head. 'I left Mala in the kitchen. Her husband brought her in to feed her. Poor man, he's dried up like a twig. Tending to her, doing his work in the gardens, as well as her chores.' Dilkash tilted her face heavenwards and spread out her palms. 'Only God Almighty can help her now,' she muttered. 'She's beyond the reach of doctors.'

'I want to see her,' Hana said. 'Bring her to me when she's finished eating.' She narrowed her eyes as someone walked past her door. 'Who was that?'

Dilkash felt stiff as she stood up; she pressed her palm hard against her waist to ease her back as she walked to the door and looked out.

'It's Mumtaz Bibi,' she said.

'Tell her I want to see her,' Hana commanded. 'I haven't seen her since this morning.'

'Eat your food first,' Dilkash said. 'It's getting cold.'

'Okay, okay,' Hana said, picking up the spoon. 'I can feed myself. Go and get Mumtaz.' She took a spoonful of soup and watched Dilkash bolt down the corridor to Mumtaz's room.

Dilkash returned a few moments later. 'She's gone for a bath.'

'A bath? At this time? I thought she had her bath in the afternoon, before tea.'

'Well, she got soaked through in the rain.'

'The rain?' The look of confusion on Hana's face slid slowly away and one of recognition replaced it. Dilkash knew the game was up. Hana had guessed that the woman in the courtyard was Mumtaz! Why was she in the courtyard so late? And what was she carrying?

'Where's Sama? Mumtaz had her.'

'She's with the ayah.'

'Bring her to me.'

Dilkash fled from the room to summon the ayah, happy to be out of her mistress' sight when she was thinking so hard. When Dilkash returned, Hana pounced on her like an owl on a timid mouse. What business could Mumtaz possibly have by the gate, near the staff quarters? Only the men lived in the gatehouse block – the munshi and the driver. Dilkash gasped as Hana stopped and grabbed her shoulders with such force, she thought her end was nigh.

'The animal sheds!' she blurted. 'That's probably where she went.' Mumtaz liked to check on the animals. She had obsessed lately that the servants were stealing milk from the cow or eggs from the chicken coop, even the odd chicken. And if she found a brooding hen, she would bring it into the fort, give it a dozen eggs to sit on and keep it on the terrace across from the Oval Garden. She'd look after it until it hatched and she was surrounded by a lot of fluffy chickens. Sometimes she put a couple of duck's eggs in with the rest and once she had bred a flock of turkeys the same way. Ugly brutes.

'That's it! Mumtaz was with the animals. And she took Sama with her, to show her.'

Sama was sluggish when the ayah brought her in. Hana held her in her arms for a while, fed her, tried to play with her. But Sama was content to snuggle in her mother's arms and let her eyelids drift shut. It pleased Dilkash to see the maternal instinct in Hana as she murmured, 'She has such long, curly eyelashes. She's lovely, isn't she, Dilkash? So much like her father.' Hana blew gently on the damp curls plastered to Sama's forehead. This summer heat was too much for infants. Sama's forehead was hot. She felt the back of her neck, checking for a temperature, feeling anxious. Surely not? She was just hot and drowsy and it was time for her to sleep.

'Bring her cot here,' she told the ayah. 'Let her sleep here tonight. Bring your bedding too.'

The weather was oppressive, so Hana waved her fan of peacock feathers gently over Sama for a while. Dilkash shuddered. She would get rid of the wretched thing as soon as she had a chance. Peacocks were creatures of the wilderness and she knew well that every part of them longed for the wilderness. But would Hana listen? Oh no! She knew best and rejected the age-old business as nonsense.

'Lie down, Bibi,' Dilkash said when the infant was breathing evenly. Hana lay down, absently fanning herself.

'I wish Sultan was here,' she said. 'He would know what to do.'

Hana dropped off to sleep waiting for Mumtaz. Dilkash watched over her. It was not the sleep of peace. The girl tossed and turned and, an hour or so later, she sat upright in bed, eyes wide.

'Something is wrong,' she muttered, like a haunted thing. She flicked on the bedside lamp and looked at the clock. Half past two in the morning. She got out of bed and looked at Sama, who was sleeping deeply. Gently, she stroked her cheek with her forefinger, disentangled the muslin sheet from her legs and pulled it over.

She turned off the lamp and tried to sleep but something was plaguing her because she turned the light on again and tried to read. No good. Dilkash could see she couldn't concentrate. She pulled on her dressing gown and strode along the gallery. Lord, she was determined to talk to Mumtaz at once!

From the door of the Green Room, Dilkash watched as she knocked on Mumtaz's door. No answer. She pushed it gently open and held the curtain aside. Dilkash could see from the gallery that the mosquito net was down and she could just discern an inert form on the bed. Hana crossed over to the other side of the room, to the door which led out on to the veranda. The outside light would be gentler. Dilkash ran, crouching, along the balcony and to Mumtaz's door.

Hana stepped out on to the veranda, stretching her hand to the switch. Then she stopped. On the large cushion-laden dais in the verandah lay Mumtaz – with a man! One of his hands clutched a naked breast, the other had disappeared into Mumtaz's clothes and his wrist flicked and twitched grotesquely between her thighs like an amputation. Hana grasped for the door frame, balanced herself and turned very quietly. She crossed the room to the gallery, hardly daring to breathe. Outside in the corridor, she retched. Holding her throat, she turned the corner of the gallery and ran through the long sitting room into her suite. Frantically, she snatched the washbasin beneath her bed and threw up.

Dilkash mopped Hana's brow with a damp cloth, helping her wash, and cleared away the basin, thanking God she had managed to get back into the room before Hana returned to the Green Room.

Back in bed, Hana tossed and turned.

'Oh Dilkash,' she said. 'Why didn't I see it?' Then came the moment Dilkash had been dreading. 'Did you know about it, Dilkash?'

'I knew what others knew.' Dilkash cowered as she spoke.

'Others? Who else knows?'

Dilkash protected her face with her forearms. 'Some of the women. They saw her going to the menagerie.'

Hana grabbed Dilkash's arms. 'Why are you doing that? Have I ever hit you?'

'No,' Dilkash's voice came out like a croak. 'But the sky and earth are changing places here, why not you?'

'Dilkash, explain why, why didn't you tell me what was going on?'

Dilkash shook her head. 'What could I say, Huzur? You've had so much to worry about since you got married. You were happy ...'

Hana dropped on to the bed. 'What will I do? How will I tell Sultan?'

Dilkash gasped. 'Tell Shaikh Saheb? Never. You mustn't.'

'Oh, so I must hush it up and let him find out for himself?'

'Oh God, rid us of this blight, please, Lord,' Dilkash wailed. 'Save our faces. Deflect our shame.'

A spluttering noise came from Sama's cot. The ayah leaped out of her mattress and was beside her in a flash, lifting her out of her cot. Hana walked across and took the baby in her arms.

'My goodness! She's really hot.'

Sama looked up at her mother with glazed eyes. The fire inside had reddened her cheeks and dried her skin. Hana forgot everything else.

'Fetch a basin of tepid water, quick. And a thermometer. Send the driver out for the doctor.'

'The driver's gone with Shaikh Saheb,' Dilkash reminded her.

'Send for Billo's son, then. He can drive.' By the time Hana rang the doctor, the car was on its way to fetch him.

'Send for the munshi, Dilkash,' she said. 'I need to talk to him before your master returns.'

'For heaven's sake, Huzur. Think of yourself, for once. Let them burn in their own hellfire.'

'Do as I say.'

Hana washed Sama down with a tepid sponge as she spoke to the munshi. 'I want you to leave Qila immediately. No packing, no farewells. Just leave. Your possessions will be sent on with three months' salary. So long as you leave immediately, I will make sure you get a good reference from Shaikh Saheb. I believe you know why I have to do this.'

Then she sent for Mumtaz. 'I've dismissed Munshi ji. Don't try to say goodbye or to contact him ever again. Or your brother will have to deal with you.'

Mumtaz couldn't tear her eyes away from Sama. 'Is she okay? What's wrong with her?'

'She's caught a fever.'

Sama's small body was flaccid as Hana lifted her into her arms and every so often she coughed, a wrenching, hacking cough that turned her little form inside out. The doctor arrived and gave her an injection.

'You have to wait,' he said. 'There's nothing else to be done – we can only wait.'

Mumtaz slipped away. The doctor asked the women questions. How were the baby's bottles and milk sterilized? What had her movements been in the last day or so?

'Could it have been the rain?' Hana asked.

'More likely a virus,' the doctor said. 'But ...'

Hana thrust through the group of servants and ran through the door, along the gallery and into Mumtaz's room, bursting with rage. The room was empty. The wardrobes stood open, their shelves bare. Mumtaz was gone.

Sultan returned home to find Hana engrossed in the baby. She looked at him with mournful eyes, unable to speak.

'The doctor said we need to keep her fever down and wait,' Dilkash explained.

Sultan tried to comfort Hana. She looked up at him then and said simply, 'You went away. I had to deal with everything. You left me, and you see I didn't prove equal to the task.'

'Children get ill all the time,' Sultan reassured her. 'But look. This was what I went for.'

He drew out a velvet-covered roll from a tubular box. In it was a pair of bangles, enamelled in cream with green vines on the inside and on the outside in grey-blue, inlaid with cabochon diamonds and rubies. The edges were studded with perfect pearls.

'From one queen to another. These belonged to Empress Noor Jehan – now they are yours. They have a long history, within our family and outside it. Put them on for me. One day, I'd like you to give them to Sama. When you do, you'll look back on this day and smile, to remember how anxious her first illness made you.'

Dilkash was aghast as Hana tore her wrist away from him and ran to Sama's bedside. She was sleeping peacefully. Hana went suddenly stiff. She did not touch her, she did not check her pulse or ask the doctor for his verdict. She knew her child was no more.

'She will never wear these bangles,' Hana whispered, lifting Sama. 'And nor will I.'

The sight of Hana would remain with Dilkash forever: holding her infant close, her small head against her chin, impassive except for the rhythmic jerking of her body and a damp sheen on her cheeks.

Sultan lurched forward and enclosed them both in his arms. He clung to them for a long while and in the end she had to push him gently away, whispering, 'Sama needs air.' Sultan dropped heavily on to a chair and cried at her words. He cried more than Dilkash had ever seen a man cry and his strapping body shook unstoppably. But Hana was motionless except for her fingers smoothing Baby Sama's hair, occasionally making a barely audible crooning noise.

Later that day Hana told Sultan bluntly that Mumtaz had run away with the munshi. It was a triple disgrace. Not only had she eloped, but with an employee and that too a Hindu.

'You were right,' he said. 'I can only apologize for burdening you with more than you could manage. I will never stop paying for it.'

He walked out of the Green Room.

Did he wait to see how Hana was feeling after the loss? Or to arrange Sama's funeral now that the munshi was gone? No, he jumped into his jeep and drove out of the large iron gates of the fortress as if a demon army was pursuing him.

A few weeks later Hana realized she was pregnant again; she sent Sultan no message but luckily Nyla was with her and made sure all the formalities were fulfilled. They were, after all, daughters of a high household and knew about protocol. Her ruby-child stopped going out. Sultan returned from time to time to keep up appearances: when Saif was born, to attend official occasions and ceremonies like the festival and on the birthdays of the new child, Saif and, later, Zara, in whom he saw the daughter he had lost.

III

23

Sharmeen flew down the stairs, eyes wide. 'Mummy! There're men at the front. They've got big-big cameras.'

Pebbles appeared through the curtains of her room and looked down at the men in the inner courtyard.

A man in jeans and a leather jacket moved out through the arch. 'Namaskar. I am here to speak to Shaikh Saheb Saifuddin Ramzi.'

'He's gone to ... he's away on business at the moment.'

The reporter held up a large mic. 'Business, you said?'

'Work,' Pebbles said. 'He's away on work. Who are you, anyway?'

'Ahhh.' The man felt around his jacket and held up a card marked 'Press'. 'From TV station.'

'Which TV station?' Pebbles asked.

'Local.' The man was being cagey – he was probably from a fascist network.

'What do you want to know?' Pebbles asked.

Zara stepped out of the long sitting room. 'Come in, Pebbles. Don't engage with them.'

'Get back in!' Pebbles hissed. 'Don't let them see you.'

The man had pushed a camera through into the inner courtyard and was filming Pebbles and Zara. Through the arch, Zara could see Kamran talking to the crew. The reporter near the camera turned to listen and walked a few steps back towards the arch. Kamran was pointing to the gate now. As the men spoke, a ball of grey and white hurled itself towards the camera, knocking down the tripod then falling to the ground with a loud yelp.

'What ...?' Pebbles said. 'Oh my god. It's Littl'un. What does she think she's up to?' She ran towards the kitchen. 'Millo. Chhoti.

Someone. Go down and help Littl'un. She's hurt herself. Get the doctor.'

She shot through the long sitting room into the Green Room. Zara followed. A crowd had gathered outside, the courtyard dwellers forming a cordon that cut off the camera crew from possible protestors. The reporter grabbed a hand-held camera and dashed back into the courtyard. Millo and Chhoti led Littl'un into the formal drawing room. The reporter was filming the tripod on the ground with the camera attached but askew. The man was making Littl'un's pathetic lunge sound like a serious attack by a member of the Ramzi household with the reporter himself as the intended victim. A cheer went up outside.

'Abba's here!' Sharmeen shouted, looking through the curtains of the Green Room balcony. 'Thank god! Now he can fix it.'

Zara watched with Sharmeen as Saif emerged from the Oval Garden, past the shrine, and approached a car. Jay opened the car door, bowed low and folded his hands in greeting to Saif and strode towards the cameras. Behind them, Karan quickly dashed out of his vehicle. He walked quickly, blocking Saif and Jay from the crew, waving his arms over his head.

'What do you think you're doing?' he said to the gaping crew. 'This is private property. You can't come in here and start filming without permission.'

'We are news company,' the man's voice was proud, 'from Janta Independent.'

'I don't care who you are.'

'We wish to speak with Shaikh Saheb.' He turned to his crew. They were star-struck by the presence of their maharaja. 'Turn on the cameras! You came here to make a tamasha, not to watch one.'

The cameraman looked helplessly at Jay. 'Mai-baap?' he mumbled the old phrase of respect, 'mother and father'. Jay shook his head and the man stepped back from the camera, arms folded.

Karan was already on his cell phone to Inspector Pandey.

'Goodie goodie, goodie!' Sharmeen said. 'The police will be here soon. And wham! These bad people will disappear.'

Zara could hear the loud noise of clanging tambourines and banging drums as a band of men walked towards the gates of Qila, ahead of a carriage-like vintage car with a small, exceptionally dark young man waving to this side and that. The car crawled to the gates of Qila and turned in. The rest of the crew reluctantly assembled their cameras, lights and suspended microphones and the reporter began speaking into his hand mic, announcing the arrival of Sardar Shinde in Gujarati.

'An attempt has been made to associate the former Maharaja of Trivikram with this terrible fraud. The courts have acknowledged the fraud implicitly by granting an injunction against the opening of the school but we have the opportunity to speak directly to Maharaja Jayendra Sinhji of Trivikrampur who is here in person. Maharaja ji?'

Karan pushed away the microphone and stood in front of Jay as the dark man, Shinde, climbed slowly out of his car and walked over to Saif, his chest puffed out like a pigeon's, and slapped a document against his chest.

'I will not let foreigner like you destroy the faith of my forefathers in the land of my fathers and my gods. I will fight the fight of very many small people such as myself who have been displaced by people like you and your murderous faith. You people who have shouted "die or convert" while you hold a sword on the bowed necks of my innocent people.'

The cameras were rolling. Saif did not touch the document and Shinde's hand remained on his breast for several seconds until Saif stepped back without a word. Jay stood motionless. The reporter spoke into his microphone.

'You can see what happened. Sardar Shinde tried to serve his papers for subpoena on Saifuddin Ramzi, to come to court and answer this charge but Ramzi refuses to take them, showing that he is in weak position.' He shoved the microphone towards Saif's face. 'You have your chance – have you anything to say in your defence?'

Jay swung his arm forward. 'Get out of here, now,' he said. 'And don't ever let me catch you speaking the Rajguru's name with disrespect again. You are not fit to utter his name.' He turned to Shinde. 'And the same goes for you.' Shinde backed away. Jay gestured to the men and women from the courtyard. 'Every one of these people and most around Trivikrampur have respected the Ramzi gurus for generations. You are not welcome here.'

Shinde shrivelled, the document still in his hand as the courtyard dwellers moved a step closer. The reporter regained his wits and held up the microphone to Jay. His hands were shaking and he cleared his throat several times.

'Your Highness knew that Shaikh ... er, the agenda behind the Academy is to convert our Hindu girls?'

'Our agenda is to drag Indian womanhood out of illiteracy and oppression where people like you keep them.' A cheer went up from the courtyard women.

'How can you be so sure that there is not some secretive intention?'

'I do not question my guru.' He bowed slightly to Saif and gestured towards the Oval Garden to bypass the crew blocking the portico.

'But Your Highness, please, how can you be ...' Shinde said.

'Speak to my lawyer,' Jay said over his shoulder.

Zara flicked the curtain away and walked in. 'I could be the lawyer. Except that I'm the damned enemy.'

24

'Don't you want to be able to say your husband is the biggest "hero" in Bollywood?'

Kamran's voice made Zara sit upright in bed. The branches of the tamarind tree swayed against a yellow-smeared sky. She looked at her clock. 6.50.

'But I don't want you to go.' Sharmeen's voice was beseeching. 'Why do you keep going away?'

'I need to work, my love. I have to make my fortune so that I can keep you like a princess.'

'But I'm not a princess. And we'll live here. And we're rich so you don't have to work and you can stay with me every minute.'

Zara rolled out of bed and inched her way to the window. Surely Kamran had not had the front to enter Hana's terrace?

Sharmeen and Kamran were talking across the void over the Oval Garden. She was leaning on the parapet, he was at his bedroom window.

Is this man real? How old is he? Kamran was wearing a grotesque white outfit made from shiny fabric – his sleeve glittered with sequins as he held it out of the window, scattering jerky points of light across the space between. Sharmeen squeaked with delight. Her body was draped across the top of the wall now, waist to hip, legs waving in the air as her flimsy nightgown fell away. It would be risqué anywhere in India – in Trivikram it was beyond shocking. Zara resisted the urge to go out and drag her in. After all, she was an outsider. That was clear.

She had to speak to Pebbles and Saif about Kamran but she needed to know more before she did.

'Come downstairs,' Sharmeen trilled. 'I want to you to see me in my new negligee. In the Oval Garden.'

'Why don't you go and get dressed first. Put on some proper clothes,' Kamran called back, softly. 'It's cold down there.'

She was petulant now. 'No. I want you to see me in my ...'

'Look. I have to get my things packed first of all.' He looked a little weary. 'After that I'll meet you. In the meantime have some breakfast and get dressed. I'll take you out to the ruins for some time. We can talk properly there. We'll have a nice chit-chat.'

'Can we sing and dance? Between the ruins? Like in the movies?'

'If we can get away,' he explained, slowly, as if speaking to a child. 'If I can get hold of a car and it's safe to go, then we'll drive out to the ruins. And if we do, then yes, of course, we can sing and dance.'

'Will you still love me even if you play opposite Madhuri?'

'Of course.'

'Juhi? Kajol? Any of the mega-heroines?'

'I will. I will. I will. Now go, go, go. You'll catch cold.'

'Only if you say you love me.'

'I love you. *Go!*'

Zara could hear them both laugh. It was a happy sound. Kamran made Sharmeen happy, so did it matter if he was also interested in her money, she reflected, as Sharmeen stepped into the long drawing room and skipped away. She wished she knew what his connection was with the troublemakers.

She pulled down her overnight case and started packing for her trip to Ahmednagar. The issues surrounding a relationship between Sharmeen and Kamran were complicated and she decided to talk to Saif at breakfast.

'No situation needs to be complicated, unless you make it so,' Saif responded. 'Why do we need to think of her marriage now? She's only just turned nineteen.' He looked at Pebbles. 'By God's grace she has every comfort here. There isn't a problem unless we create one.'

'There is a problem, though,' Pebbles exploded. 'That's the whole point. You know she's already getting proposals. We have to think, one way or another, what to say to all these people. Do we accept? Do we refuse? Do we explain and let the suitors decide? Anyhow, they're going to start gossiping soon. We have to say something.'

'Say something?'

Zara felt a tight, hysterical urge to laugh at Saif's perplexed expression.

Pebbles put her palms to her eyes and slowly dragged them down her face until her fingers rested on her eyelids. Her frustration was obvious. 'You explain, Zara. I'm so tired, really. I've been carrying this alone for too long. I get this every time. *You* tell me, what should I do? The Shamnagars are waiting for our response. Nice state, old royal family. Boy studied about hotels and catering in Switzerland. Very down-to-earth. He would be suitable. But what do I tell them?'

'Ask Sharmeen what she thinks,' Saif said. 'It's quite simple.'

The conversation she had overheard between Saif and Sharmeen flashed through her mind. Was Saif hedging to give his daughter time?

'I think you're missing the point here, Saif,' she said. 'Do you think Sharmeen can reliably make up her mind?'

'If Sharmeen is capable of getting married, she's capable of deciding.' He put down his fork and brought it neatly together with the knife. Even when they were kids, he would signal the end of a discussion by ending his present activity and walking away. He pushed his plate back an inch and stood up. 'Jay will be here soon. We're looking at some contracts, then we're out all afternoon. Don't worry about lunch.'

Zara was suddenly anxious. What if they surprised Sharmeen and Kamran? She excused herself and darted swiftly across to Hana's terrace. Kamran and Sharmeen stood to one side of the Oval Garden, behind the fully blossoming *Cestrum diurnum*, King of Day. Zara could see them through the bright green leaves studded with a million white flowers. Sharmeen was inching closer, pressing her body against Kamran's. He seemed to be threading flowers into strands of hair at her temples. Their heady fragrance wafted up to her. Sharmeen strained to kiss his lips but he was teasing, cupping her face in his hands and showering her cheeks and forehead with soft kisses. Sharmeen wanted more. For the second time today, Zara felt like a voyeur but she forced herself to watch, assess Kamran's body language. He was rejecting her advances yet his actions were drenched in tenderness. There was nothing lascivious in his manner, only deep, romantic affection. His ridiculous dress sense gave nothing away, but his behaviour with Sharmeen left Zara in no doubt about his respect and affection.

I must warn them before Saif gets down there, she thought. She leant over the wall, anxiously reminding herself that though she could see clearly from above, the bushes and trees would obscure the lovers from anyone in the dining room below. She craned her neck round to see if she could catch sight of the French windows and saw a shadow against the glass.

'Saif!' she called. Surely he wasn't downstairs already. There was no reply. She looked down into the inner courtyard. Jay was just stepping out from the formal dining room as Saif turned at the bottom of the stone stairway to greet him.

'Tea in the drawing room?' he said, leading the way.

'I noticed how well the plants are doing,' Jay commented, leaning down to flowering shrubs. 'Guruji's green fingers?'

As he spoke he looked directly at Zara. *'I'll delay him,'* his eyes seemed to say. *'Warn them.'* He had clearly spotted them as he passed the path to the Oval Garden.

Zara stepped swiftly back into the long drawing room and through it into the terrace. She looked across the Oval Garden. Sharmeen's hands were in Kamran's hair, scratching, drawing his face down to hers.

'Shhht!' Zara hissed.

Kamran heard her as he grasped Sharmeen's wrists and brought them down to his sides. He looked up at Zara, slowly reading her warning signals: *There are people coming into the dining room.* He put an arm around Sharmeen and pulled her out of sight.

Zara closed her eyes with relief then opened them in panic. For that blink of an instant her vision had been entirely filled with Jay's eyes, an intimate look that passed between them, making words unnecessary. She was trembling.

'This is why I kept away from Trivikram so long,' Zara thought, suddenly too drained to stop her mind drifting into forbidden avenues. 'The unfinished business.'

Her mind was awash with memories of her first two years in Oxford – two years of such closeness, neither she nor Jay could have imagined they would one day be virtual strangers. In fact, they had known each other better even the first time they met up at Brown's because they had played together as children. Jay had invited her to keep his promise to Saif but their common background helped them relax quickly in a new environment. They met often that first term to reminisce, or comfort each other when they missed home and, finally, because they were in love.

'Thank you soooo much, Aunty Zara. My sweet-sweet aunt,' Sharmeen emerged from the terrace stairs and startled her back into the moment.

Pebbles was waiting at the top of the gallery. 'You weren't in the Oval Garden, were you?' she snapped.

Sharmeen dropped her head. 'I like it there.'

'Well,' Pebbles said, 'I suppose it's okay if you were with your aunt.' She looked at Zara. 'I'm not too keen on her hanging around the Oval Garden or her grandmother's terrace. There's an unmarried man there – I don't want any gossip.'

Sharmeen ran down the gallery, scowling. 'I'm not a kid, Mummy. You shouldn't ...' The rest of her words were lost as Pebbles called out instructions for tea.

'Come,' she said to Zara. 'Let's see what English delights you can make for tea. His Highness is staying.'

Zara wanted to feign a headache and go to sleep. It was ridiculous how the moment's exchange with Jay had unnerved her. But

Pebbles led her to the pantry by the new kitchen and began lining up a row of baking ingredients.

'You're good at baking, no? How about you bake a cake? No, maybe so soon after the funeral it's better to bake something savoury.'

Saif was engrossed in some documents when Pebbles and Zara joined them in the drawing room downstairs. Jay stood up to greet them as they entered. Saif looked up briefly.

'Karan has found a man called Shroff, a top legal mind with sound contacts and good advisors if we need them further down the line,' Jay explained.

Pebbles gestured to Millo to set down the tray, and picked up a plate. 'Cheese scones,' she announced, passing the plate to Jay. 'Very British. Zara, you must teach Razia. This will really catch on round here. Try it, Maharaja Sa, tell us what you think.'

She pushed forward a Wedgwood plate, thin, transparent glass tinged with green and edged with gold. Zara's gaze tangled in the white whorls that circled out from a central point on the plate, and it was a moment before she noticed Jay looking at her.

'So you've become a good cook?'

No one would read anything into that remark but to Zara it brought home a whirlpool of memories of the late eighties, towards the end of her first year. It was 'naught' term and Jay was preparing diligently for his Masters. He'd spent most of the night at his friend's house, working through statistics for his thesis.

Jay took studies far more seriously than she ever could. It was part of the noblesse oblige, the duty to his family, the debt to destiny. And this release from the state had been hard-won, a reward for the years spent in the army.

The telephone rang at five in the morning.

'Zara. I'm at the police station. You're my phone call.'

She could hardly open her eyes. 'Oh Jay, stop messing about. It's five.'

'I'm serious. I need my passport and the car papers from the flat. Bring them to the police station. Please.'

'You are serious.'

She pulled on her jeans and ran all the way to his flat and then the police station. The police apologized. There had been several car thefts in the area and when they'd seen him driving around in a brand-new Mercedes in the wee hours, they'd assumed he had stolen it.

'He wouldn't believe me,' Jay mimicked the scornful look, the jeering tone of the officer looking at his scruffy clothes, his overgrown beard, his bleary eyes. 'So I told him I was the Maharaja of Trivikram.' Jay paused, chuckling. 'You know what he said? He said, "And I'm the Shah of Iran. But you still go'a come down the station." '

As they tumbled into her flat, exhausted, Jay told her he was starving, then dropped on the sofa and fell into a deep sleep. When he woke up, she brought him to the table with a flourish. A carefully prepared Indian meal awaited him.

'So you've finally used those spices – do they work after all these months?'

'Try it!' Zara watched his reaction. It looked and smelled authentic. Her neighbours had already commented on the 'strong' smells as she'd raced out earlier to buy some yogurt but she was too excited to do more than say a quick 'sorry'.

'Aren't you eating?' Jay was piling food on to his plate.

She shook her head. 'I was tasting as I cooked.'

Jay took an enormous morsel of lamb qorma and stopped, looking startled.

'What?' She pounced on him. 'What's wrong?'

'Wrong?' Jay blurted. 'Nothing! I'm amazed this is so good.'

She dipped a piece of naan into the sauce, popped it in her mouth and nearly choked. It tasted burnt and, as Aunt Hana might have said, 'toxically salty'.

'I must have added a second dose of salt. For god's sake, Jay. Why did you eat it?'

'It was the food of love,' he said, looking dazed. 'It was delicious.'

Afterwards they went to the Grand Cafe and had champagne and scones with a selection of little sandwiches with the crusts cut away just like the ones she and her mother had made before she left.

She looked around the brown living room, coming back into the moment.

'This is delicious,' Jay bit in, catching the crumbs on his napkin. 'Do you remember the scones at the Grand Cafe?'

'I do,' Zara murmured. She was suddenly glad she had baked cheese scones instead of the Grand Cafe kind. She turned to the others. 'It's a bit of a tradition in Oxford.'

Pebbles looked delighted. 'Maybe you shouldn't teach Razia,' she said. 'I'll make this my own little specialty. The only thing my mother used to get nostalgic about was scones with clotted cream and strawberry jam.'

'Time,' Jay mused, seeming to linger on the word. He took another morsel of his scone. 'You can never get it back. Or go back and change the past.'

'Philosophical.' Saif raised his head from the papers scattered on the table. He must have been concentrating hard because his forehead was still creased. Zara poured herself some savoury lassi from a cut-glass jug and sat back, relieved that Jay had temporarily, at least, been interrupted. She would try to look unconcerned. What did Jay want to bring back? They were both married now, he with children, politics and matters of dynasty; she with a husband, the law and her mission to find a way forward for women like Parveen. What did he want? A sordid little affair? A quick tumble in bed and poof, the trauma of their abrupt parting sublimated? But she was being unfair. Jay had made no such suggestion.

After that first term, they had become inseparable. Both had been scheduled to fly back to Trivikram for Easter but they managed to cancel their plans and stayed on, together, in Oxford. It would have been impossible to meet in Trivikram.

'No doubt,' Jay had said, 'we could do what hundreds of Indian lovers do and meet in secret but I couldn't lie to Saif. Nor could you.'

'You know you're a bit of an old man, sometimes, don't you?' she teased but regretted her faux pas when he looked uncomfortable. He found the age difference a little disturbing – at twenty-six, he was a few years older than most students and a full eight years older than Zara. 'I agree,' she conceded, squeezing his arm. 'Everyone knows everyone's business in Qila. Besides, I'd never been out alone in my life until I came here.'

Stella thought it was 'mind-boggling'. And it certainly brought home the contrast between the societies of the subcontinent and Britain, where Zara and Jay had reconnected and loved. It was stark and, for the first time, despite being able to understand both sides well, she had seen insurmountable obstacles to her happiness. Neither one spoke of them, revelling in the freedoms of the here and now. But as 'trinity' came to an end and the long summer break approached, they were both ready to go home.

'We can tell Saif how we feel or ...' she stopped, seeing the alarm on Jay's face.

'We can't tell Saif ...' he broke off, reflecting. 'Not yet, anyway.'

'Because ...?' Zara asked.

'Well, it's all so new. We have to work out what we're going to say, size up how he feels, choose the right moment.'

Zara told Stella she felt unsure after that discussion if Jay wanted to be with her but she would not debase herself by asking. Stella thought her old-fashioned.

'I know you're my best friend, Zara,' she said. 'But sometimes I just don't understand you. Ask the man what he wants. He's old enough to know, surely?'

Zara hedged. Being comfortable in two cultures should have been a good thing but, in fact, she ended up feeling awkward and apologetic about both. 'Jay probably feels it's a breach of trust. Saif trusted him ...'

'But what's he done wrong?' Stella's eyes widened. 'He hasn't even deflowered you.' Her hand flew to her mouth. 'Do you think he's a virgin? I call that downright honourable.' She rolled her eyes and grimaced. 'Rather you than me.'

Zara's face grew hot. 'It's hard to understand, I know.'

'I admit that, gladly,' Stella replied. 'He's old, he won't sleep with you and he's scared to tell Saif he's in love with you. That makes him downright weird.'

Zara could see how it must look from Stella's position. The protocol of love was very different in their countries, and her situation was further complicated by the association between the Ramzis and the Vamanas. Jay suggested they avoid each other altogether over the summer, Zara thought the suggestion outrageous. In the end, Sita Devi arranged a trip to the mountains because her doctor had recommended a cooler climate and purer air, and so Jay spent hardly any time at all in Trivikram that summer.

But back in Oxford they fell more passionately in love. That was how it was for several months. He would sweep her off her feet with extravagant gestures, take her to exotic locations all over England to declare his love. He would wine her and dine her and recite love poetry as they sat holding hands, looking out over a beauty spot. They'd watch a Highland loch solid with water lilies, a Welsh waterfall where the salmon leapt as they swam against the tide or a Cornish cove overlooked by craggy cliffs topped with green.

'Please,' she begged him one day as they picnicked on the grass after he'd recited a particularly sentimental poem. 'Stop writing poetry. There is too much good poetry around to justify such dreadful stuff. A poet you are not.'

Jay slapped his hand to his heart. 'You've broken it,' he said. 'I was up all night pouring it on to paper for you – and now you've broken it.'

'Well then, it must have been empty and useless,' she replied. 'Tonight, please, I beg of you, catch up on your sleep. Leave the verse-making to real poets.'

Sometimes she giggled, too, as he struggled to pronounce the complex sounds of Urdu. But Jay was undeterred.

'Correct me,' he demanded. 'Teach me how to say it right, you soulless creature.'

La belle dame sans merci, he had called her one day, telling her the story of the exquisite fairy maidens who took over the hearts and minds of poor innocent princes and left them in thrall, to perish and die.

'Will you do that to me?' he asked her one day, unexpectedly. She felt his concern, physically, like the sensation left behind by the sting of an apparently harmless plant. 'How will all this turn out, Zara?'

The reference to Keats' poem had unfortunate echoes. She had heard the term used to describe her mother. The air felt suddenly heavy.

'I love you, Zara,' Jay said, running his forefinger through the grass, raising himself on his elbow. 'I want to marry you. I don't want to have a relationship and then leave you to ...'

'Become like my mother?' She had to honour his directness. 'Wandering from ... who knows where to where.'

Jay looked sad, staring up at the clouds, and she watched him with something she might have defined as pride. Nyla remained a romantic presence among those who remembered her. Jay stroked Zara's hand.

'People used to say your mother's feet never touched the ground, you could never get the proper measure of her, she didn't allow herself to show much.' He plucked at the grass, reflecting. 'I've always thought of her as the lady whose grief everyone forgot. It must have been hard for you when she left.'

He kissed her then for the first time. And it was as if the cosmos was being created all over again. As if she suddenly knew that ecstasy was merely the space in the interstices of sadness. The profound war between races and religions suddenly became personal.

'Don't you, Zara?' Pebbles voice was saying. Zara was relieved to return to the present. 'I was just telling Jay you want to go to Ahmedabad,' Pebbles said.

'I'm not going to let you run away before you've visited the lodge,' Jay said. Zara felt on edge. Had anyone noticed the intensity in his voice and his gaze? 'It's been entirely refurbished,' he said. 'We'll do a bit of walking, a bit of hunting. Then a venison-and-wild fowl barbecue by the lily pond.'

He looked at Saif and Pebbles. 'Shall we leave tomorrow afternoon? We could be back to catch the express to Ahmedabad the day after. What do you say?'

Zara was startled. They had fantasized about a lily pond and a flowering arbour in the Lodge when they were in Oxford. They'd worked out where it would be sited away from prying eyes, which trees they'd plant and which flowers would grow there. Because if they were forced to part then the lily pond was going to be their meeting place. They pretended it was an elaborate joke but the motif of star-crossed lovers hung heavily over them, and the intensity of their planning and the precision of design had made their plan very real.

There was a soft knock on the open door. 'May I enter, Your Highness? Shaikh Saheb?' Karan Singh said as he came in, bowing. 'So sorry to interrupt ... there is an urgent communication from Sardar Shinde.'

'Shinde? I knew he'd come to his senses.' Jay sat up.

Karan bowed his head. 'Shinde filed an injunction to close down the Academy and suspend all related works effective immediately.'

Saif put down his pen and walked slowly round the table. 'That is ridiculous,' he said in a cold, quiet voice.

'I know, sir,' Karan's mouth was obviously dry as he spoke. 'I told him there must be some mistake.'

'It's no mistake,' Saif said. 'This man is deliberately making trouble. Shinde can withdraw his claim or he can find out the hard way that nothing will prevent us fulfilling our commitments.'

Jay's face creased into a slow, proud smile. Pebbles smiled, too, slightly tearful.

'At last,' she said. 'At last you're going to stand up to them.'

Jay rose. 'Good thing we're going to the lodge,' he said. 'It's probably the best place to discuss how to deal with this Shinde.'

25

Zara decided to be gracious. She resented being back in Sita Devi's apartment after virtually being turned out on her last visit. But Pebbles had been in such a flutter, rushing in with her hair dripping, insisting Zara 'freshen up' immediately and go down to the car 'Her Highness Rajmata has kindly sent'. Now they were playing out a strange scenario. Sita Devi nodded a greeting and motioned her to come in, then gestured again to offer her a seat.

'My son has invited you to the hunting lodge,' Sita Devi said.

Zara was about to say that Saif and Pebbles were invited, too, but reminded herself she owed the Rajmata no explanation. 'Is that what he told you?'

Sita Devi's laugh was bitter. 'Jay sent a forward party to prepare for y'all.' She was silent for a few moments, assessing Zara. 'I wish you to refuse the invitation.'

Zara heard the sound of her own laugh, ugly, like an eruption.

Sita Devi was still, distant. 'Maybe the break-up of a marriage is funny for you. For me, marriage is dharma. I endured much to remain by my husband's side and support him. No thanks to your mother.'

Hana had told her about an encounter between the two women but surely Sita Devi would not have read anything into that. Hari and Sita had invited the Ramzis to a small private dinner on one of Saif's visits to Trivikram. Nyla was there, recently widowed. After dinner some of the guests performed – a poet recited some fresh verse, a lady-in-waiting famous for her bhajan singing, sang for them. When she finished, the musical atmosphere lingered.

'What talented friends we have, Sita,' Hari said. 'Is there anyone else we can persuade to sing for us? We're among friends here. Begum Saheb?'

Hana shrank into her chair. 'Not me. I can't ...' But all eyes turned on her.

'Nyla,' she said. 'My sister has a beautiful voice. Sing, Nyla.'

Nyla sang without the customary false protest, as if she could not hold the song inside anymore.

Khusrau on my wedding night I went to my lover's land
My heart my Love's, my body mine – thus body and heart did blend.

The waves of melody, slow, contemplative, referred to union – the union of the Lover with the Beloved – the devotee with the divine. Nyla's loss loomed large in the room. Hana could feel the tears prickling inside her eyes. She could see through lowered lashes that others, too, were moved.

And then, after a moment's pause, just long enough to make people wonder if she would continue, Nyla resumed her song. The slow introduction was exploding now into a wild, desperate lament of longing.

My youth's passing away, Beloved, return to me soon.
My saffron beloved, come Lord, grace me, come to me soon.

The maand raga melody was the soul and spirit of these parts, so everyone responded from their depths. Hana was always struck by the easy acceptance from her restrained society of the naked longing and stark desire expressed in the lyrics. The meaning, she thought, was mellowed by familiarity, tradition and the passage of centuries, contextualized by spiritual resonance. The listener reacted only to the lingering pain, love of the land, an understanding of something lost flickering just out of reach. And that evening, there was the added dimension of Nyla's recent loss. Widowhood stretched ahead of her. She was the essence of innocent youth at the sacrificial altar. The bride bereft on her wedding bed. Every trill, every nuance, every syllable vibrated with her recent tragedy.

All too soon, her song ended. For several moments the audience sat stunned by something being taken away. Slowly, Hari started to clap. Sultan followed suit. It was almost a travesty to fill the space sanctified by Nyla's voice but everyone joined them.

'Do you know,' the lady-in-waiting said, 'Maharani Sita Devi Sa has a beautiful voice, too. I have been honoured to hear her in her prayer chamber.'

Sita protested. She looked at her husband. He sat still, dignified, choosing not to intervene.

'Please, Maharani Saheb. Sing for us. A bhajan, maybe.'

To resist anymore in the face of her guests' pleading would have been crass. Sita Devi cleared her throat and began to sing. Even Hana was surprised. The sedate, reserved matron, still a little heavy and soft from giving birth to her fourth child, opened her throat and produced the trained, controlled tones of a professional. Her song was a bhajan, a hymn, the impassioned love song of the devotee Radha yearning for Krishna, her beloved flute-playing god. She sang just one verse so as not to offend her guests by refusing. Then she looked pointedly at Nyla and stopped. There was a challenge in that look that Hana was sure no one missed.

Early the next morning, Sita arrived at the fort. She told Hana that after the guests left, Hari took her to their bedroom and hit her – on her face, on her back, on her skull. Each time he struck her, he accused her of disgracing him before his guests by behaving like a whore.

'How dare he?' Hana breathed. 'How damn well dare he?' She stood up. 'Sultan doesn't speak much to me anymore but he's going to do something about this.'

Sita grabbed her hand, forced her to sit down. 'Hana, no. It'll make things worse. I should have known it would be wrong in the circumstances. That it would bring back memories for Hari.'

Hana was intrigued.

'The singing,' Sita explained. 'Couldn't you tell my voice is trained?'

'I don't understand.'

'I was a professional, Hana. If it hadn't been for Hari I really would have ended up a whore.'

Hana hugged her fiercely and Sita crumpled into her like an infant. Vulnerable and desperate, Sita Devi, Maharani of Trivikrampur confessed that her father, a younger cousin of a ruling family from south India, had gambled away all his wealth and turned to alcohol. One day, he heard her singing and discovered a potential source of income. Her mother and her brothers begged him to spare her, but he was determined she would be a recording artist and make him millions. He moved his family to Ahmedabad, where he thought she would have more opportunities. His family stopped helping him. A classical singer he knew was instructed by a local prince to set up a small concert, and Sita was invited to make her debut. The prince was entertaining an important maharaja and wanted to make an impression. As he delivered her there, her father told her he permitted her to do what was necessary as long as she was paid above a certain sum.

The maharaja was Hari. He spoke to her after the others left and discovered who she was, how she came to be here. She had chosen a hymn to the terrible power of Mother Kali, hoping it would protect her from ruin. He told her later that he had fallen in love with her dignity and modesty and that even as she performed she had the air of a goddess, pure and chaste.

'He was right,' Hana said, cradling her friend, stroking her hair. 'You are all those things, dignified and modest and chaste. And if he's forgotten, then he's the one who should be beaten, not you.'

Sita gasped and pulled away. 'Don't talk about him like that, Hana. Hari's my husband. Besides, I have nowhere else to go. I can't go back to my family. He supports them, anyway.'

'Would you stay for that?'

She shook her head. 'I love him. If it was not for him god knows what might have happened. Till now he's given me a perfect life.'

Hana blamed herself. If she had not asked Nyla to sing, the apparently charmed evening would not have become an unsavoury drama – all for a song. She exiled Nyla to the sanctuary at Ramzi Bagh. A retreat had been set up near the main centre where women, mostly bereaved women, went to meditate upon their life and future and took instruction from the Sufis. Nyla would heal her wounds and decide what to do with her life. And Sita would have the opportunity to work things out with Hari.

Sita Devi broke into Zara's reverie. 'Despite what you may think, this request is not selfish. You may never know why I'm asking – but you would thank me for averting a calamity. It is to do with the generations past and how they affect the present. Don't question me. Just stay away from Jay. He is a Vamana – his duty to uphold right is far more than that of ordinary people. Vamana, you may know, was the first incarnation of Lord Vishnu. That is Jay's ancestry. He is descended from God. When gods break the rules, their punishment is visited on hundreds of generations to come.'

Zara locked her fingers around her knees and bowed her head. She could see Sita Devi struggling to conceal her anxiety. Why should she care about this woman who had abandoned Aunty Hana and lost no opportunity to revile Nyla and who had taken Jay from her? Still, despite herself, she felt for her.

'I promise to think about it.'

Sita Devi reached for an envelope by her desk. 'It is from my lawyer. Please give it to Pir Saheb. I took the initiative to oppose the injunction. It was withdrawn an hour ago.'

26

Jay grabbed a child's rubber ball from the glove compartment as he jumped out of his jeep, threw it high in the air and leapt up after it as the others climbed out. The resident driver at the hunting lodge climbed into the seat and drove off to park the car.

'The Rajmata has turned up trumps!' Jay said. 'Who would have thought it?'

Pebbles laughed. 'Your Highness underestimates Rajmata Sa,' she said. 'She's an exceptionally great lady. And so powerful now. But amazing she broke the news to Zara.'

Zara was light-headed with relief. Saif had been lucky and the trouble had gone away this time, but she felt a certain unease. This was not the end of Shinde.

'I think I'll work in the garden for a bit,' Saif said.

Jay frowned. 'Some tea before that?'

'Send it to me, in a mug.' Saif walked towards a thicket where an ancient gardener was working.

Zara watched him pat the man's back and fold his hands in response to the man's greeting before looking through some of the tools laid out on the grass. The gardener pointed proudly to his own implements neatly arranged in the pockets of a sheath strapped to his body, then turned to point to the columns of rose bushes. Saif shook his head, chose a couple of long-handled implements and stalked away into the distance.

'He's going to find some scraggy land,' Pebbles said. 'Somewhere he can work off energy and think. He always needs scraggy, unyielding ground when he's thinking.'

'Then, in a few weeks, plants and shoots appear and flowers grow,' Jay said. But he looked worried.

'He's struggling, I know,' Zara said, softly. 'He's got a lot on his mind.'

Pebbles sighed. 'He complicates his own life,' she said. 'Sometimes you're allowed to just be pleased about something, or angry – whatever.'

Zara agreed. 'Sometimes, as Peter says, a cigar is just a cigar.'

'I presume he credits it properly to Mr Freud?'

Zara was surprised by the sharp note in Jay's voice.

'Dr Freud, actually,' she said.

She walked over to Sharmeen who was fiddling with her mobile phone, restlessly moving from one spot to another.

'I can't get a signal.' The girl looked up at the large building in its acres of land, snuggling in a semi-circle of forested hills. 'It's because we're in some godforsaken ...'

'Tea in the garden?' Jay called, pointing to a circular area, part paved and part lawn. He led them to the chairs.

After tea, they went in search of Saif. He was standing by a pit, stripped to the waist and surrounded by mounds of clay. 'Good rose soil. But you've already got enough of those, I reckon.'

'What, then?' Jay asked. 'I'll tell the gardener.'

'No,' Saif said looking at his handiwork. 'I'll do it.'

'What will you grow, Abba?' Sharmeen asked.

'I think, my darling,' Saif said, 'I'll make a medicine wheel and fill it with plants which are good for our health and well-being. I'll do it slowly and I'll do it myself.'

'All praise to the Rajguru,' Jay said. 'But the gardener can at least buy the seeds and ...'

'I'll get them from Bowl Lake,' Saif said. 'I know those plants are effective.'

A liveried butler came to tell them it was time to eat. At the far end of the garden where tea had been served, three men, similarly dressed, stood at an enormous barbecue and a row of terracotta tandoors. The atmosphere smelled vaguely of a chemical used to dispel mosquitoes from the rooms; outside, small smoking coils were dotted around to discourage them.

Politics seemed to take over and Zara listened with interest. There was something visceral and impulsive about politics here that was, to her, almost unconvincing.

'Enough of these discussions,' Pebbles said. 'My brain's exhausted.' She and Saif drifted off to bed around 10.30. Sharmeen, sullen because she had been 'forced' to come, had spent the afternoon slinking off to remote corners of the lodge, returning more petulant after each disappearance.

'There's no signal area anywhere, Aunty Zara,' she complained, corralling Zara in a corner of the shrubbery. 'Nowhere. Why did we have to come here just before Kamran's going away?' She stamped her foot. 'Don't want to be in this stupid place.'

'You couldn't be left alone, Sharmeen, you know that.'

'Alone? The place is full-ll of people. Not fair!'

Zara said a silent thanks – left alone for a day with Kamran, Sharmeen might well break down his resistance. The horrors of the girl getting pregnant flashed through her mind. Here in Trivikram, the position of the family would complicate the issues ten-fold. Zara shuddered – it was far better to put up with her adolescent grumbling. Around midnight, Sharmeen accepted that her grumpiness would not persuade anyone to return to Trivikram and went to sleep.

Alone in the garden with Jay, Zara looked around her. The lights embedded in the ground created a dusky space around the paved area where they sat framed by frangipani trees and jacaranda. She inhaled long and deep. 'I can smell jasmine,' she said, looking around for the source of the fragrance.

Jay stood up and offered her his hand, guiding her past the carpet of purple jacaranda blossom into a grotto.

'Look here.' He closed his eyes and inhaled. The smell was exquisite. '*Gladiolus jasminoides*.'

'Motia!' Fat round buds exploding with sensational scent. 'I'd forgotten – you don't see them much in London.'

She stopped, overwhelmed by wistfulness for something lost. 'I bought some once, from a nursery in Richmond. Soon after you left. The florist said they had to be fed mineral water.' She bent, breathing their scent. 'They died anyway.' The sound that came from her was neither laugh nor sob but something between. 'I'm prattling.'

'As I recall,' Jay said, his voice soft, 'you do that when there's something you don't want to say.'

She turned to him. 'Why, Jay? Why? Why all this when ...?'

'I wanted to redeem some part of what we had – all that was left unlived.'

'And this is your memorial.'

'A promise fulfilled.'

'If we can't be together,' she repeated slowly, *'then I'll build a perfect spot in the lodge, hidden away from prying eyes where we will consummate our love.'*

It had sounded romantic then but now she felt embarrassed. Still, she let him pull her close. She thought she heard him whisper, *'Beloved.'*

'My god, Zara,' he said now, his body perfectly still. 'I don't know how I've lived so long without you.'

She felt guilty. Her life had been full. There had been Peter, their romance passionate and exuberant and such a relief in contrast to the sad, sweet love before, beset with blocks from the start. In two years they had never slept together.

'I respect you too much,' Jay said. Zara knew this was true. If they were forced to part and she married someone else, she must be a virgin. It was expected in their society. Then one day they decided they could hold back no longer.

Zara bunked her tutorial and blew her monthly budget on flowers, Egyptian cotton sheets and a bottle of champagne which she put immediately on ice. She cleaned and tidied the flat and floated fragrant candles in ornate glass bowls. She hulled strawberries until her fingernails ached, then chopped them up and put them in crystal goblets in the fridge. Finally, she went into the shower, came out fresh and fragrant.

As her head surfaced between wispy fronds of lingerie, she looked at the clock. The light on the telephone was flashing. He must have called while she was in the shower. She stabbed the button.

'Zara – I'm at Heathrow. My mother's had a cardiac arrest. The doctor says it's serious.' His voice changed, dropped. 'I am *so sorry, beloved. So sorry*. I love you. Will always love you.' His voice changed again. 'I'll be in touch as soon as I can.'

As soon as I can. That was not Jay's style. He was brought up a maharaja – authoritative, decisive, confident. It was only in matters of state and dynasty that he handed over his agency. She knew, in that moment, that Jay would never put his personal needs or desires above those of his birth.

She wanted to tell him now how she had watched her world freeze. If Sita Devi died he would be instantly drawn into matters of state. If she survived he would stay by her side to run affairs. Zara had lost him. The idyll was over. The dream had ended.

She slept in the cotton sheets while the strawberries rotted in the fridge and the champagne grew lukewarm in the bucket. Four days later, Stella banged on the door so long and so hard, that Zara heaved herself out of bed and opened it to stop her smashing it in.

'I've just heard he's gone,' Stella said, looking stricken. 'Bastard!'

Three weeks later Jay wrote to say his mother had arranged his wedding to a princess from Bengal because she wished to see him married before she died. Hana told her that the sixteen-year-old maharani, Anapurna, was provincial, self-indulgent, skittish and uneducated.

All these years later, the pain was so fresh as she stood in the circle of Jay's arms in the grotto of their fantasy, her head resting on his chest, that it was like being in that moment again. Jay raised her face to his, searched it. He guided a strand of hair from her cheek to her hairline. His finger stroked her eyelids, traced her brow. She could feel his breath on her face.

She moved closer. Jay held her tight. He kissed her hair, her neck then slowly, he kissed her mouth. She knew the shape of his lips as if there had never been an interruption.

'What a damned coward I was.' His voice was hard. 'I would happily have given up all this ...' She turned her face up to his. 'I blamed my mother at first. But it was my own weakness. My fault. My mother only stopped ...'

Zara froze. Sita Devi! What had she been trying to tell her? Zara shook her head to clear the echoing in her ears and looked around to see where the noise was coming from.

'This is not a selfish request. A calamity brought about by past generations. Nyla had something to do with it.'

Zara pulled away from Jay and he grasped a branch to steady himself.

'No, no,' she said. 'Get away from me.'

Jay was beside her, trying to calm her. 'Zara, I'm so sorry. I thought ... I ...'

'You don't understand,' she heard herself repeating. At last, she calmed down enough to speak.

'Zara? What is it? What happened?'

Zara clenched her eyes and slumped forward, her arms folded over her stomach. 'I was with your mother today. I think ... I think she was saying we have the same father.'

27

Jay had said something when she told him what she thought but she could not remember because a phrase repeated itself in her mind in time to the continuously clacking engine of the train to Ahmedabad. 'It can't be true. It can't be true.' Or was it: 'She's lying a-gain. She's lying a-gain'?

If Sita was telling the truth why had she not been more explicit? The veiled references, the nods to a past amour between Hari and Nyla suggested that the reality was unbearable for Sita. It was unlike her to choose subtlety over bluntness.

She took out her mobile and clicked on Sita Devi's number.

'What happened?' Sita Devi said when she heard her voice. 'Did anything happen?'

'No,' Zara replied. 'Is he my brother?' Zara heard a sharp intake of breath.

'I can't say anything.'

Zara's voice was sharp. 'You owe me the truth.'

'All I know is, your mother came here a widow. Late His Highness was clearly ... interested. When she left to go back to Pakistan you could see she was pregnant. Some months later, she had a baby. A girl. You. That is the simple truth as Vishnu-god is my witness. May he judge me if I'm lying.'

Zara locked herself in her compartment then and phoned Stella.

'Oh fuck!' Stella gasped. 'Thank god for his self-restraint! I used to think he's mad. But thank goodness for his madness. Oh god, Zara, how awful. Are you sure?'

'Sita Devi swore it was true. I don't believe she would swear to a lie.'

'I saw a documentary once about how blood families have a tendency to fall in love if they haven't grown up together.' She stopped. 'Wrong thing to say. Sorry. Sorry, Zara. I'm not good at this. Talk to Peter.'

Zara needed to hear Peter's voice, his reassurance. She phoned him. 'I've had a terrible shock,' she said, holding back the sobs. She desperately wanted to avoid hurting him. 'Sita Devi says my mother had an affair with Hari Vamana – I'm the result.' She thought of Peter, alone. Would he guess she had been on the verge of betraying him? His voice was strong and warm.

'Do you want me to come?' She did still matter to him. She felt an unexpected yearning to be near him. She did still matter to him.

'I feel completely lost, Peter. I feel adrift – like a severed kite. It's like a nightmare I used to have as a kid, of levitating above Qila, showing off, then suddenly I'd realize I couldn't get myself down.'

'I could be there in a couple of days.'

'I have to resolve this myself, Peter.' He had often told her she was running away; well, she would hold her ground now, though everything inside her screamed to get on a plane and fly back to the safety of home. She had promises to keep – to Aunty Hana and to Parveen. Neither one could release her from her vows.

She had never doubted that Jameel Usman was her father, a loving husband who died young. In her grief, Nyla had not noticed the signs of pregnancy. She returned to Pakistan to her husband's family, to deliver Zara. Things did not work out but because Nyla inherited her husband's vast personal empire plus his interest in Usman Industries. His family made a deal: Nyla gave them all they wanted, except Zara, and took to an itinerant life with the still enormous fortune she had left and a massive trust fund for Zara. Zara never had a home with Nyla; instead, she was deposited with Hana for long spells while her mother travelled the world chasing secret dreams.

Yesterday, standing in the fantasy bower made for her by Jay, Nyla lost her father, too. Fleetingly, she imagined asking Nyla about the situation – but she had been in the fantasy before.

As the train pulled into Ahmedabad station, she felt nauseous.

28

76 Chandni Marg. The big tea house. A woman would be waiting to meet Zara at three. It was just twelve noon. She had time to book into her hotel and afterwards take a taxi to see Hirani, jeweller to the rulers of Gujarat. He had always been a mystery figure to Zara as she grew up. The first time she'd visited him with Nyla, she'd experienced surprise upon surprise. The gateway to his establishment was a tiny wooden door, embedded in a plaster wall on a narrow, curving street. The unpretentious door swung back to reveal eight stone steps, steep and narrow, leading to another door, this one much grander, dark teak, finely carved and inlaid with ivory and minute mirrors. It opened on to a narrow balcony, running above the edge of the courtyard like the one in Qila. Below, the inner courtyard was alive with activity. Men, women and children worked in the open, artisans in the making, and the children of retired craftsmen whose skills were in danger of being forgotten.

There was a bell at the door now. Zara pressed it and immediately a man opened it. 'I've come from Qila, Trivikrampur,' Zara said.

'Lalaji is ready for you,' the man replied, bowing deeply. 'Follow me, please.'

Though he led the way, everything about him communicated respect and humility. His saffron-tinged safa sat proudly on his head and his back and shoulders were as straight as if he had been presenting a martial award.

A smoky fragrance infused the air as Zara approached Hirani's inner sanctum. *Sandalwood*, Zara thought. *Nothing changes in this place.*

The attendant opened the door slightly and looked in. 'Lalaji, Sahebzadi Zara from Qila.' He stepped back, nodded, pushed the door wide open. Hirani put both his hands to his face, fingers spread, signalling the end of his prayers. He rose to his feet and came to the door. This was one of the mysteries about this man. No one knew his religion. His surname was ambiguous and so was his honorific. The title 'lala' traditionally referred to Pathans of the Northwest Frontier Provinces but was widely used now. And his first name was pronounced Amar by those who assumed he was a Hindu, Aamer by those who thought him a Muslim, though Hana said this was irrelevant since no one ever used it. She said she had asked him once and he had responded with a verse from the poet Mir.

The bigoted Vaiz thinks me a kafir, the kafir thinks I'm a Mussalman
But, why does it not occur to them that I'm merely human?

'Aaiye, aaiye,' Lalaji said, ushering her in. 'It's been a long time. I last saw you when you were so big.' He tapped himself mid-thigh with the side of his palm. 'A little girl.' He turned to the attendant hovering in the doorway. 'Bring drinks, hot and cold.'

'Please, Lalaji,' Zara said. 'No formality. I'm fine.'

'How can that be?' Lalaji insisted.

Zara remembered the protocol. She had no wish to offend Lalaji. 'Some water will be nice.'

Lalaji nodded, pleased. 'Bring cold water ...'

Lalaji spoke fluently in Hindi softly tinged with the musical rhythms and phrases of Saurashtra. 'How is Pir Saheb? Well, I hope. May the Lord keep the family strong in their loss.'

Zara felt an unexpected surge of emotion. Lalaji didn't miss a trick.

'Be strong,' he said, pointing upwards with his forefinger. 'He will give you strength. People do not belong to us, they belong to Him. When someone is called away, the Muslims say, *'Inna i'illahi wa'inna alaihi raji'un – Verily we belong to God and to him we will return.'*

That is where the soul is happiest – with him. Huzur Saheb was a good person. She'll be happy to cast off the burden of the body.'

Zara nodded. 'She asked me to complete some work for her,' she said, swallowing hard. 'Only she ... she ... went before she could explain. I believe she may have mentioned something ...' Zara could hardly complete her sentence.

'Peace,' Lalaji intoned. 'Be courageous. Aap sabr karo, Hukam. Sab kuch theek ho jayega. Have patience, all will be well.' He gazed into the smoke curling up in a triple spiral, his hands lying loosely together on his lap. 'Noor Jehan's bangles?'

Zara nodded. 'Could be.'

'Yes. I have heard they are lost.' He sighed. 'You wish me to tell you if I hear of their whereabouts?'

Zara nodded again. The attendant entered. He bowed and proffered the tray and Lalaji picked up a tumbler of chased silver studded with lapis lazuli and moonstone and held it out to Zara, making a bowl of his palms.

'We keep it in our matkas. The terracotta keeps it cool. Ice is also made from our own well-water.'

Zara took the water eagerly. She could taste the subtle tinge of earth. It infused her mind with memories of picnics on overcast days just after the rain had fallen or when it was expected, and the smell of grass and earth rose into the atmosphere. Once, on an outing at Trivikram dam, Nyla had clamped her shoulder so hard she would have screamed if Nyla had not put a finger to her lips.

'The peacock.'

Slowly, she pointed. Framed by a canopy of low-growing palm fronds was a peacock, rocking from one foot to another, his feathers beginning to rise from his sides until, within moments, his plume fanned out and filled the surrounding space. Jewel colours, amethyst, lapis, sapphire, emerald shimmered and glowed in a strange, majestic ritual, scattering rays of light extravagantly into the air.

'The power of memories is incomparable, is it not?' Lalaji's voice seemed to float above her consciousness, somewhere. 'Our desires gild them and enamel them, stud them with jewels and make them so much the creatures of our need. But tell me, Princess, do you really believe that your aunt would have summoned you all the way from England for the bangles?'

Zara's skin tingled. Hirani knew something. 'You don't think so?'

Lalaji shifted his position. 'You see, the bangles are significant. There is no doubt about that. But my feeling is that there is far more at stake.'

'Your feeling?'

'You see, when I spoke to Huzur Saheb, she was leading up to something far more important. Something no one else knew about. That was why she took all the trouble of coming here. To Ahmedabad.'

'Aunt Hana *came here*?' As far as she knew, Hana had not left Qila since Sultan's death twenty-odd years ago. Why had she come to see Hirani when he would willingly have visited her? Once more, Lalaji responded as if he'd heard the question in her mind.

'It was to do with privacy,' he said. 'Huzur Saheb was concerned that ... others should not know.'

Lalaji continued, slowly, faltering, as if playing for time. 'I believe, at least, that her request to you was connected to her visit here.'

Zara took a deep breath and tried to still herself. 'When? When did she visit?'

Lalaji considered a moment. 'Two, maybe one year back. I remember, two – it was one-two months before Pir Saheb's aunt returned to Qila. Huzur Saheb wanted my humble advice on ... how to get certain ancient artifacts out of the country and into Europe where they might be sold to a reputable international museum. But she did not wish them to be traced back to her.'

'And these artifacts?'

He shook his head. 'She said she would tell me when the time was right.' He hesitated. 'Not jewellery, for sure. A manuscript? But I cannot say. The object was not yet in her possession.'

'Not in her possession? And you're sure it was not the bangles?'

'We spoke of the bangles. She said she had no use for them. She believed they had never found the wrists for which they were intended.' Lalaji shook his head. 'As you can imagine, I have been very much curious. But what struck me as most intriguing was to send something out of the country – something precious – when she has heirs here. I suspect it was to fund something else altogether. Something ... big.'

'You mean property abroad?'

'Perhaps,' Lalaji replied. 'Or a cause of some kind here, perhaps?'

Zara's heart contracted. 'A cause?'

'Something political.' Was Lalaji suggesting that Aunt Hana was involved in the communal riots? That she was financing a militant group?

Lalaji's voice continued: 'Some charitable operation? Like a girls' school, or a women's co-operative?'

He's fishing, Zara thought. Trying to discover what I know. And whose side are you on, she wondered, with your opaque name and your enigmatic life.

Zara took another gulp of water and stood up. 'You have been so helpful, Lalaji. It's good to see you after all this time. Everything here is just the same as before.' Lalaji stood up, too, his eyes alert. Zara smiled. 'If you think of anything that might help my search, please let me know.'

Lalaji inclined his head. 'It is my dharma to do so.'

Outside on the balcony, Zara looked down at the hustle and bustle of the artisans in the courtyard. The sun was high now and they had moved into the shade of the awnings and colonnades. The attendant with the saffron turban reappeared and guided her to the door, opened it and stood back. Zara slipped down the stairs, eager, for some reason, to get out of Hirani's environment and into the road. She walked along the street for a few moments, looking up and down for the car that had brought her here. There was no sign of it. It was probably parked on the wider, tarred road about fifty yards down.

She passed a bandhni shop. A woman and her child were unpicking the tie-and-dye threads with powerful but nimble tugs from a length of fabric, stretching it to reveal the gem-like colours created by the process.

'Mrs Zara?'

Zara started then turned to see a woman, tall for an Indian, wearing a muslin sari.

'I'm Kamini. We had an appointment to meet at Chandni Marg? I finished my meeting early so I thought I would wait for you here.'

'But how did you know ...?'

'Please don't worry, Mrs Zara. Everything's okay. You're safe in our hands.'

Kamini's English was fluent and melodious. But she was clearly not of the Indian elite who mainly spoke English.

'Shall we take the car?'

Kamini looked disdainful. 'Car? Definitely no.'

'I'll let him go, then,' Zara said. 'I'm not sure where he is.'

'Might be better to leave him here. He'll wait till you come back.'

Kamini's cloak-and-dagger manner was making Zara uneasy. 'He'll get terribly hot, and thirsty. He hasn't eaten yet.'

Kamini smiled. 'He's used to it. He'll be okay. He can look after himself. We should go.'

Used to what, Zara wondered. To being treated less than an animal? Their meeting could take an hour, maybe more. Was this man to be left in the baking heat of the bazaar?

Kamini was sizing her up; she could see it, wondering about these strange Indian women who came back with memsaab attitudes, thinking the locals needed to be looked after. Even Dilkash had been scornful when Nyla insisted on treating servants as equals.

'They'll jump on your head if you go on like this,' she'd squawked. 'And when you go, they'll be no good for anywhere. They'll think they can sit around wearing ankle-bells instead of working like ordinary servants. What do they benefit from your treatment? A queen for a week and back to slavery. Who is that good for?'

'Is Lalaji a good man?' Zara asked as Kamini glanced up at the jeweller's window.

Kamini shrugged again. It made her oddly unattractive. 'Who can tell? We heard he helped a lot of people during the troubles. We hear stories from both sides. He could be a great man.' She turned a corner and pulled Zara behind her. 'On the other hand, he could be a Mussolini. There's no way to know.'

Clearly, this was a culture of mistrust. Anyone could turn out to be a hidden enemy or a guardian angel – even Aunty Hana. People prepared for the first and were thankful for the second.

After a short, silent walk, Kamini stopped at a gleaming glass door proclaiming Reshma's Chaat Palace. Its brass handles shone with a high polish. A uniformed doorman stood outside the door, in a deep brown uniform edged in gold trim. He bowed then extended a gloved hand and opened the door. Kamini stood back.

Zara walked into the cool, womb-like silence of the room. It was a hot afternoon and the room was dark. Potential customers had clearly opted for an afternoon siesta. Zara felt suddenly weary, disheartened. Was this all a fool's errand, she wondered. Would a single one of these people ever manage to help her? Be willing, even? As she slipped behind the table, three men walked in.

Kamini turned to greet them, folding her hands. The men returned the gesture and then extended it to Zara as they pulled back chairs and settled in.

'Pleasure, ma'am. I am Samir. This is my colleague Aman. And Sahil.'

More ambiguous names: were they Hindu or Muslim? Zara sat up straight. *I mustn't get into this mindset. I don't care whether they are Muslim or Hindu. I have clients of all denominations. I'm here for all of them.* 'Save the women,' Parveen had said. She had not specified the religion.

Samir took the initiative. 'So you know our friend Swami Ramcharan?'

'I asked his advice about contacting this network.'

Samir was not enthusiastic. 'The swami is highly respected amongst the activists here – that's the reason we agreed to meet you. He is one of the few people who can be trusted.'

Aman spoke now. 'We have to be very careful. I mean, even people who are being deported, you know, it's possible that they, you know, can look helpless to you in England but here they have a power base.'

'Are you saying you can't help?'

Aman held up both palms. 'No, no, no. Only, we're saying, we can't rush in. We must think and plan carefully. If these people are trying to infiltrate then our operation can be destroyed.'

'I understand,' Zara replied. 'What exactly is your operation?'

The members of Ankahi exchanged glances. 'What did my uncle tell you?' Kamini asked.

'Swami Ramcharan is your uncle?'

'We're from the same village. What did he say?'

'Only that you have a wide network and you would help. And that there would be risks.'

Kamini looked doubtful.

Samir took over. 'You have to understand we have to be really careful. Our network is basically for protection of various of communities who might be getting into troubles through no faults of their own. Helpless people. If our identity or our work is disclosed to the wrong parties a lot of innocent people will be plunged into suffering.'

'Is there a way you can help?'

Sahil leaned forward. 'Please tell us why you did not approach a well-known organization?'

'As I told Swamiji,' Zara said, 'the danger arises when a woman is alone and without backing. The other networks find her work and a place to stay and then leave her to get on with it. But that's the problem; she's alone again and the trouble starts.'

There was silence in the group then Aman spoke. 'Are you aware that you could be at risk here in India?' He was looking down at his fingernails.

Zara shook her head. 'I haven't been here for ten years. No one knows me.'

Aman pulled out some sheets of crumpled paper from his pocket. 'Zara Hamilton, born Zara Usman in Pakistan. Thirty-four years of age. Human rights lawyer. Husband, Peter, English. Member of the Ramzi family of Trivikrampur and brought up by her aunt, recently deceased Hana Ramzi ...'

Zara felt goosebumps on her arms. 'That information is not secret or incriminating. Why should I be in danger?'

'They no longer need reason to be violent in this state, Mrs Zara.' Kamini's eyes were flashing, her face wore a ruthless expression and at the same time looked tragic. 'We have become primitive people. A savage streak has been released. The state ministers play on the fears and resentments of the people. They truly believe that we must kill all the Muslims or they will kill us. Even educated people.' She scrabbled around in her bag and brought out some pieces of paper. 'Read them. They are all reports from the English newspapers of India. Our own people are shocked and unable to understand the impulses of some people. Read them, Mrs Zara, and then ask me if we need to take any actions, even, to put ourselves into danger. Noth-thing. We simply need to be here, present. And then, you? You are rich. You are Muslim. You are connected with Pakistan. You are a lawyer in England. They will say you spoil our name and our reputation out there in UK. You work with the traitors we throw out and you corrupt our women, tell them we are the bad ones to upkeep our moral code. That they are right to run away and live alone in a country full of immoral people.'

Kamini sat forward, her elbows on the table, her face in her hands. She paused for a moment, catching her breath as Zara looked over the documents. Fascism is alive and living in Gujarat, wrote Arundhati Roy.

'These are two years old,' Zara responded. 'They are out of date.'

'They are not out of date. It is still occurring.' Aman's words seemed to fall, heavily, one by one, on to the wooden table. Kamini reached forward and snatched one of the papers back from Zara.

'This VHP leaflet. It is still in circulation. I saw them distributing it just last week.'

'Mrs Zara, please tell me one thing. Why did you come to Trivikrampur at this par-ticular time?' Kamini asked.

'My aunt was ill. She wanted me here. At the same time, my client killed herself because she had nowhere to return to in India. She asked me to do something for the women.'

Kamini's eyes filled up but her questioning remained strident.

'Best is, you talk to our Trivikrampur representative.' Samir scribbled on a piece of paper. 'Already there is very good work going on there.' He thrust the paper at her. 'This man, Talwar Barot, is very active member of our group. He will help you make plans.' He sat back in his chair and looked around the table with the air of a generous benefactor.

'Now, my friends, we will take tea and snacks.'

29

The fortress felt eerily quiet as Zara walked up to her room and took a bath. She had read the documents Kamini thrust at her at Reshma's and was overwhelmed by the prejudice her clients had experienced; that she had spoken to, and touched and even challenged survivors of such emotional brutality. Both sides of a conflict suffered and inflicted suffering. 'It is still occurring,' Aman had said, despite the change of government and the ongoing probes and inquiries of Parliament.

Zara shuddered as hard drops from the shower struck like pellets against her shoulders.

'Zara Bibi.' Littl'un was hovering by the bathroom door. 'Do you need anything?'

'Nothing, thanks, Littl'un. I'm fine.'

'Okay. Leave the light on. If you touch the switch with wet hands you'll get a bad electric shock. Use the wooden stick. Or leave it. I'll do it later.'

Obviously, Littl'un had something on her mind but it was hopeless trying to conduct a conversation from the shower. Zara washed out her shampoo and came out wrapped in a towel.

'She thinks you took them,' Littl'un said. 'She grabbed me by both shoulders and shook me. She said I stole them for you.'

'What are you talking about, Littl'un?'

'The bangles. She said you wouldn't let her come to Ahmedabad because you wanted to get them priced and smuggled out to London.'

Zara was appalled. 'But I wasn't even here when they disappeared. I never expressed the least interest in owning them.'

Littl'un's expression was full of intrigue. *I'm getting sucked into something here,* Zara thought. *I shouldn't be listening. This is an irrational accusation. How dare Pebbles suggest I'm a thief?*

'Huzur Saheb was really upset, too, you know,' Littl'un said. 'She tried so many times, so many ways to prove to Bahurani that she hadn't got the bangles. She even went through the list of family jewels with her. But it's hard to refute something if you are not directly accused, isn't that so? They talked about it all the time. Round and round and round. Huzur Saheb didn't know what else to say or do. She gave up in the end, you know.'

Perhaps Peter was right and people only believed what suited them. Zara shuddered. Did Hana want the bangles sent out of the country where they could not harm her family? Or was there, as Hirani suggested, something else on her mind?

'Littl'un,' Zara asked, 'do you know why Aunty went to Ahmedabad?'

Littl'un cackled. 'Why would she need to go to Ahmedabad when Ahmedabad would come to her on bended knees with hands outspread? Hiraman has been begging her for years to let him come.'

'You mean Hirani?

Littl'un took the comb from Zara's hand and slowly ran it through her hair, tenderly disentangling the knots.

'Listen,' Littl'un came very close and took her hand, 'I've been trying to tell you.' She dragged Zara along the balcony until they came to the back kitchen and positioned her at one of the windows.

Littl'un pushed a raffia stool forward, dusting its woven surface and motioning her to sit. 'Down there.'

An old crone sat in the middle of a large group of courtyard people who lived in the shade of the fort's back buttress.

'She's one of the new people. One of the artisans. I'm not sure what she does, exactly. Came five-six years ago. She's well known for her readings. She can always identify a thief.'

'That's terrible.' Zara jumped up from the stool and headed for the steep stone staircase leading to the backyard. A crackly voice was reading lines from the Quran. The servants were clustered around the foot of the stairs. Zara saw terror in their faces. Clearly, Pebbles had forced them to be present.

So I'm not the only suspect, Zara thought. Her heart thumped at the idea of being singled out by the diviner. Did the woman not worry that she might implicate the wrong person, someone innocent, someone with dependents, maybe?

In front of the crone an aluminium pitcher floated in a large brass basin filled with water. She held it down. Her eyes were shut and she was chanting in a loud voice. Suddenly she opened one eye, raised her eyebrow and swung the pitcher round, her face turning with it, in bizarrely synchronized movements. Pebbles knew her cue. She bent forward instantly and lowered her cupped hands, tipping several tubes of rolled paper into the bowl. They bobbed and floated as they swirled into the water. The crone squared herself, opened her eyes and let go of the pitcher with a mighty whirl.

' In God's name! Point to the thief,' she screeched.

With a gasp, the servants and courtyard dwellers stepped back. The pitcher spun onerously for a moment or two then slowed down, swaying and heaving. The people in line with its spout twitched and fidgeted, trying to inch out of its radius.

Zara darted down the stairs as the pitcher rocked slightly before bobbing to a stop. Quickly, she stepped forward and stood in front of the spout. She clapped her hands. 'Come on, all of you. Back to work. Get on. The show's over.'

She turned to the old woman. 'God knows how many innocent people you've harmed with your silly little spells. If I hear you've been up to your tricks here again, I'll report you to Pir Saheb and you'll be out, do you hear?'

Zara turned to walk back up the stairs then stopped, mesmerized. Pebbles sat in a trance, her eyes rolled upwards beneath heavy lids, the trace of a smile flickering on her lips as she looked at Zara.

She thinks I've been proven guilty! The thought chilled Zara but she decided to say nothing more to Pebbles. Better that she believed it was Zara than some innocent servant who she could victimize. But she felt shaken by the sight of a crazed Pebbles. Was she mad? Had she passed down some terrible mental condition to Sharmeen?

Pebbles called after her. 'You sound just like your aunty.'

Zara did not turn around. Her body felt stiff and graceless as she walked back upstairs, sensing a mad spectre behind her. One look back would probably dispel the feeling of being watched by something Pebbles had unleashed but it made her heart thump harder than the thought of the fascists in Ahmedabad.

30

Zara stood facing the magnificent building. Vikram Bhavan. They had played here together: she, Saif, Jay, Karan and Raju, the son of the chief driver, who had been her best friend amongst the children of the palace staff. Vikram Bhavan had stood empty for years, uninhabited except for the gatehouse where the caretaker and his family lived. She remembered sneaking in from the bottom end of the Deer Park, thrusting through the vines and bushes, tumbling down a steep grassy slope to the huge green bowl punctuated with tall trees garlanded with vines. It was a secret garden where they spent many hours playing until eventually they scrambled up the other end and emerged into the gardens of Vikram Bhavan. They were not manicured and tended like the other gardens in those days but they had been magnificently laid out; colourful wild flowers replaced the cultivated roses and lilies of its glory days. Now it had been brought back, if not to a former glory, then certainly a groomed, contemporary state, minimal, functional, striking.

She looked at the magnificent lake. That, at least, was the same; still, glass-clear and dotted with water lilies except at the far end where they clustered in such dense masses that it seemed possible to walk over them without sinking. The light caught the ripples 'as if a celestial hand has scattered silver dust across the surface', Saif had said once.

She tore herself away from the lake and walked round the main entrance to the bistro at the back. Zara was both relieved and surprised that the Ankahi contact wanted to meet in such a public place.

She looked at the damask-covered tables with elegant flower-filled glass bowls. Several were still empty. She pulled back a wrought iron chair, sat down and looked through the menu.

'Hello, Aunty Zara.'

Zara looked up startled. 'Kamran!'

'May I sit down?'

Kamran shimmered from shoulder to toe in white and silver, the caricature of Michael Jackson.

'Sorry,' she replied, then lowered her voice. 'I mean, I have a meeting here in a minute. Sorry.'

Kamran ran his left hand through his thick brush of hair and put his right hand out, Bollywood megastar style. His eyebrows came together, his eyelashes flickered. 'Your meeting is with me.'

Zara smiled, shaking her head. 'It definitely is not.'

'Talwar Barot. The dynamite sword. That's me.'

'You are Talwar Barot?'

'I am. Meet Ankahi's representative in Trivikram.' He bowed low.

Zara stood up. 'Is this a joke?'

'Kindly sit.' Kamran's face was serious. 'Let me explain.' He laughed but his tone was earnest. 'Obviously I can't show you identification. You see, every character who's dubbed an "enemy of the nation" or "the invisible hand of the enemy" seems to carry around a passport, according to our politicians. They are supposed to be Pakistani spies, usually. Mad guys, these Pakistani spies, it seems to me. They carry around passport and identification when they come here undercover to blow up our country. Am I right to assume you have one too?' Zara was mesmerized. Kamran sat down. 'Let me get you something to drink. This place makes *ex*cellent fruit juices. Freshly squeezed on the premises after you place your order. Anar, ganna ... that means ...'

'Pomegranate and ...' she paused, her mind blank, though she could see the woody golden rounds. 'What's ganna in English? I swear I've known all my life.'

'Sugar cane,' they both said together.

'I'll have ganna,' she said, sitting down again. 'With lots of lemon juice. But later. Let's talk first.'

Zara's instincts and rational self felt out of step with each other. Be careful, a part of her was saying. He's not to be trusted. But another side felt open to his presence. She looked across at him. She would get past the Bollywood caricature.

'There is no reason for you to trust me,' he said. 'We have only just met. But let me tell you how I came to be a member of Ankahi. With your permission.'

Zara nodded.

'Well, you know already about my grandmother, Mumtaz. She left Qila suddenly with the Ramzis' munshi ji, my Dada Jan. He was Hindu. She gave birth to my father soon afterwards. My Dada Jan had no problem getting a good job with the British. They couldn't live like Dadima was used to but she had jewellery and art objects which she sold for a lot of money, I'm told. She always says that Ramzi riches and palaces did not bring any woman the love she had with Dada Jan.

'But when my dad grew up, my grandma changed. She didn't like him to work for people whom her family would never condescend to talk to, even. She started taking steps to get a part of the Ramzi estate. More than wealth she wanted status; she wanted to be reinstated in Qila. Dada Jan thought it would never happen. The courts here mostly don't consider women's claims to property. And then the Hindu-Muslim marriage, that would be like nuclear bomb in the wrong hands.

'Everyone in India has some enemy or another. It's a way of life. Dadi Ma, she said she could destroy the Ramzi Order. Khatam. Khallas.' He clapped his hands and dusted his palms. 'Dada Jan said noth-thing. But definitely she held a pow-erful bomb in her hand.

'But then a bomb imploded in our family itself. My father fell in love with a rich Hindu girl – his boss' daughter. A real cliché, no? From one side her father objected, from the other side, Dadi Ma objected. Anyway, short time after I was born they killed themselves. Grandfather found me a few days afterwards. He thought I was dead.' He stopped, jogging his knee. 'But, of course, I am alive. He took me home. Dadi Ma was grateful to have me.

She could forget about Papa's past and take me to her heart. She showered me with love and kindness and here I am.'

'Your other grandparents?'

'They didn't want to know me. A half-caste in this society is worse than a cripple. People used to say in school about me: "Poor fellow. Don't blame him for being of mixed-up race." '

Zara squeezed his hand.

'But Aunty Zara, I can call you that? You have an idea how this-all feels. You also lost your parents. I mean, I know your mom's alive ...'

'I've always wondered if that makes it better or worse,' Zara heard the words sliding out.

'Well, I mean, at least there's a chance you might meet again,' Kamran murmured, his head bowed, his hair veiling his face.

'I suppose. But you live with the feeling that your mother doesn't want you.'

His head jolted up in surprise. 'Sorry? I live with ...?' His lips stretched slowly into a sad smile. 'Oh yes, I see. I was reading a book once, pop psychology. It says we use the word "you" instead of "I" when we want to make something impersonal. But when you said "you", I thought at first you were talking about me. You see? Like my mom was ...' he broke off. 'Sorry. I'm talking too much.'

He folded his starchy napkin carefully into a small, tight square. 'We're sort of in the same position that way.'

He placed the tiny white square on the table. It sprang open like a live thing and settled back into its original folds.

Kamran was lost in thought. Zara noticed she was holding the small glass vase. Perhaps she'd grabbed it to prevent a spill when the napkin unfolded. She looked up from the petals of the rose in full bloom. *The rose that once has bloomed forever dies.*

'Your ganna juice.' Kamran jumped to his feet and waved his arm around. A liveried waiter appeared.

'Ek ganna, ek anar,' he said. 'Ekdam thanda. Completely cold.'

'How did you come to be so, er, into Bollywood?' Zara asked.

Kamran looked intense. 'Dreams come true in Bollywood. I used to go to the movies to resolve the melodrama of my life. And there was always – well, nearly always – a happy ending. At least for the hero, you know, the star. That's who you identify with, right?'

'But you must like to dress up,' Zara teased.

'Defi-nitely. One reason why I decided to join the film industry. Then I became involved in politics. It became a good cover. People think you're a mass-sive idiot, just following around movie sets like a camp-follower. They don't take you seriously and you can get to all sorts of places, meet all kinds of useful people – and dangerous ones. It's fan-tastic.'

She could see how the cover would work.

'Of course you meet quite a few stars with a strong sense of respons'bility. You must have heard of the whole Sanjay Dutt thing. He got accused of supplying Muslim militants.'

'Religion is used to destabilize societies,' she said.

'Right, right,' he said. 'You've heard of the Pepsi and Coke wars, no?'

Zara nodded.

'Ya, ya. Hrithik modelled for Pepsi. Shahrukh Khan was the "face" of Coke. The RSS and their people started demonstrating outside Shahrukh's house. They were accusing him of opposing Hrithik because he was a Hindu. Those guys are good friends. They rock! The battle was commercial – between Coke and Pepsi. Noth-thing to do with religion. But people use it to suit their purpose.' He shrugged.

Zara braced herself. 'And what about Ankahi? How did you get involved with them?'

'I went through a rebellious stage. I was with a gang of boys who just went about making a big noise. Nothing harmful, you know. Worst we did was smash a headlamp here and there, basically just making a halla-gulla. Then some of the boys in our gang got caught up in this communal rioting. There were news reports – state was involved in Gujarat massacres and all. People were getting worried if this was really true. They tried to recruit people who were not bothered by this religious stuff. I was in Mumbai where, basically, you know, only politicians care about that stuff. The man in the street will have three, four, five religious talismans on his chain: Allah, Om, the cross, Ganesha, Buddha. So that's how I became involved. My parents, my grandma both destroyed their kids' life because of this religious stuff. And mine, too. So I joined up with Ankahi.'

'And what exactly do you do? I mean, Ankahi?'

Kamran responded more readily than she had expected. 'Basically, we find out what's going on with communal groups. If someone's in trouble we try to get them out and find them a safe place – here, there and everywhere. Also, we want to find the troublemakers and break their power base.'

'Have you had much success?'

Kamran laughed. 'Defi-nitely. But we're million miles from damaging the movements. Here and there we break up cells but others soon come together. Individuals, yes. Movements, no. Religion is a big thing in this country, still. A very alive thing. But you know, every aaye-Ram gaye-Ram – sorry – Tom, Dick and Harry thinks he's a patriot. They jump on the communal bandwagon and try to do their own thing. Kidnapping, lynching, arson. Exploit religion and someone will fund you for sure. They're all the same, Muslims, Hindus ... and the poor man is left with the problem.'

'Do you think you can help me?'

'Defin-nitely. We have areas where we can "lose" people out of the eyes of the authorities and their own families if they're being pursued. We just, you know, disappear them. India's a big place. Life is expensive to live, cheap to lose. We "lose" people. No one comes looking. Same with your deportees. We can lose them and find them something to do, somewhere to live. They'll just mix up with our own refugees. You call them asylum-seekers. We have them too. In fact, everyone's an asylum-seeker in one way or another, isn't it? Even you and me.'

Zara's head felt heavy on her neck. 'I suppose we are.'

The waiter returned with a silver tray bearing a memo. ‘Excuse me madam, message for you. From car.’

Zara took the message and stood up. ‘Saif’s sent the car. Are you going home? I’ll give you a lift.’

Kamran looked uncomfortable. ‘I have to go somewhere else. But you can contact me any time to discuss further details. We will help you.’

Zara wondered if she was wrong to trust Kamran. She had not, in any case, given anything away. But she felt warmth from him, not for the first time. She nodded, slightly brusque. ‘As you wish. I’ll see you back at Qila. We’ll talk more.’

Now that she had a direct line to him, she was determined to find out his intentions towards Sharmeen.

A feeling of distress washed over Zara as she opened her eyes. With a jolt, she recalled the nightmare realization that Jay could be her brother. She threw off her fine cotton sheet and ran to the bathroom. She had to wash. The shock of cold water down her spine made her gasp. She sucked in air, imagining it working its way round her insides, cleaning, clearing, until she could hold it no more and the pressure from her lungs forced it out again.

She could not bear to face Jay again. She shuddered. But something told her Jay was not, could not, be her brother. Was that denial? What would Peter say? Was this one of those moments he would ask her to rely on her instincts? Or would he say her mind was ‘in denial from a truth that challenged her inner survival structures’. Littl’un yanked aside the curtain and came into the bedroom with a self-important swagger.

‘Saif Baba wants to see you.’

Zara reached out and slipped on a striped Moroccan abaya.

‘Come in, Saif. I’m decent.’

Saif stepped into the room. ‘Everything okay?’

Zara looked at the clock on her bedside table. ‘Good lord. 9.30. I hope you didn’t wait for breakfast?’

Saif shook his head and sat down. 'You're okay, though?'

'Fine. Fine.' She did not mention the succession of bad dreams of magic and incest. 'I woke up early. Must have drifted off again.'

Saif pulled forward a chair. It was the first time he'd come into Hana's room since her death, as far as Zara was aware. Suddenly, she was self-conscious about being in his mother's bed.

'You don't mind ...?'

'Not a bit. It's a good feeling. Continuity.'

'You look worried.'

'Look, I didn't want to disturb you. Only, I have to rush off. And Jay called – he wants to talk to you urgently. It's about some information his mother might have given you. He sounded anxious.'

'I don't want to see him.'

Saif looked shocked.

'I mean – oh god, it's complicated. Look, Saif, I'll just blurt it out. Sita Devi says Jay could be my brother.'

She could not read Saif's reaction. 'Those were her words?'

'Pretty much.'

'Incorrect.'

Zara wondered whether she was shaking from shock or relief. 'Are you sure?'

Saif nodded. 'Not that it matters. Does it?'

'Did my mother have an ... affair with her husband?'

'Bahurani's looking for you, Baba,' Littl'un squawked suddenly, pointing to the silhouette behind the curtain.

Pebbles lifted the curtain and stepped in. 'Oh, there you are. I've been looking for you everywhere.' Her eyes narrowed as she took in the question still on Zara's face, Saif's troubled expression.

'What's the matter? Something's the matter.'

Why did she always sound so hostile, Zara wanted to ask. She tingled, wanting to pick a fight. 'Nothing you need bother about.'

Pebbles' eyes glided from Saif to Zara. 'Exciting trip to Ahmedabad?'

'Not as exciting as it was to come back.' Zara shivered.

'What's the matter, Zara?' Pebbles said, her voice deep and languorous. 'Feeling cold?'

'Creepy,' Zara said. 'As if strange things are going on that shouldn't be happening.'

Pebbles' startled eyes darted to Saif's face but she saw that the exchange had passed him by. She fixed her gaze on Zara's.

'Maybe,' she said, 'you don't understand our little, uneventful lives any more. As they say, "A half-apothecary is the enemy of life." '

'Good heavens, Pebbles,' Saif interrupted, 'what are you two talking about?'

'Zara should stop worrying. She needs to grieve and heal and go home to her husband.' She tucked her arm into her husband's and guided him out of the room.

Saif paused by the curtain. 'I'll deal with Jay's query.'

What, she wondered, would Saif say to Jay. She felt her insides lurch, threw off her dressing gown and ran into the lavatory.

31

A mist, the texture of longing, hung around the shrine of Dost Pir, the Friendly Sage, the founder of the Ramzi Order. No one knew exactly when he had arrived in this remote forest on the desert's edge, this secret spot, which became a sanctuary for his followers and a retreat for new disciples. Lack of curiosity was essential to the ethos of the Order. Seekers did not look back to its roots and foundations. A Lover, like a newborn, had no past.

It was all obscure to Saif when he first heard it at the age of eleven. Later he found that if he replaced an impersonal word like 'object' with a precise one such as 'God', then the meaning was clearer. Someone with a name as cozy and reassuring as Friendly Sage would have chosen simplicity, Saif thought. The task he chose for initiates was simple – working the earth, growing things. He asked his followers to look to nature for all exemplars. Each novice was given a patch of land to work. The output of the crop would determine his dedication. Blessings and abundance would follow – plants for eating and for healing, for earth-nurturing and for maintaining the natural ecology.

Saif enjoyed the gardening but questions clamoured inside him. His father, an astute diagnostician of the soul's disorders, saw immediately, when he began his training, that Saif's base nature, or nafs, manifested as curiosity. He told Saif that curiosity was an aspect of power-lust. Desire in humankind had to be brought under control. The disciple's aim was to seek Truth. Sultan gave Saif a rocky piece of land to work. He must dig though the land did not yield until his desire to dominate was subdued; the rewards would come when Saif deserved them.

Saif worked his patch of land, digging out the outcrops of rock, heaving them from the earth and piling them up to build himself a meditation 'cave'. Often, he became so engrossed in his work that he did not notice the sky grow grey and the darkness spread like a veil.

And it was one such night when he returned to the sanctuary, that he saw her.

Darkness surrounded Nyla's curled-up body like a smoky hollow, the winged back of the chair like two sentinels guarding her. When had she come to Ramzi Bagh? Had she looked for him?

He jerked back from the window as his father entered the room. His expression was beneficent. Saif edged nearer to the window.

'Can't get to sleep?' he heard Sultan ask. Nyla shook her head. Sultan walked over to the sofa. 'Will it help to talk?'

Nyla shook her head without looking at him. It was barely fifty days since Jameel had died. She looked so distressed that Saif wanted to run in and hug her. Sultan sat down. Saif could see only his back. Nyla shook her head but Sultan settled back into the sofa as if preparing to stay. Perhaps, Saif thought, he would teach her about achieving peace by accepting God's will.

They sat in silence, Nyla looking wary and watchful. The curl of her body tightened; she was like a wild animal preparing for predators.

Saif saw his father pat the sofa beside him. Nyla wrapped her arms around herself. She looked confused, then afraid. Saif felt a twinge of anger. Was his father as harsh to all his disciples as he had been to him? Was he telling Nyla she must cure her nafs?

Sultan stood up and walked towards Nyla; she shrunk into herself. Saif turned and ran into the night. The next day, Nyla found him.

'I had to see you before I left,' she said. 'I can't stay.'

'Why?' he managed to choke out. 'Why did you come here? Was it so that I wouldn't be lonely?'

'Of course not,' she said, ruffling the back of his head. 'Hana Apa made me.'

Nyla hugged him tight. Her fingers clawed his back. 'If this how it's going to be,' she said, 'I don't want to live.'

When Nyla returned a year later with infant Zara, she seemed sure of herself again. But Saif recalled an uncanny feeling that she might break. Between the death of her husband and the birth of her child, a liaison with Maharaja Hari Sinhji would have been impossible. His mother had made sure of that for the sake of her dearest friend.

32

Jameel Usman had never been a significant presence in Zara's mind so she was surprised by the depth of her reaction. But then, who considered the ground beneath their feet? Now one of the few fixed elements of her life had shifted and she felt destabilized.

She looked through Hana's bookshelf in the long sitting room. She knew every book on the old bookshelf. They hadn't changed much over the years: the selections of Somerset Maugham, Pearl S. Buck, an assorted medley of books by Russian authors – *The Brothers Karamzov, Dr Zhivago, War and Peace.* And the Indo-Anglian writers – R. K. Narayan, the poems of Sarojini Naidu, the novels of her niece, Nayantara Sehgal, a volume by Amrita Shergill. And then a shelf full of Urdu poetry. Zara pulled out a slim edition of Iqbal. *Asrar-e-Khudi, The Secrets of the Self.* His work always absorbed her but this time her mind wandered. Perhaps, she thought, she should go back to the bedroom.

This was silly; she was making excuses to avoid Pebbles until Saif came back at lunchtime. She would stop lurking and face Pebbles.

She put down her book and walked through the dining room into the back verandah. The cooker gleamed beside the work-surface. It replaced the one Aunt Hana and Nyla had used when she was a child, experimenting with western dishes. It was where she had baked her first cakes, biscuits and meringues. The square, open space was still paved with the medieval flagstones from when the fort was first built. But over the years the spaces were adjusted and remodelled to suit the needs of generations of Ramzis.

Off to the right were a few steps going down into a dim, cavernous space that was now the kitchen. Zara tried to remember what had been there before. Slowly, a wall came into her vision and she remembered a door through the dining room into a massive Aladdin's cave full of large gunny sacks of grain of all kinds, weighing scales with round brass discs of varying thickness and diameter. The room, dark in any case, was hazy with flour and the dust of other grains and pulses. Zara could taste the atmosphere – sometimes she identified besan, gram flour, dry and chalky, sometimes cornmeal. Chhoti the cook used to scoop up the various grains and load one of the round trays on the scales. On the other side she placed the gota, slate-grey discs of iron to weigh against them, adding a little one, removing a bigger one while the two trays swung and descended, rose, hovering in slow, measured contest until they finally came to settle. When they were even, Zara knew the right weight had been reached and Chhoti moved on to the next item.

Zara went down the steps by the cooker and peered to the right. The women looked a little surprised and the younger ones scuttled around for a moment but quickly got back to lunch preparation and ignored her. The door was still embedded in the wall. The old kitchen had more or less been replicated. Small three-legged stools no higher than foot-stools were dotted around braziers and a couple of clay stoves. The storeroom had clearly been divided to bring the kitchen closer to the dining room. It made more sense than carrying food down the gallery and through the living room. But there was a pang in Zara's chest as she came back up into the open.

The sunlight in her eyes was painful. She walked quickly across the paving stones, half taking in the clusters of activity in the backyard below, and walked to the covered space where Pebbles sat watching a Hindi movie. She looked up at Zara but said nothing.

'What's going on down there?'

'Where?' Pebbles looked disgruntled.

'At the back. Looks like an event in the courtyard.'

Pebbles raised herself on one shoulder and glanced over. She was nervy, snappy. 'They live there.'

'What, all of them?'

Pebbles snorted. 'Haven't you Britishers heard of the population explosion here?'

'Not like this!'

'There are some newcomers. I was ... made to sell one of my buildings to incomers. They rent down there for their servants. Workers call their relatives. You know how they are, these people. They're given something good and they pull in all and sundry to overcrowd it.'

She picked up the remote control as if to switch off.

Zara gazed at the television screen. The images were familiar. 'My goodness, I saw that when I was a kid.'

Pebbles looked baffled. 'You?'

'Oh yes. I was obsessed with Hindi movies. Especially after,' she paused to detach from emotions that suddenly swamped her, 'after my mother left.' Her voice dropped to a whisper. 'I kept hoping she'd walk in while I watched, especially these black-and-white ones ... she loved them.'

Pebbles looked at her with hooded eyes. 'This one is about a girl who's been adopted. An untouchable. And the man they want for their own daughter falls in love with the adopted daughter.'

Zara's life seemed to be full of mirrors at the moment, each reflecting elements from different angles.

Pebbles switched off the screen. 'We have suffered similarly, you and I,' Pebbles said, softly. 'We should have been friends.'

So why are we sometimes adversaries, Zara wanted to ask. She wanted to hug Pebbles, stuck in this all-enveloping world of Qila. Her brain clamoured to be occupied, her talents were rusting with disuse. No wonder she had become entangled in the oppressive demands of being a Ramzi. She was defining herself by the space that imprisoned her. She was mistress of Qila now but instead of feeling free, she had been taken over by that familiar obsession that Hana had clung to all her married life. Qila must be protected and passed on to the rightful heir. Pebbles felt compelled to ensure that Sharmeen would be the next owner. But who was standing in her way? Unless, of course, she herself decided to sell it and move on.

Strange thought. What if Saif and she left Trivikram altogether, as she had, and discovered their identities as anonymous individuals instead of dynastic representatives, owned by history, owned by edifices, owned by time itself?

A faint memory hovered in her mind, of terrible anxiety. Clinging. What was she worried about? She peered into the memory cloud and saw herself beside her mother, asking if she'd stop being a part of Qila if she went away. Nyla was leaving on one of her trips and no one was sure she'd take eight-year-old Zara with her. Aunt Hana wanted Zara to stay. Nyla seemed unsure.

'It's my place,' Zara insisted, weary of strange locations, new people, being dragged around museums and old buildings. 'My trees. My garden. My room. But if I'm not here then it won't be mine anymore. So I can't leave.'

She felt a smile inside, recalling how Hana had encouraged her to say that. Nyla's expression had been mysterious.

'Hello?' Pebbles was waving a hand in front of her eyes. 'You've vanished.'

'I was thinking,' Zara said, feeling for the right words, 'that places like Qila that have been coated for years in the aura and voices and emotions of a single family – if they own you, can you leave them and move on? Or do they hold on to you? Do you ever break free?' Her voice broke and she got up to pour herself a glass of water from the fridge in the dining room.

'Have you ever thought of moving?' she asked when she returned.

'Why would I?' Pebbles asked. 'Who would I be?'

'Yourself.'

Pebbles' body shook with soundless laughter. 'And you think that's worth anything? You live in another world, Mrs Zara Hamilton.' Her eyes wandered to the screen. 'This is India.' She flicked on the television and was immediately absorbed.

Millo came in from the kitchen. 'Pir Saheb's back for lunch.' She lingered, her eyes magnetized to the screen. Slowly, Pebbles detached herself from the screen and flicked off the television.

'What are you waiting for, Millo? Go on – start bringing lunch to the table.' But her voice had none of the fire of her words.

Suddenly, Zara had a sense of Pebbles' predicament; a tornado of women's loss and grief through the centuries seemed to have come to reside in her. Zara put her arm around her.

'We should be friends,' Pebbles said again, stiffening. 'And yet you persist ...' She turned and walked away.

'Wait, Pebbles, listen to me. What is it you think I'm doing?'

Pebbles tossed her hair, turned back to the door and nearly collided with Saif.

'Don't worry about lunch, my love,' he said. He looked solemn. 'Get some essential things together, Zara. You have to spend a few days with the Rajmata.'

A snort burst through Zara's nose, something masquerading as a laugh. 'With the Rajmata?'

'There may be trouble. We have to get you somewhere safe.'

'Trouble,' Pebbles muttered, storming out of the room. 'I knew she'd bring trouble.'

Saif looked as if he was about to respond, then changed his mind. 'We should get cracking, Zara. Pack for a week.'

33

As the car pulled out of the gates, Saif handed Zara a faxed typescript of a newspaper.

> PAKISTANI SPY FREE TO TRAVEL LENGTH AND BREADTH OF INDIA
> A lady spy from Pakistan is travelling freely and boldly in Gujarat state. Purporting to be on a visit to attend a family funeral, this modern Mata Hari has already visited Ahmedabad since she arrived in India's Gujarat state last week. In Ahmedabad two days ago, she was seen to be in conference with known troublemakers and dissidents. It is suspected that she wishes to pass information for anti-Indian plans being hatched in the UK where she has had recent contact with at least two high-level Indian traitors seeking asylum in Britain. This spy disguises as a human rights lawyer to work regularly with Indian anti-nationals who abandon their country and work to bring India into disrepute in foreign lands. She is currently staying in Trivikrampur with relatives, a well-known Muslim family who have, in recent years, fallen out with the revered Rajmata of Trivikrampur following her association with the VHP party, showing their disdain for all things Hindu.

Surely no one was going to take this report seriously, Zara thought. But Saif's silence indicated otherwise.

'How serious is this likely to get?'

Saif was strumming his thigh with his fingers. 'It'll blow over, hopefully.'

'Worst-case scenario?'

'It's a matter of time before the story hits the Trivikram papers. The Gujarati papers. On the whole, the English-language papers are fair – passionate but rigorous. We need to get you out of the way. We can weather the storm. We've dealt with them before.'

Saif's evasive answers were frightening. 'Saif, please. Please tell me what they're likely to do?'

'Who can tell? The point is, they're after you. If you're not here, they'll go.'

She felt as if Saif had punched her. 'And if they find out I'm with the Rajmata?'

'Even better. If she speaks up it'll be seen as the nonsense it is ...'

'But she won't, will she? She dislikes me. Always has.'

'At times like this, personal likes and dislikes are irrelevant. She's a wise lady. She'll do what she has to do.'

'Do you think the protestors will go there? To the palace, I mean?'

'Unlikely. It's possible you'll be taken away. To the lodge, maybe. We simply have to wait.'

'I'm so sorry.'

Saif squeezed her hand. 'No need. This is all tied in with the opposition to the Academy. We're in troubled times. This isn't the India you lived in.'

'So, I cause trouble and then vanish and leave you to bear the brunt of it?' She felt utterly helpless.

'Inspector Pandey is watching out for us,' Saif was saying. 'His men will be at Qila by now. And he'll go personally at the first sign of trouble.'

'Is this my fault?'

Saif turned in his seat and faced Zara. 'Answer me a couple of questions. Are you a spy? No. Did your visit to Ahmedabad involve meeting up with traitors planning the destruction of the Indian government? I think not. It's not you. Absolutely anything could trigger this. In fact, maybe you've been targeted because of us.'

Zara said nothing. She could sense Saif wanted to withdraw and reflect. Randomly, she thought how near the annual Festival of the Green-clad Man was. 'What happens at the festival? Are people peaceful?'

'So far. Most still respect the divine. The people of Trivikram believe profoundly in the power of the festival. Of course, we have many incomers now. They join – all Indians love a festial. The troublemakers are generally organized groups – Inspector Pandey thinks they come from other areas – professional troublemakers.'

'Shiv Sena?'

'Hard to tell. Could be, or rogue cells operating independently. It doesn't take much organization for a bunch of thugs to cause damage. The festival is definitely vulnerable. I believe it's been safe so far because Jay's presence highlights the mixed religious element. Actually, so does the Rajmata's. Her patronage counts immensely with the extremists.'

'I can't imagine she'll be thrilled to have me foisted on her.'

'It was she who invited you,' Saif replied. 'I think you imagine her dislike.'

'Honestly, I don't. It's like Peter's "generational transmission" – she hated my mother.' She saw Saif's expression and held up her hands. 'Okay, okay. I'm a wreck. Aunty would ...' She hated it when her voice broke. 'Do you know, it's not even ten days since she went? Sometimes I think she's still here. It feels like an age ...'

'She'd rise to the occasion with gusto,' Saif patted her hand. 'Try not to get sucked into talk of blame and guilt. Allow yourself to just be. That resolves most dilemmas.'

The car drove through the palace gates and Saif touched her arm. 'You may have to spend some time with Jay.' He looked awkward. 'I love him like a brother. But he too is human. He met the sudden demands of his position with such commitment. Sadly, he never had the chance to develop his emotional side. It has been hard for poor Ana.'

The car came to a stop before Zara could ask Saif to clarify. She saw Jay come towards the drive and prepared to face him.

34

Jay's smile was warm. Had Sita Devi reassured Jay that Zara was not his half-sister?

'We'll lunch in the summer garden,' he said. 'It's pleasant there. Zara, the Rajmata's resting right now. She's sorry she couldn't receive you. You're staying in her wing.'

Zara thought she might take the opportunity to clear up the matter of her relationship to Jay. She made up her mind to be direct.

Jay ushered them through an ante-room to a verandah on the far side. Down a few steps was a Turkish garden, with small kushiks scattered around. Poppies, azaleas and eglantine grew all around and flowering vines draped themselves around ornate arches. Jay pointed to an umbrella structure, like a bandstand, where lunch had been laid out on a marble-topped table. On the side, another table was covered in a starched white tablecloth and set with three services. Various dishes were lined up beside buckets of ice, jugs full of lassi and freshly squeezed lime juice.

'This looks wonderful,' Saif said. He inhaled appreciatively. 'But I'm afraid I must go. You understand. I must be at home with Pebbles and Sharmeen.'

Jay's face filled with sympathy.

'I hope all goes well,' Saif said. He raised his hand. 'I'll see myself out. Take care, Zara.'

The butlers served their meal and stood back by the side table. Zara cleared her throat. 'Saif said you wanted to talk to me.'

Jay paused, gazing into his *citronne presse.* 'I did, yes. It was about my mother's accusation ... I can assure you she was wrong.'

'But how do you know?'

Jay looked awkward. His unease was palpable. Zara felt her teeth clamp.

'Kids hear things. My mother suspected my father and Aunty Nyla. There was nothing. I heard my father swear to Guruji Sultan that he would never even look at his sister-in-law in that way.'

Zara could hear the hysteria in her own voice. 'How can you be so sure he meant it?'

Jay shrugged. 'Call it devotion. Call it judgement. It's something you've lost touch with, Zara.'

Suddenly Zara was exhausted. 'I'm sorry – that sounded rude. Someone up there keeps throwing things at me. First, Aunt Hana and her unfinished business. Now this ludicrous spy thing – and somewhere in between, my paternity is in question and I'm flirting with incest ...' Jay winced. 'I don't want to offend you, Jay. Truly. But even if you're not my ... if your father ...'

She couldn't speak. The tears were threatening to come. She took a deep breath and let her chin sink into to her chest. 'It's too much. I mean, is Jameel Usman still my father?'

It was useless trying to stop the sobs now. She sensed Jay's arms go out to hold her. She must have flinched because she heard the clink of cutlery and glass as his hands dropped back on the table.

'Your father is the one you thought he was, Zara.'

'Oh Jay, you're so uncomplicated.'

'Not so. You were born around nine months after his death. Your father's family accepted you without question.'

Zara slumped back in her chair. 'I wish I felt so sure.'

Jay fidgeted with his cufflink. 'Let's have a DNA test.'

Zara sat bolt upright in her chair. 'Sounds like something out of a dodgy chat show.'

'It happens all the time.'

Zara smiled. Jay was one of the kindest men she knew. 'I hope you're right,' she said.

'You should rest now. It's quiet in the Rajmata's wing. Browse through my father's library – it's not far from your room. Hopelessly underused. Help yourself. You'll also find videos and DVDs there.

There's a screen in the library and in your suite. I'll send word when the doctor's here.'

Zara could taste the air-conditioning. Other than that the room was a homage to F. Scott Fitzgerald's descriptions of the magnificent home of Jay Gatsby. New wings had been built on to existing palaces all over India in the wake of the novel. Zara remembered people discussing how one maharaja had instructed his architect to replicate the Great Gatsby home, complete with identical interior. It had become the maharaja's main claim to fame.

'He's got a tiny kingdom,' Sita Devi had reminisced once. 'It would fit inside your palm. Hari says that the maharaja is a canny businessman.' She shuddered. 'How awful, no? A maharaja being a middleman, like a pimp, buying and selling ...'

'Not a pimp, exactly,' Hana protested.

'Well, a middleman, then, a dalal. Same thing. He took commission for selling things to Europe and America.' She shuddered, then dropped her voice to a whisper. 'Can you believe it, *trading ...*'

Zara looked around her, at the curtains and upholstery, the bedspread and other details. The Gatsby maharaja might have lowered himself to businessman status but that had not stopped Sita Devi building her own wing and decorating it in the style of the same book!

The bed looked welcoming with its covers elegantly turned. Zara lay back against the pillows. The room was done up in soft pinks, satin and lace like a Hollywood star's boudoir from the fifties.

Zara felt drowsy. She turned on her side, snuggled into the mattresses to get comfortable. The pillow felt the wrong shape. She reached up to adjust it. Her hand touched something hard. She pulled out a small notebook. On the cover was pinned a note: *To Zara, the princess and the pea.*

What the hell was Jay doing? She slid the diary down to the edge of the pillow then opened it.

'Do you remember that magical time when we were caught in the snow, on a hilltop in the highlands, watching Mount Suilven? And we stayed until the flurry of snow turned into a thick, almost solid veil which cut the black hill from view. And you said ... "I'm sure that under that veil of snow, the mountain is still proud and naked and glistening." '

Zara was surprised to hear her voice echoing the words from so long ago. She let the covers of the notebook close over her forefinger and rolled back in bed.

It had been a freak snowstorm during a December visit to Lochinver. They'd been grateful for their four-wheel drive, heaving up through narrow winding roads, heavily snow-feathered. The mountainside rose sheer on one side and rolled down on the other to vast sheets of glass, sinister with suggestions of thick, writhing foliage, defiant creepers, virulent roots fighting for existence beneath.

The fear added a frisson. Lochinver was a summer town. Few hotels or bed-and-breakfasts were open this time of year and they had wandered a long way from their rented cottage. At last they found a room in a hotel in a nearby town.

They stumbled up the stairs, cold and relieved, the fear of perhaps having to spend a night in the car still clinging. Jay's hands shook as he fumbled with the key. She wasn't sure if his clumsiness was caused by nerves or the warmth beginning to flood back into his cold-deadened fingertips. Amazing how a few moments from car to pub had frozen them both into stalagmites. It was such a relief for them to find the room that they forgot their usual snobbery about their surroundings, their acerbic comments about the tired decor of never-ending thin corridors, déclassé carpets with flattened pile and 'naf' walls.

The door opened. Zara's eyes fell on a colossal bed. A four-poster of gleaming brass draped in lace and sequin-spangled net, so soft and pliable that it draped like chiffon. Bordello, she thought, but waited for Jay to be the arbiter of her final decision. Would the fabulous bed be beautiful or horrendous?

'Goodness gracious!' Jay breathed. They stared at each other. Zara knew Jay felt the same. He was waiting for her to decide.

'Stunning!' she said, still tiptoeing on glass.

'Astonishing!' Jay responded.

Zara began to giggle. They were still laughing several minutes later. Zara sobered for an instant, considering what she wanted from Jay. All she knew was, it had to be more than before. Jay was restrained, self-controlled, always concerned for her honour; what if – what if they never got married? What if they split up? What if Zara married some ultra-traditional Indian aristocrat who expected her to be a virgin? It frustrated her sometimes that Jay couldn't see beyond the issues and repercussions, that his passion didn't overwhelm him enough to smash through the barriers of fear and custom.

'I'm willing to throw myself into it, Stella,' she said. 'Just ride out the worst.'

'That's a rape fantasy if I ever I heard one,' Stella said. 'You know how I feel about this weird chastity thing you guys have. But if it is such a big deal then I suppose it's a good thing he's doing.'

Zara understood Jay's reasons. Of course she did. But here, rolling about, laughing in this great invitation of a bed, in the middle of the Scottish Highlands, surrounded by drifts of snow, her desire overrode caution and consequence. Jay must have sensed her intensity because he reached across and prodded her in the ribs. She sprang back from his touch.

'It's astonishing,' he repeated.

She saw his hand still beside her body. 'Good astonishing?' she said, trying to swallow the thickness in her voice. 'Or bad astonishing?'

Jay said nothing, rolling closer to her, trying to disguise his passion as play. He snatched at a frond of her hair and stroked his lips with it then catching her eye, moved it up, curling it like the twirling mustachios of a hussar. Her fingers wandered to his forehead, stroking back a lock of hair. She always teased him about the solitary wave that crested his forehead like the coiffed plume of a rock star. But his was natural, she thought, overcome with emotion. Suddenly, everything depended on how they would define the bed.

'Palace? Or bordello?'

Jay took her other hand and held it to his cheek. 'What do you think?'

'I can't make up my mind.'

'Mmm. Palace, I think.' He kissed the back of her hand then unfurled each finger to its full length, dreamily kissing each digit, starting at the bottom and finishing with the tip. 'With you in it, a palace, definitely. You transform anywhere into a palace. There must be a bed like this in Qila, surely?'

She could feel Jay's breath on her neck as he leaned his head against her shoulder.

If heaven is on the face of earth
Then it is here, it is here, it is here.

She wanted to make one of her usual jokes. Her mind had already articulated a response: '*Wow, Jay. How original. One of the most famous verses ever – composed by Jehangir in Kashmir for his beloved Noor Jehan.*' But, instead, she let the pleasure sink in. There was a stirring inside that seemed to make every part of her body yearn and she was unsure how to handle it. This was why, this was exactly why she joked every time Jay tried to be romantic.

Was he feeling as she did? She turned up her face and kissed him softly on the lips then let her head drop so that her forehead rested against his cheek. He placed a finger beneath her chin and brought her face up again. She imagined she could distinguish the shape of his lips as they kissed her fully, firmly on her closed lips, wondering if he would think her shameless if she opened her mouth. Suddenly her body felt active, frenetic, blood coursing, ears humming; her breath came in gasps and spurts, forcing her to inhale deeply. She was aware her body was trying to fix itself into his shape. Her hands seemed to move of their own volition, stroking, caressing. And, always, surge upon surge of sensation.

'It's like the ocean inside.' Jay was kissing her throat, the base of her neck and she could almost see a small purple blob of light fall on the spot his lips touched, drawing all her sensations towards it. Slowly, she realized he was saying something.

'You never told me about the bedrooms in Qila,' he murmured. His speech made a whirring sensation against her neck.

'Hmmm? Spartan.'

He moved away so that they were face to face again. 'Really? I remember green Venetian mirrors.'

'The Green Room.' She stroked the back of his neck. 'But it's a fortress, not a palace.'

Jay reflected a moment. 'I suppose you're right. I remember the portraits of the Ramzi rulers, though, just like our place, but then, palaces do tend to stay the same.'

Zara laughed. 'They weren't rulers, remember? They're ascetics.'

Jay disentangled his fingers from Zara's. 'I can't imagine Saif will leave us all and go away to the forest one day.' He moved away.

He would always move away from her, Zara thought, feeling the spell break. 'No messiah for broken glass', went the poem. Every time the centuries'-old relationship between the Ramzis and the Vamanas came up, every time Jay thought of facing Saif again, Zara would be between them, either as a secret or as a wife. In Jay's mind, a sacred trust had been violated. Zara knew well that in Trivikrampur society, at least, Jay would be pitied for being ensnared by the daughter of the enchantress – Nyla.

When she admitted the next morning that she hadn't slept well, he asked why. She shook her head, rubbing a sore spot on her hip, wondering if her wild thoughts had kept her awake or the unanswerable questions about her future, or a hard object beneath the bedding driving into her flesh so that she had to keep manoeuvring her body out of its orbit.

'Some hard, poky thing under the sheets,' she said. 'I feel black and blue.'

'Heads will roll.' Laughing, Jay pulled off the sheet. 'Nothing!' he exclaimed, removing the next layer, feathery and soft, beneath. 'Nor here!'

Finally, he pulled off a blanket placed over the mattress and found a white shirt button. 'The culprit!' he said, pouncing on it. Then he stopped suddenly, his face full of wonder. 'I can't believe you felt that under all those layers. You're like that girl who found the pea! And you shall marry the prince.'

They had fallen silent then – and the silence had remained throughout breakfast and the drive back.

Zara snatched the notebook and slid off the bed, pacing the room. 'I lost. Again and again and again, I have lost. My mother. Qila. Aunty Hana. Jay.'

She would have given up everything for him, she realized. But her willingness then to exchange her beloved Qila for a London life with a successful career and anonymity didn't take into account the strings of heritage that twitched at Jay's actions. Sita Devi was simply a catalyst. The split would have happened one way or another. But would it have been worse if they had slept together? They could have enjoyed a sense of belonging as they negotiated their separate futures. There was something profound between them, or so she had thought at the time. She didn't fool herself that their passion was unique.

She raised the notebook, flicking through it, unable to read because of the tears. Clearly Jay was also searching for something lost. She brushed her eyes with the back of her hand, peering into the pages, trying to read the crumbling words.

From young blood's impassioned highways
Arms cried out, bodies called

Too beloved, though, the yearning for dawn's face
Too close, the skirts of the Beauties of Light
Longing fleet-footed
Fatigue suppressed.
Word is, light and dark are already split
Station and goal already united
So changed the rites of the People of the Wound
The ecstasies of union, legitimized
The anguish of separation outlawed
In the heaviness of night no relief yet
For the eye or heart, no reprieve yet
Let's go on, the goal's not reached yet.

And then a note in Jay's copper-plate hand: *We were meant to be. We must be. There's no point stopping it.* Jay was writing lovelorn notes like a teenager. What did he think he was up to?

Zara flung herself into the armchair by the window and began reading through the notebook again. Poem after poem carefully translated; poems Zara knew well in the original and had probably read to him in Oxford. And he'd taken the trouble to remember them, look them out, translate them and collect them into a book. Or had he done a Cyrano de Bergerac and had them translated? She brushed away the thought. There was something in these words of Jay's essence, his turn of phrase, even his way of thinking. Frenetically, she looked through. And there it was. 'No Messiah for Glass'.

So he had felt the void of that lost encounter. He had carried it all these years. And he felt it so powerfully that he had raised its immolated phoenix inside her.

She lay down on the bed. The four-poster bed. If Jay still wanted her, he must be sure they were not siblings. Was this what it was all about? The offer of the DNA test? The confrontation with his mother? All, so that he could redeem the chance still dangling before them like a mirage?

She walked over to the long mirror panel tilted slightly back at the base of its art deco frame, to allow a clear look at the feet – or rather sari border – of the user. Zara looked squarely into her own eyes, pushing away the phantom of Peter on the periphery of her imagination. 'Now is the moment. I'll make love to you, Jay. I'll risk everything and afterwards I'll go wherever it takes me. But I'll do it.'

Like magic, the spell worked. The turmoil settled. Zara flopped into bed. She would see if there was a future for her and Jay.

But would Jay have the courage, this time, to take risks and make sacrifices?

Sita Devi looked as confident as ever at tea when she apologized about her 'prevarication', as she called it.

'It was my duty to prevent you and my son ... even if there was the slightest chance that you are related.'

There was no point now in contradicting her. The crisis was over, her decision made. She and Jay would redeem their missed opportunity. They both felt it; they were both too sensible to jeopardize the rest of their lives for something that wouldn't work permanently. She smiled to herself as she imagined Stella's response: 'Whatever floats your boat, sweetheart.' But what if the boat hits stormy waters, she thought. What if we're all stuck in a maelstrom and can't get out? What then?

This tacky sentimentality was not her style at all. In spite of the situation, she wanted to giggle at the purple phrases in her mind. Sita Devi was staring at her, and Zara wondered fleetingly if she could see into her mind and know her intentions. She shook away the irrational thought and waited. Sita Devi spoke into the silence.

'You aren't staying in Trivikram for Jay's sake, are you?'

Zara frowned. 'I'm here because Aunt Hana sent me an SOS. I intend to stay until I find out what it was.'

'And this other business? The newspaper report? Is there any truth in that?'

Zara nodded. 'I met up with some people. It was to do with work.'

'Pakistan?'

'I've never been there – not after my birth.'

'Your mother?'

'I don't know.'

'Does she have a connection with Pakistan?'

'Look, I haven't seen her since I was ten.'

Sita Devi looked shocked. 'She keeps in touch, though?'

Zara shook her head and sat back in her chair. 'Maharani Saheb, this is turning into an interrogation. I'm grateful for your protection. And I understand that you need to clarify some points ... but really, it has no connection with my mother.'

'You would not be here if I had not already decided to help. I want to know how much I am going to risk. Nyla was a passionate Pakistani.'

'I was too young to know that.'

'The people you saw in Ahmedabad?'

'It was in connection with my legal work. We occasionally need reliable local specialists to verify the claims of our clients.

'Immigration or asylum?'

'That's the kind of thing that needs verification.'

'Can you give me an example?'

'One woman claimed to be persecuted because of an inter-racial marriage. We needed to verify her marriage records.' Zara felt uncomfortable. 'I can't say any more. You'll appreciate it's confidential.'

'So you'd be using Indian professionals for a professional fee?'

Zara nodded.

Sita Devi's mouth suggested a smile. 'I can see a strategy. You happen to have been born in Pakistan but you never visit it. You work with Indians wanting to make a life in Britain. You are here to further their cause and forge links with local professionals who you will pay in foreign currency.' She sighed and sat back. 'It's hanging in the air. It simply has to be said. I want to offer an olive branch. You were right when you said I never had much time for you. Because you could be – have been – a permanent sign of my husband's disloyalty. But that is no fault of yours. I see that you are honest and direct. I like that.

'I will issue a statement to the press, if they request it, but only to the national press, laying out what I have just outlined to you. Local papers won't make a difference.' Her laugh was grim. 'They think they're judge and jury.

'I have information which might help you,' she continued. 'There's a Durga Das Rai, retired curator of the Trivikrampur National Museum; Hana gave him some items to verify. He has been involved in researching that for a while now. He's currently in Ahmedabad, I believe. I will try to obtain further information.'

'I'm grateful. For everything.' Zara rose. 'May I ask just one question?'

Sita Devi tensed.

'Did you truly believe what you said to me about Jay?'

'I believed it possible.'

'Then what changed your mind?'

'Saif, Pir Saheb. He dispelled the lingering doubt of thirty-five years.'

Jay burst into the room. He bowed to his mother, briefly joining his hands in greeting, and turned to Zara. 'There's trouble at Qila. We must get you to the lodge.'

'Welcome, son. It's sad, no, the first time you visit my apartments in two years, it is with bad news.'

'That's right, Mother,' Jay's tone echoed his mother's sarcasm. 'But no sadder than not visiting at all for two years.'

Sita Devi nodded. 'It is a good thing Anapurna is so dutiful. I wish she would return soon. I miss her, and my grandchildren.'

Jay turned to Zara. His gaze was hypnotic, despite his brusque manner. Zara felt hot. She looked quickly at Sita Devi. Jay was at Zara's side, touching her elbow, ushering her to the door.

'Thank you, Rajmata Saheba,' Zara said. 'I'm grateful for everything. I won't forget.'

'My welfare doesn't depend on your remembering,' Sita Devi said, her voice thin and curt, again. 'But yours does depend on getting away to safety. What about Pir Saheb and his family, Jay? Do you propose to take them to the lodge as well?'

'Of course. Naturally,' Jay responded. 'Later. At present, the police are trying to disperse the protestors from Qila.'

Zara felt the tightening of Jay's hand on her elbow; his body was close as he steered her from the room into the corridor.

'This is my fault. I have to get out of Trivikram. I'm causing trouble for all of you.'

Jay paused mid-stride and Zara had to lean her tense body against him to regain her balance. His hands cupped her face. 'Listen to me,' he said, his breath soft against her lips. 'I don't give a damn how much trouble you cause or what you do. I've found you again and I'll die to keep you by my side.'

She let go of the tension then, relieved by his words. Dramatic he may sound, but she savoured it.

I miss it, she thought suddenly. *I actually miss this sentimentality. I miss the romantic schlock and the completeness and openness with which love is declared here.*

'Surely,' Jay continued, 'you must realize by now that I love you? My greatest mistake was leaving you. For what?' He looked around him. 'None of this means anything. I don't enjoy it. I don't live my life without thinking of you, longing for you, regretting my cowardice. The truth is, I didn't realize, until far too late, that nothing matters as much as love.'

'I feel it, too, Jay. But who knows, if we'd done it the other way round, we may have found a different truth.'

He snorted, slightly, and shook his head. 'I doubt it. My only regret would have been Saif. But he would have forgiven me, I'm sure.'

And now, he was hurrying her down the corridor again.

35

The atmosphere in Jay's car was intense and strangely familiar. Zara kept quiet to avoid a kind of teenage embarrassment. When she was eighteen and they were on one of their endless drives into the English countryside, this same tension had been exciting. And here it was again, fifteen years later, still exciting, still brimming with risk, still without a future.

She turned her head now, absorbed Jay's profile, his alert, straight-backed body driving the car. She could have felt resentful – cautious, at least – but all she felt was adolescent impatience, sadness for the way life was arbitrated by duty and social obligation. His abandonment and its aftermath was remote – a misunderstanding of Jay's actions.

She had a sudden image of the large, feathered brushes of a car wash they had sat in together, once, pounding softly against all the glass panes, rocking them from side to side, back to front but remaining beyond the barriers of glass and metal. There was something surreal about it – like now, looking at Jay, longing to be in his arms.

The phone rang. Jay hesitated. 'Shall I ignore it?'

'It could be important,' Zara said.

Jay looked at the screen of his mobile phone. 'Oh god,' he said. 'It's Guruji.' Swiftly, he spoke into the mouthpiece. 'Saif? Yes. Fine. On the way to the lodge with Zara. Much safer there.'

His hand swerved on the steering wheel. 'Any damage?'

He listened silently for a few moments while Zara held on to her questions. 'Thank god! Karan is at your disposal. Let me know if I'm needed.' He flung the phone on the dashboard.

Zara felt her blood buzz in her ears. 'What's happened?'

Jay looked stonily ahead. 'It's turned into a riot at Qila.'

'This is my fault,' Zara could hear the shrillness in her voice. She felt hot and clammy at the same time.

Jay shook his head. 'That news report would have antagonized a lot of people.' He stroked her hand. 'It's not because of you.'

Her fingertips curled over his. 'I want to think not – but it is.'

Jay's grip on her hand tightened. 'I don't care,' he said. 'We'll weather it. Together.'

Zara was not sure how to respond; Jay sounded irrational, childish even. They drove silently for the rest of the way. As he stopped the car at the lodge, a number of guards moved forward. One opened the door and stood back, bowing, as Jay and Zara stepped out. Jay dismissed them with a nod, instructing them crisply to ensure that the place was well guarded and that lines to the police superintendent were open. Then he led Zara to the door.

Inside the hall, they stood facing each other. Jay looked like a gloomy, confused child.

'What can we do?' she said.

He shrugged, adding, 'You look miserable.'

Zara caught a glimpse of herself in the mirror behind him, partly obscured by a scarf suspended from a coat stand, and saw the same expression of unhappy confusion on her own face. Spontaneously, they laughed.

'This is hysteria,' she said, sobering up.

'Releasing tension,' he agreed.

Suddenly, she thought of the all-night horror shows in Piccadilly which she and Peter often found themselves in, where the goriest scenes were followed first by a gasp from the auditorium and then a titter of relief. Still, she was uneasy – how could she be here, in these circumstances, while Saif took another body blow? She dropped her head. Jay reached out to stroke her cheek, but she stepped back and looked away.

'We should be with Saif,' she murmured. 'Or you should.'

'I can't leave you alone here,' he said, and she had to smile at his horrified expression.

'I will be fine. You have a fine library.' The look on Jay's face was trance-like. She turned her face away, embarrassed by the love-lorn expression. A few moments ago she had felt the same.

A butler appeared soundlessly from a corridor, bearing a tray, then silently turned back and walked away.

'Being diplomatic,' Jay said.

'He doesn't ...?'

They could hear the clink of glasses on a metal tray, a knock and a firm clearing of the throat before another, older butler came in. Zara smiled; she could see, in his aged face, the outlines of a middle-aged one with high cheekbones and a strong, angular jaw. He was less straight-backed now and his arms cuddled the tray to his body for support.

'Gulab!' she said. 'How are you?' He bowed his head, touched his chest in brief acknowledgement, his eyes averted, and mumbled to Jay that the servants would leave in half an hour.

'Do you require anything before that?' he asked. Jay shook his head.

'Any instructions for the bodyguards?'

'Alert them,' Jay said. 'They might be needed.'

'Hukam. As you command.' Gulab raised his right hand to his brow and left with his eyes still lowered.

Zara flushed with humiliation. Gulab Khan had known her as a child. He had always made it a point of serving her a small plate of Nice biscuits after noticing she liked dipping them in her lemon pressé. She wished desperately that she had not been so enthusiastic about greeting him. He could not have forgotten her, surely? Perhaps the protocol with adults was different. Or had he guessed ...? No, she thought, he didn't recognize me. In that case, the thought was slow but definite; this was not the first time Jay had brought a woman here.

'A drink? Tea? Something cold?'

Zara shook her head. 'It's going to rain,' she said, watching a bank of dark rainclouds. 'I'd forgotten how beautiful they looked.'

Suddenly, they were in each other's arms. '*When Harry Met Sally*,' Jay murmured. 'We've beaten their eleven years.'

Jay moved towards the drawing room, turned on the music. The deep, warm voice of Mohammed Rafi filled the room as Jay led her out into the garden, the grove that he had constructed for her.

'*I've seen you in flowerland*,' the voice on the speakers crooned, '*found heaven on this earth*.'

Zara smiled to herself. She had loved the song and could remember the megastar Dharmendra lifting thick ropes of roses and marigold and motia hanging from frames above the bed to look at his bride, played by the legendary Meena Kumari. Again, she tried to override her embarrassment about Jay's mawkish sense of the romantic.

She was outside now, in the grove. Jay chose a chair, bent to make sure with the palm of his hand that it was clean, then pulled out a snow-white linen handkerchief and wiped away the dewy dampness. 'Please,' he said, stepping back.

Zara dropped into the chair, aware of a bizarre preliminary ritual that had always been part of her relationship with Jay. Not so with Peter. They had grabbed and hugged each other spontaneously, uninhibitedly, bursting through the door and practically pulling off each other's clothes even before they had slammed it shut behind them. Once they had been so impatient, Zara ended up with carpet burns.

'Next time,' Peter said with a show of gallantry, as he massaged some ointment into her skin, 'I will be the one underneath. You shall be Lilith, the woman on top, shocking the cosmos and the Ineffable. But I shall be far more chivalrous than Adam and I shall not let the Ineffable cast you from Eden.'

'You're mad,' Zara replied. The next moment, Peter threw himself on to the bed and swung her on to his torso.

Jay lit some lanterns with a flare. Zara felt a twinge – thinking of Peter made this feel like a transgression.

'I'll be back in a moment,' Jay said, going in.

It was a mistake to return to this spot after their last experience here. Yet, she wanted to snatch every moment before it slipped away forever. Despite Jay's passionate remarks, this would not last. There was too much to lose. The protests were an indication.

She stood up and paced the small paved area. The smell of jasmine was almost overwhelming. Where was Jay? What was he up to? She couldn't bear these silly delays.

Zara went into the main drawing room. The CD track began to repeat – he must have put it on replay. She walked towards the bedroom. Jay was there. He'd obviously seen the movie too. The bed was strewn with rose petals and jasmine. She glanced quickly at the posters on the bed and relaxed, seeing that the polished mahogany frame was ornamented only by the thick, soft folds of a snow-white mosquito net. No ropes of flowers in grotesque imitation of the movie. How embarrassing that would have been! The guards, the servants who had been asked to do it – she shuddered at the thought of being the illicit lover sneaked in by the maharaja for a sleazy rendezvous.

Jay was holding out his arms. Zara took a few steps towards him. Her heart was thumping, her mouth dry. Gulab had known. They all knew. The guards were familiar with escapades like this. This was not the first time Jay had sneaked in a woman here for sex! That was why Anapurna had been so anxious.

'Sorry, Jay.' She turned and walked out of the bedroom.

'What's the matter, Zara?' He went after her, seized her by the shoulders. She no longer felt the electric charge of his hands. The magic was gone. His arms fell limply to his side. 'What went wrong?'

She shook her head, desperate to console him. But the truth would have been too harsh. The husky, sex-laden voice in the background filled her with disgust. The fabulous verses piled into a diary for her attention, felt cloying. This, all this – it felt crass, a tacky seduction effort.

Suddenly she realized what Saif had meant when he said that Jay had not developed emotionally, that Anapurna was unhappy.

The truth was, Jay had not moved on – at least, not in this context. He had gone from education and romance into family duties, negotiations with the government, the transforming of what was once state responsibility into business development and a political career. He had neglected his interrupted love life and made a marriage of convenience – and his sentimental, over-romantic side had never been fulfilled. A moment's envy streaked through her as she thought of Jay romancing Anapurna. She took a step towards him, wondering if she would regret losing the opportunity to complete the unfinished business of so many years. Sublimation, Peter would have called it. The healing of an old psychic wound.

'Zara?' He was standing very close.

'I'm sorry, Jay,' she said. 'It's me. I can't do it. I've changed too much. And you ... you're just like you were in Oxford.'

Jay hung his head. 'Let me order some food. Let's just relax and talk. Then I'll leave.'

Zara breathed deeply. 'I can't stay, Jay.'

'But it's dangerous, Zara. I can't let you ...'

'Please, Jay. I have to go.'

He looked bewildered.

'Can you organize a car to take me to Ahmedabad? I want to get out of here – of Trivikrampur. I don't want to return to Qila yet. I've caused enough trouble.'

Jay opened his mouth to protest or defend her right or declare his love – she'd never know because, thankfully, he said nothing. Instead, he nodded. 'I'll drive you.'

'No,' Zara said. 'No. I'd rather you got one of your staff to do it. I'll be more anonymous that way. And you can see to Qila.'

Zara was relieved that Raju was driving her. Raju, who had grown up with them.

'Do you remember, Princess,' he said, 'when you and the other children used to call our Maharaja Saheb "Prince Three-steps".

Look at him now. A great ruler and an important politician. Like a true descendant of Vishnu-god.'

'You're right.' Zara was only half-listening. She hoped that Raju suspected nothing of the underhand set-up she had left behind. Probably not – Jay had brought her to the lodge to get her away from the rioters.

She turned her thoughts to Ahmedabad – how her secret visit had turned into a rod to beat her back. What if all this had an effect on the Ankahi operatives?

Who, she thought in panic, in God's name could have given the papers the story of her visit to Ahmedabad? No one knew where she went.

Was it someone from Lalaji's establishment?

Raju waved at three sentries who stood to attention as he drove past. He grinned.

'Do you recognize that boy, Princess? That's Vijay, grandson of Gulab, the head butler – he used to think he was the boss of all the staff.' He chuckled. 'But when it came to his son, he wanted him to do an independent job. So he had a choice: driver or guard. That way you don't have to serve people. My father was the same. The other two guards are his cousins from his village.'

'It's a good thing you're all still at the palace, in the same family.'

'We will be here until our line dies out,' Raju said. His voice was soft. He briefly removed his hands from the wheel, folded them together and bowed his forehead to touch them. 'The Vamanas are our gods.'

The journey to the station was mostly silent. Through the window Zara could see the dust rise beneath the wheels. Despite the darkness children played all the way along, quick to cluster around the windows when the car stopped, begging in languages ranging from the local Gujarati to Hindi, English and even Russian.

It was dark when they arrived at Nandpur Station. She had passed the platform several times as a child, on the train to or from Trivikram, and was surprised to see a miniature version of one of the grand Victorian stations left by the British in large Indian towns. Zara stepped out of the car. Raju darted forward to the ticket office, checked on train times and accompanied her to the platform with her overnight bag.

'Don't wait, Raju.' Zara held out some money.

Raju shook his head. 'Don't shame me, Princess. Do you think so little of me? After all these years?'

Zara apologized. 'I– it's past dinner time.' She put away the money. 'Your family. How are they?'

'They're all fine, by God's mercy. Maharaja Sa bought my father some land in the village when he retired. He has a neem tree plantation. He feels like a zamindar.' He chuckled. 'From driver to landowner!' Raju's voice was suddenly robust. 'The train will be a little while. I'll be here until you are safely on it.'

He set down his burden and picked up a hamper. Ceremoniously he threw back the lid, took out a tablecloth and spread it on a bench. He detached a plate and some cutlery from the strapping and laid it on the dazzling damask cloth.

'This is amazing,' Zara laughed. 'But really, Raju, I'm not hungry.'

He laid out some containers. She laughed again. 'Mind you, if it had been a tiffin-carrier from your mother, it might be too tempting to refuse. Do you still use tiffin-carriers in India? Or is it plastic boxes like England?'

'A moment.' Raju disappeared through the entrance area of the station and reappeared with a tiffin-carrier. 'If I'm not offending you?'

Zara sat up, excited. The tiffin-carrier was smaller than the ones she remembered but then in those days they had catered for at least four. Each of its neatly stacked brass bowls gleamed, catching the light of the naked bulbs on the platform. Beneath the gleam, she could see fine scratches left by bits of coal in the unsifted ashes used to scrub the containers. Raju released the catch on the solid brass bands that held the stacked pots together. It loosened. He slipped it off and slowly removed the top container.

'Methi-alu!' Zara breathed in the aroma of the bright green fenugreek leaves studding potato chunks golden with turmeric.

Raju held out the second bowl and revealed round discs of crumbly bread. 'Garnished bread', it translated as roghni roti because it was coated with a little ghee or butter. 'Your mother's?'

Raju nodded, smiling happily. 'You remember.'

'Of course I remember.' Zara lifted one out of the bowl and ladled some methi-alu on it.

'We ate this when we went hunting.' They spoke the words together and Raju suddenly fell silent.

'Raju, what's the matter?'

'I– just. I'm sorry, I got carried away. Talking to you like this.'

'Nonsense, Raju. You've made me very happy. I miss your mother's cooking in London.' She wanted to squeeze his arm but it would be inappropriate. An English woman might get away with it but she was still part of a big family and its tradition. 'Does she still make that chutney? You know, the one with dried red chilli? And garlic? With lots of ghee.'

'Absolutely. With millet bread. You remember? Or khichri.'

'We have to make our own khichri in London.'

'But you must have good restaurants there.'

'The Indian food in restaurants is not like this,' Zara confessed. She stuffed another morsel into her mouth. 'This is wonderful.'

She laughed at Raju's shocked expression. She had a sudden image of a bowl of khichri, white rice studded with tiny yellow lentils, and its comforting bouquet of cloves and black pepper. 'When I get back, bring your mother to see me. And make sure she cooks some of her lovely khichri, and the chutney.' Her voice was drowned in the dogged rumbling of an approaching train.

Raju stacked the brass bowls together and lifted the luggage. He strode alongside the train, looking expertly through the train windows until he spotted a relatively empty carriage.

'I'm sorry, Princess. There was no advance reservation so I might not find an exclusive carriage.'

Zara shook her head. 'It's only a short journey.'

Raju looked around impatiently. 'Where's the station master?'

Further down the platform, the uniformed station master was strutting up and down. Raju spoke to him in a low voice and he approached a carriage. A few people stepped out of it and into another one. The station master's voice was conciliatory, his manner solicitous as he ushered them in. Raju walked towards him, bowing as he motioned Zara forward.

'I've cleared this carriage,' he said. 'Are you travelling with the Princess?'

Raju shook his head. 'Make sure she's taken care of. She's the Maharaja's own guest. Personal guest. The sister of ...' He choked back his words.

'Family.'

'Rajkumari.' The man gave Zara a surreptitious glance and bowed. She was relieved the man had assumed she was Hindu. Raju settled her into the carriage, dusting the windows, wiping down the faux leather seat. He placed her luggage carefully on the overhead rack, then took it down and settled it on the seat opposite.

'You won't need to trouble yourself to lift it up and down now,' he said. The shrill whistle sounded. 'Your permission, Princess?'

Raju remained standing inside until Zara had nodded and thanked him.

'Thank you, Raju. Go on, hurry. The train's moving.'

He bowed low and, with a swift leap, landed nimbly on the platform. Zara watched him, a warm fragment of her childhood, as still as one of the station columns, transfixed, eyes fixed on her carriage window as the train moved out of the station. An era gone. A forgotten memory revived. A past enriched.

She stood up to get a book out of her overnight case and there, beside the Fortnum's hamper, was the gleaming brass tiffin-carrier. Raju had given her his food. And now he would drive back hungry. She picked up the tiffin-carrier and held it close. Her tears were hot. They fell on the pristine, gleaming surface of the metal container. She rubbed frantically with her handkerchief. She couldn't, under any circumstances, let Raju's gift get dirty.

IV

36

She must have fallen asleep because the sign for an unfamiliar station drifted into her vision.

A few men boarded the train, peering into her carriage as they passed. She hated this open curiosity and looked out of the window, willing them to disappear, but they returned.

'This carriage is reserved,' Zara said.

A man stepped inside and signalled his companions to enter. The small compartment was crowded. Zara felt claustrophobic.

'I'm sorry. This carriage is reserved.'

The man looked at a piece of paper. 'Reserved from where?'

'Nandpur.'

'It doesn't state this here, madam.'

'Well it was done – at the station.'

'By whom?'

'Trivikram Maharaja – his personal chauffeur booked it.'

The man paused, taking her in slowly. There was a swagger to his movements – as if he thought himself beyond the station master's authority, maybe even the maharaja's. His gaze was offensive as it scraped her body, full of entitlement. He looked, alert, at the tiffin-carrier clutched tight in her arms.

'Please come with me, madam,' he said.

'Come where?'

The man turned around and muttered a long stream of words in a language she couldn't place, ending in a command. 'Rekha, come here.' A female in salwar-kurta stepped into the carriage.

'Mrs Zara Hamilton, please?'

Zara nodded. Who were these people? The woman's voice dropped. 'You've come here for a meeting, yes?'

'Not here.'

'I know I know, I know.' The woman spoke rapidly. 'You're on your way to Ahmedabad.'

'I am.'

'We've come to get you, madam. News gone ahead already, you're expected in Ahmedabad. Much safer you get off here and come with us.'

Ankahi. They had come to collect her before she got into trouble. Impressed, Zara stood up. 'Who told you I was on this train?'

Something about Rekha's gap-toothed grin made Zara uncomfortable and she looked away.

'We have our sources everywhere. Please come with me, Mrs Zahhra,' Rekha said.

A sense of *déjà vu* dangled in Zara's mind when Rekha introduced the 'h' into her name – something intangible that made her cringe. A few curious faces peeped in through the window.

'They're beg'ning to think why train is so long in station,' Rekha said. 'We should go before anyone becomes shuspicious.' She grasped Zara's elbow and guided her out of the carriage, then paused, grabbed the tiffin-carrier and walked her to a people-carrier with muddy wheels and a damaged body. The man who had spoken earlier slid behind the steering wheel, the others piled into the back row and the driving cabin, leaving the middle seats free for Rekha and Zara.

'Where are we going?' Zara asked as the car drove quickly out of town and on to a dirt track along the base of a range of mountains.

'We are obliged not to talk about it,' the driver said.

'Is all this secrecy necessary?' Zara challenged. The driver turned and stared at her from behind his seat.

'Think about it, Mrs Hamilton. We knew exactly how to find you. In spite that it was the last-minute decision and no one had been informed of your movements. You think we are only ones and others cannot do same like us?'

Zara preferred the more vocal, direct Ankahi members she'd met before. These people were menacing. She shuddered. 'How do I know you are who you say you are? You could be anyone.'

Rekha gave her a warning look as the car swung to the right and up a steep gradient. She unscrewed the lid of a small stainless steel flask, poured out some coffee and thrust it at Zara. 'Yes, madam. You are right, Mrs HAM-milton. We could be anyone. No need for you to find out that information. So no point to think about it, madam.'

The coffee tasted bad, gritty. Zara took another gulp and looked out of the window. The last streaks of light were casting a glow over parts of the mountainside. The skirt of the mountain, she thought, recalling a line from a poem. Would the grass be springy, she wondered, if she were to open the door and leap out? Could she roll down and conceal herself in the folds of this magnificent skirt? Her hand tightened on the door-handle. But why, she asked herself sharply. Why would I want to jump? These people are here to help me. It doesn't matter if they're a bit rough and ready.

'I know now,' she said, 'why you call yourself Ankahi. Unspoken. You really don't give away anything, do you?' Her face muscles felt stiff.

She flinched as a man's voice boomed from in front. 'Who is this Ankahi?'

'She's nearly gone, sir,' Rekha said. 'She's talking nonsense.'

In the distance, Zara could see something glint in the luminous saffron sky-shroud. The car jerked violently. Zara's head snapped back from her neck. The pain was like a screwdriver twisting between her neck and shoulders. She strained to open her eyes, listening for the screams she was sure were coming from her throat. But no one responded and she seemed to have no control over her body.

'Still sleeping.' Rekha was climbing out of the car. 'She can stay.'

'Water. Please, I need water.' Rekha paid no attention. Couldn't she hear? 'Please, water, please,' Zara begged, trying to follow her out.

The men had walked on ahead and stood cocooned in the light of an oil lamp held up by a man swathed in saffron. All around them the deep black night was closing in, leaving four men and a Brahmin priest suspended within a small hollow of light. Which part of it was real, Zara wondered – the darkness or the tableau in the spotlight?

She curled herself into a tight ball then let her body spring back, screaming with all the power she could muster. 'No!'

The priest looked at the car. He raised the lamp, stepped out of the tableau and walked towards her. The men followed. 'This woman is sick,' the man said. 'Why did you not bring her in for help?'

'We didn't want to bother you, Swamiji.'

She heard what could have been anger in the priest's voice. 'Bother me? This is a place of God. It is our dharma to tend to the needy here.' He paused. 'We fed you and rested you, did we not? Yet you were hale and hearty.'

'She's not sick, too, Maharaj. She's just tired – sleeping.'

Zara felt a hand, soft as cotton wool, sweep down her face, and shame when the priest spoke again. 'She has been sick.'

Immediately, Rekha stood between the priest and Zara.

'Move out of my way, please, young woman.' The priest's voice was firm. 'This person needs seeing to.'

'No, no, Maharaj.'

'It is inappropriate,' he said, 'for you to prevent a holy man from carrying out his duty.'

'Only because, Your Grace, because, you know. She's ... we ... we don't wish to contaminate ...'

'Service does not contaminate, it elevates. Please step aside.'

'She's a *Muslim*!' Rekha spluttered.

'A Muslim!'

'We usually don't talk to these 'Ms, Maharaj – she was on the roadside ... we couldn't leave her and now ... she's a druggie.'

The priest placed a hand on Rekha's shoulder and moved her aside. His face was glowing in the light of the flickering lamp. 'You think I will be contaminated by tending to a Muslim? Do you know this temple was rebuilt and guarded by a Muslim when we were forced to leave it two years ago?'

'Please,' Zara was relieved to hear her own whisper through rubbery lips. 'Water.'

She was being lifted out of the people-carrier by saffron-clad bodies. Water, blessed water, trickled into her mouth and poured over her face, sliding through her hair, spilling down her body, washing away the dirt of the journey, the smells of sweat and regurgitated coffee.

She remembered coming to the guest house with the Vamanas and Saif before Aunty Hana stopped going out. There was a warm-water spring. She was five, or younger. Jay had told her that it was where Vamana, the incarnation of Vishnu, had planted a fourth, secret footstep. The large indentation left by the foot of the god was filled with water from sulphur springs. It was a temple of healing. Beautiful.

'When it's light,' she burbled, 'there are mountains. Just behind the rooms there, at the back. Gypsies came, too. Every year in winter ... to dance for the Vamanas.' She opened her eyes and looked into the face of the swami. 'I'm so sorry,' she said. I'm imagining things. My mind is ... there's something wrong with me.'

The priest was listening carefully. 'Never doubt your instincts, child. We don't remember what happened in another lifetime except in blessed, lucid moments when we are hovering at the edge of consciousness.'

She could hear voices approaching. 'Say nothing more, child,' the Swami whispered. 'What is private is sacrosanct. Not for everyone's ears. May Vishnu bless and protect you.'

Someone was placing her in the car beside Rekha, who pulled at her. Then there was sleep.

37

The car swung off the track on to a scrubby verge. Zara sat up with a jolt. The driver was about to drive off the edge of the mountain. The car seemed to nosedive. Gravel crunched beneath its wheels as it slid down an almost vertical slope and screeched to a halt.

Rekha opened the door of the car and Zara retched at the terrible stench. She covered her nose with a scarf and shoved Zara out as if she were a parcel, keeping hold of her arm as she marched her into a yard.

The driver pointed to a door at the end of the row on the left. Rekha guided Zara to the door as another man unlocked it. Inside there was a bed and two chairs. Zara stopped. 'What's going on?'

'Come. Sit. I'll get tea.'

'Where are the others?'

'What others?' the driver asked, sharply.

'My friends. The people I met before.'

'What friends? You haven't been to our country for twenty years.'

'I have friends, nevertheless.'

'Naver theee lass,' the man mimicked. Then he straightened himself up. 'You have no friends here and you are no one's friend. You are a spy.'

'A spy?' Zara said. 'Oh yes, of course, for the Pakistanis.'

There was complete silence. Zara wrenched her arm away from Rekha and faced the men. 'Look, if Ankahi has changed its mind about helping me, that's fine. I can't force you. This is a labour of love. But there's no need for all this elaborate stuff.' She looked around her. 'I'd like to go home now, please.' No one moved. 'Well, in that case, I suppose I'll have to start walking. Someone will give me a lift.'

Rekha looked as if she was about to speak but the driver spoke again, sneering. 'Did you see any single vehicle or personage when we came up?'

'Look, it is already dark,' Rekha said. 'Let us all calm. Mrs Hamilton, sleep now. In the morning we will decide what to do next.'

Zara could hear her voice grow sharp. 'Decide what? I want to go to Ahmedabad and that's all there is to it. If you can't drive me, I'll make my own way.' She turned to the door.

Rekha shoved her hard and she staggered backward through the doorway and grabbed a chair to break her fall. Quickly, Rekha stepped in after her and shut the door, 'These men are patriots. They will do whatsoever it will take them to protect their country. They will give their own life as easily as they will take yours. They are not this Ankahi you keep talking about.'

Zara's tongue clung to the roof of her mouth and her head banged as if her heart had climbed into it. She could hardly hear Rekha speak. 'I don't know what you're talking about. Protect their country from whom?'

Rekha's mouth literally fell open. 'You are still pretending you don't know nothing about why you were brought here?'

'I don't know what you are thinking. You've misunderstood ...' Rekha looked confused. Zara repeated herself. 'Aap log pata nahin kya soch rahe hain. Aap ko galat fehmi ho gayi hai.'

'Don't you speak to me in that horrible tongue! What do you think I am? Do you think I can't even speak English? Hunh? You speak always English with the mens and with me you speak that dirty Urdu language.'

'You don't watch Hindi movies? Listen to the radio, watch TV?'

'I watch. That is Hindi language, not Urdu.'

'What's the difference?'

'*You* speak, makes it different. You're a dirty Muslim. Worser even. You're a traitor.'

Suddenly, she looked different. Her bushy eyebrows came together into a fierce mono-brow beneath her deeply ridged forehead. Her voice was shrill and sharp and the words streamed from her mouth. Rekha seemed to be ranting about news reports, informants who had confirmed that Zara worked for Pakistanis, that she was here to discredit India's name abroad. That her chambers in London took on anti-nationals, traitors out to destroy India, and rewarded them handsomely for stirring up strife and riots and fomenting discontent in India. The people Zara called 'deportees', they were none other than 'plants' from the Pakistani government. She had an elaborate system which she used to exploit British immigration, swapping Pakistanis and Indian Muslims to legitimate Indian Hindu immigrants or even Sri Lankan asylum-seekers. And how could she do this unless she was getting 'big bucks' from somewhere? Who but the Pakistani government itself! People like her were responsible for making Indian Muslims feel strong with promises of Pakistan, whose aim it was to get enough power to invade Gujarat at the Sind-India border while everyone else was concentrating on Kashmir.

This is a delusion, Zara thought. I'm having a nightmare. The troubles of the past couple of days have unhinged me. This kind of thing doesn't happen – not to people like me. A great wave of revulsion heaved up her stomach to her throat. She ran to a bucket in the corner and retched violently. Nothing came. She remained hunched for a while, clutching at her ribs.

She felt the hardness of the bed meet her body. The sheets smelled of carbolic. It was a relief from the pervasive stench. Best to sleep. She closed her eyes. When she woke again, the nightmare would be over and she would be at Ahmedabad Station. It occurred to her, as she drifted off, that her trip had been impromptu and she had made no contact with Ankahi.

Zara's eyes flickered open, registering the wall in front of her. Where was she? Her eyes began to focus and her memory with them. Her heart throbbed uncomfortably in her throat. Had she been drugged? Not possible. She'd had nothing to eat or drink since coming here. She shuddered at the memory of the hideous coffee. It must have been drugged. This was as far-fetched as Rekha's ranting.

She lay down again. Saif would have heard by now and if Jay hadn't instructed these people to get her back to Trivikram immediately, then Saif certainly would. Some light was beginning to leak into the darkness though a few stars still studded the sky.

Lying down again was a bad move. She sprang up and lurched to the bucket. Nothing. She banged on the door. It opened immediately and a man looked in.

'Kya baat hai? What's the matter?'

'I want to go to Trivikram.'

'So jao. So jao. Go to isleep. They will come morning time.'

The man was carrying a rifle.

'Is that to kill me with?'

The man shrugged.

'Call Rekha.'

'Rekha isleep. Everyone isleep. You isleeping also.' He prodded her with the rifle point and banged the door shut.

Zara climbed on to the bed, shuffled her body around and leaned against the stone wall. She could see out of the slit. She looked up at the sky and saw a star – the poor thing was fading. *Please don't die,* she thought desperately. Suddenly she was shaking with sobs – stars didn't die. They just faded and then regenerated the next night, as luminous as before.

A rickety trestle table was being dragged into her cell. Two men stood in two corners of the room. Rekha was hovering over her bed.

'What do you want?'

Rekha looked startled. 'What do I want? Get up.'

There was a thud and the door flew open. The 'colonel' who had sat beside the driver the night before marched in. His army boot had left a scuffed dent on the door where he had kicked it.

'Did you drug me last night?' Zara angled her head towards Rekha. 'That coffee. There was something in it, wasn't there?'

'I am the person who is asking the questions,' the colonel snapped. 'But since you ask, yes, we thought we might do you kindness to give you something for sleeping.'

Rekha propelled her towards a chair.

'Very kind,' Zara said. 'Thanks. Now let's just get this stuff over so that I can get on with my plans.'

The colonel jumped at her words. 'Plan? What plan?'

Unbelievably, Rekha was tying her hands to the chair with a rope.

'You've been watching too many movies,' Zara said. 'You think I'm fooled by all this? I'm an international lawyer. I know the Indian government would not use such ridiculous tactics.'

'So you admit you know about our government tactics? How did you come by that information?'

Zara could hear her own laughter, a dry cackle that burst out of her throat. Two pairs of eyes glowered at her. The colonel spoke.

'I am Colonel Solanki. I came to apprehend you as a Pakistani agent who is here for the express purpose of contacting insurgents and setting up local networks to foment trouble in Gujarat. If you answer my questions, it could be we will release and deport you to UK. If not, you will ... disappear. Your arrest is nowhere on record.'

'Okay. When are you taking me back to Trivikram? Or Ahmedabad?'

The colonel's eyes slid away. Rekha tightened the cord around Zara's wrist, and then again, so that it chafed and stung. Zara writhed as the two strands pulled together and pinched her flesh.

'What was your mission in coming to India?' the colonel asked.

'My aunt was dying – she asked me to sort out her will.'

'Let us dispense with the cover story. I will do whatsoever is necessary for getting information from you.' The colonel leant forward and the smell of coffee on stale breath snaked out of his mouth. She recoiled. It was like the stench of a dead rat.

'What are you after? What do you want from me?' she said.

'Names, dates and locations.'

'What the hell are you talking about?' Zara was alarmed.

The colonel stepped back and signalled the two guards. One grabbed her by the shoulders while the other punched her in the stomach. Zara's back hit the metal corner of the table. The man raised his rifle butt and brought it down just beneath her ribs. The pain of the metal corner was so intense she felt nothing else.

Rekha looked at the uneaten food on Zara's bed. 'Our simple food is not good enough for you?'

Zara could not be bothered to reply. The pain in her body was severe and she had slept so much she had no sense of time.

'You have good job. You are lawyer, why you do this kind of bad work?' Rekha asked. Zara ignored her. The stupid woman had taken to asking facetious questions about life in England. She pushed. 'Must be nice there, no? Everyone is rich.'

'No.'

Rekha scowled. 'You think I'm fool? I know people whose relatives come back to visit. They always bring expensive items.'

'When can I get out of here?'

Rekha shrugged. 'Give them their informations.'

'I haven't got any. How many times do I have to tell you?'

'We know you are lying. If you are here for your aunt, you should be gone after burial. Why you made riots in Qila?'

'I did not cause riots.'

'Hunh! Just like your mother was not a prostitute.'

'What did you say?'

Rekha's face was like a storm cloud. 'You are living like princess. Look at my life. You know how I grew up? Like outcast. Everybody look down on me.'

Rekha raised her outstretched palm and shook it in Zara's face. 'I curse you – all your Muslim people.'

The door burst open and the colonel came in, waving a piece of paper. 'Proof. Your father was activist – Sindhi nationalist who worked with Muslims in Rajasthan to secede and declare their independence.'

'My father died before I was born. He was an industrialist.'

'Legacies like this are handed down generations.'

38

Saif had eventually built the small stone room in his teens out of the stones he excavated from that first piece of land he worked in Ramzi Bagh more than a quarter century ago. He opened the door and smelled the familiar damp. Lighting the brazier would soon dispel it but he could not bear to enter. He felt contaminated by recent events and did not want to sully the purity of this simple space.

Zara had disappeared. He believed that had it been possible, she would have contacted him. A week was ample time to work through any confusion or distress. Something was wrong. Peter concurred and agreed to allow a few days before contacting the foreign office. Zara had often fantasized about 'going underground' for a while. Perhaps in a crisis she had acted it out.

Saif looked again into the cool darkness of the stone shelter then turned and walked through the thriving herbs and plants he had nurtured in this lush space on the ledge of a hill. He would take some back to the lodge for his medicine wheel. With his back to the hill, he looked up at the sky and then across at the nearest mountain in the crescent that circled one side of Ramzi Bagh. It brought back a flash of his single rebel act when he joined the army after university to flee a future tied to the Ramzi legacy.

The past month had drawn him into the push and pull of worldly concerns, a reminder that detachment was not always possible. It reminded him how lucky he was to have Pebbles who accepted his function and allowed him to live the life for which he had been ear-marked. When he looked at each aspect of life laid out like a blanket, he was astonished at how differently people lived. How so-called 'normal' life was filled with an excess of activity and emotion and how the likelihood of satisfaction and fulfilment was continually pushed out of reach by resentment and avarice. What amazed him was the sheer triviality of it.

So much of his life was simplified; the petty struggles of proving the right and wrong of minutiae which segued into the endlessly growing need to be in command, to steer events beyond the capability of individual commands were, to him, irrelevant, redundant. He recalled a rare affectionate memory of his father and smiled. Sultan always said, 'Let the sky take care of it.' His followers shortened it amongst themselves and when they wanted to guide a fellow disciple or a novice struggling with the need to take control, they simply pointed upward and said, 'Sky.'

Nothing was comparable to the relief and liberation of that instant of letting go. But these last weeks, life's impurities and pettiness had surrounded him and clung to him like filth from a sewer. There had been moments when he felt himself sucked into the heavy sludge. Was there a message for him in this, Saif wondered. Was there something he was missing?

He went carefully through the events, stopping mid-stride as he made his way up to the peak of the hill, to shake off the chaos that had entered his life. There had been the mess created by Shinde.

He paused, squaring his shoulders to distribute the weight that each memory seemed physically to lay across them so that, for the first time he could recall, the summit looked too far to reach. But he was determined to keep climbing. There, he felt sure he would evade the grasping, demanding fingers that pinched and pulled at his coherence and, once again, even if very briefly, experience peace.

Ah, Zara! Had she any idea, at all, how much she had shaken the equilibrium of the worlds between which she moved? Her colleagues were ready to turn it into an international media circus; Peter believed the British government needed to be involved and Jay agreed with him, devastated that he had allowed this to happen. News had reached Anapurna who was burning in the flames of her own jealousy. There were moments when he questioned his own understanding of his faith – was this an event which must be left to God? Or was this where action and control contested blind trust and the individual took things into his own hands? In such moments Saif, like Ana, felt all the grief and torment of a jilted lover – as if his beloved was abandoning him and he was lost.

He looked up and saw the sky revolve around him. He reached for a rock and leant against it. The familiar contours of the boulders and rises above him looked suddenly alien. It is a reflection, he thought, of how things look from varying perspectives. He felt a great exhaustion as he straightened himself. Why, he asked himself, why should I be so weary? World-weary, another part of himself seemed to say. Perhaps the time was approaching. The moment was coming when he was to make the transition. Would he have felt the deep, singeing sensation of loss had this immersion in gross chaos not reignited the disintegrating fragments of worldly attachment, the demand to control? But there was always a mirror – could it be that this was the last confrontation, the meeting that reflected something beyond the confines of his chosen perspective, like a mirror contains images beyond its physical frame?

He stood up, swaying a little from the vision of the distance between himself and the mountain peak. Did he really need to drag himself to the top? To what end? He knew God was to be found everywhere. He looked back. The skirts of the hill stretched far below, a fabulous combination of patchwork, alive, springing from the earth, ribboned with delicately wavering streams and falls.

He turned and walked upwards. His body was energized and in his mind he saw roses in bloom. Roses he had planted with Sultan when he was fifteen, on his first trip to the top. 'Why not?' his father had asked when he hesitated. 'Your function is to make the conditions conducive to planting. It is not up to you to make the plants grow or the roses bloom. You are the gardener – the worker. Your function is to plant, so plant. Remember it when you are surrounded by eager acolytes who cannot grasp the ramz – tell them: "Plant and nurture to the best of your ability; do not look for results – the outcome is not your concern."'

Now he was soaring up to the summit on a wind of memory, icy, compelling. He could remember his lifetime encapsulated in a moment when he sat beneath a glacier in Kashmir amid the eternal boundary skirmishes. His heart split just like the country was split at the Partition of India and the governments of both sides sent innocent men to kill each other because there was no other way for the two sides to interact. The troubles that assailed Trivikram now were on the continuum of that sinister schism leading to 1947. But he had touched peace. And that peace was not around him but within. It came, he could see, not from withdrawal and isolation but in those moments of intense attachment, of life and death, when white became red with splashes of fresh blood and hot blasts of gunpowder scorched the virgin snows. He could, then, with all the love and sympathy possible in the human organism, look to God and open himself without request or complaint and let Him see inside. How often he forgot that simple lesson taught so many times: 'Your duty is merely to do your best.'

The essence of detachment was to accept your limitations. He had collected the ruptured dead, his tears had mingled with their blood, he had suffered. But he had, for the first time, known that to detach was not to eschew suffering and strife. It was merely to continue doing one's job.

I am a gardener, he thought, his elation making him fly. He felt weightless and like a husk, nearly formless, knowing that one day he would dissolve into the atmosphere.

As he reached the top of the mountain, he saw roses, red and white, and a curious, deep red that was almost black.

39

Zara scratched a line on the floor with a piece of slate. Nine lines marked nine days. Her arms shook as she placed a table on the bed and a chair on top. She leant on the wall for support as she clambered up and looked out of the chink. The desert sand rippled across to the horizon where it joined the sky, featureless, uninhabited. No cars, no locals, not even the odd camel with its leader. Here was heaven turning into hell. She had never dreamed that she would ever wish away her desert. But right now, she would give all for a busy road.

Somehow, high up here, she felt safer, cleaner than below where one of the soldiers had tried to rape her. He went away when she buried a shard of wood into his cheek and told him she was suffering from AIDS.

'You think I am stupid?' he snarled. But he slunk away.

'What is like to marry an English?' Rekha kept asking.

'All Englishmen are not the same.' Zara felt dizzy.

'But still. They must be different from our Hindu men, no?'

'Are all Indian men the same?'

Rekha scowled. 'All are maamaa's boys. Does your husband listen to his mother or to you?'

'That's my business.' Zara rolled her food on her tongue. 'You've put something in the dal. You've drugged me again. You know it's against the law ...' What law? She was in some abandoned cell in the middle of the desert held by vigilantes. Would she ever get out of here?

She needed to get Rekha on her side but it was the hardest thing she'd ever had to try. She could cope with the nasty stuff – it was the perpetual drone of resentment, the drip-drip questions about England and her privileged life that drove her mad.

'They say firangis don't care if girls have sex with other men before marriage. He bhagvan! Oh god!' She grabbed her ears then smacked her cheeks. 'Indian man will kill wife and whole family if they gave him non-virgin.'

Zara knew from clients that this was sometimes true. 'Some might,' she snapped. 'Not all.'

'Now you know better than me. Haven't you heard of dowry deaths?'

Had she heard of dowry death? It was one of the human rights abuses that had brought her into the field.

'Tell me, what is your husband like?'

Peter was a good man. Why was she so dissatisfied with him? Perhaps being dissatisfied was her preferred mode of living. It must exasperate him to hear her drone on about Nyla yet do nothing about contacting her.

Peter had made her happy and given her a sense of belonging. It was a closeness that transcended cities and buildings and nations. That sense of belonging had its source in a mutual dream.

She felt dejected, sad that she had not been able to take pleasure in Peter's new dream. She had failed without trying. The more settled he was the less fulfilled she felt. He had seized his dream by stamping on hers. But would she have been happier the other way round, knowing she had strangled his?

Night and the silence were the hardest. Nothing to do, no one to speak to. There was so much she needed to say and do. She needed to look at herself instead of pointing the finger at Peter.

Sometimes when she blinked, the gap between opening and shutting her eyes was like a slideshow or a scene change in a movie. There was a blank or 'wipe' like a colourful curtain, dancing patterns separating one instant from another. Anything could follow, often without sequence or logic.

Questions gathered from all over; she could see a great, heaving ocean, glitter and sparkle, but she knew that beneath its tantalizing, alluring surface was an infinitely deep, dark abyss.

Look into it, Zara. You might find what you're seeking.

'I won't!' she screamed. 'I won't. I don't want to look.'

'What are you frightened of finding?'

She sat up with a jerk. There was a twinge in her neck. It bolted through into her skull, behind her ear. Was Peter here? That was Peter's voice. Then she saw his face, distorted, scornful, scoffing and she knew her imagination was playing tricks again.

They kept slipping things into her food and water. She'd thought of refusing to eat and drink but they didn't care. They didn't care if she died. Now she knew what it was like to be alone in a world where she was insignificant and unwanted. Like Peter's clients. And hers.

Beware: if you look into the abyss, the abyss will look back into you, Nietzsche warned. And here she was now, beside the abyss. Or was she in it – avoiding contamination by refusing to look?

Stillness! I feared it would catch up with me. Now it has. And it's worse than I imagined.

She closed her eyes. Let it devour her. She would stop fighting.

Dreams, memories, imaginings tumbled into the space left by resignation. In the light from the niche she saw scenes from the past. The curtains at the window in the long drawing room at Qila – soft muslin printed with bold bunches of violet. She liked the fine green stems and leaves. Now they flowed out of their space and trailed around her chair, binding her as Aunty Hana spoke without trying to free her.

'Things have always come easy to Nyla,' she said. 'Her husband's devotion. The way men fall in love with her. How she feels she has a right to freedom – you see how easily she flits from one country to another? Nothing holds her down, nothing defeats her. She's weightless, insubstantial. You, Zara, you are like Urdu, dispossessed, a citizen of no state, undervalued, unable to lay claim to any territory.'

Hana had a history and tradition which she honoured, which gave her gravitas. Nyla was a free spirit. Zara was driftwood.

Zara's bones and muscles were filled with liquid tiredness and the pain moved when she moved. She tucked her clasped hands beneath her cheek and snuggled down into the luxury of the soft bed. Her body suddenly realized how much it had longed for – needed – the comfort of lying down. But she felt triumphant. She had prolonged the day as much as she could. The day out with Mama at the Taj Mahal. Of course it wouldn't have mattered where she was, as long as she was with Nyla in this loving, indulgent mood. It was unusual. Nyla was changeable. It made Zara jittery. One moment she was telling a story with verve, changing her voice to suit each character, diving into digressions about the story or its writer then returning to the main tale; the next she'd rush to the end and withdraw, as if her clockwork had run down and there was no one to wind her up again. No amount of cajoling and coaxing would work. And if Zara persisted, Nyla might snap at her, or just get up and walk away. That was the worst of all.

Zara had been good all day, and even when she forgot and became too high-spirited, Nyla's good mood continued. Once or twice, Zara caught her gazing at her face with an intensity that scared her. As if Mama was memorizing her. Zara wanted the day not to end. She said nothing when the small of her back ached, the calves of her legs pinched from deep inside and her shoulders felt weary. There was a pain deep, deep in her stomach. A very different pain.

She flopped on her stomach when they got home, her arms flung above her head. Oh! The pain in her tiny breasts was dreadful, as if a golf ball was pressing into them. She sat up, flushed, her heart throbbing. She was ill. Should she tell someone? No, she would go to sleep. She'd be fine in the morning. She was just overtired.

She closed her eyes and conjured up her favourite moments of the day. The picnic on the grass by the fountains, the tour of the shrines of Mumtaz and Shah Jehan, in a chamber below ground. Nyla had covered her hair and raised her hands in prayer. Like many others in the tomb, they read the Fateha for the peace of the lovers' souls. Suddenly, Zara was aware of Nyla's tension.

'Subhan'Allah!' the mullah said – Zara saw that he was not praising Allah, but her mother's beauty. She nudged Nyla, who finished her prayers swiftly, grabbed Zara by the shoulder and hurried her out, scowling. Oh no, Zara thought, I've ruined it now. She's going to stop having fun. But the moment they were out, Nyla released her and laughed out loud. 'Dirty sod!' she breathed. 'He's supposed to be ministering to the souls of the dead, not ogling pilgrims!'

'Well, I guess it is a romantic story,' Zara ventured.

'Zara!' Nyla gasped, shocked. But it was only pretend shock, because she dropped to the grass and hugged her. 'My little girl is growing up.' She stared into her eyes, cupped her face in her hands. Zara thought she looked as if she was seeing her for the first time. Nyla pressed her head to her shoulder and held her close for ages. Zara was sad when it ended but she could hear her mother's repeated, fierce whisper – 'I love you. I love you. I love you' – like a heartbeat for the rest of the day. So she drew out the day. Every time going home was mentioned she distracted her mother and eked out more moments.

She closed her eyes, now, and imagined her mother's words in time to her heartbeat. Just like when she was a baby – Nyla said that as she lay with her in the night, she would find herself breathing in time with infant Zara. Sometimes the baby's breathing felt deeper and longer, sometimes shallower than her own and she would adapt her pattern so that they breathed in rhythm. And in those moments, Mama couldn't explain why, but the harmony felt vital.

She could feel her mother's arms around her in bed as she drifted, despite the pain. She did not dare to move as Nyla's slender fingers moved in her hair, in case the fantasy dissipated and she found herself alone in bed. In case even today's magical trip turned out to be imagined and Nyla was still away, drifting from one universe to another, free, unhampered by her daughter. She kept her eyes firmly shut, remaining motionless, sensing that their breathing was in consonance again. Was Nyla doing it on purpose?

She felt something hot, liquid at the nape of her neck. Tears! She swirled round in the bed. Nyla's hair was damp with tears. Zara stroked them away, her own pain forgotten. 'Don't cry, Mama.' Then tense, desperate. 'Why are you crying? Have I done something?'

Nyla hid her face in Zara's hair. 'No, no, my darling. You've been lovely. I'm just being silly. I had such a wonderful day with you today. I was thinking how happy we were. Feeling cross with myself that I hadn't made sure we had more days like that. Silly, isn't it, how happiness can make you cry?'

They lay there for a long time, mostly in silence, but occasionally Nyla would whisper words of love or advice. 'Whatever happens, Zara, always remember I love you. You are the most precious thing in my life.'

'What could happen?' Zara whispered, anxious, wanting to believe it would be like this for the rest of her life.

'Nothing. Nothing will happen to you. Your life will be perfect,' Nyla said. Then she had added, 'Things happen. People argue. Things get in the way ... people get in the way.'

Zara put her hands over Nyla's mouth. '*No!* Don't say that. Nothing's going to happen to you.'

'Of course it's not,' Nyla said robustly. 'I'm a survivor. And you, my darling, are surrounded with love. Always will be. Now, sleep.'

When Zara woke up, Nyla was not in bed. She could vaguely hear a goodbye whispered in her ear from somewhere afar. She reached up and felt the strands of hair around her ear and cheek were damp. Nyla had been crying again.

She sat up in bed. Everything was silent. She tiptoed into Hana's room. The lights were out and Hana was sleeping her usual light, tormented sleep. Zara could not breathe. She ran into the Green Room where Nyla was staying. The bed was empty. She snatched open the tall Venetian glass doors; their mirrored, jewelled handles glinted and glittered – the wardrobes were empty. Zara looked at the handles again. They were glittering yellow. Artificial lights. She dashed to the balcony. The small car was driving slowly towards the gates. So slowly that she could have walked faster. Mama. Mama's going away. She's leaving me and going away.

She must have screamed because everyone was surrounding her a few moments later when she opened her eyes on Hana's lap.

'My mother! Has she gone?'

Hana hugged her close. 'She has, my darling. But you'll be fine. You'll be just fine. We all love you very much. You'll be just fine here.'

'When is she coming back?' Zara still remembered the despair plumb deeper into her belly as Hana shook her head.

'I am not the most precious thing in her life,' Zara said, very slowly. 'My mother lied to me.'

She sat up, thinking: *I remembered the lie and forgot her love.*

That made her inexpressibly sad.

There was a puff of dust in the distance. Someone was coming. A vehicle? She stood still; movement could discharge the image into a mirage. The desert was a trickster.

But no, the sun was catching something tangible that scraped the desert sand, reflecting off its surface as the dust cloud came closer, never rising too far above ground level. Not a car.

She knew those glimmering clusters of light well; they reflected through the atmosphere, creating small, watery worms and circlets of light. The mirrors on the tunics of gipsy women!

They moved closer and the brown ovals of their faces became distinguishable. Through the dust fumes a man emerged, put his hand to his eyes against the sun and glared back at it.

He was in shadow, she couldn't see him. But she could see his hair coiffed Bollywood-'hero' style. How much of his earnings did this poor man spend to have his hair done like this? It was madness. He was turning now to someone beside him and talking as he pointed to the bunker to which they had brought her. These people would probably kill her anyway. He was walking out of her range of vision towards the building.

Loud voices. Doors banging. She could hear the odd phrase, the man requesting food for his band of nomads. If not food, he was saying, then water. Then there was silence. They would be given water.

Soon the gypsies were singing and dancing, entertaining the men. Waves of emptiness made Zara's mind and body sway. With all her will, she focused hard. There was something strange about that song. It was from a movie! Life was imitating art.

The door burst open and a man walked in with a tin tray. Zara felt anxious. Lunch should have been a while ago but she had forgotten about it. Now she felt hungry. The sight of the mess on the plate made her heave – two globs of muck on a banana leaf. Someone had chewed the food and regurgitated it. She could smell the putrid stomach enzymes. She could feel the fire in her eyes as she looked at the man's grinning face. She wondered if she should throw it in his face. Her glance wavered to the space behind him. Could she make a run for it? There was a movement in the background. A man was hovering some distance behind the guard. He looked familiar. The effort of focusing made her stagger. Her eyes ached all the time now. The guard must have noticed her looking. He turned to shut the door and in that instant she saw the man behind him. Kamran! The quiff, the tall, lean frame – he was leading the gypsy troop. And now he was inside.

Perhaps he would make a heroic attempt, in Bollywood style, to rescue her. She would be ready.

He did not.

The sun passed its meridian, the dust rose again and swallowed them. The gypsies had gone. She hadn't a hope in hell.

Kamran was the traitor. It was he who Ankahi had asked to handle her mission – it was he who must have tipped off these people. Would she ever have the chance to warn Sharmeen?

And Raju? His poignant gift of the tiffin-carrier could have been the sign that identified her to the vigilantes.

It didn't matter. Nothing mattered.

The furniture staircase worked well. She amused herself by climbing it. After the daily morning interrogation everything went quiet for a few hours. Unless of course Rekha wandered in, bored, with a puerile set of questions. Sometimes she pretended to be concerned for Zara's wounded body – when the colonel or one of his men had hit her particularly hard. The beatings didn't hurt so much anymore.

Acceptance had taken away the fear, reduced the impact of physical pain. Like the dogs in the experiment with the electrified floor. They clung to the sides of the cage to avoid the shocks until they accepted the situation. Then they wandered on and off. Yes, resignation did bring relief.

40

Large, dark stains appeared on the beach the day Peter told her about changing his career. She felt panicky. They had appeared suddenly. She wanted to leave them behind but they moved, swiftly, strongly along the sands in front of her.

'Why are you running?' Peter asked, keeping pace.

'Those black shadows. What are they?'

'Cloud shadows.' He relaxed. 'Look up.' She could hear his voice smiling.

She looked at the skies. A flotilla of clouds moved swiftly along, casting a dense, ominous shadow on the sands. It felt like the kind of thing you read about.

That was the day Peter told her about his change of plan.

Zara stalked towards the car park through tall clumps of grass surrounded by scrubby dunes. 'No India anymore then?'

Peter stared into the distance. 'Peter?'

He stood very still, leaning slightly against the car door, then mumbled something and began plodding up the dune back towards the beach. Zara leapt out of the car and followed him. 'I'm right, aren't I? This changes everything.'

Zara did not know if she was more shocked by the decision or by the complete change in Peter who had always been so direct, so clear about what he was thinking, what he wanted. His underlying message was clear: 'I will do exactly as I like, even if it hurts you, but I'll try to make it as easy as I can for you.'

She clenched her fist so hard she could feel twinges of pain. As she released it she knew she was letting something go.

The clouds drifted out of range quite swiftly, to empty their doom elsewhere, no doubt. She wished she could do the same.

She blamed Peter and resented him for the emptiness. It was easier than admitting the void had always been there. Had she failed to fight for her fantasy because she was unsure of ever filling the hollow inside?

She would probably never have the chance, now, to tell Peter what she had discovered. But it was time to stop blaming him and the world for her grief, trying to pin her misery on people and places. To let herself stop and breathe instead of being in a constant state of striving – for what?

She laughed. How ironic life was. Here she sat, locked in a cell, marooned with a bunch of brutal captors with the first real chance of achieving a sense of contentment. This was probably why hermits could be contented. They were cut off and at ease with themselves. Their surroundings didn't matter. Captivity liberated them. But she was not done – not yet, anyway.

Her small piece of charcoal had rubbed away to nothing. She ran her palm gently along the floor, feeling for any tiny object to use instead. She felt something sharp and applied pressure to it so that it would stick to her skin. Her calloused palms felt nothing. She brought her hand up to her eyes. A thrill of pain told her the object was still in her hand – she had not lost it. Carefully, she fanned out her fingers. A dusty bloodstain at the base of her forefinger – in it, a tiny, glittering splinter of glass.

Her body shook. Tears dribbled from her eyes. What did it matter, anyway, how many days she had been here? How many bits of rubbish was she going to collect before it all finally ended?

She didn't know how many days later it was that the cars arrived. Armoured cars at the front of the building. She looked at them dully from her perch. More people. More questions. More beatings. More of the same stupid, bloody accusations.

Her door flew open. The guards were used to her peering out of the chink. They beat her and castigated her for doing it but no one confiscated the furniture. They did try to break her down in other ways. Like the time they starved her then brought her dal. Zara was about to stuff it into her mouth when Rekha said: 'Are you so hungry you'll eat food with piss in it? You know the guard, the one who wants to ...' She rolled her fists into balls and shoved her right thumb in and out of the left. 'The one who ... likes you – he went to toilet on the way here. He put it on the floor. You know how those dug-out toilets cause splashing?'

'I'll leave it for you, Rekha,' Zara replied and was satisfied by the look of fury on her face. But in the moment between Rekha's comment and her own retort, she had wondered if she might eat the food anyway.

The man in the doorway was a stranger. Behind him was one of the old guards with a bunch of keys.

'Please step down from the window,' the stranger said in English. 'I am Inspector K. C. Thakur. You will come with me, please.'

So the police were involved now. She would go through more sophisticated forms of torture and interrogation. Zara came down cautiously. 'Where are you taking me?'

The inspector's voice was gentle. 'Back to civilization, ma'am. You will be safe now.'

He stepped closer and began to usher her out. Zara became conscious of her own smell. In the corridor, uniformed officers were smashing open cell doors. She watched as some men carried out body bags. The stench! The unbearable smell she'd wondered about since the moment she came. She saw the colonel and his gang, in irons from wrist to ankle, pushed into an armoured van. As the inspector ushered her to his car, Zara began to retch. The smell was no longer bearable now that she could be rid of it.

'Please, Inspector,' she said. 'Can I wash before I get into your car?'

41

Zara felt a muted sense of triumph among the police officers as they leapt out of the van with their prisoners outside the police station. The staff at the station peered out of the upper windows, waving, while those on the ground floor gathered at the doors and waited on the steps, smiling and saluting.

'We have a lot of problems with Solanki's type of people,' Inspector Thakur said. 'They operate independently with members of Bajrang Dal and Durga Vahini – they are no better than the goondas and common criminals. He waved to the men and returned their salutes. 'The men are happy because we've captured them and no one can accuse the police of letting anti-Muslim operators off the hook. It's a good day for us.'

The uniformed crowd on the steps separated to let through Saif, who came quickly down. Behind him was Peter. Zara's spine turned limp. Swiftly she grabbed the inspector's arm, steadied herself and stumbled towards Peter. His arms around her felt secure, comforting. She could still meld into his shape. There was a cheer from the crowd of policemen. Zara noticed the tears of emotion in their eyes and looked down at her strange outfit.

Peter had brought her a set of her own clothes. 'I knew you'd want your own,' he said. A shock of guilt ran through her – he was a kind, considerate man. It was one of the many things that made her love him.

'I'm sorry. I'm so sorry ... for being ... for blaming you ...'

'Heyyyy.' He stroked her hair. 'None of that.'

She stood back slightly and looked at him. 'You've got thin.'

He smiled, shakily. 'Ditto.'

She slipped back into his arms. 'How long have you been here?'

'Thirty-nine days. Saif called me four days after you were abducted.'

'Only forty-three days?' The weight of time had been heavy. She thought a moment. 'A fortnight after I stopped counting.' Time had lost its importance once she gave up hope of rescue.

'We were on the verge of involving the international media,' Peter said. 'But the government wanted to avoid unnecessary publicity. They're image-conscious.'

Zara shuddered. 'I'm glad I'm not an "international incident". I'd look like an idiot.'

Peter squeezed her. 'Saif's waiting by the car.'

Saif was smiling. He spread out his arms when he saw them coming and walked briskly towards her, radiant in his white pyjama-kurta and a beige Kashmir shawl. 'Little Zara. When are you going to stop getting into trouble?' He held her close, gently stroking her hair.

'Saif. I saw Kamran there. Is everything ... I mean ...?' Her anxiety was suddenly unbearable. It was important to protect Sharmeen.

Saif smiled. 'When we'd had word from the priests at Vikram Giri, Kamran volunteered to go with a band of his actor friends and check out the base.'

'The priests?'

'Do you remember stopping at a mandir?'

Zara's thoughts whirled through a long, dark funnel. She nodded, beginning to shake.

'The chief priest was sure you had visited as a child. Apparently you described the royal apartments. They made inquiries. Your so-called "colonel" was a breakaway from the Bajrang Dal who'd got some ex-soldiers to work for him. He thought he'd serve the nation by grabbing a Pakistani secret agent and squeezing information from her – about an attack against India.'

'Secret ...? Me? I'm sorry, Saif. I really am.'

'Don't be silly. If anything, it's the Ramzi connection.'

'Kamran spotted you in a room ...'

Zara closed her eyes. She swallowed hard. 'All I want is to see what the curator knows about the will. Then I'll go home ... to uncomplicated Aylesbury Avenue. Has anyone seen him?'

'Steady on,' Peter said, squeezing her hand.

'He was in Europe,' Saif said. 'A conference. We'll let him know you're back.'

Zara looked from one man to the other. 'What?'

Peter leaned forward so that he could look directly into her face. 'Prepare yourself,' he said softly.

'I'm prepared for anything.'

He held her hand between both of his. 'Your mother has been in touch. She wants to speak to you – if you'd like.'

Zara heard a strangulated sound wrench itself from her throat. Then she clung to Peter and safety.

Littl'un followed Zara around like a shadow the day she returned to Qila. 'My heart', she said, 'is flowering like a garden seeing you here and safe. But how thin you've become, my precious one, and how lacklustre.'

She tried to feed Zara strong-smelling concoctions of herbs, spices and exotic roots to help her regain her strength, and sat watching her when she dozed. She insisted on keeping vigil when she showered and even when everyone else disappeared to allow Zara privacy to telephone Nyla, she sat at her feet clutching her hand. The only other person in the room was Peter.

Zara's mind seized up when Nyla answered her call. She swallowed. Who was she to ask for? Nyla? Mama? 'This is Zara.'

'Di mio! Zara!' Nyla's voice was exactly as she remembered. Except for a tinge of Italian. 'Thank god. Thank god. I didn't know if you would call.'

The questions tumbled into Zara's head. How could her mother doubt she would call? How could she give her up and never spare her another thought?

'How long have you lived in Italy?'

'Twenty-two years.' There was a pause. 'I remarried.'

Zara wondered of Nyla had other children. 'Do you like it there?' Her laugh was like a snuffle. 'You sound a bit Italian.'

'Oh, my darling child. I have missed you every moment of my life. I did the most terrible thing ... it was the most hideous mistake.'

Zara could hear the tears in her mother's voice. 'Why, Mama? Why did you?' The word 'mama' sounded odd from a mature woman.

'I was unstable. Not a good mother.'

'So it was for my sake?' Zara thought Nyla had put down the phone but then she spoke.

'I was restless and unstable. I couldn't settle. I left you for long spells at Qila.' Zara could hear her mother taking a deep breath. 'Hana Apa said you missed me unbearably – she said I would damage you, everyone was saying it. I could either take you with me for good or I could leave and you'd have a stable home with her.'

'Why didn't you tell me?'

'Tell you what?' Nyla sobbed. 'That I was abandoning you because I hated Qila – which you loved? That I was hardly capable of looking after myself? I couldn't give you what Hana Apa and Saif did. They adored you.'

'You could have taken me.'

'I was on ... medication. To sleep, to get through the days. I took too much once. She thought I'd be a danger ...'

'You acted as if you were dead.'

'Don't ... please.'

Questions held in for years tumbled out and Nyla tried to explain. She had called as soon as she landed at Santa Cruz Airport in Mumbai – Hana told her the call would distress Zara. She had tried calling a hundred times over the next few days and weeks. There was never a good time to talk to Zara. So she wrote. Hana wrote back and told her not to contact Zara. She explained that after a long period of grieving Zara had accepted her mother's abandonment. She was now well settled but easily upset by mention of Nyla.

'I wondered if she told you I was dead,' Nyla sobbed.

'No,' said Zara. 'Never. She didn't say that.' She did not tell her that Aunty Hana refused to discuss making contact with Nyla not because she was angry with her but because Zara was the best thing in her life.

Zara laid her head on Peter's shoulder. She would take it slowly with Nyla. She knew nothing about her mother's situation, her personality – if there was even a space in her life for Zara.

'Odd,' she said, 'Mama hated Qila. I thought it was me she hated.'

A sticky sleepiness had seeped into her bones, her muscles and her mind. Her lids were drawn down and held together. 'I can't believe Aunty Hana did that.'

'Sleep,' Peter said, plumping up her pillows and drawing a sheet over her. 'We can talk about it later.'

Zara formulated words through layers of drowsiness. 'In a way I'm relieved she did.'

Every time Zara woke up and saw Peter, she touched him to convince herself she was back in Qila, in Hana's room, and he was sitting beside her in flesh and blood. She was aware of talking to people who came in and out: Saif, Sharmeen, Pebbles, the family doctor. Often, she drifted off without hearing much – explanations were not important.

The branches of the tamarind tree swayed at the window. Zara pressed her body into the mattress – it was soft. Peter was not there but beside her was the imprint of his lean, tall body – like a mirage. The desert cell and Hana's room were like alternate dimensions, disconnected zones which still somehow bled into each other.

She felt peaceful in her body though she was still trying to absorb the fact that her mother had spoken to her – and that Hana was responsible for their separation.

'Can I come in?' Saif's voice said. He dropped a kiss on Zara's forehead and perched on the divan. 'How do you feel?'

'Great. Trying to take it all in. Where's Peter?'

'Walking. Thought he'd take in Bowl Lake.'

'Long walk.'

Saif laughed. 'The Bentley was ferrying a group to Ramzi Bagh. He went along.' He patted her shoulder and stood up. 'Well, I'd better be off. Plans for the festival.'

Then, 'Jay sent his best. He'll come to see you later.' He hesitated. 'No pressure, but when you're ready it might be a nice idea to visit Sita Devi.'

'She's put a lot of effort into ... well, all this. She was a good friend to my mother ...'

Zara sighed. More unfinished business. She longed to find out about Hana's rift with Sita.

Zara rolled over on to her side and ran her fingers along the impression of Peter's body. Fleetingly, she was touched by an evocation of happy days with Peter. She had despaired of ever being able to recapture the sweetness and intimacy between them, but their relationship felt different. So much of what bothered her seemed trivial now. So much of what she found reprehensible about people and cultures was universal.

'I've understood at last,' she said when Peter returned that night from Bowl Lake, 'that once something has happened it's gone – if you can't fix it, leave it. I have never been good at letting go.'

Peter walked over to the window, gazing at the tamarind tree. 'I walked quite a way past Bowl Lake today,' he said. 'I stopped to eat. I spoke to people.' He ran his hand through his hair and turned to face her. 'I was overwhelmed by the forbearance of the people. They keep calling it "sabr" – is that patience? But it's really deep resignation. Some of those places haven't been updated since before 1946.' He drew up a chair and sat astride it, resting his chin on its back.

Zara felt a little rush of emotion. His voice, the way he sat reminded her of how he used to be. His eyes sparkled. 'They need help, Zara. They need us.' He stood up again. 'I let go of that dream too easily – I've had a lot of time to think. I visited places I'd been to before. I won't try to explain – I don't know if we can understand our own profound impulses, we can only take them on board.'

'Perhaps if I had challenged you instead of shutting off ...'

'Perhaps. But I was hasty; deep down I knew if I stopped to think, I would not have stayed in England. I was unsure if I'd fit into your family. I dreaded trying to live up to their expectations, be something I'm not. And at that time it didn't fit with my self-image. I was ... well, I was scared and I got it wrong. I'm so sorry.'

'I was, too,' she said. 'What I should have done was start a row.'

He flopped down on the bed beside her, laid his head in her lap. Zara stroked his hair, grateful they were speaking again.

42

Now that Zara was back, Saif had just one more job to do before returning to sanity.

He went to his office behind the dining room and unlocked the top shelf of his cabinet. He still had the original key two centuries after the wood had been shaped into a cabinet, carved lovingly and put to so many different uses over the years. Hana had believed that objects, even small ones like iron keys, remained safe when they were kept in the same place. The cabinet was said to have been assembled in the downstairs room when it had been the service area, to house the paraphernalia of formal dinner services. When the room became Saif's study three decades ago, it still occupied the same space.

He lifted out a slim briefcase and pulled out some papers. They had been in the drawer since Jay handed them to him five weeks ago after Shinde had laid claim to the riverside land.

Saif released the documents from the leather case. Karan had been meticulous. The file was prefaced by a contents list which included a summary of the case, a précis of the correspondence and the ownership documents, safely zipped into a plastic pocket. Shinde was claiming the riverside property for its 'rightful owner'.

'Just take it out of your cabinet and hand it over,' Pebbles had said. 'Let Karan do the rest.'

But Saif was resistant. The documents would establish his ownership of the land but violate his grandmother's taboo. She did not want her name 'bandied about all over the show'. Once the documents were presented in court, her name would be in every newspaper. 'I don't want butchers wrapping meat in my name and sopping up the mess, or people lining their drawers with it. Or mispronouncing it at breakfast,' she had said with a shudder. Saif shuddered, now, nearly forty years on.

Shinde's documents had been authenticated by the court and all that remained was Saif's response. He detached the photocopy of the land deeds. The land seemed to be owned by a Colonel Deendayal. He unlocked the bottom drawer of the cabinet. It resisted, as if aware of his will. He shifted it from side to side and worked it open an inch, then slid his fingers inside and pulled. It inched out stiffly. Saif delved into the bundles of papers. It always fascinated him to see how dust collected in perfectly enclosed spaces.

He lifted the deeds out of the brocade bundle in which Grandmother had wrapped them and leafed through, stroking each page to retrace the surface she had touched. Grandmother's signature was nowhere but the colonel's was. He peered at the faded date – a date like a burning ember in his mind – the last day before he was forced to spend all his school holidays at Ramzi Bagh. And just above it his own childish signature.

With a spurt of energy he searched the bundle until he found a power of attorney assigned to Colonel Deendayal Sinhji of Vajhna, a small state not far from Daulatnagar. The colonel had bought the riverside property in his name, on Grandmother's instructions to be transferred to Saif 'with the utmost discretion' when the boy came of age.

Saif's body flooded with lightness. He could release the deeds without revealing Grandmother's name. He reached for the telephone.

Members of Colonel Deendayal's family continued to live in their ancestral home. Saif introduced himself and was directed to the eldest son. Ajit Singh sounded eager. The colonel had developed dementia, he explained, and the family had struggled, after his death some twenty years ago, to make sense of the papers he left behind. Saif described the documents before him.

'Indeed,' Ajit replied, 'those ones I do remember. I came back from the US when my father passed away. They were damaged; white ants – you know what a problem they are in old buildings. But we managed to decipher the Daulatnagar connection. Papa was very close to Their Highnesses, particularly Begum Saheb. You know they were brought up together – like siblings – even though Papa was much older. Trouble was, they had both passed away.'

A cold hand clutched at Saif's heart as Ajit Singh described how the old palace at Daulatnagar had been taken over by branches of the family who had not maintained it well, plundering its movable treasures and even removing ancient windows, ceiling bosses and stone features of the structure itself, to sell. He could hear the apology in Ajit's voice, his attempts to be diplomatic, but the disgust showed through.

'They were desperate for me to sign over the deeds to them. One of the guys even turned up in Vajhna, at the house with thugs, threatening me.'

Saif apologized for the unpleasantness. He had no idea that there were thugs amongst the Daulatnagars. How had he been so unaware of the current state of affairs? Had he been negligent? Why had he never tried to find out about the property? It belonged to his family, after all.

'It's an age-old story,' Ajit Singh was answering his unarticulated questions. 'Family members all have their own homes and if there are no direct male descendants then it turns into a free-for-all.' He was apologetic all of a sudden. 'Of course I'm not sure what the situation was ...'

'As you describe, I imagine,' Saif said, heavy-hearted yet aware that he was grieving for sticks and stones. But what a life they had possessed, what they had witnessed and how much tenderness he had known in their confines.

'I'm sorry, sir,' Ajit said. 'I'm a lawyer. I come across this kind of thing all the time. I didn't mean anything personal.' Saif reassured Ajit that he had not taken offence.

'May I ask you a few questions about your documents, sir?' Ajit said.

Saif answered questions, about dates and places and the minutiae of wording. 'I'm satisfied your claim is entirely legitimate, sir,' Ajit said, in the end. 'I have my father's power of attorney and with your originals, there should be no insurmountable problems.' He hesitated a moment. 'I'll be happy to attend court, sir, or send in a deposition. If you give me the contact details of your lawyers we can liaise directly.'

Saif put down the phone and stood up. His job was done. It was a matter of time before things were settled and the Academy was on its way again.

He would work for a while on the Oval Garden. He had not worked there since Mumtaz's arrival to avoid giving offence. But she had shown no interest in it before or since Zara and Sharmeen had begun using it.

He might, he thought, replant poppies and rushes around the pond. Maybe even water lilies.

43

There was an air of tension in the formal drawing room as they waited for the curator to arrive.

'I am absolutely fed up with secrets,' Zara said. 'But Aunty Hana told me I should receive her parcel in private. I'm really sorry.' She looked at Peter for approval and he squeezed her hand.

Pebbles pursed her lips. 'It is unacceptable for you to ban us from a meeting about the Ramzi inheritance, in the Ramzi home, which will most certainly have a bearing on the Ramzi future.' She turned to Saif. 'Surely you must agree?'

Saif looked uninterested. 'I'm all for banning secrets but my secret is mine to give. If you entrust me with yours, then I'm honour-bound to hang on to it. It's amana – a sacred trust.'

'We don't need your two paisa worth of philosophizing, thank you, Saif.' Pebbles' voice was harsh.

Zara was shocked by her vehemence. 'Aunty repeatedly instructed me not tell anyone. It's part of her final wishes.' Zara paused a moment, considering, then spoke. 'I must see the curator on my own.' She knew immediately that her decision was wrong. It felt wrong. 'Let me see him alone first.'

'I'm the outsider here,' Peter said. 'But I agree with Saif. Zara's following her aunt's instructions about confidentiality just as she would any other client's.'

Pebbles snorted. 'It's just a pair of bangles, for god's sake. What's the great drama?'

Zara could hold back no longer. 'The drama, Pebbles, is something you've been creating since I got here – and before.'

'We all know you and my mother-in-law had some conspiracy about the bangles. You should just hand them over.'

'So you know it's all about the bangles, do you, Pebbles?'

Pebbles shrugged and stood up. 'I put it to you, *Counsellor*, that I have been kept in the dark about what is mine.'

'I must do what Aunty said,' Zara said, half-heartedly.

Pebbles narrowed her eyes. 'And how do you propose to get rid of me?' she challenged. Zara wondered briefly about walking out of the room. The curator wouldn't disclose anything in her absence, surely? Or she could meet him at a hotel. That would be unseemly and would embarrass Pebbles.

The old Bentley crunched on the gravel and Saif stood up. Zara slumped on the sofa. 'Look Pebbles. Let's just take it calmly. There's no conspiracy against you.'

Saif returned and introduced the curator. Zara was disconcerted to see Pebbles' face wreathed in smiles. Suddenly she was the perfect hostess, solicitous, concerned.

'Millo, bring tea. Go on, quick, quick. Rai Saheb, how was the drive? Not too, you know, tiring, I hope? Did Ajay drive carefully? He loves the Bentley. We don't really let him drive it too often but his dad was away. He's gone to his village for a few days to settle his mother into his new house.'

Zara was dismayed to see that Dr Rai did not have a case with him. Ajay walked through the door, carrying a tubular metal container. Zara's heart lurched. Pebbles voice trailed away.

'Rai Saheb,' she said after a moment. 'How rude of me. Have you met my cousin? Zara Hamilton. Huzur Saheb's sister's ...'

Rai raised a hand. 'I know, I know, I know who she is. Her mother Nyla Raje was the regular patron of museum. Zara Raje used to come from very young, like this ...' He waved his hand to indicate her height. 'Always asking, "Rai Saheb, please, what time is sound and light exhibition of Trivikram battle in 1857?" ' He looked awkwardly at Peter. 'She was only the child, you know. Only nine, ten years. They learned about the history, 1857 great uprising, contribution of maharajas.' He paused and held his forefinger and thumb to the corners of his mouth. 'After, I used to tell Zara Raje, always is sound and light time, baba, when you are here.' He laughed. 'All local poor kids would come running in when they saw Zara Raje come. They knew now will be son et lumière show.'

Ajay stood awkwardly, holding the metal tube across his chest.

'On the table? Is that okay, Rai Saheb?'

The curator did not notice the subterranean tension in the room. 'Idhar dena. Give here.' He held his arms out for the container and Ajay placed it carefully on his lap.

'Zara Raje? Please come, sit here. Jara idhar padharo, Hukam.' He patted the seat beside him.

The respectful phrases were comforting. She walked over and sat on the sofa. Rai pulled out a pair of white gloves, opened the container and reached deep inside.

'Papers!' Pebbles exclaimed. 'Is that it? What about the bangles?'

Rai looked up, startled. 'We have not got bangles,' he said. He adjusted his glasses and shot Pebbles a curious look. Zara watched him unfurl the paper with the tenderness of a mother holding her newborn.

'These, Pir Saheb – these are invaluable,' he said, 'They are hitherto unknown manuscripts from Emperor Jehangir's collection.' He held up a series of Green Man images. Around them were notes in seventeenth-century Persian script. 'We can identify the hand of the artist Mansur from court of Emperor Jehangir.'

Saif's forehead wrinkled in concentration. 'My grandfather spoke about these,' he said. 'He must have given them to my mother.'

'This manuscript establishes that Emperor Jehangir travelled to Ramzi Bagh to pay respects to Dost Pir Saheb. Huzur Saheb, she told me she had never looked at this small bundle of folios. They have been wrapped up in this selfsame blue silk and kept inside trunk. Also there was this leather-bound manuscript. She did not wish to touch it. When I came to see her, she said, "Might as well show folios to Rai to see what he says." I was very much excited.'

Rai wiped away an imaginary speck from the table. He pushed back his teacup and saucer and cleared a space, then drew a manuscript from his briefcase and placed it on the table.

The book! Zara leant forward to look but decided not to bring attention to it. Rai stood up and folded his hands. 'I think perhaps that the rest is for the family to consider in private. I should take my leave. It has been a long day.' He bowed to everyone around the table. 'Pir Saheb, Begum Saheba, Zara Raje. With your permission, I will retire.'

He picked up the leather-bound manuscript from the sofa and handed it to Zara. 'Zara Raje, this is marked for your confidential attention. And Huzur Saheb asked me to personally hand you this envelope.' Zara clutched the manuscript for a moment, then laid it down on a stool beside her and began to open the envelope.

Saif rose. 'I'll take you to your room,' he said to Rai.

'No, please. You have important matters to discuss here.' Rai saw Ajay standing in a corner. He stood up, nodded around the room, hands joined, and followed Ajay out.

Zara tore open the envelope, sat close to Peter and began to read.

Beloved Zara,

If God gives me life, I'll tell you myself about all this but I'm not sure I'll see you before I go. I have been ill – nothing specific – little body shocks that leave me weaker each time. I trust you to carry out my instructions to the letter.

1. If Saif and Pebbles agree to the marriage of Sharmeen and Kamran, you must personally draft an agreement that Kamran will leave his portion of Qila to Sharmeen or any children they may have. Furthermore, their children must carry the Ramzi name. I believe Mumtaz will agree to this.
2. The Green Man folios by Mansur are for Pebbles. I trust her judgement on how to deal with them. I thank her from the heart for the work she has done in the courtyard. Without her help many lives would have been lost. The project must remain a secret so that it may continue. I fear we have a long way to travel before our oppressive customs change.

3. The book must leave the country. Saif must never know about it. It explains the origin of the Ramzi Order. It is said that if the Ramzi leader reads it, he and the Order will die.

There was a muffled scream. Pebbles stuffed the edge of her sari into her mouth and sobbed, biting at the filmy material, as she rocked back and forth. Saif laid the manuscript on the table and walked to her side. He sat beside her, holding her close.

'You read it. Oh my god, you read the manuscript. It's my fault,' she sobbed. 'I forced Zara to do this in public. I've caused ... Saif, what have I done?'

'What? What did you do?' Zara could hear the desperate demand for contradiction in her own voice. 'You're not saying you believe this stuff? Saif, why is she ...?'

'I forced y'all to break the taboo! That's what I mean.' Pebbles' voice was a high-pitched shriek. She rushed out of the room, hair wild, careering from side to side. Saif strode out after her.

Zara could feel the familiar feeling of pressure building in her chest. She tried to push past it, to breathe deeply. She felt her stomach tighten. Peter held up the leather-bound manuscript open a few pages in and began to read. He glanced at Zara. 'It's a fairytale, Zara. Saif will be fine.'

Zara nodded, unable to think.

'I'll summarize,' Peter said. 'It says a princess fell in love with a healer in the forest near the Bowl Lake. They married and gathered quite a following and learned about healing and horticulture. They were known as sabz-poshis.' Peter stumbled over the unfamiliar word.

'It means "green-clad",' Zara said.

'So that's where it comes from,' Peter said. 'Anyway, the local priests were angry so when the princess was giving birth, they murdered them both. The king sent the infant away to a Sufi community in Multan. And he didn't want his name connected to ... how do you say it?'

'Sabz-posh,' said Zara.

'Right. So when the kid came back after twenty years, he was renamed Ramzi, because of his secret. After a bit he took over as leader and became known as Dost Pir.'

'The Friendly Sage,' Zara whispered. 'That's who he was – son of a Hindu princess and a Sufi healer.'

Peter put down the book. Zara clutched his arm desperately.

'Saif is not going to die,' she said. 'It was a ploy, wasn't it, so that they wouldn't find out the Green-clad Man was not a supernatural being.' Yet she was confused and frightened. She looked at Peter – if anyone could allay her fears, he could.

Peter returned her gaze. 'Of course Saif will die, Zara – one day.'

She glared at him. 'But not because of a curse? He will die when his time comes. Like the rest of us.' Zara leaned her head against Peter's shoulder. 'I should have kept the book away from Saif.'

Saif and Pebbles came in. Pebbles was sobbing. 'I don't know how to apologize.'

'If anyone's to blame, it's me.' Zara picked up the will from her lap and began reading.

4. I believe Qila should go to Pebbles as my father-in-law left it to me. But your father wished you to have it so I leave it to you. I would ask you to bequeath it to Sharmeen. It is my dearest wish that the whole of the property, divided as the result of my mistakes for the first time since it was built, should once again belong to a Ramzi.

'I don't understand.' Zara's voice was dull, listless. 'My father?' Peter took her by the shoulders. 'You must ask your mother.'

Zara felt Littl'un's hand shuffling on her knee. 'Pir Sultan Ramzi was your father.'

'No!' Zara shouted. 'No! How? When?'

'Zara Bibi, listen to me. Your mother was young. Just widowed. Huzur Saheb sent her away to Ramzi Bagh, on a retreat. She was confused. She didn't know what was going on. He, he ...'

'She betrayed Aunty Hana – her own sister?'

'No! Not at all!' Saif said. 'She was too frightened to resist. I think I saw it.'

Zara tried to absorb the information. She was a Ramzi. How often she had wished for that as a child. Now she felt battered.

'Watch what you wish for,' Dilkash used to mutter. 'It could be the "time of acceptance" but no guarantee it'll come out like you want it.'

How right she had been.

Zara crossed the room and put her arms around Saif. 'I always felt you were my brother. I'm really glad you are.' Saif squeezed her shoulder, dropped a kiss on her hair.

'Deep down, I suppose I always knew too. From the day I heard Nyla Khala insist on leaving the retreat.'

'Was that why, do you think, Aunty stopped my mother seeing me?'

'Jealousy,' Saif replied, his voice flat. 'My father was coming to Qila for a while. My mother thought Nyla Khala would damage her chances of a reconciliation.'

'I should be angry with Aunty, I suppose,' Zara said. 'But I understand even more why she didn't want to lose me. I think she was trying to– to make things safe.'

44

'Can't sleep?' Peter murmured, half-awake.

'I've been restless all night,' Zara replied.

He pulled her close. The room was suffused with a soft, pre-dawn glow. The foliage of the tamarind tree scraped against the windowpane. The birdsong was unusually loud. Zara snuggled up against Peter. 'I've been thinking a lot about home. Missing it.'

Peter raised himself on one elbow and looked at her.

'It's okay,' she said, squeezing his arm. 'I'm not running away this time.'

'Nobody would blame you if you did.'

'It's strange,' she said. 'I've always felt I was a Ramzi and now I feel like a fake.' Her voice dropped. 'Nyla and Sultan, though. Can't bear to ...'

'And ... Qila?'

She searched Pete's face for signs of concern. 'It feels easier to walk away from.' She frowned. 'Is that perverse?' Peter shook his head. 'The truth is,' she continued. 'Qila's not mine. No more than it's always been. Places like this – well, they just want caretakers, don't they?'

Peter was gazing at her. She flushed. Despite feeling close to him again she had not told him the details of being Solanki's captive. She stroked his lip with her forefinger and a charge ran through her body. She remembered that passion – he had never resisted an overture from her since they had met, but she hesitated. Maybe he needed time.

'Is there anything that you want to know ... about the desert? I mean, if ...'

Peter held up his hand. 'Only if you want to tell me.'

Her voice trembled. 'The thing is ... I wondered if you had any questions. I mean, like if the guards ...'

Peter got out of bed and sat in the armchair, facing her. 'It doesn't affect my feelings. You're still you.'

'You must wonder.'

He took her face in his hands. 'I don't wonder. I only want you to be okay.' He walked to the window. 'If it helps, feel free.'

She took a deep breath. 'No one laid a finger on me except to hit me.' She laughed shakily. 'Even that was mostly with truncheons and ...' Peter was on his knees beside her, wiping her tears, raking back her hair, cradling her.

'I love you,' she whispered, as if she was saying the words for the first time. He grasped her hair gently by the temples, eased back her head and kissed her.

'My goodness,' she said trying to catch her breath. 'I'd forgotten a kiss could be so exciting.'

She could see the first streaks of the sun streaking the sky.

'It's not morning yet,' Peter said, following her gaze. 'Let's be decadent.'

45

Zara still felt as if she were floating around outside her mind. She looked at the brown velvet sofas, the glass windows, the Oval Garden outside. This place she loved had been left to her. Those men in the portraits on the wall were her ancestors. She was part of a long, established line of people whose home had been Qila for many centuries. She wondered if it would change anything. Her vision blurred.

She heard a snatch of conversation from the group on the sofas – she felt remote from it.

'I never gave it any credence,' Saif was saying. 'If I had seen the book before, I would have looked in it. The profound mystery is not whether the taboo is prophetic – it is humankind's fear of death. But death is simply a transformation of the mineral, Rumi would say, that has outlived its use.'

'When you come to it,' Peter said, 'a great mystery has grown from a minute kernel.' Zara felt a whirr of pleasure as he spoke and she wanted to reach out and touch him. He was relaxed, blending effortlessly with the family.

Jay looked grave, his head slightly inclined, his hands making a steeple of thumbs and fingertips. Seeing him again was not as difficult as she had expected. She felt sorry for him.

'You don't know how I cursed myself for letting you go that night,' he said. 'Or not giving Raju explicit instructions to drive you all the way to Ahmedabad even if you ...' he broke off, shaking his head.

'I've caused everyone a lot of anxiety.' Zara said, shakily. 'But it's finished now, thank goodness.' She held his gaze easily without tension or frisson. He looked lost. Strange, he understood little of metaphysics despite it being part of his life for so long, yet she had expected it of Peter. But now she wanted to talk about recent discoveries – her paternity, the curse of the broken taboo.

Pebbles leapt to her feet. 'I'm going next door.'

Zara dashed out after her. 'To Mumtaz?'

'It's about time she answered some questions. I mean, the worst is done. We deserve answers.'

Zara followed Pebbles across the Oval Garden. Pebbles pushed her weight against the heavy timber door. The top end wanted to move, the bottom held heavily to the wooden threshold. Pebbles kicked it, flinching only slightly, then ploughed in. Zara could feel her heartbeat as she followed.

Pebbles was in truculent mode: chin thrust out, shoulders following, hair flying, she pushed past the heavy door and mounted the stairs leading to Mumtaz's terrace.

A child wandered on to the scene followed by the maid.

'Tell your mistress I'm here,' Pebbles commanded. The woman clearly knew Pebbles' reputation. She opened her red mouth and shut it again. 'Oi. What are you waiting for? Go! Quickly! I'm Pebbles, from the Ramzi family.'

'From the Ramzi family? And who exactly do you think I am? A beggar from the street?' Mumtaz stood in the archway. 'How dare you barge in here like some maharani?'

Pebbles breathed deeply, like an animal preparing for a fight. 'My husband has seen the book.' Her voice was surprisingly quiet and steady. 'Tell me whatever you know.'

Mumtaz froze. Pebbles sank down on a wooden bench against the wall, swaying slightly as if she might faint. Strands of the bougainvillea creeper hung down and framed her face. Zara saw, for the first time, the beauty that enchanted Saif when he looked at his wife.

Mumtaz snapped her fingers as if someone had released the image from stillness to motion. 'Water!' she shouted. 'Chairs'.

Three servants arrived with chairs. The maid scuttled in

with a tray of glasses in jewel colours and diverse shapes. Oddly beautiful, preserved in the great store cupboards left behind when the decision was made to divide Qila. Mumtaz picked up a glass and held it to Pebbles' mouth. The maid brought the tray to Zara. Quickly Zara picked up an amethyst-tinted glass that had been hers before Aunty closed this wing. Pebbles put down her glass, wiped her mouth with the back of her hand. 'Please. The book. I need to know.'

Mumtaz shrugged. 'Secrets have destroyed this family.' She ran a roughened hand down the back of Pebbles' unkempt hair. 'It was all to preserve this ...' she chuckled a bitter sound. 'The great Ramzi clan, huh? But let me not waste time. I'll tell it to you what happened.' She sat back, preparing to confess. 'I contacted Hana Bhabhi a few years back and informed her that I wanted my share of the Ramzi inheritance. She was prepared to give me money and even some property but she refused any part of Qila which my father had gifted to her. I told her I had the famous book and would show it to Saif. So she gave me this part of the house.'

Pebbles looked at her in horror. 'And you'd have shown it to him?'

'I don't believe in curses. It was manmade.' She stopped then began again. 'Peacocks danced by the Bowl ... at least when I was a girl. People say their piercing cry comes from pain of the massacre of the Green-clad Sage and his beloved. There was a local tradition that all his followers turned into peacocks. And he vowed that his descendants would lay down their lives for the Vamanas as he had for his wife, the Vamana princess.

'Then and now, so many lives destroyed through communal prejudice,' Mumtaz's voice was dull as she twiddled the thin, curving end of her tightly woven plait. 'Think about it. My family. Sultan Bhai and Hana Bhabhi ...' she gestured dismissively. 'Jaane do. Let it go. It was all a long time ago. But now, even Sita Devi ...'

Mumtaz sighed then ran both hands over her face. 'So much tragedy would have been avoided if I had not run away. I lost everything because I chose my husband.'

Pebbles entire body seemed to let out a hiss of air. 'You exploited my mother-in-law.'

Mumtaz's voice was shrill. 'I lost too much. I had to give something back to my grandson.'

There was nothing left to say. Zara was uncomfortable with the silence yet she could not break it.

'Greetings. May I come in?' Saif's voice said. Mumtaz stood up and walked over to him. She had to raise her arms well above her head to put them around his neck. Her tears were flowing again.

'How these arms have longed to embrace you.'

'Then why ...?' Saif looked bemused.

She shook her head. 'It was part of the agreement with your mother. I was to have no contact with you. I might have told you about the book. She was someone who liked to control things. That was why I did not attend her funeral.'

'But I hope,' said Saif, 'that you will take part in the festival.'

46

Zara awoke to see Peter watching her.

'Oh no,' she said. 'Did I go to sleep again?'

He laughed. 'It's nearly seven.'

Zara stretched, arching her body, enjoying her new sense of well-being. It was like the beginning of an affair.

'Stop that,' Peter warned, still watching her. She knew he could see her body through her voile gown. 'Or we'll be the laughing stock of the maids.'

She heard Pebbles' voice from the kitchen.

'All this prophecy stuff makes me jittery,' Zara said. 'Saif and Pebbles don't act any different but I'm sure she believes it.'

'You don't think there's a subtle change in Saif's behaviour?'

She looked at him, startled. 'Do you? How?'

He was sitting up now. 'Hard to say, exactly. But he's – preparing.'

'He is. The festival's tomorrow.'

'I meant preparing to ... go.' Zara winced and he squeezed her shoulder. 'Sorry. Putting matters in order, like mending the fences with Mumtaz. Fixing things.'

Something was dawning on Zara. 'Pebbles, too. She seems to be making peace with the world.' She leaped out of bed. 'How ghastly! I didn't think ... *She believes it! She thinks her husband's going to die.*'

She grabbed a shawl and ran from the room, wrapping it around her shoulders. The fragrance of din ka raja wafted up like an invisible cloud, surrounding her. She could smell the faint whiff of earth, as if it had rained. The clouds were heavy in the sky. An unexpected spring shower?

Pebbles was on Hana's terrace, her body draped across the parapet. She turned as Zara called, her finger on her lips.

'Look!' She was pointing to a bird perched on the old telegraph wires strung across the Oval Garden. It was a plain-looking creature. 'You don't recognize it? Just wait and watch.'

The bird took wing. As it rose, its body flashed vivid turquoise beneath its wings. 'It's called a chahe. They say there's a fine line of gold around its eyes.'

It felt surreal, she and Pebbles standing unoccupied on Hana's terrace talking about birds.

'You're welcome to stay as long as you like,' Pebbles said suddenly. 'With or without Peter. Forever, if you want.'

Zara squeezed her arm. 'Thanks.'

Pebbles gazed into space. 'I've not been welcoming ... but I want you to feel Qila is your home – not just because it is officially yours.'

Zara was moved. 'Can Qila really belong to anyone? Aren't we the ones who belong to it?'

'I've always noticed this thing you have about home. This– I don't know, like, torment.' She pushed back a strand of hair. 'It was the opposite for me. I moved from my father's home to this home. No period of adjustment, no questioning. I thought you unnecessarily complicate things. But never questioning is just as complicated.' She blinked away a tear. 'This ... this, you know, the prophecy. It's terrible to say ... but it's almost a relief to just know ... I've been dreading ...' She ended on a sob and quickly regained control.

Zara grasped her hands. 'You ... believe it? The prophecy.'

Pebbles took a deep breath. 'I believe it.' She pulled her hand away. 'I've been tortured all my married life with the Ramzi burden, the Ramzi mystery. The day Saif would leave me for the Divine Beloved. I've died many deaths thinking of it; every time he went to Ramzi Bagh on a long retreat I asked myself – have I lost him? But to accept the Ramzi burden is to be released from its terror. I've let my life be ruled by a fairytale. When you love someone with a passion all else fades. Saif and I know that love.'

The silence between them felt comfortable as they stood looking out at the sunrise.

'It smells like rain.' Pebbles said. 'Wrong time of the year – but it'll wash away the dirt.'

Was she talking metaphorically, Zara wondered.

'You should stay, Zara. Who knows when he'll find the light.'

Zara wanted to stamp her feet, shout, protest. 'I can't believe you're so serene about it.'

Pebbles reached down and unhooked the large bunch of keys from her waistband. 'They're yours.'

'No, Pebbles. They're yours. And one day they'll be Sharmeen's.' Pebbles opened her mouth to protest. 'Please,' Zara said. 'I broke my promise to Aunty Hana about keeping the book from Saif; let me at least do what she wants with this. Let Qila belong to the Ramzi line.'

Pebbles did not replace the bunch of keys immediately. 'All these years, the fortress tethered me to itself. I think it was like that for my mother-in-law. It would stretch to let her move then the chains would again tighten. You agonize about things that, in the end, are trivial. I don't go anywhere in case I miss something vital going on here. But now I'm liberated. Qila is not mine and I'm free to leave it. I feel at peace.' She smiled. 'Saif thinks I should visit the UK. Saif will be with me wherever I am. He has always felt it helps to know that divinity is all around.'

She shivered slightly. Her gaze drifted past Zara. Saif stood by the door. Both were transfixed, looking at each other as the glow of the dawn sun deepened and framed them.

This was the Pebbles that Saif knew beneath the maddening ways, beyond the self-doubt, the tense entanglements with trivia. His faith in her had delivered her to herself.

Zara slipped away as they moved towards each other in a daze.

47

Littl'un staggered up to the coffee table, carrying a silver tray. 'She's sent this. Goodness knows what she's after.' She set it down on a table. 'If it wasn't from *her*, I'd say it's almost auspicious.'

'Her?' Zara frowned, putting aside the files from the curator. The notes on the bangles made for fascinating reading. She must have mused aloud; Littl'un's bewildered expression made her laugh. 'Sorry Littl'un, I was miles away.'

'The gift. Her from the other side sent it. I said it's almost auspicious, except what would she know of graciousness?'

Zara picked up the envelope. It was addressed to her.

'Careful! Have a care! Invoke God's name for safety before you touch it. There might be some bad spell in it. And she's written in that devilish firangi language. Satan doesn't lose his power over you just because you live in England. There may be no Devil there, but here he's still throbbing with life.'

'The Devil?'

'He guides people like her. That was his parting condition to God when he was banished – *I'll attack Your creation from behind and before and all sides.*' She shuddered. 'You make me so nervous with your ... recklessness.'

Zara took the letter from the envelope, ignoring Littl'un's ramblings.

'La haul wa la quwwati illa b'illahi ...' Littl'un intoned the familiar Arabic words of protection as Zara read Mumtaz's carefully composed English. There is no terror or power greater than Allah.

> My dear Zara Begum,
> Following our family reunion this morning, I am experiencing a great relief and now feel able to make a proposal which has been very near to my heart for some few months.

I know you are aware that my beloved grandson Kamran and your darling niece Sharmeen love each other. I don't want this to be disrupted or to poison their futures as mine was poisoned because of barriers of faith and class. These are prejudices which-all we must get together and destroy. I think so his wife does not object to my grandson only she does not like idea of her daughter starting relationship before marriage.

I therefore take my courage in both hands and ask you to intercede with your dear cousin brother, Pir Saheb Saifuddin Ramzi, who is also present head of Ramzi Order, to please agree to accept the hand of said grandson with Pir Saheb's daughter Sharmeen.

I leave my dignity in your hands and hope to hear from you positive news, very soon.

This is up to your powers of persuasion.

With love and blessings,

Mumtaz Phuppi

Littl'un jumped up, fanning Zara's face with a magazine. 'Hai hai Bibi. What has happened? You've gone white. I told you to pray before ...'

'Littl'un, I'm fine.' She jumped up. 'Where's Pebbles?'

She grabbed the heavy silver tray and dashed towards Pebbles' room, Littl'un panting noisily behind her.

'Pebbles!' Zara yelled. 'Where are you? Pebbles!'

Plait swinging, Pebbles appeared at her door. Zara looked across the open square dividing her from Pebbles and wished for a moment she could fly across, instead of racing around the gallery to reach her. Pebbles was moving towards her now. Quicker because she was unencumbered.

'What is it? What's happened? What's wrong?'

'Nothing's wrong!'

Pebbles held back the curtain and waited at the door. 'In here. What's that?'

'I don't know.' Zara set the tray down on the table. 'It's very heavy.'

Pebbles eyed the covered tray.

'From next door,' Littl'un said. '*She* sent it.'

'Something for the festival, maybe,' Pebbles said, slumping a little.

'No, no! Look. Pebbles. Listen. Sit down.'

'For heaven's sake, Zara,' Pebbles said. 'What is it?'

'Mumtaz. Sharmeen. I mean for Kamran!' Zara stopped and took a deep breath. 'Mumtaz has sent a marriage proposal for Sharmeen. She wants her to marry Kamran.'

Pebbles let out a long wail. 'Oh god! I can't believe this.'

Sharmeen appeared at the door. Zara saw a whirl of colour as Sharmeen launched herself on her mother with yelps of joy. Littl'un screamed, realized she'd committed an indiscretion and began cracking her knuckles against her temples, muttering blessings.

'Do you really think it'll take away the evil eye, Littl'un?' Zara said.

'Don't mock traditions that have been passed down the centuries. They've come from those whose wisdom was famed a thousand years before someone put a brain cell in your head, much less intelligence in that brain cell.'

Sharmeen danced around the room. 'I knew it. I knew it. I knew it.'

'You did?' Zara was amused. Had she never noticed Mumtaz's hostility?

'Yes. She promised me a long time back. She said: "My little jagmag jugnu ..." That means "glittering firefly", Aunty Zara ...'

'If you guys don't stop translating for me,' Zara said, 'I'm going to throw a tantrum.'

'She calls me "jugnu", you know. She said, "My little jagmag jugnu, I'll make sure you marry Kamran before I die. However long I have to live, even fifty years more, I won't go till I've done it. Only one condition. You two don't touch each other now, okay? Be together but apart." '

Pebbles laughed softly. 'Strange woman. Saif was saying to me last night, "*She's an unlikely oracle of love.*" But maybe not that unlikely, hunh? Her story is quite a love story too, isn't it? I mean, eloping and all. Even tougher in her time. No?'

'I guess. I've always thought her a bit of a ...'

Zara nodded. 'Thing is, if you like someone, their love story is beautiful; if not, it's disgusting.'

'He's a decent boy, Zara.' There was a note of pleading in Pebbles' voice. 'All that Bollywood obsession and all, I'm sure he'll get over it as he matures.' She looked tearful. 'I was against them meeting in secret but he ... at least he understands Sharmeen.'

'You knew?' Zara said.

Sharmeen was hovering around the tray, stroking its shiny satin cover. 'What's inside?' she asked.

'Let's have a look.' Pebbles leaned forward.

Sharmeen whipped off the gold-edged cloth.

'My god, Sharmeen. Don't be so rough!' Pebbles voice was sharp. 'Be gentle, darling. You're going to be a bride. A married woman.'

One side of the tray was piled with boxes, each with a name on it. There were sweetmeats from the most exclusive halvai; scented essential oils from the oldest families of attars, distillers of fragrant oils. On the other side was a large, flat box covered in dark red velvet, addressed to Sharmeen. Pebbles handed it to her. Inside, nestling on pearly-cream satin, stained with age, was a magnificent necklace with matching bangles and earrings.

'Wait, wait, wait,' Pebbles gasped as Sharmeen lifted out the necklace. 'What am I doing? Put it back! Sorry, darling. I'm not thinking straight. It's a bit premature. I mean sweets and attar is fine but sending jewels like this before we've accepted the proposal? We'll call your father then we'll let Mumtaz know what we've decided. We can open the boxes after that.'

Sharmeen's face crumpled. Pebbles struggled for a moment. Then her scowl disappeared and she put an arm around Sharmeen. 'We have to follow the rules, my darling. But it will be okay.'

She took the jewels from Sharmeen's fingers.

'Abba will agree, I know,' Sharmeen insisted. 'Just wait and see.'

Pebbles nodded. 'I hope you're right. Now, Millo's waiting to talk to you about lunch.'

Sharmeen hesitated a moment, pensive, before disappearing through the covered terrace. Pebbles leaned towards Zara in a conspiratorial manner.

'Very genuine, I think,' she said. 'I think Mumtaz realizes about Sharmeen's problem. How down-to-earth she turned out.'

She snatched up the phone, went next door and came back in a few moments, beaming. 'He says if Sharmeen's happy, he's happy.'

Pebbles turned to Zara. 'I believe you've done quite a bit of work without me or Sharmeen knowing. Y'all-all have been discussing Kamran and Sharmeen, yes?'

'We have. He's a good boy.' *A good boy?* Zara could not resist a smile. It didn't take much to slip in and out of old patterns.

'We know he's trustworthy like Hirani,' Pebbles said. 'He, too, knew what we were doing here, at the back. He sent a few people for help. But Kamran worked solidly.'

Sharmeen came in, skipping. 'Am I getting married?'

Pebbles hugged her. 'I spoke to Abba. He says yes.'

Sharmeen screamed. 'Really? You're not joking?'

'Did you say Hirani was helping?' Zara asked suddenly.

Pebbles blinked. 'Yes. Why?'

'The bangles! Do you think Aunty gave him the bangles in exchange for ...?'

'Which bangles?' Sharmeen asked.

'Just a minute, Sharmeen.' Pebbles turned back to Zara. 'What did he say about them?'

'He denied all knowledge of them – but he said Aunt Hana had been to see him. Could she have asked him to sell them?'

Pebbles clutched her head in her hands. 'No. How did he explain her visit?'

'He said something about sending something abroad.'

Pebbles' eyes grew wide. 'The manuscript of the old paintings. She wanted to send it abroad, like she said in the letter. Maybe she asked Hirani about raising funds for ...' She flicked away a tear. 'How could I have been so wrong? She was trying to protect her son. But I was so obsessed with what she would give you – Qila, the bangles ...'

'What bangles?' Sharmeen asked again.

Pebbles was exasperated. 'Sharmeen, please darling. We're talking. Can you wait a moment?' Sharmeen tore out of the room.

'Oh dear,' Zara said, 'we've upset her.'

Pebbles was deep in thought. 'I knew there was a visit to Hirani – to enlist his help. But I was not thinking straight.'

Sharmeen barged into the room and slammed a jewellery box on Pebbles' lap. 'Mumma. Please. Look.' She opened the box and reached into it. 'Are these the bangles y'all keep talking about?' She held them up. 'These ones? Noor Jehan's bangles?'

Pebbles held the bangles at arm's length then hunched over to examine them. She passed it to Zara, then turned to Sharmeen and held her anxious face in both hands as she knelt beside her. 'Where did you find these, darling?'

'I took them from Dadi Huzur's cupboard. Why?' She looked from one face to another. 'They're mine anyway, aren't they?'

'But why didn't you tell anyone?'

'I forgot. They got to the bottom of the box and I forgot.'

'They're really precious, and important.'

Sharmeen looked tearful. 'But Dadi Huzur said they were mine.'

'And so they are.'

'Can I keep them?'

'You can, my love.' Sharmeen threw her arms around her mother's neck. Pebbles held Sharmeen at a distance. 'But you know what would be really nice?' she whispered. 'If you present them to Rajmata Saheba for the Trivikrampur Museum.'

'I like Sita Devi,' Sharmeen announced. 'And I never wear them anyway.'

Pebbles sat head in hands. 'I can't believe it. I just can't believe it. That box is full of fake rubbish.' Pebbles sighed. 'I've been wrong about so many things.'

Mumtaz's eyes brimmed as she leant forward and lifted the gold-fringed rectangle of pink lamé from the tray. Pebbles looked satisfied as the array of special sweets was displayed. The bhatyaran had sent word to the top halvai for the unexpected order and served up her usual standard of celebratory sweets, including halva coated in silver leaf – grains of silver beaten so fine that they became fragile, edible sheets – and tiny, sugared pastry lozenges decorated with preserved, crystallized rose petals. One end of the huge dining table was covered in silver trays piled with enormous dried dates, plums, apricots, raisins and sultanas, along with pistachios, almonds and cashew nuts. Next to them were the eternal flower garlands, fat mogra buds interspersed with roses – coiled, fat and juicy with droplets of moisture still glistening on them like diamond studs.

Zara heard an unexpected snatch of her mother laughing as she herself toddled about trying to scoop dewdrops from flowers early in the morning, in the Oval Garden, then looked at her wet palms, perplexed, as they dripped water.

Mumtaz's fingertips trailed across the garlands. 'Let us call in the children,' she whispered.

Kamran was low-key as he greeted everyone, head modestly bowed, then sat down beside his grandmother. Sharmeen bounced in with Littl'un, ran instantly to Mumtaz and flung her arms around her neck. Mumtaz hugged her back.

Garlands were exchanged all around. Mumtaz produced a ring from a small box and handed it to Kamran.

'For your bride,' she said.

Sharmeen put her hand out straightaway. Pebbles moved up behind her and whispered in her ear. 'Be patient, darling. Be dignified, please.'

Pebbles squeezed her shoulder and handed her a small velvet-covered box. 'For Kamran,' she whispered. Sharmeen opened it and squealed at the sight of the ruby in its chunky square setting. 'Look, Kamran. Now we're really going to be engaged!'

Sharmeen flashed her hand around, showing off her sparkling emerald-cut diamond. Suddenly everyone was hugging everyone else, talking, laughing, congratulating each other.

The maid appeared at the door. Pebbles pressed some money into her hand. The woman made the usual gestures of refusal then on Mumtaz's nod, took the money with a show of reluctance, bobbed her head and saluted her thanks. She moved quickly to Kamran.

'Kamran baba. People have come to see you.'

Mumtaz whirled round. 'Don't you see we have important guests? Ill-mannered wretch!'

'Sow-ree.' The maid looked sulky. 'They say it's very urgent.'

Kamran tensed. 'I'm sorry ... there could be trouble. I should ...'

'Go!' Pebbles said. The tension in her voice was electric.

Kamran nodded briefly and half-ran, looking back quickly at Sharmeen as he went through the door. Pebbles stared after him, her hands clasped together. 'Be safe,' she whispered. 'Allah Hafiz.'

48

Littl'un waved her hands wildly from the balcony as Zara and Pebbles worked on the plants in the inner courtyard. Pebbles looked up sharply as Littl'un tumbled out of the long sitting room.

'The bhatyaran ...' she cried out. 'I knew something was the matter when I went to order the sweets. It turns out someone tried to grab one of her daughters-in-law. You know, her nephew's wife? They were claiming her nephew abducted a Hindu girl. They tried to kidnap her to take her back to her family.'

Littl'un ran in a frenzy along the balcony rails to get to the top of the stairs.

'Slow down,' Zara called. Her fragile frame would be shattered if she fell. 'We're not going anywhere.'

'I need to come and tell you the story.'

'This could mean the news has got out about our work,' Pebbles said. 'It could be dangerous if it has. We've only just sorted out the Academy stuff ...'

'Shall I call the police?'

Pebbles shook her head. 'Intruders – they attacked the bhatyaran's house. We don't need the police yet, she handled the situation. We'll just order the back gates to be kept shut. The men will do guard duty. We have to monitor who comes and goes.'

It sounded grim but far-fetched. 'Are the Ramzis in danger? What about Sharmeen?'

'She knows not to go into the courtyard without asking. I'm not too worried.'

'What about the festival?' Zara was breathless. 'Can everyone come still?'

'There's a large police presence on the day. The inspector is usually present. Most people come out of devotion; if there's trouble it's from casuals a few days after. People are still concerned about offending the divinities on the festival day.'

'And the attack downstairs? That will be reported?'

Pebbles was silent for a moment. 'I don't know. Let's see what Kamran says.'

Zara looked into the courtyard. There was no sign of discord. It was a sea of small triangular flags waving from every little house. The place was alive. In front of Amina's house, four vats bubbled as she dipped fabrics in, stirred, checked on other items. Clouds of smoke billowed over the old kitchen block.

'The old kitchen's being used,' Zara mused. 'Like the old days.'

'Only once a year, for the urs,' Littl'un croaked. 'The bhatyaran uses it. She needs the extra capacity.'

'How many to feed?' Zara asked.

Littl'un was evasive. 'Well, you know, people visit ...'

Zara hugged the old woman. She was still guarding Hana's secret. Littl'un pushed her away. 'Get away with you. You're not a baby anymore.' Her eyes filled as Zara echoed the words in Littl'un's accent and she shook her head. 'Who can believe she's an educated young woman living in Ing-laind for twenty years. She sounds like a Gujarati peasant.' She composed herself and peered down. 'Unbelievable! Look, she's back at the fire pit. She's solid material. That's what I was telling you.' Littl'un was excited again. 'This morning, when she heard the commotion, she was slicing onions. She went to investigate with an onion and the knife still in her hands. A man was trying to grab her daughter-in-law – she shoved the onion in the attacker's face. His companion saw the knife in her hand – he just ran.'

'Did they catch him?'

'They disappeared like the horns off an ass's head. No sign of them.'

'And the one she attacked with the onion?' Zara was laughing so much her words came out in small explosions.

Littl'un's mind was on the story. 'She said it wasn't as good as the women in that Gujarati film – you know the one where they threw dried chilli at the invaders?'

'*Mirch Masala*,' Pebbles said. 'Wonderful picture! These women worked in a spice factory, packing dried red chilli – they attacked their enemies with chilli powder. Woman power.'

'Not really funny, though,' Zara was sober, remembering what had happened to her, wondering if this young woman would have had a similar experience in store. 'Why do you think they picked her?'

'Laow merrij,' Littl'un muttered.

Zara was laughing again. 'Did she run away to have her "love marriage"?'

Littl'un shrugged. 'Why do you faarin-return people always mock everything?'

Zara put her arm around Littl'un. 'Go on, I'm listening.'

'Nothing to tell. No more jokes about miserable runaways seeking scraps ...'

'Oh come on, Littl'un,' Zara said. 'Don't be offended. There's so much horrible stuff happening, we have to laugh or we'd die of misery.'

Littl'un clicked her tongue repeatedly. 'My darling baby. May the Devil be struck deaf. Don't let such bad thoughts come to your lips. May you be happy forever. May you flower and fruit ...'

'So tell us what happened?'

'Chameli ran way with a Muslim boy from another village. Huzur Saheb persuaded the bhatyaran to take them in. It was one of the first "adoptions". Eight, ten years ago. The bhatyaran had so many children already, may God give them all long lives, hardly anyone noticed from outside. Inside the fort they just said he was a nephew and his wife come to make a living. Amina was next. She brought in some girls who had been ... they'd suffered badly ... in riots. They couldn't face their families. Then men came – people were boycotting their produce and shops, not letting them sit exams, turning them out of their jobs.'

'I was told – by a yogi I met in London.' She felt suddenly weak.

'Zara?' Pebbles said. 'Are you okay?'

'I was thinking,' replied Zara. 'If I'd known about the courtyard work, I wouldn't have had to meet Ankahi at all. Your operation is exactly what I was looking for.'

49

Zara, Peter and Littl'un watched the forecourt from the balcony of the Green Room. The sun was strong for a February morning. The road beyond was decorated with flowers and flags. The last few shopkeepers, open to serve last-minute festival-goers looking for offerings of sweets and flowers, were locking up. Zara was happy to see the vast iron gates of the fortress wide open. Inside, workers were setting up a large stage in the centre of the front courtyard for Jay and Saif to preside over the festival. Four throne-like chairs from the shrine were arranged in the centre, two slightly smaller ones, also ornate and decorated in gold, on the side. Behind them was a row of dining chairs. Men and women were setting up trestle tables on the edges of the space.

Sharmeen popped her head around the corner. 'Are you going to take all day, Zara Aunty? You have to come down.' She grabbed Zara's wrist and dragged her back from the balcony into the Green Room. In her other hand, she held the bangles. 'They're waiting.'

'Uncle Peter and I will watch from here, with Littl'un.' Zara's voice was gentle. 'It's a great view.'

Sharmeen's lower lip quivered. 'You don't want to come and watch me give Rajmata Sa these? You can sit in the side row with me.' She waggled her hand. The emeralds in the bangles caught the light and cast green-tinted reflections around the walls, bouncing back from the mirror, illuminating the room like a cave. Sharmeen stood transfixed.

'Everything's glowing today,' she said at last. She gazed off into space. 'Abba's leaving, isn't he? He's going today.'

'Going where, sweetheart?'

'To the ocean of light.'

Littl'un hugged her. 'Sweet thing,' she whispered. 'He's going nowhere. Who's been telling you ...?'

'Abba's been telling me about the ocean of light for a long, long time.' Sharmeen smiled. 'It's a nice place and he's always wanted to go. It's even prettier than this room or the meditation chamber – all dazzling. He's not sure he'll go there but he says he'll become a little fleck of light and dance around the Great Blaze until he's worthy to join it. Funny to imagine Abba dancing ... Sometimes he'll be a little droplet of foam and leap out of the infinite ocean. And sometimes he'll be a speck of dust and whirl in the vast desert. And he'll reflect, like these stones, in everything. So I'll be able to see him and feel him in all the specks everywhere. It makes me feel better about him going away.'

Zara stared. 'He's been telling you this since you were little?'

Sharmeen nodded. 'He used to show me the light in everything. How the desert glints and the sea shimmers and the sky lights up.'

Zara walked out again into the freshness of the balcony and watched with Peter as Sita Devi climbed on stage, flanked by two aides. Anapurna was trailing behind her, head bowed, dressed in a sari of fresh green. Jay climbed up behind her, attentive, solicitous. They looked small from here. Little people who had transformed her life.

Someone carried a large tray of garlands on to the dais and placed it on a chair. Saif bounded up the stairs and joined the group. A shaikh in white with a green scarf about his shoulders followed him. He took the flowers from the tray and garlanded all four of them.

Sharmeen squealed. 'We'd better hurry or they'll get started. I have to give her these before they start.' She ran through the room then stopped at the door. 'Come on then, Uncle Peter, Aunty Zara – or I'm not going ...' Zara grabbed Peter's hand and they dashed behind Sharmeen on to the stage.

'My little moonbeam. Why the rush? Welcome.' Saif was radiant.

Sharmeen threw her arms around her father and whispered frenetically, waving the bangles. Saif disentangled himself and guided her to Sita Devi. Sharmeen thrust the bangles at her.

'I had them all the time,' she said. 'Mummy says they're precious and I should let you decide what to do with them.'

Sita Devi flinched, then composed herself and held out her hand to Sharmeen. 'That's wonderful.' Her face looked tense for a moment, then softened. 'Thank you very much.'

She led Sharmeen to the two smaller chairs and they sat down together. Sita took Sharmeen's hands in hers. 'You know, your grandmother and I used to squabble about these bangles. I thought they belonged to my family, she thought they belonged to yours. But they belonged to neither. They were the Empress Noor Jehan's.' She polished the foliate heads with her forefinger. 'You know, Sharmeen, I don't think they were ever meant to be worn. I think the empress wanted them to go to our first guruji.'

Sharmeen whooped. 'So they were Ramzi bangles after all. Grandma won!'

Sita Devi smiled. 'Yes, she won. But then, she always did. I am – was – used to that.' She stroked Sharmeen's hand. 'You know what we should do?'

Sharmeen grew wide-eyed. 'You won't throw them away?'

Sita Devi smiled. 'After all the trouble they've caused? Never! We should put them on display. What do you think about giving them to the museum?'

Sharmeen tipped her head back and narrowed her eyes, thinking hard before she jumped up and clapped her hands. 'Yes! Yes! Yes! That's what Mummy said. The museum! In the Ramzi section?'

Sita nodded. 'The uprising of 1857. It was actually recovered in the trunk of gold and gems Trivikram Maharaj gave to the Ramzi guru to raise an army ...'

'... the Ramzi warriors.'

'... who always saved Trivikrampur lives and honour.' Jay leaped lightly up and came over to them. Saif bowed his head. A warm smile passed between them. Facing Saif, Jay looked quite overcome. 'You have been everything to me. My brother, my guardian ... my guru.' He dropped to his knees and touched Saif's feet. Saif swooped down and raised him up. They embraced without words.

The crowd cheered. Zara looked at the throng – hundreds of people moving around – inspecting the food stalls and the various artefacts on display. She felt disoriented, as if the stage was moving in different directions. She closed her eyes for a second then focused on the shrine beneath the tamarind tree. Its tiny courtyard was filled with devotees, tying their gold and silver strings to the pierced marble surround of the sanctuary

'Dreams fulfilled,' she thought. She had made a promise there once in secret, with Littl'un by her side. For Nyla to return or at least to reveal where she was. She could finally fulfil it, too.

'Is it okay, Abba?' Sharmeen asked. 'The museum? Should we?'

'Absolutely!' Saif said. 'Nothing would make me happier.'

'I know,' Sharmeen nodded sagely. 'Material possessions are a burden and the easiest things to shed to lighten our spiritual journey.'

The Keepers of the Ramzi shrine were approaching the dais. The leader nodded to a row of drummers standing ready by the side of the shrine. A strong, sombre rhythm rumbled through the atmosphere. A memory awoke inside Zara. The earth's heartbeat, she used to call it when she was a child. A group of people scuttled up the steps and lifted the covered trays.

'Where is my beloved bride?' Saif said, rubbing his palms together. 'It's noon. Time to begin the ceremonies.'

Zara looked round. On cue, Pebbles appeared from the Oval Garden across by the shrine and stood, slightly uncertain, looking this way and that.

'It's her first time without Aunty Hana,' she whispered to Peter.

Pebbles' hair was swept off her face and the flames and mirrors from the dancers' thalis acted like prisms, rotating rainbow light clusters around her face.

Zara could see that Pebbles alone filled Saif's vision. Her hair was covered lightly with the sequinned border of her sari. Later today it would be torn into squares and used to parcel food and gifts to be blessed and given in charity.

Sharmeen jumped up, pointing wildly. 'Look! Look! Kamran's granny's coming.'

Mumtaz had come out of the house and was covering Pebbles in a green mantle.

'Light and verdure, manifestations of the Almighty,' Saif murmured as Pebbles and Mumtaz walked to the stage. As they approached the steps, Saif, followed by Jay, stepped forward to help them. They took their seats, Pebbles on one of the throne chairs and Mumtaz on the peacock chair.

A large circle formed around the stage as the breath of the players floated through the reed flutes. Zara could feel Peter's enthusiasm. The dancers were holding sticks in preparation for the traditional dandiya raas of the desert. They stood in pairs and, on either side of each pair, a dancer carried a tray filled with lit candles and mirrors representing Bowl Lake. Each couple rotated within the circle, creating a rhythm with the clash of the sticks, echoed by the drummers. The dance had begun.

Slowly, gradually, the rhythm picked up, became faster, more exhilarating. Small circles formed spontaneously among the crowd, joining the dance. People had brought along their own sticks in preparation, others clapped instead.

Zara looked around for Kamran and saw him standing well back from the stage with a group of other young men dressed like Bollywood 'heroes'. How different it had been when she first saw him with them before the protest at Hana's funeral. She clutched at Peter.

Jay and Saif looked at each other with quiet pleasure. A decorated platter was placed between Pebbles and Anapurna. They rose together to lift it. Sita Devi stood up behind them. Saif looked over at Mumtaz and nodded so slightly that Zara wondered if it was intentional. Mumtaz walked silently to the front. Once again, in perfect harmony, Saif and Jay walked to the side of their wives.

The dancers picked up speed, moving to the far side of the stage. Pebbles and Anapurna brought forward their tray and placed it on a low table. Together they lifted a cloth and released a dozen tiny chicks. There was a rush of hands at the edge of the stage as members of the crowd reached out frenetically to grab them.

Peter leaned towards Zara. 'Fertility symbols, I presume?' Zara nodded. 'I once pestered Littl'un to smuggle out half a dozen for me – turned out she got the cook to buy some from a backyard breeder.'

The two women lifted the first of the fruit and flowers and vegetables of the season. The dancers on stage crowded round, hands reaching out, clamouring for a blessed gift, then resumed their circumambulation.

One of the men in white held up his right hand. The stage became still and silent. A group of people marched on to the dais, carrying a bundle. A saffron-clad priest held out a swaddled bundle. Anapurna took it, then stooped and placed it on the tray. Immediately, another priest shook out red streamers, waving them over the baby to represent blood.

'It makes sense at last,' Zara breathed. 'It's the baby who survived when the first sage and his wife were killed.'

'Dost Pir,' Peter said. 'The baby who came back.'

Kamran darted towards Saif and whispered something. Jay was inclining his neck now, allowing the priests to garland him. For a moment he was obscured by marigold, roses and gardenia. There was a loud sizzle, followed by a large puff of smoke, as a priest threw handfuls of incense into an open grate. A flame sprang upward. Its strong scent overpowered Zara.

The dance came to full momentum. The dancers whirled around the stage, clashing sticks. The drumbeat mounted. The crowd became frenzied. Zara felt oppressed.

How could Saif look so serene despite the clamour, noise of fireworks, interruptions? Did he feel calm, Zara wondered. She saw him tense and followed his gaze past the rituals, into the crowd. She saw a light eruption, heard a dissonant boom. At the periphery of her vision, she sensed a discordant movement. A decisive movement, on stage, violating the rhythmic, repetitive leaps and revolutions of the dancing crowd. Kamran shot past Saif towards Jay. Saif's body streaked across, knocking down both men, sending chairs crashing, flew into the air as if leaping, exultant, then swivelled and crashed. His green cloak came off and floated up. A jagged hole in it seemed, bizarrely, to bleed, as a red-brown stain seeped out to surround its charred edges.

Saif lay on the stage, red and white. Damp red streamers covered his body. Jay was scrabbling on the ground, frenetically pulling at the streamers, one hand cradling Saif's head.

Sharmeen and Pebbles moved towards each other in slow motion. Their shoulders joined, arms close, entwined as they dropped to their knees beside Saif. Pebbles caught the end of her sari and wiped his face clean. The crowd was stampeding. The Keeper of the Shrine whispered to Jay who held up his hands and said something to the crowd.

Zara looked around wildly and saw Kamran pushing through the crowds towards a small cluster of people. Amid them was Rekha, holding a gun.

The crowd seemed to rise like an angry breaker, then crest and curve until Rekha was surrounded by a wave of protestors, ready to lynch her.

'Do something, Jay, do something!' Anapurna wailed.

'What can he do?' Sita said drily. 'Destiny has spoken. The prophecy has been fulfilled. The yogi, the book ... the Lord has spoken. This is how it has always been, how it will always be.' She got up slowly, her body suddenly stiff like an old woman's. 'The Green-clad Man has yet again sacrificed a Ramzi to save a Vamana.'

Three police trucks ploughed in through the gates. Ear-shattering feedback obscured the words coming from the microphones. Policemen thronged around Rekha, shoving Kamran out of the way.

Mumtaz clutched at Pebbles. Zara held Sharmeen as Kamran joined them. Her chest was tight, as if her breath didn't want to come. Peter stood close beside her.

The police dispersed the last of the crowds. Inspector Pandey came towards Pebbles. His steps fell heavily on the hollow floor of the stage. 'I'm very sorry for your loss, Begum Saheb. I must ask you all to go inside now. We will defer questions until you are able to ...'

Pebbles stepped out of Mumtaz's arms. 'I will stay until my husband is carried in. Then I will be ready to deal with your queries.'

Zara felt suspended, as if she and the others were temporarily enveloped in a respite from grief. The occasional feelings of normality and relief seemed inexplicable. How could they chat and go about ordinary business when they had lost Saif?

'It's the mind's way of relieving stress,' Peter said.

Zara could hardly believe that Saif had died three days ago. Even more baffling was Pebbles' decision to fly to London with Sharmeen in April.

'I don't want to think about it at all until the forty days of mourning are over,' she insisted, leaving Peter and Zara to deal with the logistics. 'There is so much to do before I can go. Jay will supervise the courtyard activities, with Kamran. After that, a change will be good for Sharmeen and me.'

The far end of the formal dining room was so full of flowers it looked like part of the Oval Garden. They stood in buckets, cauldrons and tubs. Pebbles prepared the stems of a bunch of lilies. Sharmeen spun around, picking out flower heads and decorative foliage for an enormous crystal bowl.

'So many flowers you've brought, Uncle Peter!' she said. 'It's like a wedding.'

Peter flushed. 'Oh dear,' he said softly. 'I apologize if it's inappropriate.'

Pebbles looked up from her lilies. 'Apologize for what, Peter? It's a lovely thing to do. Fortress Florist must have been overjoyed. I bet he's never sold so many flowers in a week, let alone a day!' She smiled. 'Saif would have been chuffed.'

Sharmeen laughed too. 'When we drove past Fortress on the way back, we saw he'd closed his shop. Uncle Peter bought *everything*.'

'I know Saif loved flowers.'

Zara stared at Peter and saw that Sharmeen and Pebbles were staring too.

'What?' he asked, flushing again.

'How did you know that?' Pebbles asked.

Peter shrugged. 'The way he talks– talked. I saw how he was around anything that grew.'

Pebbles shook her head, smiling. 'He was a mystery to me. How he showed different sides of himself to different people. All I know is, he was really into his roses here in Qila, especially those white ones in the inner courtyard.' She looked out and caught her breath. Her eyes glistened. 'He was telling me the morning of the festival how he was looking forward to them blooming – he was sure they'd be budding by this week.' Her voice trembled. 'They are – I noticed this morning.'

Sharmeen hugged her mother. 'We'll take them to him in Ramzi Bagh, Mummy,' she said. 'He'll like that.' Her eyes drifted upwards. 'How beautiful it was for his funeral. When he went to his Divine Beloved.'

The image of the wild flowers in the woods revolved in Zara's eyes. It was the best time of the year for colour and freshness in Trivikram. Multi-coloured lantana heads, tiny mauve touch-me-nots, clusters of grass-hugging white blossoms beneath the towering plumbago. The woods surrounding the Ramzi mausoleum had been alive with people. He was buried beneath a plain umbrella structure hewn from local red stone surrounded by greenery. A stream trickled down a four-foot-high grass mound to a rocky pond alongside the clearing. Pebbles believed in the tradition that women should not go to the graveside, and Zara did not challenge her. This was her call.

Their car was positioned for the best view without obstructing the mourners. Peter sat with the women while Ajay, the driver, joined the crowd. But as the ceremony began, a shaikh invited him to join them. He knew, he said, that Shaikh Saif Ramzi held him in high esteem.

After the ceremony was over, Sharmeen recited a verse, barely above a whisper, then turned to Peter. 'It means, "Once again the tulip's lamp has lit the hills and vales,/Again, the garden bird arouses me with splendid songs".'

'Plenty of tulips, Uncle Peter,' Sharmeen said, now lifting a bunch.

'Thanks to that lovely verse you recited,' Peter said.

'My father taught it to me,' Sharmeen said proudly. She seized her mother's hand. 'Please can we put that on Abba's tomb, Mummy? Please?'

Millo staggered in clutching a cardboard carton filled with vases and bowls and flower-arranging implements, followed by Ajay carrying another. Pebbles strode across directing them, swooping on dry sponges and ikebana platters. Sharmeen gazed at the spring flowers on the table, picking them up with delicate fingers and sniffing.

'Rose, lily, narcissus and eglantine/the ever-martyred poppy, in its blood-drenched shrine,' she chanted softly. 'Which do you think would be better for Abba's shrine?' she asked, burying her face in her hands. 'Oh oh oh! I'm drowning in flower verses, I don't know what's happening.'

Pebbles hugged her. 'There's no hurry to decide,' she said.

Sharmeen pulled away. 'But I might forget.'

Pebbles turned back to her flowers and in a moment she had created a sculptural ikebana bonsai. Sharmeen looked distressed.

Peter reached into his pocket and pulled out a crumpled notebook. 'I have a nicer one upstairs which you're welcome to,' he said. 'But look, I write down all my ideas here and then I don't forget. You could do the same. Then, when you've got them all down, you can choose your favourites.'

Sharmeen clapped, then skipped forward and hugged Peter. There was a movement in the Oval Garden. Pebbles darted to the glass door.

'Welcome, Rajmata Sa,' she said, bowing in greeting and ushering her in. 'Such an honour.'

'I hope you don't mind I came in through this way,' said Sita Devi, signalling Raju to return to the car. 'There is still quite a crowd at the front entrance. I told Raju to drive to the side.'

'Of course not,' Pebbles ushered her to a seat. 'Welcome. You are welcome through every door.' As Sita Devi sat, Pebbles turned to Sharmeen, mouthing, 'Tea.'

Sharmeen slipped out of the room.

'I'm glad that it is only family here,' Sita Devi said. 'I was afraid you would have a lot of guests. I mean, what I have to say is for family alone.' She shifted uncomfortably in her seat. 'I owe this family an explanation, at the very least, if not also an apology.'

Pebbles sat down beside her. 'Please, Rajmata Sa. There is no need.'

Sita Devi raised her hand; she stroked Pebbles' cheek and let her hand trail down her shoulder. She shook her head, almost imperceptibly. 'It seems that the Vamanas are constantly responsible for the sorrows of the Ramzis.'

Zara saw Pebbles clench and unclench her fists, keeping control of her emotions, preserving the tradition of dignity in grief.

'I must explain why Hana and I saw ...' Sita Devi struggled to find words, '... less of each other recently.' She clasped her hands tightly together. 'It goes back a long time.' Suddenly she snorted, looking at Zara. 'Would I give up someone so dear to me for a pair of bangles? True, we disagreed but, pfff. It was the other business. Your mother and Hari.'

Zara's voice was cold as a shard of ice. 'I thought you said there was nothing ...'

Sita Devi laughed a snuffling, half-bitter laugh. She rearranged her cream chanderi sari. 'I had reason to believe Nyla was having an affair with my husband. Soon after, she was widowed.' Her voice quavered and she pressed together her lips. 'Our Shaikh Saheb, her husband, had told her Hari was innocent. She knew how unhappy I was ...' She shifted on her seat and readjusted her sari around her hair. 'She kept the truth from me. She was the only person who knew it was killing me to keep up the pretence of a perfect marriage, that I had never forgiven Hari's betrayal. Even when he was dying of cancer, she didn't tell me my Hari was innocent. She deprived me of my last chance to make things up. She stole my married life – nearly three decades of my life which should have been happy. That was how I felt when she finally told me.'

Zara gasped. 'So you knew that Hari was not my father?'

Rajmata's glance darted to Peter. 'I had believed for thirty yars that he was. It was hard to expunge ... then Saif reassured me.' She traced the pattern on her sari. 'I have come to believe that your Aunty Hana did not act out of malice.' She shook her head and picked an imaginary speck from the sofa. 'She was guarding the Ramzi honour. There was one person she cared for above all of us. That was Guruji Sultan. And he dealt the deepest possible wound to her pride – he made her think she was not worthy of being a Ramzi.'

She dabbed her eye with the corner of a folded tissue. 'May God forgive me for questioning our Guruji Sultan. But if I'm honest, I have questioned it often – when I finally found out. Well, what can I say?'

Sita Devi tried to continue then pressed hard on her upper lip. 'And now I think how much the Ramzis have lost because of the Vamanas. Had I not complained to Hana about Hari – mistakenly, as it turns out – then she would not have sent her sister to Ramzi Bagh and, who knows, she and Guruji Sultan might have been reconciled. When she told me the truth, finally, I thought this may have been a subtle form of revenge. But I know my Hana would never do that. She was committed to action – never revenge. Now, once again, she has made a sacrifice. Her son has laid down his life for my son.'

Sharmeen returned to the room, followed by Millo bearing a tray of tea. Behind her another maid carried a tray of savouries.

Sita Devi sat back in the sofa. She thrust out her neck and spoke softly to Pebbles as Sharmeen directed the maids.

'I have told you what I came to say and I apologize deeply for the distress I have caused.'

Pebbles grasped Sita Devi's hands. 'It is not for you to apologize for any of this. It was meant to be.'

Sita Devi patted Pebbles' knee. 'You are a bride worthy of the Ramzis.' She paused. 'Jay and I have spoken. We are both happy you are going to England. Beautiful place. We have agreed that he and I will attend to courtyard matters – with the guidance of Kamran. And also, he has asked me to assist him in the work of the Girls' Academy.'

Sharmeen thrust a bunch of freesias and narcissi into Sita Devi's hands. 'For you. Uncle Peter says that in England you can see these actually growing wild in the parks, not just at florists'. They smell so nice.' She inhaled noisily. 'See?'

Sita Devi took the flowers and thanked Sharmeen, then looked round to find Peter and nodded. 'Will you join us for tea?'

Peter laid down his bunch of flowers. 'Thank you. I'm not making a good job of this at all.'

Zara laughed. 'I'm not sure why you even tried.' Then she sobered up; how could she laugh at a time like this? Peter sat down beside her.

'Uncle Peter says that next month in London the parks will be full of these flowers and crocuses and daffodils.' Her eyes widened. 'They grow in Aunty Zara's garden as well, and poppies and tulips, too.'

Zara could see Sharmeen cavorting in her garden and Pebbles out and about in London, putting together her daughter's trousseau. She felt warm at the thought of Peter unloading their luggage from the car as she put the key to the front door and ushered her family into her home.

Acknowledgements

Thanks to my agent Toby Eady for placing the novel instantly and saving me the arduous process of multiple rejections; to Alison Fell for being my first reader and giving me invaluable guidance; to Christopher Shackle for keeping the nourishment flowing while I wrote and for the long drives in the East Sussex countryside when I needed to clear the cobwebs.

I also want to acknowledge the use of Faiz Ahmed Faiz's poem 'Mere dil mere musafir' and the line 'Chaman se aaj saba beqaraar guzri hai' from (an early version) the poem 'Tum ae ho na shab-e-intezaar guzri hai' which inspired the title; and two lines from the poem 'Qaid-e-tanhai': 'Koi naghma, koi khushbu, koi kafir surat/ Adam abad-e-judai mein musafir surat' in my translation as 'A lyric, a fragrance, a kafir face/In separation's Nowhereland, a travelling face' incorporated into the text.

Last but not least, my grateful thanks to my editors Saugata Mukherjee and Pallavi Narayan for their gratifying response to my book and for their work on the manuscript.

I couldn't have done it without you.

Acknowledgements

7